The
Tenth
Song

Also by Naomi Ragen

The Saturday Wife

The Covenant

Chains Around the Grass

The Ghost of Hannah Mendes

The Sacrifice of Tamar

Jephte's Daughter

Sotah

Women's Minyan: A Play

The Tenth Song

Naomi Ragen

St. Martin's Griffin

New York

THE TENTH SONG. Copyright © 2010 by Naomi Ragen. All rights reserved. Printed in the United States of America. For information, address St. Martin's Press, 175 Fifth Avenue, New York, N.Y. 10010.

www.stmartins.com

The Library of Congress has cataloged the hardcover edition as follows:

Ragen, Naomi.
     The tenth song / Naomi Ragen.—1st ed.
         p. cm.
     ISBN 978-0-312-57017-0
     1. Jewish women—Fiction. 2. Mothers and daughters—Fiction. 3. Life change events—Fiction. 4. Domestic fiction. 5. Psychological fiction. I. Title. II. Title: 10th song.
PS3568.A4118T46 2010
813'.54—dc22

                                                                                    2010029213

ISBN 978-0-312-57018-7 (trade paperback)

First St. Martin's Griffin Edition: October 2011

10 9 8 7 6 5 4 3 2 1

To Alex

There is nothing so whole as a broken heart.

Rav Nachman of Breslav

Acknowledgments

The writing of this book took place during one of the most challenging experiences of my life. That this experience resulted in the writing of a book, rather than depression, alcoholism, or gaining ninety pounds, is due to the help, love, and guidance I received from many wonderful people.

I would like to thank those whose lectures helped me not only to envision and express the wisdom of Rav Natan, but to stretch and grow instead of breaking: Rav Yechial Michael Yosefi, Rabbi Natan Ophir, and the Rav (who wishes to remain anonymous) who taught me about the miracles that lie in our ordeals, about the Tenth Song and the days of the Messiah. In addition, I would like to thank Hannah-Sara Zeller, for sharing her late husband David's remarkable book with me: *The Soul of the Story*, from which I have taken the quote from Rabbi Shlomo Carlebach.

My thanks to Steven Emerson of the Investigative Project on Terrorism (http://www.investigativeproject.org) for putting me in touch with a federal prosecutor who provided invaluable information on how terror suspects are investigated and tried.

My thanks to Stuart Fund for answering my questions about the accounting profession and to Talia Siman-Tov for the camp stories.

Many thanks must also go to Dr. Asher Ragen, whose valuable insights on the entire manuscript were extremely helpful.

My heartfelt thanks to Rabbi Aaron Rakefet-Rothkoff, who showed me by his personal example what generosity and true spiritual greatness look like. Heartfelt thanks must also go to Professor Emily Budick of The Hebrew University of Jerusalem for her priceless support and encouragement, which allowed me to continue writing. To my dear friend and marvelous fellow author Yehudit Rotem, I give my deepest appreciation for her unending kindnesses.

I thank Mibi Moser, Tamir Gluck, and Yaron Hanin for being my knights in shining armor and for teaching me many valuable lessons about the legal profession. In addition, the following books were very helpful in forming my understanding of what it's like to be a student of the law: *Ivy Briefs* by Martha Kimes and *Law School Confidential* by Robert H. Miller.

I thank Daniela and Yehuda Cohen, founding members of beautiful Kibbutz Ein Gedi, for showing me the miracles of making the desert bloom. My thanks also to Dr. Gideon Hadass for a fascinating private tour of his archaeological sites in the desert.

A very special thanks must go to my editor, Jennifer Weis, who helped me to realize my vision of what this book should be. Thank you, Jennifer!

And last, but not least, my deepest thanks to my husband, Alex, who has made this book, and my life, possible.

The Tenth Song

1

It happened, like all horrible things happen, at the most inconvenient time.

Abigail Samuels awoke as the sun streamed through the leaded glass of her beautiful French patio doors. Her eyes opened slowly, taking in the delicate lace of her curtains and the polished wood of her antique canopy bed. Her husband's gentle kiss lingered on her lips, a faint, sweet memory. It was Tuesday, her day off, and he had tried not to wake her before leaving for work.

I'm so lucky, she thought, humming her most recent download from iTunes—a catchy paean of love and longing written and performed by a sixteen-year-old. She might be getting old, but her taste in music hadn't changed; she still loved anything that made her want to dance. That, too, made her happy.

The water was hot enough to burn you, she thought with pleasure, adjusting the temperature controls on the frighteningly expensive mixer faucet. She remembered their leaner years, the first apartment with the broken-down shower that only gave you lukewarm water until noon, and then only enough for one.

She reached for a thick, fluffy bath sheet, catching a glimpse of her nude body in the mirror. Staring at her overlarge breasts, her rounded stomach and thighs, she wondered where her own body had gone. She looked like a Renoir painting, *Baigneuse,* or *Bather Arranging Her Hair,* unfashionably heavy, but not unattractive. To her surprise, instead of being depressed, she felt the word "sexuality" echo in her head. She wondered what that meant at her age, with a husband who had been her boyfriend, and who loved her—with this body and the original—and whom she had loved back now for forty-odd years?

Wrapping the towel around her, she looked into the mirror, combing her wet hair. It had retained its thickness and its sheen, although the days when it flowed down her back like a dark river were long gone, along with her natural mahogany color. It was short and honey brown now, a color that came from bottles and tubes, and was applied with plastic gloves. And while her face had retained its lean shape and had surprisingly few wrinkles—testifying to a calm, pampered, and, for the most part, happy life—her eyelids had begun to droop and her forehead crease. Only in her eyes—large, dark brown ovals that still flashed with amusement and curiosity—did she sometimes glimpse the person she remembered as herself.

Impulsively, she threw open the patio doors, stepping out onto the veranda. "*What a lark! What a plunge . . . ! Like the flap of a wave . . . the kiss of a wave,*" she thought, remembering the words from *Mrs. Dalloway* she had just taught her eleventh-graders. The pungent scent of damp fall leaves rose up to meet her, the crisp Boston air like chilled cider, intoxicating.

She loved the fall, all the sun-faded colors of summer repainted by vivid reds and golds still clinging fragilely to branches that would soon be covered with snow.

What a wonder! My lovely home. My marvelous garden as big as a park, tended by meticulous gardeners. My daughter's engagement. Planning her party. The blue Boston sky. She pirouetted around the room. It would not rain today, no matter what the weather report predicted. Today would be perfect, she thought, slipping on clothes that were unseasonably light.

Walking down the hallway, she could already hear the buzz of the vacuum cleaner as the household began its day without her. No matter how many years she had employed cleaning help, she still hadn't gotten used to it. Perhaps the housekeepers could feel her discomfort. They never stayed very long.

Esmeralda had been with them for six months now. She was in the dining room, working on the carpets. When she saw Abigail, she turned off the machine, her round face, creaseless as a fall apple, looking up warily.

"No, don't stop! I just wanted to say good morning and to tell you I'm going out for a while, to make some arrangements for the party."

"The engagement party. For your daughter. Miss Kayla." The woman nodded and smiled politely, pretending to care. Abigail smiled back graciously, pretending to believe she cared.

Lovely to be walking down the street in the early part of the day instead of stuck in a classroom! She exulted like Clarissa Dalloway, loving *". . . the wing, tramp, and trudge; . . . the bellow and uproar; . . . the motor cars, omnibuses, vans . . . the triumph and jingle and the strange high singing of some aeroplane overhead;"* life, Boston, this moment of September.

She smiled at her shadow as though it were a companion, delighted at the kindly angle of the sun that had airbrushed all the sordid details of aging. But then she noticed the little tufts of hair that stood up waving in the wind—another expensive hairdresser's experiment gone wrong. Ah, well; she smiled to herself, patting them down. What was such a whisper of annoyance next to the ode to joy resonating loudly throughout every fiber of her being?

She raised her face to the sky, beaming at God.

So perfect!

The words had become almost a mantra over the last month, beginning the moment Kayla—her hand clasped tightly in Seth's—announced: "We're engaged!"

She closed her eyes for a moment, savoring the memory: her youngest child's shining face, her big, hazel eyes full of glint and sparkle, like well-cut jewels, revealing their many facets. She recalled clearly the pride and triumph, but somehow the happiness and love were more elusive, like water in sand, absorbed and swallowed. But those things were a given, were they not?

For what was there not to be happy about? Even Kayla, used to golden fleeces falling into her lap without any long quests, must appreciate the answer to every Jewish mother's prayer who would soon, God willing, be her husband. Congratulating them was like making the blessing over a perfect fruit that you hadn't tasted for a long time, Abigail thought: two Harvard Law School students, both Jewish, both from well-to-do families, members of the same synagogue in an exclusive Boston suburb.

But even as she exhaled gratitude like a prayer, she acknowledged it wasn't all luck. I had *something* to do with it, she told herself, almost giddy with triumph. What *hadn't* she done to nurture Kayla? The bedtime stories, the elaborate birthday parties, the shopping trips, the decorator bedroom, the private tutors, the long talks, the faithful attendance at every class assembly, play, and athletic event . . . And Kayla had repaid her beyond her wildest dreams. Straight A's, valedictorian, youth ambassador to Norway . . . And now, soon to be a Harvard Law School graduate.

Like an athlete standing on a podium about to hear the national anthem played before the world because they had jumped the highest, run the fastest, thrown the farthest, Abigail exulted in her motherly triumph. Her nerves rock steady, her hands and feet swift and unswerving, she had run all the hurdles of modern motherhood with this child, if not with her older brother and sister, perfecting her mothering skills. Too bad they didn't give out medals. With Kayla, she had certainly earned the gold.

She heard a car honking and turned around. It was Judith, the rabbi's wife. She had a huge smile on her face as she mouthed the words *Mazal tov!* behind her windshield.

There had been no official announcement yet. Still, everyone had heard through the grapevine.

Thank you! Abigail mouthed back. At just that moment, she saw Mrs. Schwartz walking across the street in the opposite direction.

"Abigail! Just heard about Kayla! How wonderful!" She cupped her mouth, shouting.

Abigail waved, delighted. "Thank you! Thank you!" She shouted back. "Are you coming to the party?"

"I wouldn't miss it!"

She felt almost like a celebrity, as if she owned the town.

A motorcycle roared past, shearing the air and cutting off her thoughts. She looked up at the swaying old trees, suddenly feeling afraid. Her grandmother would have said "*kenina hora*" meaning, more or less, "may the Evil Eye keep shut." In the Middle Ages, all good fortune would have routinely filled the recipients with dread, she comforted herself. One would have had to bang pots or compose and wear amulets to ward off the furies set loose by such joy as hers.

She took a deep breath, exhaling all bad thoughts, focusing. The caterer, then the florist. Check the hotel reservations at the Marriott for the out-of-town uncles and Adam's sister and brother-in-law. Check Printers Inc. for place cards and probably Grace After Meal booklets with a photo of the young couple, although Adam might be right in thinking that would be overkill, since they'd have to be reordered for the wedding. But she wasn't feeling frugal.

They'd moved up far in the world. From the salary of a lowly junior accountant to the earnings of their own accounting firm, whose clients headlined articles in *Fortune* magazine. It had taken a long time. Their eldest, Joshua, had just gotten into high school when they'd finally bought their dream house, a historic colonial on a block of sought-after homes a short commute from downtown and Harvard. The renovation had taken years.

She turned the corner into Harvard Square. The students who rented out the smallest apartments had already taken up residence. They crowded the streets, their trim figures still in shorts and sleeveless tops, as if their defiance was enough to keep winter at bay.

She had been teaching high-school English for close to thirty-five years now. She liked young people. She liked looking at them: their bright, smooth, open faces, their supple, shapely bodies, their smiles. She liked their intelligent rebellion against forced compromises with conventional wisdom, often thinking that she learned as much as she taught. That, perhaps, had been her greatest fear about her profession: the *bloody-mindedness* as D. H. Lawrence—that rebel against hypocrisy—had called it; the repetitiveness of it all. The need to "cover material," dulling the senses of the fresh enthusiastic human beings who, for the first time, were about to encounter a world of infinite wonders.

That had not happened, at least not too often. When she assigned Willa Cather's *My Antonia,* or Steinbeck's *Grapes of Wrath,* or *The Diary of Anne Frank,* she felt like a bystander to a thrilling event about to unfold before her very eyes. Sometimes, she admitted to herself sheepishly, she even felt a little like she'd coauthored the book, deserving part of the credit for its wondrous qualities.

The kids were always such fresh challenges—not unlike the books themselves. At the beginning of each new school year she felt as if she were peeling back the covers from their stiff bindings, each one a unique and fascinating story. She'd begin her relationship with each one hopefully, hanging in there, looking for the good things until forced to admit otherwise. That did not happen often. If you looked hard enough and refused to give up hope long enough, you could always find something.

How lovely to be young and unwrinkled, with so many unspent days and months and years ahead! How lovely to have strong bones and white, glistening teeth straightened to perfection by expensive orthodontia. Her tongue navigated her own less-than-perfect smile. Some women her age got them straightened—there were invisible braces nowadays, and porcelain veneers . . . But it seemed so vain and extravagant, not to mention bothersome. Besides, she had a man who had been telling her for the last forty years she was the most beautiful woman in the world.

She smiled to herself, waiting on the corner for the light to change.

The Body Shop window had cranberry-scented candles in little straw holders. But might it be too obvious to use a fall decorating scheme for the party? Pumpkins and squash, cranberries and apples? Adam would love it. Orange was his favorite color—any shade. The kids often poked gentle fun at him for wardrobe disasters that could be chalked up to this enthusiasm. Since he never shopped unless forced to by dire necessity—like running out of socks—his purchases were often spontaneous impulses that overtook him when passing outlet stores with signs that read EVERYTHING REDUCED 70%. Inevitably, those drastic reductions included some article of men's apparel dyed a shocking— and consequently unsalable—shade of unbelievable orange: jackets, shirts, vests, ties, raincoats, even boots.

She shook her head. Goodwill always had a supply of excellent high-quality items in those shades courtesy of Adam Samuels. They hardly ever sold. Even poor people had some standards.

She walked into the shop, fingering the waxy shapes, breathing in the spicy smells. There was still time to make these decisions. So far Kayla had been very breezy "whatever" about the engagement party, except for defining the absolute parameters: Evening. Black tie. Top-notch catering. And one-twenty to one-fifty guests, max.

"Abigail?"

She turned her head. It was Sandra something, a woman she knew vaguely from synagogue functions; someone who wore strange, baggy designer clothes and had her hair cut brutally short. She and her husband were the kind of people who always wanted something: free tax advice, investment tips, donations for obscure causes, or to enlist you in time-consuming volunteer schemes that would make themselves look good. She smiled.

The woman put her arms around her, kissing her cheek: "*Mazal tov!* I just heard. Wonderful about your daughter's engagement!"

"Oh, how did you . . . ?"

"Your friend Doris told me. So exciting!"

Doris? "Yes, thanks so much," Abigail said with an inward sigh, mentally adding her name and the vaguely remembered Doris's to a guest list already bloated with people she had to invite or risk insulting. Suddenly, when a party was in the offing, people seemed to sniff it out, ratcheting up their friendliness quotient to be included.

"Well, see you in *shul*!" Abigail waved, hurriedly leaving the store.

As she walked toward the caterer, Abigail felt herself tense. She hoped there wouldn't be a fight with Kayla, but there was no way she was going to insult Arthur Cohen (who was, after all, a fellow synagogue member and an old friend) by going elsewhere.

She remembered Adam's fiftieth birthday bash. Even though Abigail had done all the work, Kayla felt she had a right to decide the guest list. "You don't want them. They are so boring," she'd said, putting a line through Henrietta and Stephen.

They were old, old friends, people she and Adam had known from the first week they'd moved to Boston. They had been to all each other's milestone celebrations, shared Sabbath evening dinners, planned joint vacations. They were like family.

"But we were invited to Stephen's fiftieth!" Abigail protested.

"Oh, he's such a bag of wind. And she's even worse . . ." Kayla scrunched up her pretty nose in distaste. "I thought we would just have—you know—the family," she continued, crossing off another two of their oldest friends.

Abigail said nothing but invited whom she pleased.

It was a surprise party. She'd expected all the kids to arrange something special for Adam. Joshua, of course, did, preparing a heartfelt video in which he interviewed all their friends and relatives, putting together a lovely tribute. And Shoshana, even though she was eight months pregnant and had a toddler of two to look after, made all the flower arrangements, handwrote all the place cards, and baked hundreds of those sugar cookies she was famous for. Kayla, in contrast, breezed in the night of the party, an hour later than Abigail had asked her to come, wanting to know how she could help.

"Nothing, darling. It's all been arranged. I'm just so happy you're here." Abigail smiled at her sweetly, swallowing hard. "Daddy will be here soon. Would you be an angel and answer the door?"

It was Stephen and Henrietta, followed by Arthur and Helen, and a few more of Kayla's cross-offs. Kayla gave them a bare smile, then sulked the entire evening, until finally she left early without saying good-bye.

"Her Majesty is not happy with her subjects," Adam murmured dryly, when Abigail filled him in on the details.

The next day, of course, Kayla was contrite and apologetic. "I just had something really private and special planned for Daddy. I had this whole speech. . . ."

Abigail felt a pang of guilt. Perhaps she had ruined some lovely, special moment between father and daughter? Perhaps there had been an excellent reason for her bratty behavior? Perhaps Kayla was on a higher level—a place Abigail couldn't see even in her imagination?

Or perhaps not.

As always, they both apologized, hugged, and let it pass. What was the name of that organization founded by a billionaire to help Bill Clinton out of the Monica Lewinsky morass? Getoverit.org? Or something like that. Exactly.

For a moment, she thought about discussing this openly with her daughter. She rummaged through her purse for her cell phone, then suddenly remembered it was on her desk recharging.

Just as well. She just wouldn't bring the subject up. Kayla wouldn't remember anyhow, she thought, recalling her sweet sixteen party. For months, every time the subject had come up, she'd feigned disinterest, saying it was silly and childish, like kids' "theme" parties. And so Abigail had ordered a cake and invited the family and a handful of Kayla's friends. But then after attending a friend's sweet sixteen in a theme park, with a party held afterward in the Hilton ballroom in Back Bay, with a live performance by a popular local band, Kayla had changed her mind.

Of course, things were arranged: the band, the hall, the works, all at the very last minute. Kayla had been adorably grateful and happy. She had enjoyed every minute. And Abigail, exhausted, had spent the next week in bed. Now, except for the caterer and the guest list, Abigail was perfectly happy to do anything her daughter wanted—if only Kayla would say what that was. On time.

Oh my goodness, she scolded herself. *The bride is too pretty.* Was this stuff worth worrying about? You have a beautiful daughter. A Harvard Law School student. A girl who is engaged to a Jewish mother's dream. A *nachas* bonanza. Give it a rest!

Maybe she'd just buy a few cranberry candles and show them to Kayla.

But first—she wanted to settle with the caterer.

"Hi, Gayle," she said, walking into the catering and takeout shop. "Is your dad in?"

"Oh, Mrs. Samuels!" The girl looked up from her computer, hastily slamming it shut. Her face turned the color of the tomato salsa featured in the refrigerator case, Abigail thought, wondering if it had been that color when she walked in, and she just hadn't noticed. She stood staring in wonder, watching the color deepen to scarlet. "Oh, I'll . . . just get Dad," the girl said, fleeing.

A tiny stab of unease suddenly pierced Abigail Samuels. A prescient moment, absolutely baseless, began to send a wave of nausea and nervous tension through her body. She was the kind of person who always unconsciously identified with the person she was with—a remnant of her childhood inferiority complex, which insisted she be a chameleon to court favor. Everyone had to love her. And if you were just like the person you were with at the moment, it helped.

"Oh, Albert."

His face was pleasant but not welcoming, with a strange crease of discomfort between the brows. "Abigail."

There was an awkward silence as she tried to figure out where she was and what had happened. Did she owe him money? Adam always paid the bills and paid them promptly. Perhaps Kayla had slipped and told one of her friends about the outside catering, and word had gotten back to him? But she was here now, ready to order . . .

"I'm—so sorry," he finally said.

Like a character in a bad play, she looked behind her to see who he could be talking to. There was no one there.

"What's wrong, Al?"

His face took on a sense of shock. "It was on the Internet. Gayle showed it to me . . ." He paused, horrified as the realization struck that he would be the one breaking this kind of news to a person he knew and liked, the kind of news that should be heard among your own people, in your own home, surrounded by people you loved.

2

The only way a blunt cut looked good on anyone was if it was done perfectly, Kayla Samuels thought, trying to coax some of her recalcitrant wisps into sweeping inward just below her chin, very Posh Spice. This was the third hairdresser she had gone to in the last six months trying to achieve that effortlessly perfect look that went so well with business suits. It had been to no avail. No matter their reputation, Boston hairdressers were all ridiculously overpriced provincial hacks, she thought. To the simple fact that the cut imposed unrealistic demands on her naturally curly hair, which was constantly looking for ways to bolt its man-made confines, she gave no quarter. It was her hair, and it would obey.

She sat down on the steps of the gothic brick building housing law-school classrooms, looking at her watch. He was already ten minutes late. Given that her fiancé, Seth, was an annoying stickler for punctuality, this surprised her, even evoking a mild concern. What could be keeping him? she wondered, caressing the fine leather of the briefcase in her lap, a gift from her thrilled parents when the Harvard acceptance letter arrived. She opened it, taking out her compact and staring at her nose. To her horror, she saw that her freckles were visible. She hurriedly covered them with makeup. There was nothing that made her look less like a lawyer than freckles, except if it was curly hair as Seth always said.

For months she had been resisting his advice to go to a real salon in Manhattan to get it properly straightened. But she realized now that she had absolutely no choice. She couldn't very well go to her own engagement party looking like a "crash and burn One L."

One L. The first year of law school in that private language that conjured up harried, privileged, and near-neurotic inductees into a secret society. But it hadn't been so bad. *Paper Chase* and Scott Turow's *One L* were really history. There was a gentler, kinder cloud hanging over Harvard Law these days. A new dean had banished the ogres and injected some Technicolor into the aging sepia overtones of a school drowning in tradition. The curriculum had undergone the most radical changes in a hundred years, making Harvard Law less "the factory" its cynical graduates had nicknamed it—a mass-production line for legal hacks to defend corporate sharks—and more, as the new dean said, a place for: "engagement with the world . . . a place . . . for people who love ideas, because ideas make a difference."

Even the old campus buildings—she looked behind her at stately Austin Hall where Professor Dumbledore would have felt at home—were soon going to be relics, overtaken by the new Northwest Corner expansion, which would transform the musty halls of power into a magnificent modern enterprise.

Although Yale was still being listed on Web sites as the premier law school in America, no one actually believed that.

She remembered her first day of classes, standing in the hallway outside Ames Moot Court in Austin Hall waiting to be officially "welcomed." Leaning shyly against the wall, she took a leisurely survey of her fellow students. They stood in conversation knots: skullcaps talking to skullcaps; stiletto heels talking to preppies; Midwesterners talking to people from New Jersey. Chosen from over seven thousand applicants, the privileged five hundred or so of the entering class of 2006 would soon be divided into sections. She wondered which of them would constitute her friends, competitors, and classmates for the most challenging year of her life.

She saw him standing in the middle of a group of laughing men and women, people magically at ease, filled with the open friendliness that comes from extreme self-confidence. He was tall and slim, with shining blond hair that caught the light, distracting her from whatever blah, blah was being said. When they were finally divided into sections, she was disappointed to find he wasn't in hers.

She soon forgot about it. She had no time for a social life anyway, she told herself, as the incredible pace of study, classwork, and exams swung into full gear. She was overwhelmed, wracked with doubts, wondering when and if she would finally crash-land into the side of the mountain she was trying so desperately to clear. More than that, the coursework itself began to fill her heart with fears. Torts, especially, gave her nightmares, filled as it was with way-out scenarios of horrible things one person did to another intentionally or unintentionally. Take the case of the poor woman who was on a subway on the way to the beach when someone dropped firecrackers on the tracks, resulting in a huge scale hitting her on the head from the other side of the platform. Life, Kayla began to realize, was totally unpredictable. And so was the law.

She didn't dare admit any of this, of course. She felt isolated and lonely, walking a fine line in class between showing off and shirking participation. And while she met people, and joined study groups, she never felt she was making new friends. Everyone seemed to have an agenda, the same agenda: to live through year one and pass all their courses. To that end, it was a community of moles, blindly dedicated to self-preservation, competing for sustenance, i.e., help with notes and outlines, and a good word from any professor. They were in a race, charging toward the finish line and the honors that came with the best grades. She had no illusion of being a worthy contender. She just wanted to keep her head above water.

In the middle of her first year, after four months of hibernation, her best friend, Shana, insisted on fixing her up on a blind date.

"He's my boyfriend Mark's second cousin. He's twenty-eight. He was a few years ahead of us at Hebrew Day School. He's also just started Harvard Law. He has a B.A. from the University of Massachusetts, Boston, in anthropology and international relations."

"A state school?"

"His parents are wealthy, but cheap, Mark's mother says. He managed to get into the MBA program at Stanford and wound up winning the Siebel Scholars jackpot, $25,000 a year for the remainder of the program!"

"He's got an MBA from Stanford? So what's he doing in law school?"

"Mark says he went to work for a high-tech company in Silicon Valley but didn't like it. But he stayed there a few years to make enough money to partially fund law school."

"Sounds indecisive. Or is he just one of those perpetual students?"

"Are you kidding me? With an MBA from Stanford and a law degree from Harvard, he'll be able to write his own ticket! Not to mention he looks like Brad Pitt in *Thelma and Louise*. Stop being stubborn! You'll kiss my feet when you meet him."

"Shana, I appreciate it. But I just don't think dating and law school are ever going to mix. First of all, there is no time! Second of all, there is no way you can fit a male Harvard Law student and his ego into the same part of the city, let alone the same restaurant! Besides, if he's as gorgeous as all that, he's probably gone out with every single available Jewish princess in Brookline already."

This turned out to be true. It also turned to be irrelevant.

She looked down at her engagement ring. The stone wasn't large, but it was absolutely flawless. And the setting, a custom-made platinum band with two small rubies, was special.

She leaned back on the steps, looking at her watch again. He was now twenty minutes late. A sudden chill gust made her fingertips tingle. She zipped up her jacket, sorry she hadn't worn a warmer one. She folded her arms across her chest and closed her eyes. Her lids felt warm.

Somehow, she'd gotten through her first year. The second year had been easier.

For one thing, unlike her first year, which was pretty much mapped out with requirements, she had had the opportunity to choose her classes. Her first instinct had been to enroll in Child Advocacy; Child Exploitation, Pornography, and the Internet; Law and Social Change; or Bioethics. But following a long and heated argument, Seth had talked her out of it. "When the recruiters start wining and dining you, what are you going to offer them? Little Orphan Annie law? If you want to pay back the thousands of dollars a year for your student loans, you better take Bankruptcy, Corporation and Taxation, and Securities and Regulation. And throw in Business Strategies for Lawyers for fun."

She didn't remind him that she, at least, didn't have thousands of dollars in student loans. In fact, she had no loans at all, a sore point between them since his parents had refused "on principle" to help him pay his tuition. While he had some money saved from his high-tech days, it was not nearly enough for three years at $42,000 a year plus living expenses, forcing him into serious hock.

But whenever the subject came up, Seth declared that not only did he understand his parents, he even agreed with them, defending them, Kayla thought, a little too passionately.

"I'm going to do the same with my kids . . ."

"Our kids . . ."

"Our kids. Why should anyone think they deserve a free ride through life? Besides, how can you connect with clients who have money problems if you've never experienced any? You live such a sheltered existence, Kayla, and your parents are such enablers!"

"And your parents are cheapskates, and snobs, and social climbers . . ." she'd replied with hurtful accuracy, thinking it wasn't her fault if her parents were too rich for her to apply for a scholarship. Why should she be punished by being forced to take expensive, interest-bearing loans from strangers; people who would not be as understanding as Daddy when or if she had cash-flow problems?

They didn't speak for days. Although she tried to convince herself that she wasn't in Harvard Law just for the money, she had to be honest: She wanted the American life. The good life. The life of her parents. The life she was used to. Although she knew her parents would pay for her education and would be generous when it came to a down payment on her first home, after that, it would be considered in bad taste to ask them for anything. And even though she knew Seth would likely be earning a top living in one of the best law firms, she also knew that both their tastes were very, very expensive. In addition, the statistics about divorce were not encouraging. She wanted to be able to depend on herself.

The recruiters, she knew, held the key to all her dreams. They'd be looking for the top students in the areas that made the top money. Harvard Law had often been accused of training lawyers to serve the upper 10 percent of the nation's earners. Kayla knew that for many of her classmates, that was not so much an insult as a description of aspirations.

Going against her instincts, she'd enrolled in Civil Procedures; Legislation and Regulation; Bankruptcy; Administrative Law; and three other courses that were sure to be difficult and time-consuming and consummately boring. At least, she had no interest in them. Seven classes was a ridiculous workload. She knew it would be torture. She also knew she'd do well. She always did. Now she was beginning her third year, and the recruiters were knocking on her door.

She jumped up. He was now officially twenty-five unforgivable minutes late. At this point, she was really more alarmed than angry. That was *really* not like him. She dialed his number for the third time. Again, it was busy. She hated that, hated that he was involved with someone else when he should have been there with her, on time. Unless, of course, he'd been in a car accident, and the phone was lying in the gutter beeping away just as the ambulance drove off with him. But in that case, it would just ring until the voice message came on.

Ten more minutes, she thought, feeling a knot grow and expand in her stomach. If he's not here by then, and I still can't get through, I'll start calling his parents, his friends, the police. I'll walk over to his house. Because thirty-five minutes would mean that some of the world's unpredictability had finally caught up with them.

3

"Seth, come look at this . . ."

"In a minute, Medgar," he said without raising his head. "I'm in the middle of memorizing a casemap for Civil Procedures, and I've got at least another ninety pages of reading for my contract class. On top of that, I've got to meet Kayla in fifteen minutes. So, if it can wait . . ."

"It can't," his roommate answered decisively, tapping him insistently on the shoulder, then pushing a laptop into his face. Seth reeled back in surprise. "What the hell . . . !"

Medgar, a black honor student from Brooklyn College who had been rooming with him for fourteen months, was levelheaded and quiet, a person who studied hard and respected boundaries. This was totally out of character.

"Just look at it," he insisted quietly.

Seth stared, grabbing the computer with white-knuckled fists. "It's got to be some kind of mistake!" His eyes pored over the screen, taking in the images and the words in growing disbelief. "My God!"

"Too bad A. J. Hurling is involved. He's practically an icon. You know the story: a street hood who rose up from his prison background, founded a successful software company, becoming a role model, a contributor to urban charities. . . ."

People are going to be outraged that Mr. Samuels involved him in a dirty scheme to fund terror networks who are killing American soldiers . . ."

It was a nightmare. "People are innocent until proven guilty . . . icon or no. It could just be yellow journalism," Seth protested weakly.

"For sure. But once the press gets hold of you . . ." Medgar shrugged, gently prying away his laptop and closing it, erasing the offensive images. "Did Kayla mention anything?"

Seth shook his head. "I . . . Nothing. She hasn't said anything . . ." At least not to me, he thought bitterly. He reached for the phone to call her, but it was already ringing. "Father. No, no. I didn't. I don't know anything. She didn't mention . . . I'm just about to meet her. I'm sure she would have told me if . . ." He pressed his lips together furiously. "What is that supposed to mean? She wouldn't do that. She would never hide something like this, not from me!"

Even as he said the words, a small doubt crept into his heart. "No, I don't agree. I don't think postponing the party is a good idea. It's not up to Mom! It's up to us. Look, I'm late for an appointment. I'll call you later. Yes . . . yes, I'll think about it. Good-bye."

He hung up and immediately began to dial Kayla's number, but something stopped him. He put down the phone. How was it possible she hadn't known? Surely her father had warned the family he was in trouble. But it would be better to discuss this face-to-face, he thought, putting on his shoes, his jaw flexing in fury.

His phone buzzed. He glanced at the screen, his eyes rolling as he considered his options. If he switched it off, she'd just call back.

"Mother." He closed his eyes, pressing the phone to his ear. "Look, I'll know more when I talk to Kayla. Yes, I'm just about to see her. . . . What do you mean? That's ridiculous! There aren't going to be any reporters lurking behind the bushes on Harvard's campus! Why would you say that? She's my fiancée, and he's her father! You're being hysterical." He fell silent, listening intently for a long time. He closed his eyes, taking a deep breath. "Don't cry. I said I'd think about it! Good-bye." He turned his cell phone off, then slammed it shut.

Medgar squeezed his shoulder sympathetically. "Hey, man, whatever I can do . . ."

"Yeah, thanks."

"And Seth?"

"Yes?"

"She's worth it."

He shrugged. "Yeah. I know."

"See you later, bro."

With relief, Seth watched the door close behind him.

He needed to be alone. He needed peace and quiet and time to make up his own mind and decide what it was he thought and what he was going to do about it. His mother was beyond hysterical. She was talking about calling off the engagement altogether, not just postponing the party. She felt tricked, betrayed.

"You can't get involved in this. It will ruin you, Seth," was what she had said.

He grabbed one knee to his chest, resting his chin on it, in shock. How could this have happened so quickly, from one moment to the next? What was needed was a cold-blooded damage assessment, he told himself, steadying his nerves.

There was Brad Atkinson, of Atkinson, Marciano and Lowe, the top law firm in Chicago, who was flying him out for an interview in three days. There was no reason for anyone there to connect him to Adam Samuels. They weren't married yet. They weren't even officially engaged—nothing had appeared in the social columns of the papers. In fact, the subject of an official engagement announcement had only just come up. Mostly his mother's idea; Kayla couldn't have cared less. And once they were married, she'd have his name.

The biggest problem, as far as he could see, was all those callback interviews Kayla had set up for herself in New York. She had done so well on the initial interviews . . . Damn! With a swift and brutal motion, he swept his arm across his desk, sending everything smashing to the floor. They'd been counting on two incomes, to pay off their (his, he reminded himself) school loan debt and have a reasonably comfortable lifestyle. Was it cowardly for a person to want to protect everything he'd worked so hard to achieve?

From his parents he had received amazingly little. Although they lived in a very expensive house in the most expensive neighborhood in Boston, and went on extravagant vacations twice a year, they never bothered to have their children's teeth regularly checked by a dentist, something he and his sister had paid for dearly once they got into college. His father was a member of several country clubs, and always bid for the highest honors in the synagogue, but refused to give his children a penny toward their college tuition. It would take years to pay off Seth's loans if he did it alone while supporting a family.

He was already twenty-five minutes late. She'd be furious or worried. His gut told him to run to her as fast as he could. But something else was in charge of him, he realized. Some powerful tenacious force had wrapped its tentacles around his heart like a python, squeezing out all feeling except self-preservation.

4

There was only one other explanation, Adam Samuels thought as he looked at the men who had invaded his office: that he was in the middle of a nightmare. Sometimes they seemed so real: that sinking feel you got when it all turned too horribly complicated to unravel; the feeling of fighting your way to the surface, the blessed realization that all you had to do to unravel it all was simply open your eyes. The problem was, he felt as if his eyes were already open.

He had been at his desk only fifteen minutes that morning when he heard the voices rising in his outer office. He pressed the intercom: "Is everything all right, Ida?"

The heavy oak door to his office opened.

"Mr. Samuels . . ."

She came in, half-turned around, facing the three strangers who surrounded her like basketball players trying to prevent a pass.

"Mr. Samuels, I told them they couldn't just . . . but they insisted . . ."

"It's all right, Ida." He looked at them and smiled, rising from his chair. They looked like colleagues, fellow accountants, in their dark suits, white shirts, and ties. "Can I help you gentlemen?"

The impassive hardness of their faces betrayed nothing.

"Are you Mr. Adam Samuels?" one asked politely. He was a muscular man with a large frame that seemed unnaturally confined inside his grey business suit, his belt straining against his large gut.

"Yes, I am. How can I help you?" he repeated, confused now.

"Mr. Samuels. We are agents of the Federal Bureau of Investigation and you are under arrest," the second one said. He was smaller but seemed somehow more menacing, his pale face as waxy as a root vegetable, his small eyes as dark and hard as river stones.

The secretary made a strangled sound, clutching her mouth with her hand.

Adam's head swam. "What?" Then he suddenly relaxed, looking up over their shoulders to the corners of the room, searching for the hidden cameras. "You're friends of my son Josh, right? From out in Hollywood?" They would show the film at his birthday party. Everyone would be falling out of their chairs in hysterics. He winked.

The men lifted their eyebrows at each other.

His heart began to race. "This is some kind of prank, isn't it?"

"I'm afraid not, Mr. Samuels," said the muscular one without expression. "We're here to take you into custody. We hope for your own sake, you'll co-operate."

"Mr. Samuels!" his secretary said, her voice rising hysterically.

"Please tell your secretary to go back to her desk and not to interfere, or she'll be charged with obstruction of justice and arrested."

"Ida, please, do as they say!"

"All right, if you're sure, Mr. Samuels . . ." Her hands shaking, she closed the door reluctantly behind her.

"What do you think I've done, for God's sake? Please, can't you at least tell me that?" he begged.

"You have the right to remain silent. Anything you say can and will be used against you in a court of law . . ." they continued, ignoring him.

How many times had he watched scenes like this on television dramas? It was impossible to imagine yourself part of it, he thought. All the worries that keep a person from sleeping at night, that fill him with fear and apprehension, never include these things. They are too outlandish and theatrical. Or, perhaps, he thought, there was some kind of self-preservation mechanism that prevented people from envisioning catastrophes on such a scale.

Adam sat down, barricading himself behind his desk. "Okay then. I'd like to see your warrant please, and some kind of identification."

The menacing one took out a piece of paper from the inside pocket of his jacket, placing it on the desk, while the others reached into their pockets, extracting badges with identification. Adam grabbed the paper frantically. A federal warrant for his arrest! And the badges and the IDs looked real enough, but how could you know?

"Mr. Samuels, don't make this harder on yourself than you have to," warned the muscular one, who looked as if he was capable of making it a lot harder.

"I want to call my lawyer."

"You can call your lawyer when we reach our headquarters."

Something white-hot and electric spread through him. He felt a fury that filled him with adrenaline. "NO! NOW YOU LOOK!" he screamed. "I don't know who you think you are, but you can't do things like this! I'm a U.S. citizen. I've got some rights!" He slammed his fists against the smooth wood of his desktop.

That, he realized too late, was a huge mistake. The muscular one moved quickly around the desk, pulling him out of his chair. Levering his body, he pushed Adam's head against the wall, pulling his arms backward as he snapped on handcuffs.

The cold metal burned against Adam's skin. He struggled to free his wrists, shocked. "You can't just come barging into a man's office with absolutely no warning, threatening him. . . ."

"Yes," the third man finally spoke, selecting every word with care, "we can." He was tall and slender, more like a college student than a cop, with reddish hair and blue eyes. He seemed reasonable, not like the others. "We are authorized to do exactly that by the FBI's Terrorist Financing Operations Section, which was created by the Patriot Act. You and your client have been under surveillance for almost two years for transferring money to support terrorist organizations that are responsible for the death of dozens of American soldiers."

"American soldiers? Terrorist organizations?" Adam went limp. He felt breathless, his expression changing from outrage, to confusion, then finally to terror. "This is a horrible mistake, gentlemen," he pleaded helplessly, his voice lowering from a shout to a whisper. "I don't have any clients who would be involved with terrorists, who would—God forbid!—want to hurt our soldiers! I'm just an accountant. I'm Jewish. I wouldn't help terrorists! I'm a Jew! I support Israel! I'm even in favor of the Patriot Act!"

Not a muscle moved in their passive faces, Adam realized in despair. There was an invisible shield between them. Nothing he could say would penetrate it.

"At least let me tell my wife what's going on! I can't just disappear!" he appealed to the one with red hair, while the others put their arms through his. He felt his feet digging long ridges through the new carpeting as they dragged him to the door.

"Once more, as my fellow officers explained, we are authorized to discuss all these things with you at headquarters, sir," the redhead said politely, opening the office door.

Coffee, recently swallowed, rose back up into Adam's throat. Suddenly, horribly, he felt his bowels loosen. "Please, can I use the bathroom?"

They looked at him, expressionless. "Where is it?"

He nodded toward a door, glad now he had insisted on putting one in his office and would not have to be taken down the hall to the public toilet where everyone on the floor might see him.

"Just leave the door open."

He nodded. "Could you take off the cuffs, please? Just for a moment?"

The menacing one began to shake his head at the others, but the redhead nodded, unlocking him.

"Thank you," he said hoarsely.

He sat down on the toilet, embarrassed by the explosive sounds coming out of his body. When he was finished, he washed his hands, staring into his own eyes. Who are you? he thought. What do they see when they look at you?

When he came out, they held out the cuffs.

"Please, are the cuffs really necessary? I'm not dangerous."

"It's just procedure, Mr. Samuels. Nothing personal," said the muscular one.

"Well, at least cuff them in front of me then, not in back."

"It's against regulations." The menacing one shook his head.

"But if my nose runs, or my face itches . . . please," he begged.

"Cuff him in front," the redhead told the others.

He held out his hands gratefully, already behaving like a prisoner, used to the rules, sinking into the new landscape of his life. It swallowed him like quicksand.

Was this real?

If it was a dream, it had not all been a nightmare.

He remembered the part where he had pressed his lips warmly against Abigail's forehead as she slept before leaving the bedroom that morning; the scent of damp fall leaves crushed underfoot as he walked down the driveway to his car; the chill of the cool leather seats; and the rhythm of the windshield wipers sweeping away the dew. He remembered standing on line in Starbucks, ordering a caramel macchiato for his secretary and his own latte, and how the combined aromas had made the office a momentarily festive place.

But if it was all real, then how could the universe have participated so fully in keeping his fate from him? There should have been some omen: a razor nick that brought blood, a shattered glass nudged off the kitchen counter, something to presage what was coming. It was the same complaint, he knew, that Holocaust survivors had voiced against the sun, which continued to rise and set, unaffected and indifferent to gas chambers and crematoria.

He leaned his head against the hard, polished wood of his office door, gathering strength for the ordeal of being dragged out in front of his secretary. Her horrified face and tear-filled eyes made him feel like a murderer fleeing the scene of his crime. Choking on a wad of phlegm, he coughed until his eyes filled with tears.

"Ida, call Abby!" he called back to her, as they hurried him out of the office.

He saw his young associates lean out of their cubicles. Mark, the newest hire, a Stanford honor student, wooed from a dozen other companies, had a look of frozen disbelief. Phillip, who had been with him longest, kindly turned away, hiding himself as quickly as he could. They were young people who had trusted him, putting their bright futures into his hands. Now those futures were tarnished, he thought, wiping away tears of shame. They hurried him into the elevator.

Any illusion of fighting for his good name was suffocated in an avalanche of howling reporters and photographers who ambushed him just as he left the building.

"Where did they come from?" he heard the redhead mutter under his breath.

"Who in our office has a girlfriend that works at the *Herald*?" the muscular one answered cynically.

Instinctively, Adam flung his arms across his eyes, shielding them from the harsh flashing lights, the hostile stares of strangers.

The newspaper editors would choose that one, he thought as he sat in the back of a car with tinted windows, pressed between the thighs of two beefy strangers. The wire services would pick it up. Unless his lawyers could find some way to stop it, by tomorrow morning—or sooner—it would be everywhere, along with heartbreaking photos of dead American soldiers killed by terrorists, illustrating the screaming headlines:

BOSTON C.P.A. ARRESTED FOR FUNDING

TERROR AGAINST AMERICAN SOLDIERS

He imagined his children, his relatives, his clients, his friends in synagogue . . . his rabbi, picking up the paper.

He imagined Abigail.

It was inexcusable he'd left that phone call to his secretary. But what other choice did he have? He was under arrest.

Under arrest.

His phone vibrated, dancing with festive lights, buzzing away. He knew it must be her. Where was she calling from? he wondered. The florist? The caterer? He imagined her voice, that breathless tone she got when she was busy and joyful with some urgent question about salmon versus mushroom crepes, or whether the flowers should be local or imported. She was so happy about Kayla and the upcoming festivities. He didn't take this for granted.

She was odd that way, unpredictable. Take the house. While most women would have been thrilled to decorate a beautiful house to their heart's content, Abigail had—more or less and despite her best efforts to hide it—hated it. And now, here she was, floating around Coolidge Corner, choosing roses and lilies and canapés, filled with joy.

"We'll take that for now," the muscular man said authoritatively, reaching over and grabbing the cell phone. Slowly, deliberately, he pressed his thumb down, turning it off and placing it in his pocket. It went dark and silent. "Evidence," he murmured.

Adam pressed both palms against his eyes, his fingers gripping his head on either side as if it were a coconut that had been cracked and was about to halve. Strange thoughts rushed by, then images: holding Kayla in his lap on a park swing when she was still too young to sit upright, both of them swinging toward Abigail, who stood in front, her arms outstretched, the baby's big smile reflected on her face as she looked back into his eyes, acknowledging the perfect joy of the moment; the cork popping out of the bottle of Israeli champagne in their tiny Queens living room the day he'd signed the contract with his first big client, transforming himself from a lowly accountant to a "trusted advisor."

Many clients had followed. People with computer start-ups and manufacturing plants, doctors branching out in their practices. In fact, almost all the successful people in his synagogue had begged him to do their books. He had given them all excellent advice, nurturing and sheltering their money, their work, and their vision as if it were his own.

He loved it. He loved being part of their adventure without shouldering any of the risks, and without limiting himself to one narrow field of activity. Every day he learned something new. It was like living a few lifetimes simultaneously, having people trust him, and trusting them, becoming part of their families, their lives.

He looked through the greyed-out FBI car window, glimpsing the Esplanade and Hatch Shell, where he and Abigail had taken the children on warm summer evenings to listen to concerts. And there was the shining surface of the Charles River. He loved the way the sun transformed it into a jeweled carpet. A team of college rowers were making their way swiftly through the waters. They looked strong and carefree. And young. So young.

He'd loved this city, he thought, from the moment he'd set eyes on it; loved its refined buildings and cultured, educated people, the fact that there was so little prejudice, and no rampant crime or corruption. It was a quintessential place to enjoy the blessings of being an American.

He thought of his father, Alex, born in a little village in the Carpathian Mountains, a place that had changed loyalties and languages with each new conqueror. He had never really spoken about what he had been through during the war. But then, when Adam turned eighteen, his father had come into his room, reaching inside his jacket to take out a peeling, sepia photograph of a slim, pretty young woman in an old-fashioned dress with thick black hair and beautiful dark eyes. In her lap was a little girl wearing a frilly dress and hair bows, and on her right a sturdy, handsome little boy. "Your half brother and sister," his father whispered. "My first wife. The Hungarians made me slave labor for the Germans. And when I got back, my neighbors told me they'd all been deported. To Auschwitz."

It was the first and last time they'd ever spoken about it. But when his father died a few years back, and they'd buried him beside Adam's mother, he and Abigail decided to have the names of his first wife and children etched on his tombstone, finally giving them a gravesite.

They say when you are about to die, your whole life flashes before your eyes, like a video on fast-forward. But he wasn't dying, he thought. This was nothing like his battle with cancer.

For months, he had avoided doing anything about the little lump in his chest. And then, when he finally showed it to Dr. Siegel, the young doctor's reassurances had been so emphatic and convincing that he felt no sense of urgency at all about following his advice to "get a biopsy just to put your mind at rest."

His mind was at rest.

He'd only known Siegel a few months. He was a kid compared to wise, grey-haired Dr. Arnold who had been his doctor for several decades before retiring to take Lindblad cruises to Antarctica. But he had instantly liked the bright, friendly thirty-two-year-old with diplomas from Columbia and Harvard hanging in glorified lamination on his office wall. His desk photos of a perky blond woman and three adorable little kids made Adam like and trust him even more. Besides, he felt sure Dr. Arnold would not have handed over his practice to someone less than excellent.

And Siegel was—an excellent doctor, thorough and caring. Adam didn't blame him for not catching the cancer earlier. A malignant sarcoma was so rare that many GPs never came across one in their entire practices. Rare, and for the most part, untreatable, chemo having no effect on them whatsoever. All you could do was cut them out, zap them with radiation, then hope for the best.

For some reason, he had greeted this terrifying news with stoicism. He was shocked, but somehow not really surprised. Many people his age wound up getting something for no good reason. It had just been his time. God had been good to him all his life. He had no complaints. He was willing to do what he had to do, then leave it up to fate. He made an appointment with the young surgeon that Siegel recommended.

But when he broke the news to Abigail, she was—to his mind at least— hysterical. After urgent, nonstop phone calls to every person who might be in a position to know, she'd zeroed in on the undisputed sarcoma king of America, or perhaps Planet Earth. At twelve midnight the same day, he had an appointment. He didn't ask her for details about how she'd managed that when the specialist's appointment book was crammed up to nine months in advance. He knew better.

While part of him was grateful for her concern and no-stone-left-unturned whirlwind of activity on his behalf, truthfully, a part of him resented her interference. He'd been perfectly fine with the young surgeon Siegel had recommended, a choice Abigail had viewed as tantamount to being operated on in the park by a wino with paper cutters . . .

She was furious at Siegel for not catching the cancer earlier, unforgiving of his original mistaken diagnosis. And Adam had been furious at her for being furious, accusing her of making things worse. She'd been devastated, breaking down for the first time, her frenzy of activity lapsing into mourning.

Repentant at seeing her in such pain, he'd reluctantly agreed to see Dr. Sarcoma King. He was glad he did. Because even Abigail had had to accept it when the great man said: "We'll cut it out, then radiate. But only God knows why sometimes that works and sometimes it doesn't."

That had been five years ago. His chest scars had healed along with the radiation burns, a hairless patch of smooth white skin the only memento of his journey through hell. And even hell had not been so bad. It had been quick, and not particularly painful. Healing had been fast. The worry—well, coming to terms with your mortality was deeper than just worry, he thought—bearable.

The moment of diagnosis—though shocking and depressing—had not felt like the end of the world, just the beginning of a trip you were being forced to make to a third-world country full of inedible food, bad hotels, and dangerous natives. But something inside him had assured him he'd purchased a round-trip ticket, and would be arriving home again, a little battered but safe and sound.

This was different.

He clasped his fingers together in a tight grip that slowly drained them of color. Bringing them to his mouth, he gnawed on his knuckle until he tasted blood.

This was worse. Much worse.

With cancer, he had been cast in the role of innocent victim and embattled hero, surrounded by loving family and friends who sympathized and encouraged, deploring his tough break and praising his forbearance. This, he sensed, was quite a different role. Even if after a long, hard fight he was proven innocent, no one would think of him as a victim. "Where there is smoke there is fire" was the mentality of most average people, who had been turned into wide-eyed morons by too many years of feeding on half-baked stories written by hasty, irresponsible opinionated reporters with egos the size of the Grand Canyon.

The average person, ignoring the growing mountain of debunked information in the press, still read newspapers with a trust best reserved for religious texts. If something was "written in the newspaper," they assumed it had gone through some kind of rigorous scrutiny, when the truth was it was no more reliable than the things your friends told you about sex in the third grade. Until they read about themselves in the papers, few people cared to acknowledge this fact.

Yet—a small surge of hope welled up, like the bubble from a fish exhaling underwater confirming its unseen presence—he was innocent! No one who knew him could possibly believe these outlandish charges. Still!—WHAT IS GOING ON HERE? WHAT WAS THIS ALL ABOUT! HOW COULD THEY POSSIBLY ACCUSE ME OF THIS! his mind repeated incessantly, scurrying from place to place, seeking answers the way a small creature fleeing a huge predator seeks refuge.

Maybe it wouldn't make the national wire services, and would be confined to Boston? Even then. Just the thought of Seth's parents' reaction was like a brutal boot stomping out his delicate, meager hopes, the way you stamp out the dying embers of a discarded cigarette, determined to kill any potential it might have to flare up again and start a forest fire. Somehow, as he was from an older generation, the idea of any other source of news other than a newspaper never crossed his mind.

Then he suddenly remembered: the Internet.

He sank back into his seat, his knees buckling, his heart beating fast. He felt suffocated. He wiped the sweat from his forehead with his sleeve. He had to call them all before they read about it online.

"Please, can I have a drink?"

"We'll be there in twenty minutes."

"Where?"

"Our headquarters. And then to the initial arraignment in federal court."

"But please, why? I haven't even seen a lawyer yet! Maybe we could just clear this up . . . ?"

He had been hoping he could somehow settle this before it got to court—after all, it was too absurd! He remembered that movie *My Cousin Vinny*. It didn't matter what kind of evidence they had against you if you were really innocent. He certainly hadn't violated any antiterrorism laws. It was ridiculous!

Or was it?

He searched desperately for something to hold on to, some innocent thing that had been misconstrued. Was it the Donleavy account, perhaps? They did a lot of outsourcing to places like Bangladesh and Pakistan. Or was it, perhaps, Milton Ornby Ltd., the recycling plant, which sold quantities of raw material to Indonesia? None of it made sense. They were all invested in U.S. stocks and bonds . . .

And then, suddenly, to his horror, something occurred to him.

Christopher Dorset.

It was at the mixer for Harvard Law parents. Adam had been surprised and flattered that the high-rolling tax attorney even remembered his name, let alone bothered to come over. He was the kind of person who hung out with CEOs, movie stars, and media bigwigs; the kind whose name and photo with a blond bimbo showed up in gossip columns on the backdrop of Las Vegas casinos.

They had met only once before, briefly, when Dorset had been consulting for one of Adam's largest clients on a major case. They didn't really know each other. He remembered being in a kind of daze at the unexpected attention. And then Dorset had introduced him to Gregory Van, who, according to Dorset, had been his friend at Cambridge, and was now the financial world's most-well-kept secret: "the most successful hedge-fund operator in Europe," according to Dorset. Adam had been even more surprised that Van had lingered, making no attempt to mingle with the far more powerful and interesting mix of people around them.

What had they spoken about? Adam tried to remember, his dry lips gnawing each other, peeling off the chapped skin. Had there been any warning signs that he'd registered but ignored? All he could recall was a vague sense that the hedge-fund man knew how to dress, and that his suit was no doubt bespoke. The introduction by Dorset had been enough to convince him to listen in fascination to Van's long and complicated tale of banking and investments all over Europe. "We are developing some very interesting financial instruments," he'd said, sounding like Prince Philip. (What was it about that clipped, upper-class British accent that puts Americans off guard, making them feel inferior and worshipful?) Was it that?

At the time, he'd felt the meeting was serendipitous. Only weeks before, A. J. Hurling had called him out of the blue, claiming to have read about Adam in *Fortune* magazine. Adam remembered the article. In it, the CEO of a small but successful start-up that made software for farmers had been kind enough to thank Adam for his guidance and support. Adam had been thrilled that the piece had attracted someone of Hurling's stature, who asked for guidance in investing the millions his software-security company had been raking in over the past year.

Adam had agreed to look around and get back to him. But until the meeting with Van, nothing seemed to fit the bill. He'd listened, wondering at the remarkable coincidence of finding exactly the financial instruments Hurling seemed to be looking for. It was a match made in heaven that had just fallen into his lap. He calculated that his fees alone would be close to a million a year.

And he really needed the money.

The house had eaten up so much, more than he'd ever dreamed possible. And then there was Kayla's tuition, and helping Shoshana and Matthew finance the dream house that he'd been told was going at a bargain price, a beautiful home for his grandchildren. Not to mention Joshua's incessant demands for money to keep his company afloat, demands his wife knew nothing about, and Adam wanted to keep that way.

All he'd wanted—ever wanted—was to keep his family and his clients happy. To do his job well. Had he taken shortcuts? Had he investigated Van properly? Or had he, even unknowingly, slacked off, the lure of profit too strong for him? He felt a sudden panic.

What if it was all true? What if he had unwittingly become part of something evil, and dragged his family and his client into it?

Oh, my God! he thought. Oh, my God!

What, he thought with horror, if I am guilty?

NO, no, no. He had not done anything wrong at all! He hadn't set up the tax shelter, and he wasn't the only financial investor using it. Dozens, if not hundreds, of other clients from very respectable firms had jumped on board. At least, that is what he had been led to believe by men he thought he could trust. He had even traveled to London to check the books twice a year. But what . . . what if it wasn't true? If A. J. Hurling was the only investor? My name and signature are on every single piece of paper. It all leads back to me, he realized with a sense of impending doom.

It's not my fault! he shouted silently to the cynical voice inside him, which sat in silent observation, unmoved and unconvinced. "Okay. Perhaps I was naïve. Perhaps I should have been more suspicious, checked things out more thoroughly. But that would have been like exchanging a beautiful gift for a credit slip when there was absolutely nothing better to buy.

"GREEDY," the ugly, unforgiving voice shouted in his ear.

"HARDWORKING AND CLEVER!" he shouted back.

"Irresponsible and dishonest toward a client," the voice changed tack, whispering.

This cut him to the quick: "NO, NO, HOW CAN YOU SAY THAT! I'M INNOCENT, INNOCENT."

Only when the man next to him said: "What?" did he open his eyes, realizing that his thoughts had found voice.

5

When Abigail came home, she ran up the stairs to find her cell phone. It had twenty-five unanswered calls.

After speaking to Ida, she frantically called their lawyer, Louis, and a taxi service, not trusting herself to drive. All the way to the courthouse, only one thing went through her head: Adam Samuels was the most honest man she had ever known. If he lost luggage and collected insurance money, he actually wrote to return the money when the suitcase showed up ten months later. "They probably have to hire a person to staff a whole new department to handle your letter," Abigail had teased him. "It's never happened before."

But deep down, she was proud to be married to such a man. He never cheated on his income tax. Even when he had legitimate business expenses, like dinners. If he so much as invited Abigail along, he refused to deduct it as a business expense.

These things hadn't surprised her. From the beginning of their relationship, she had seen this in his character. It was one of the reasons she'd fallen in love with him.

They'd met as young singles at a party given by a college fraternity for observant Jews at Brooklyn College. Except they didn't call it a party but a lecture or—better yet—a *symposium,* all the better to deodorize such a gathering from the smell of desperation that clung to Young Israel singles weekends. No one still in college could admit they needed rabbis involved to facilitate their social lives.

So there had been a speaker talking about Soviet Jewry and how to get Anatoly Sharansky and other prisoners of Zion out of the gulag. Afterward, the discussion about the efficacy of public protests versus quiet diplomacy had become a nasty shouting match.

Elliot Reich, the boy she had come with, had loudly defended all the clandestine negotiations supposedly going on between the Kremlin and certain Hasidic rabbis which—according to Elliot—were just on the verge of achieving miraculous results that would be blown to bits by rude public demonstrations insulting to the Soviets. Others had shouted him down, mocking his theories: "Right—the rabbis sitting in Crown Heights have a hotline to the Kremlin! We need to boycott Soviet goods and demand America stop exporting wheat to them. Let them all starve until they open the prison gates for our people!"

Then the room suddenly turned ugly.

"You are just like the American Jews who sat back and did nothing when they were gassing Jews in the concentration camps!" someone shouted.

That was the moment she'd first seen Adam. He took a few steps forward, raising his fingers, his palms outstretched. The room suddenly went quiet, as if something reasonable had been said that everyone could agree with. People seemed to know him, she thought, impressed, looking around.

He spoke so softly that she had to strain to hear him. "Three men are seated on a plane: a Communist, a Fascist, and a Russian Jew. The plane begins to shake, and the three cry out to heaven to save them. An angel appears and says: 'God has heard your prayers. He will keep the plane from going down. More than that—He was so impressed with all of you, that He's decided to grant you each a wish!' The Communist wishes that all Fascists would disappear from the earth. The Fascist wishes the same for all Communists. The Jew says, 'If you are going to grant their wishes, I'll just take a cup of coffee.'" Laughter broke around the room. Then he turned serious. "Maybe we can't do much about

Soviet Jews at the moment, except jaw, but there are still plenty of other tragedies going on in the world where we can be helpful. Like the famine in Biafra."

Suddenly, magically, the atmosphere changed. People's faces unfroze as
they lifted paper cups filled with harmless soft drinks to their lips. It turned
back into the social event it was meant to be. How had he managed that so
easily? she wondered, her eyes following him with admiration and curiosity as
he walked around the room collecting money in an empty ice bucket. Then he
was suddenly standing in front of her.

He was taller than he'd seemed from across the room, but not too tall. She
hated the neck-bending required to communicate with towering males, feeling
as if looking up to someone physically ensured her an inferior position in the
relationship. It made her feel childish and vulnerable. With Adam, all she had
to do was slightly lift her chin.

She studied his eyes, which were a calm, dark brown, very steady, behind
the awful nerdy black-framed glasses of the late sixties. But somehow, because
his face was so large and handsome, his jaw so square, he pulled it off Clark-
Kentishly. He had thick, badly cut black hair and a girl on his arm—a sorority
type, the doctor's daughter or the daughter of people determined she'd be the
doctor's wife—wearing a twinset and wildly expensive yellow patent-leather
Italian flats that were the latest status symbol among rich Jewish college girls.

Right then and there, Abigail had given up hope, almost simultaneously
with the flash of recognition that she had hope. She was not competitive when
it came to men and had an abiding sense of inferiority toward anyone who
looked as if they'd been brought up carefully by nurturing parents with high
expectations and demands—the opposite of her own.

"You've got to be kidding!" Elliot snorted with derision, looking into the
bucket. For the first time, Abigail realized what a condescending jerk he was.
But thrown off kilter by her own nervous attraction, she found herself giggling.

"He's right, Adam," the girl in the twinset said, rolling her eyes and giving
his arm a tug.

"There is nothing funny about this," he said quietly to Abigail, ignoring Elliot and his girlfriend. He spoke firmly in a way that made Abigail want to sink
with misery into the ground.

"Come on, you have to admit, it's a bit of an odd venue for African fund-raising," Elliot sneered, thinking no doubt he was defending Abigail's honor. She stepped away from him, reaching into her purse and taking out ten dollars (her campus lunch money for the week) and throwing it inside with the nickels and dimes. Her eyes met Adam's.

"I know, you're right. I'm . . . I didn't mean . . . to laugh . . . It was just so . . ."

"Stupid and embarrassing?" the girl in the twinset suggested, dropping his arm and flouncing away. He looked after her, confused, but made no move to follow.

"I thought instead of fighting, we could actually accomplish some good this evening." He shrugged. "I apologize. Here . . ." He placed the ten back into her palm, closing her fingers over it. "I know you need it."

She looked out of the car window, her fingers massaging her knuckles, remembering the first time his hands had touched hers, so warm and electric that she had pulled away. She had been appalled that he'd seen through her largesse, refusing to take the money back.

"No! Please. Keep it. I mean . . . give it . . . contribute it . . . I'm . . . It wasn't . . . It was a good idea," she finally blurted out, by this time thoroughly mortified at her sudden, uncharacteristic stutter and strange discomfort.

"I'm not even sure how to get this money to any refugees . . ." he said honestly.

She laughed, and this time he joined her, his face relaxing. They moved into a quiet corner, Elliot looking after her, furious.

"Your boyfriend seems upset."

"Oh, he's not really . . . my . . ." She swallowed. "So does your girlfriend."

"Oh—Darlene. She's very opinionated. Besides, I think she's getting ready to dump me anyhow."

"Why?" She smiled, strangely at ease.

"I think I'm not what her father had in mind."

"Oh. And what would that be?"

"Premed or prelaw."

"What are you then?"

"A lowly accounting major. I've always loved numbers. I thought once I'd go into pure math. Do a Ph.D. But I'm not smart enough. Those guys are really geniuses. What about you?"

"Oh, my mother thinks I should take education courses and become a teacher."

"Your mother but not you?"

"Good guess."

"And you?"

"I've always loved words, reading. I suppose I'm still in my adolescent fantasy of becoming a writer."

"What's wrong with that?"

"It's like wanting to be an actress. Very, very high failure rate, then what?"

"Editor? Journalist? Public relations, copywriter . . . ?"

"I suppose it would be better to fail at any of those than become a successful teacher." She sighed.

"So, what *are* you majoring in?"

"English—and education . . ."

"So, you can teach English . . . ?"

"Right. Hedging all bets."

"I guess we've got a lot in common then . . ."

Abigail looked into his comfortable smiling eyes and rested there, her whole body quiet with relief.

"Give me your phone number."

She looked down at her hands, feeling almost as if he'd shaken her out of a deep sleep.

"So I can call you and tell you what I did with your money."

"Oh, of course." She smiled, deflated but never doubting this was a beginning.

She waited for his call, finding herself turning down dates, evening invitations with her friends, anything that would take her away from the phone when he might suppose her to be home.

A week went by, and she'd felt anxious. When two weeks passed, she felt disappointed but hopeful. But as weeks three, four, and five disappeared without the slightest sign he had ever existed, she found herself going through a range of emotions that began with reasonable doubt (had he lost her number?) and ended with righteous indignation bordering on anger and hopelessness. He had seemed so sincere. But perhaps, like many other people, he was just a good actor who hadn't meant a word of anything he'd said, pocketing the money and having a good laugh.

She finally took up her life again where she'd left off, agreeing to see a movie with a girlfriend. When she returned, uplifted that the spell had finally been broken, her mother said: "You had a phone call."

Of course, it was Adam.

"What'd he say?"

"That he'd call back."

"When—?"

"Well, well." Her mother had looked at her curiously. "What have we here?"

She smiled, remembering what had happened next, which had set the frank and honest tone in which their entire life together had always been lived.

The phone rang again, and this time she'd run to get it.

"Hello? Abigail? It's me. Adam."

"Adam. It's been so . . . long."

There was a beat that gave her enough time to blush at the embarrassing neediness her words revealed.

"Oh, yes. Sorry. It's taken me a while to find out where to send our Biafra money."

"Oh, that." She was both relieved at his honesty and upset that this was a business call.

"I wanted to make sure it would actually get there—so I had to check out how much overhead they take, and salaries. This organization is pretty much all volunteer, and they have been around forever . . ."

"It must have taken a lot of effort."

"Well, I have this thing about money. If you take someone's hard-earned cash, then you have a big responsibility to make sure it's used honestly."

"That is good of you."

"I'd like to send you a copy of the receipt. What's your address?"

She'd told him.

"What part of town is that?"

"Bayswater."

"A bit of a ride from Brooklyn!"

"I know. Which is why all us girls here have been designated G.U."

"G.U.?"

"Geographically undesirable."

He laughed. "That was actually my next question."

Something about what to put on the tax receipt, no doubt! she'd thought. She put her hand on her cheek now, remembering what had happened next.

"Well, I was wondering if you'd like to go out with me Saturday night?"

"I can't believe you're finally asking me out!" she'd blurted out before she could stop herself.

There was a long, silent pause. "Do you always react this way when a boy asks you out?" he'd deadpanned.

"No," she'd answered honestly. "Just you."

The interrogation had been polite but brutal. He tried to answer the questions honestly and simply, but soon found that was impossible without incriminating himself. He soon stopped cooperating, having seen enough television shows to know he shouldn't answer anything without a lawyer present. At a certain point, his interrogators gave up, and he was taken into court.

When the doors opened, he saw Abigail and his lawyer waiting for him. He searched her face, terrified of what he might find there. He saw fear, and anger, and heartbreak and even—surprisingly—guilt. He could deal with those things, he told himself, relieved, reaching out to touch her. She was shaking.

"Adam, it's all over the Internet," she told him. "Everyone knows."

He didn't move, paralyzed by what he imagined he'd seen in her eyes, the one thing he would not have been able to survive: doubt.

It was she who moved toward him, drawing him into her arms and resting her head on his shoulder, hugging him to her as if her life depended on it.

"I haven't done anything . . ." he whispered, hugging her back desperately, like a child, like a lover.

"Shush . . . shush . . . Of course. I know that. You don't even have to say it."

He meshed his fingers through hers and enfolded them. "I thought we'd have more time to prepare the family. Until tomorrow at least. Do the kids know . . . ? Kayla . . . Shoshana . . . ?"

She nodded, confirming his fears. "It will be all right, my love. I will help make it all right. I'll take care of you, Adam."

All at once, he forgot about the lawyers and the judge and the verdict. All he could think about was simply going home with Abigail, where they would sit quietly side by side at the kitchen counter enjoying a freshly prepared meal. How he would take a long hot shower, then lie down beside her on clean sheets in their big, welcoming bed. All he wanted was to get out of the clutches of these belligerent strangers and back to his life.

His lawyer asked the judge to set bail. Not a flight risk. A respected family man, homeowner, member of the community, no priors. His heart welled with hope. But the prosecutor objected. He made all kinds of vicious accusations about the damage Adam Samuels could do if he wasn't kept behind bars.

How easy it was to become a criminal, Abigail thought, feeling capable of attacking the man, with his shiny shoes, patrician nose, and thrusting, self-important chest. How could he say those things? He didn't know a single thing about Adam Samuels, the man he was so eager to destroy.

The judge sat listening without expression until both sides had finished.

"Bail is set at three hundred thousand dollars," he finally announced.

"Your Honor!" the prosecutor exclaimed shrilly, jumping up. "That's nothing for a man of Mr. Samuels's means!"

But the judge rapped his gavel against his desk, turning to Adam's lawyer. "Your client will turn over his passport."

"Yes, Your Honor. Thank you, Your Honor."

Then his lawyer leaned over and whispered in Adam's ear, and he'd nodded.

Abigail watched them, feeling excluded, a child in the next room, protected by the adults. She watched the prosecutor gather his papers together. He seemed distracted. He glanced up once. Abigail caught his gaze and stared back at him, her face etched in incomprehension and stony hatred, until, finally, it was he who turned away.

The day stretched on and on, until at long last the correct papers were signed, bail was arranged, and they were told they were free to go.

Adam held her hand as they walked down the courthouse steps.

"Your wrist?" She'd touched the angry, reddened welt rising on his irritated skin.

He'd patted her hand, looking straight ahead. "Abby, let's go home."

6

Someone held the door buzzer down insistently. Even before he opened it, Seth knew he would find Kayla standing at the threshold.

"Medgar, could you give us a little alone time, bro?"

His roommate nodded sympathetically, grabbing his windbreaker and his computer.

"Hi, Kayla," he said, without meeting her eyes. "See you later."

"Yeah, see you, Medgar," she called after him, confused at the brush-off.

She saw, with a mixture of relief and anger, that Seth was there, leaning back on his bed, his feet bare, his hair uncharacteristically disheveled, as if he had been combing it with his thumbs.

"What happened to you? I was really worried. I even started calling hospitals."

"I think if anyone should start explaining, it's you, Kayla. How could you keep this from me?"

"You want to tell me what you're talking about? You kept me waiting for over a half hour! I even called your parents . . ."

"You're kidding. What did *they* say?"

"Their phones were both busy. And then my phone started getting all these weird calls. So I shut it off."

He sat up, looking at her closely. "What kind of 'weird calls'?"

She shrugged. "You know. Wrong numbers. Reporters. Crazy stuff."

He went very still. "You really don't know, do you?"

"Brilliant deduction, counselor!"

"Kayla, your father has been arrested. It's all over the Internet."

She felt the blood rushing to her head. "That's impossible." She stumbled, then felt Seth grab her and lower her into a chair. "Show me!"

"Are you saying you are surprised? That your father never said a word to you or your mother that this was coming down the pipeline?" He shook his head incredulously.

"SHOW ME!"

He opened up his computer and typed in "Adam Samuels arrested." Hundreds of Web sites popped up. He opened one.

Kayla stared at the screen: her father trying to block his face with his hands, his wrists handcuffed. The headline:

BOSTON ACCOUNTANT ARRESTED IN TERRORIST FINANCE PLOT

"And that's the kindest one," he said, opening another screen. There was a huge picture of her father taken from below, dark shadows making him sinister, beneath a headline which read:

FINANCING TERRORISTS WHO KILL OUR SOLDIERS

"What are we going to do?" Seth cried, his head in his hands. "This could ruin us!"

She looked up at him in shock, then sank to the floor, speechless.

"Kayla, are you all right?"

She shook her head, trying to catch her breath.

"I shouldn't have been so blunt. I'm sorry. But you needed to know."

She lifted her head. "You know that none of this is true, don't you? I mean, there can't be a single doubt in your head, is there?"

"Come on! As if you're absolutely sure!"

His words were so painfully true that they could never be forgiven, Kayla thought. "This is my father! My family!"

He grabbed her by the shoulders. "Kayla, don't you understand? It doesn't matter if it's true or not. By the time the truth comes out, no one will care. This is all they'll remember. This picture, this headline. The newspapers will be calling both of us, trying to put our faces on the front pages too. Imagine how this is going to affect our job prospects. We are lawyers! We have to be above reproach."

She shook her head slowly.

"I know that you love your family, and that you are incredibly loyal. But your parents wouldn't want you to ruin your life over this. You need to distance yourself. We both do."

"What, exactly, is that supposed to mean? That I disown them? Pretend my name is Jones?"

"Don't be dramatic! You know what I mean! Don't get your picture in the papers, or your name. Or Harvard's."

Part of her saw he was just being practical, and another hated him for it. "I see. Go underground, like I have something to be ashamed of, is that your advice, Seth?"

"Just until the worst of it blows over."

"You know I have to go home now. You do understand that, don't you?"

"No, I don't! That's the last place you should go! There will be reporters crawling everywhere . . ."

"If it was your parents, what would you do?"

"I don't know," he said, avoiding her gaze.

"Yes, you do."

"Okay. I do."

"But this is my father, right? Not yours."

What could he say to that? he thought, ashamed. It was sadly true. A father-in-law, especially a prospective one, was not a father. There were no blood ties and never would be.

"I'm going now, Seth."

"What should I tell the reporters?"

"Why would they call you? Our engagement isn't even official yet. And you know what, it never has to be," she added bitterly. "So don't worry. This isn't your problem."

"Kayla," he protested, trying too late to put his arms around her. She shrugged him off.

"I know you're angry at me now. But I'm just telling you the truth. And I'll say it again, for your own good: You need to distance yourself."

"Whose idea is that anyway? Your mom's or your dad's?"

He made no reply, his face reddening.

She got up and went to the door, opening it.

"Kayla!"

But the door had already closed.

She walked aimlessly through the streets, feeling dazed, like someone who has survived a terrorist attack with no physical injuries, the horrible details running through her head like a dark, viscous liquid, clogging all her rational thoughts. What was going to happen to her parents? Knowing what she did now about the unpredictability of the law, she was terrified.

Like mercury spilling from a broken thermometer, the law was fluid and impossible to grasp. It changed and altered daily, hourly, with every judgment of every judge in every court in the world. And the legal tricks and maneuvers lawyers used to manipulate the system were really beyond the grasp and imagination of an ordinary person. Bleak House is what Dickens had called law courts. Which is why no sane person should every willingly enter one. Like people volunteering for elective surgery in the hope of emerging better off— richer, more honored, more beautiful—the great majority were badly mistaken. Except for throwing enormous amounts of money overboard, there was nothing the least bit certain about the outcome and final destination when embarking for a sail on legal seas.

But in her father's case, there was simply no choice. He had been targeted. Why, how, fairly or unfairly, she had no idea, except that there were those who would benefit from destroying him. She needed to call home but didn't know what to say or what to do.

She needed Seth's arms around her. They were engaged. He was the man who said he loved her. He was the man with all the answers.

She remembered their first blind date, how he'd knocked on her dorm room and how she had given herself a quick, clinical review in the mirror, approving her shining mass of freshly shampooed strawberry blonde curls, large hazel eyes, and rosy, freckled complexion. She'd tugged the white cashmere turtleneck down over her black-satin pants, slipping her feet into open-toed shoes with three-inch heels. Pearls to swine, she'd told herself with a groan, already regretting the hours not spent studying. She'd gone to the door reluctantly.

Then there had been that moment of shock, seeing it was him, the fair-haired boy from orientation. He stood there, not saying a word, for at least fifteen seconds. He didn't look anything like the scruffy Pitt in *Thelma and Louise,* she thought. He was the spitting image of the suave, preppy Robert Redford in *The Way We Were.*

"Did you know," he said finally, "that research has shown it takes less than thirty seconds to form a lasting impression, and it can take up to twenty-one repeated occasions for someone to alter a first impression?"

"I'm sure you're right," she answered. "And goodness knows, I'm looking for Mr. Right, as long as his first name isn't 'Always.'"

He blinked, then slowly inclined his head in admiration, nodding, the way fencing partners do to acknowledge a good thrust.

"My point is—"

"I was wondering exactly that," she cut him off, wondering if she was going to have to hunt down Shana's boyfriend and kill him.

". . . that you don't look like a One L . . ."

"What did you expect me to look like?" She bristled, annoyed, passing her fingers through her curls, trying not to notice how gorgeous he was since he was obviously hopelessly full of himself.

"Glasses. Creased around the eyes from too many nights falling face-first into books. Hair that hasn't been washed in a while because there's no time, held back by a red rubber band. Fingers stained with ink. Overweight or anorexic because of food issues triggered by the horrors of outlining and study groups and six-hour exams on tax law . . ."

"And your point is . . . ?" Her voice rose in perfect imitation of her terrifying corporate law professor's, a man fond of cryptic non sequiturs like: *"Shall we use the key rather than kick down the door?"*

"Just that you don't look like someone who needs to be fixed up with blind dates. But that's just my first impression. I'll need to meet you at least twenty-one more times to test this theory." He smiled, a big, white, charming, lopsided grin in a big, handsome face framed by perfectly cut and probably blow-dried golden hair.

She exhaled, deciding to let Shana's boyfriend live.

He took her to a Chinese vegetarian restaurant. The food was mysterious and warm, full of fungi and heady sauces. He had wonderful manners, tilting his soupspoon away from him, and bringing it to his mouth for small, noiseless sips. He cut his vegetables into neat, precise bites, and ate almost daintily, wiping his mouth discreetly at intervals even though she could see no reason for it. She watched in admiration.

"So, how do you like law school so far?" he asked.

Mellowed by the candlelight, a glass of sake drunk too fast on an empty stomach, she found tears filling her eyes.

"I just think it's a horrible mistake." She shook her head, amazed at her candor. "I can't even count the number of times I've wanted to throw my books out the window and follow them!"

"What did you think it would be like?" Seth asked her, grinning.

She wiped her eyes, embarrassed at his amusement. "I don't know. Learning about how to save the world, maybe. But what we're doing is such crap. It has nothing to do with practicing law."

He put his hand into his pocket and took out a well-worn book. It was Mark Herrmann's *The Curmudgeon's Guide to Practicing Law.* "Here, listen to this: 'You always thought law school exams were ridiculous. . . . Cram irrelevant crap into your head . . . spill it all out . . . forget about it, and move on to the next set of irrelevant crap. . . .'"

She threw back her head and laughed. "That's exactly what I think!"

"Well, according to Herrmann you're 'Wrong, wrong, and wrong again.'"

"Care to explain?"

"This is what he says: 'when [you] argue a motion [you] . . . cram irrelevant crap into your head . . . spill it all out . . . forget about it, and move on to the next set of irrelevant crap. . . .' "

"It doesn't make the profession sound very appealing. There has to be more!"

"There is!" He picked up the book again. " 'What do I do when I take a deposition?' "

"Wait, don't tell me! Cram irrelevant crap into my head; spill it out . . . forget about it, and move on."

"Exactly. According to Herrmann, 'If you don't enjoy cramming, spewing, and moving on, you picked the wrong profession.' "

"Oh, hmm, well, maybe," she'd said, laughing, filling her sake glass for the second time. "So, I guess you're just breezing through it then?"

He shrugged. "It's manageable. If you know what you're doing."

"I guess I don't then." She sniffed, searching vainly for a tissue.

"I can never resist a damsel in distress," he said, pulling a clean package of tissues from his pocket, which, for a man, was impressive as hell, she thought. "And along with the tissue, I'm now going to throw in, absolutely free of extra charge, my secret formula for One L success. "

"Better than a set of steak knives!" She smiled skeptically. "What do you have behind that curtain, Mr. Wizard?"

"Three things: One, keep up with the reading; two, don't get bogged down with details; and three, use commercial outlines," he said.

"That's it?"

He held out his hands palms upward. "Easy as that. Now, what have you got lined up for your summer internship?"

She pressed her lips together. It was a sore point. She had already been on several failed interviews, something she preferred to keep to herself. "Oh, it's too early to worry about that."

"Early? Absolutely not! It's late."

"Where are you interviewing?"

"I'm not. I've already got a job."

Of course. Figures, she thought. "Where is it?"

"Bradley, Bradley and Ehrenreich in New York."

"Wow, they don't come any bigger than that!" She wanted to ask him how he'd done it. But looking him over, she suddenly thought: Why bother? He exuded privilege, and upper-class noblesse oblige. It was no accident that recruiters on campus had zeroed in on him, and that his first job offer had started at the top.

"The truth is, I've been on a few interviews with the big law firms, but haven't gotten a single callback. They just don't seem to take me seriously. It's not my fault."

"Have you ever heard of Charlotte's Rule?"

"Huh?"

"Remember, in *Charlotte's Web,* when spider saves pig from becoming bacon by spinning a slogan over her doomed head which reads: 'One terrific pig'? Everyone believes it! People will believe about you anything you tell them to believe as long as you look the part. What did you wear to these interviews?"

"I don't remember . . . Wait. A black pantsuit. With a V-neck sweater. Why?"

"Wrong, wrong, and wrong some more! You need a dark suit in blue or grey—black is too funereal—with a skirt cut to the knee and a shirt buttoned up to the neck. What kind of shoes did you wear?"

"I wore my boots."

"No way! Shoes with heels no higher than two inches, and God forbid anything open-toed or slingback! Men never show their toes or their necklines in any formal setting; neither should women. In fact, the higher up on the neckline you wear a scarf or collar, the more in command you look. That's why airline staff always wear collars and scarves up to their chins."

"How did you become such an expert?"

"In the summer after I graduated high school, I got this minimum-wage job as an usher at a convention center that held a Dress for Success Seminar. It was a revelation. The lecturer was a little middle-aged woman wearing a blue suit and a beautiful silk scarf. She made volunteers from the audience come up one by one, then had the rest of the group guess who they were and what they did. You wouldn't believe how drastically people lowered their expectations based on the slightest imperfection. A run in a stocking made them demote a

CEO to a checkout girl in Walmart. A bad haircut convinced them a systems analyst worked frying burgers. They were merciless!"

"How nineteenth-century!"

"That's just the way the world works." He shrugged. "Employers just figure if you know how to dress and present yourself, you are probably competent in other fields as well. Get used to it. So you can retire early and wear anything you want."

"You can't be serious!"

He looked very serious. "You think because your grades were off the charts in high school and you aced college and the LSATs that your work is over? The express elevator up the corporate ladder to the six-figure paycheck isn't holding open its doors waiting for you. In case you haven't read about it, the job market out there sucks."

"That's what they always say . . ."

"Yes, but this time, it's true. That's why the likability factor is more important than ever."

"The what?"

"Let's face it. People hire people they like. Were you friendly? Did you ask them about themselves? People love to talk about themselves."

"Certain people," she murmured pointedly. "Anyhow, I'm not sure I want to work in a big firm. I'm really more interested in child advocacy, nonprofits . . ."

He looked flabbergasted. "It suicide. It means only nonprofits will consider you next summer, and then when you graduate, your résumé will have nothing to offer a top law firm. Your father must have some connections. Go down the list. Take anything. Pay them! But it's going to be hard, even with help, because you are a woman . . ."

She glared at him.

"Look, I didn't make these things up. Whom did they hire in the end, the jobs you wanted?

She shrugged. "Men."

"I rest my case, counselor. And, Kayla, one more thing . . . You are a stunningly beautiful girl. I love the way you look. But do yourself a favor. Get your hair cut and straightened. And get rid of those freckles."

"Well, it's getting late," she said, running her fingers through her curls, then looking at her watch meaningfully.

"Is it?" He looked around at the bustling restaurant, where the night was just beginning.

"I've got lots of work to do this weekend, especially since I've just learned I'm doing everything wrong."

Comprehension dawned on him. "Oh, you weren't offended, were you? I was just trying to help . . ."

"No . . . why should I be offended? Just because you've told me off, insulted my appearance, and made me feel like an idiot?" She got up abruptly.

He paid the bill, hurrying after her.

They drove back in silence.

"Look, I'm sorry I came on a little strong . . ."

A little strong?

"I'm not usually like this," he said softly.

She had one hand on the door handle, about to escape. She turned around, curious. "What are you usually like?"

"It's just . . . when you opened your door, I was just bowled over. You looked like that iconic poster of Farrah Fawcett hanging in the bedroom of every horny teenage boy in America—all hair and white teeth. Except you weren't blond and didn't exude easy virtue. And then you seemed so upset about school, and your interviews. I just wanted to help."

"And you," she told him, "reminded me of that bad performance of Ryan O'Neal in *Love Story,* trying to be witty and clever, and just sounding pushy and offensive. Let's say there are more than adequate grounds for reasonable doubt," she said in that husky low tone she found herself using when attempting to sound lawyerly.

"I am a little pushy . . . but only on matters I know about, and to people I care about." He reached out to take her hand. "Truce?"

His hand was warm. And he was so good-looking. And some of his advice, she'd already begun to admit to herself, hurtful as it was, might even prove useful.

She didn't answer, reaching out to give him her other hand.

He pulled her gently toward him, taking her in his arms and kissing her tenderly.

"I'll call you," he whispered.

She bought the commercial outlines, and kept up with her reading, not allowing herself to get stuck on the details. She bought clothes and shoes she would never before have been caught dead in except in the synagogue on Yom Kippur. She got rid of her curls and freckles, remaking herself.

To her utter amazement, she found that not only did her professors take her more seriously, but she was beginning to take herself more seriously, even if that self was a person she hardly knew when she looked in the mirror. Her father helped her arrange a number of interviews. She arrived dressed for the part, was as friendly as a Southern preacher's daughter and inquisitive as Dr. Phil. She had her pick of job offers, one of them in a Boston district court.

Seth was thrilled, except for the fact that they'd be apart all summer.

"I'll fly up to visit you on the weekends," he promised.

"And I'll come to Manhattan."

They were together every weekend, and spent many nights working together, sharing notes. The decision to sleep together came naturally as did their decision to get engaged. In fact, it happened so casually, she almost missed it.

"I'm going to have to decide about job offers," he'd said in June. "Where do you want to live?"

She twisted her engagement ring around her finger, the lovely band and stone suddenly heavy and constricting. He was never wrong about anything. But now he had given her advice she just couldn't take. She was on her own.

7

The phone began ringing that evening. Her best friend, Debra, was the first, of course.

"How are you holding up, Abby?"

"I'm not," she said, relieved she could finally tell someone the truth.

"What's going on?"

"It's all a big lie, Deb. But the worst kind, with some tiny bits of truth thrown in. Of course you know Adam would never . . ."

"Oh, please. You don't have to explain. I know Adam. So what's the story?"

"Honestly? I have no idea. All I know is that Adam innocently transferred money to an investment fund in England that turned out to be a front for Al-Qaeda and other terrorist groups. It's horrible, Deb. The phone doesn't stop ringing. I'm scared."

There was a long pause and a sigh. "Take a virtual hug," Deb said. "And you can call me anytime, day or night."

"I love you."

"And I love you. Hug Adam for me."

"Hello? Abigail. Stephen just showed me the article on the Internet. How awful! How are you both holding up?"

"Henrietta, it's so good of you to call. What can I say?"

"Is it true that he transferred money to terrorists who killed American soldiers?"

"Of course not! I mean, not knowingly. I . . . it's complicated."

"Because the Internet and that picture . . . It was unbelievably damaging. It's the kind of thing that just buries a person's reputation."

"But none of it is true!"

"Well, Stephen says the article was very well written, and they gave so many details . . . You've got to do something about this!" she said, phrasing it as though she were imparting valuable advice.

Abigail's eyes smarted. "Henrietta, there's someone else on the line, I've got to go." She hung up, feeling stunned and raw. Her hands shaking, she poured herself a cup of coffee. She opened the refrigerator for the milk, but there wasn't any. A walk will do me good, she told herself, throwing on her coat.

The weather had changed. The brief, glorious warmth of the morning was gone. The air was soggy, smelling of coming snows.

"Abigail?"

It was Sandra.

"Well, long time no see," Abigail said, trying to be jovial.

"I hope it isn't true," the woman said.

Abigail caught her breath. "You don't have to hope. I'm *telling* you it isn't true!"

"I hope it isn't true," she repeated, unforgivably.

Abigail turned away, her cheeks as red as if someone had slapped them. She paid for the milk as quickly as she could. She heard the door of the grocery slam behind her, as if someone else had wrenched it shut.

Kayla telephoned. "How's Dad?"

"All things considered, he's . . . all right."

She heard her daughter exhale. "Really?"

"I'm sure he'd like to see you. Kayla, he hasn't done anything wrong, not knowingly . . ." The more she repeated this now-familiar line, the less sure Abigail was.

"Really, Mom, I'd prefer not to talk about this over the phone," Kayla answered sharply.

"Of course," Abigail replied, hurt.

"I'll be over, Mom."

They said their good-byes, the unspoken words crowding out and canceling what was said. Abigail called Joshua, who said he was getting on a plane the next day. She called Shoshana, who told her not to worry because it was going to be just fine. She was planning on driving in.

"With Matthew?"

"Yes, of course. Matthew is very concerned."

The next day, the phone rang and rang and rang.

"Please, Abby, you pick up. I just can't," Adam begged.

Half the calls were from reporters. She gave them their lawyer's number. Then there were the clients, people she didn't really know that well. "Tell Adam that we have every confidence in his innocence. It is always the good people that they come after. Send him our love."

"I will, and thank you so much." She felt her throat ache. It was not the insults of friends, but the kindnesses of strangers—so unexpected and unearned—that made her want to cry.

What she had expected from her friends—words of concern and unconditional support—was going to be the exception, not the rule, she realized with shock. The rule was a nervous silence. The rule was the people whom you expected to call didn't get in touch at all. This rule would also be followed through, she realized, in person. There would be the conversations that stopped when she passed by; the oh-so-ingratiating smiles that disappeared like a Popsicle on a summer sidewalk the moment her back was turned.

At midmorning, Marsha, Seth's mother, called.

The conversation was filled with questions, polite concerns, and good wishes as substantial as air kisses. Then, with the niceties out of the way, she got down to business: "With *all you are going through*," she said curtly, "it is clear that the engagement party should be postponed until further notice. You've got enough on your plate already. I'm sure the kids won't mind."

"Well, Marsha, how very kind of you to be worried about *all we are going through*. Yes, we are busy. But we don't mind. We don't want to disappoint the kids."

"Seth really won't be disappointed. In fact, I think he's already discussed this with Kayla."

"Really? Did she agree? Is this what they both want?"

There was a pause. "He didn't share that information with me."

"Oh. I see."

"Has Kayla said anything to you?"

"No. Not about this . . ."

"Of course, there can be no question now of a formal announcement in the newspapers. Hello, are you still there?" Marsha said, tapping the phone.

"I'm still here, Marsha," Abigail replied, thinking of the woman's dark, light-less eyes staring out of the heavy folds of her drooping eyelids; her puffy cheeks, her stingy mouth—a dark valley amid the drooping hills of flesh.

"Oh, I thought the phone had gone dead."

Abigail pressed her lips together until she felt the veins in her throat pop up. "Let me talk it over with Kayla and get back to you."

"There's nothing to discuss, Abigail," Marsha said flatly, her high-pitched twitter suddenly gone, her voice level and cold. "There isn't going to be any an-nouncement, and there isn't going to be any party. It would be a circus."

"Well, then, Marsha. You'd feel right at home."

There was the sound of a sudden intake of breath, then a dial tone.

The next day, she called Kayla, but either her daughter's phone wasn't work-ing or Kayla was looking at her caller ID and not picking up. Exasperated, Abigail sent her an SMS about the get-together that evening. There had been no reply.

Then she called Shoshana: "Are you sure you are feeling up to the drive? Tell Matthew to take it slow."

"Listen, Mom, Matthew isn't going to be able to make it."

There was a short silence. "Why?"

"He says he's got too much work to do, but I think he's nervous about re-porters taking his picture. He's worried about his clients."

Of course he was.

"Well, I don't want you driving with the kids all by yourself in your seventh month . . ."

"Mom . . . save it. I'm coming. I'll be fine."

"Shoshana . . ."

"Mom, I'm hanging up. I will see you and Dad in a few hours."

"I love you," Abigail whispered.

She stood over the stove stirring the pumpkin soup. She had gotten almost no sleep. Her feet were tired, and her eyes had difficulty staying open. She diced the coriander, and its pungent fragrance filled the room. She added it and the garlic to the meatballs. She shuddered at the thought of them all sitting around the table. What would they talk about? It would be more like a shiva call than, say, Thanksgiving. Still, people needed to eat. She melted a large chunk of chocolate over water for the cupcakes. They were her grandson's favorite, and a pain to make. But the thought of her grandchildren making the exhausting drive with so little to look forward to when they arrived kept her stirring, beating, and melting.

Despite everything, she had to admit to herself she was selfishly looking forward to seeing them under any circumstances. It had been months. Although it was only about a three-hour drive from Shoshana and Matthew's home in Greenwich, Connecticut, she saw them only marginally more often than Joshua and Deidre, who had to fly cross-country from California.

Joshua was in the music business, a song producer. He was doing well, or so he said. But it wasn't the kind of job she'd imagined for her son. It wasn't solid enough, and it was in show business, after all, a risky and suspect branch of the economy. At least he had—at long last—married. Deidre was a singer. She was also a Methodist.

Abigail felt a dull stab whenever she remembered. She had agonized over attending a wedding in which there would be a minister and a rabbi sharing the same stage. Only at Adam's insistence had she finally given in. The ceremony had been traumatic and painful. But afterward, she had eaten and danced with everyone else. What else could she do? It was like a plague, happening to everyone, even those, like herself, who had invested so much in their children's religious educations, sending them to day schools, keeping the Sabbath and holidays as family affairs, deeply held and respected.

Maybe all those guitar lessons had been a mistake?

Shoshana, thank God, had made up for him, snaring a Jewish mergers and acquisitions expert from a prestigious Wall Street firm. Abigail stirred the soup thoughtfully, tasting it, then adding some more coriander. But she wondered sometimes if her son-in-law's success had really been such a blessing to her daughter. It had always bothered her that Shoshana seemed to be resting on her laurels, not displaying any inclination to use her expensive degree in architecture from Brown, content in her role as the perfect Greenwich hostess, mother of two beautiful children, with a third on the way. Everyone's different. Abigail shrugged, reminding herself to be grateful. Shoshana was, after all, the sole grandchild factory up and running. She opened the oven, putting in the cupcakes. But it would be good for her daughter to be working as well, if simply for her own self-respect.

She washed her hands, wiping them on her apron. That wouldn't happen to Kayla. Kayla would be her own person, ensconced in a rock-solid profession, with an encouraging partner who respected her intelligence and education. Perhaps they'd even set up a practice together? It could be a wonderful, interesting life, married to the perfect partner, personally and professionally. At least, she hoped.

She hung up her apron, walking into the living room and sitting down on the sofa. Marriage was so unpredictable. You could never know how the gears of two separate people—perfect in themselves—would mesh with one another over the long run. She thought of a friend's daughter, a dentist, who had run a dental clinic with her orthodontist husband. They had been very successful, with a sprawling house in Newton, offices in Back Bay in one of those immaculate brownstones, and children enrolled in Maimonides, where they'd learned to lead the prayers in Hebrew. It had been perfect up until the very moment her friend's daughter had run off with the contractor redoing their kitchen.

The doorbell rang at six. It was Joshua and Deidre.

"Why didn't you call? I would have picked you up!" Abigail protested weakly, enormously relieved.

"Right, Mom. Like you don't have anything else to do. Besides, Deidre wouldn't let me."

"You're a brat," she told him affectionately, thankful to Deidre, knowing Joshua wouldn't have thought twice about making her fight the rush-hour traffic to Logan Airport.

"I'm *so sorry*, Mom," he said, hugging her.

She hugged him back tightly. "I'm so sorry you had to schlep out all this way!"

Deidre hung back, unsure, until Abigail went to her. "Deidre, it was so good of you to come, to take off work and fly all the way out here. I'm so grateful."

"Of course, Abigail! There was never any question. This is where Josh and I both need to be right now."

Did she mean it? Oh, what difference did that make! a voice inside of her shouted. She's here, isn't she? And where is Matthew, your perfect Jewish son-in-law? He hadn't changed his plans. He wouldn't be coming. He hadn't even bothered to call.

Shoshana and the children arrived a little while later.

Abigail pulled six-year-old Alex—his great-grandfather's namesake—to her, hugging him tight, then reached out for twelve-year-old Ellen, who reluctantly let herself be kissed.

"Mom, are you okay?" Shoshana asked, her eyes anxious and searching.

"I'm fine, fine. Don't worry about me. How are *you*? Come in, come in."

Shoshana put her hand protectively over her rounded stomach. "We are both fine. Don't worry about us. Where's Dad?"

Abigail looked around, realizing he hadn't come down. "I don't know. Maybe he's still up in his study, or lying down?"

"Poor Dad! What do your lawyers say?"

"Don't say hi to your brother," Josh interrupted, pecking her on both cheeks.

"You're here too! When did you get in? Deidre!"

The two women hugged each other.

"Children, come in. Have something to eat!" Abigail said gaily.

The grandchildren glanced up at each other briefly, then down at the floor. They didn't move. "What's going on, kids? Why so quiet?"

"Mom, can I talk to you for a second?" Shoshana pulled her lightly toward the privacy of the kitchen.

"They saw the papers."

Abigail felt her stomach flip over. "OH, NO!"

"And . . . that's not the worst." Shoshana hesitated.

"Tell me!"

"Some moron in Ellen's class told her: 'Your grandfather helps kill American soldiers.' She took it hard."

Abigail crossed her arms over her chest. Like a wave, the feeling rose and swelled, crashing down and covering her completely. Of all the horrors she had envisioned, this one had somehow escaped her. "No, no, no, no." Her head felt loose and achy as she shook it in despair. She pinched Shoshana's sleeve, whispering fiercely: "Don't tell your father any of this!"

"Are you kidding me? Why would I do that? I spoke to the kids. They'll be fine. I'm going upstairs to get Dad."

But as they reentered the living room, he was already there. He had Alex in his lap and had one arm around Ellen, who was sitting next to him on the couch. Deidre and Josh stood behind him, gripping the sofa.

"Well, there they are, my two beautiful girls!"

Shoshana leaned over him, kissing the thinning salt-and-pepper hair on his crown. "Hi, Dad!"

"Don't look at me like that! This is all a tempest in a teapot! I've got great lawyers. This will all blow over soon . . . it's ridiculous." His jaw flinched, even as his smile never wavered. "I see the tablecloth, but no dishes or silverware. We are eating, aren't we? Did you promise them turkey, Abigail?"

"I haven't promised them anything, Adam. They didn't come to eat. They came to see you."

"They can do both. I'm starving. Right, we're starving?" he said to Alex, bouncing him on his knees. "Skin and bones, this kid! Let's fatten him up, Abigail! We can't have such a skinny person in the family. You know, for your grandma Esther, not being a 'good eater' was the worst crime a person could commit!" He laughed.

The adults cast furtive glances at each other.

"Oh, please. Don't be so serious! It's a joke! I'm not a criminal, except if stupidity is somehow a jailable offense."

"What do your lawyers say, Dad?" Josh prodded him.

"Oh, you know. Lawyers. They are so supercautious. And they're still studying everything. There's a mountain of papers. Boxes and boxes."

"Are they at least the best? You should get the best," Deidre said.

"Yes, Deidre. They are the best money can buy."

"Grandpa, it's not true, right?" Ellen burst out suddenly.

There was a collective intake of breath.

Abigail watched her husband's smile fade. He blinked, then pressed his fingertips into his eyes, his knuckles lifting his glasses above his eyebrows. He adjusted his glasses on the bridge of his slippery nose, gesturing to Ellen to come closer. "Of course it's not true, Sunshine," he whispered, hugging her.

"Let me help you set the table," Deidre offered.

"Yes," Shoshana agreed, her hands shaking. "Where's Kayla?"

"I don't know," Abigail admitted. "She's not picking up her phone."

"But you've spoken to her, right?" Shoshana pressed.

"Is this the right set?" Deidre asked, her hand suspended in midair, holding a plate.

It was the special-occasion Villeroy & Boch.

"Sure." Abigail shrugged. With an atom bomb hanging over their heads, protecting the good china seemed ridiculous.

Shoshana took some plates and placed them carefully on the table. "You mean to say, Kayla hasn't even called you or Dad today?" She shook her head, incredulous. "She is unbelievable."

"Shush. Don't be hard on your sister. Her engagement party is in two weeks, remember?" Adam said sharply.

"That's true. I completely forgot. You're going ahead with it, right?"

"Of course! Why shouldn't we?" he demanded.

Abigail shrugged. "I got a call from Seth's mother. She's adamant about canceling."

"What does she have in mind?" Adam said with quiet bitterness. "Calling up every single person who got an invitation and telling them: 'The engagement's off because my husband is a crook'?"

"She's an idiot. Don't pay attention to her." Josh nodded. "I agree with Dad."

"It's not up to me, Josh."

"That fat, social-climbing snob with her curly, dyed blond hair and perky personality!" Shoshana fumed. "It's her loss! Think of all the third-rate travel packages to Morocco she could have sold to all the hapless guests."

Abigail wanted to protest but found herself smiling instead.

"Whenever I spend time with her and her show-off of a husband, I count my teeth." Adam nodded.

"Really? I thought I was the only one who felt that way," Abigail said, strangely elated. "I wish I knew how Kayla feels about all this."

"I can't believe she hasn't been over here yet! You mean to say, Mom, you went to bail out Daddy all by yourself?"

"The lawyer met me there, Shoshana."

"She is the most selfish little brat in the world."

"Leave her alone, Shoshana!"

"Adam, don't get upset. We are just talking . . ."

"Kayla's the one who is going to suffer the most here from all of this," he continued hoarsely. "And none of this is her fault."

Shoshana knelt, hugging him. "It's not yours either, Daddy! You shouldn't let her get away with this stuff."

"She'll be here." He nodded confidently, stroking Shoshana's hair.

"The table is ready. Why don't we all sit down and eat something?" Abigail said brightly.

They settled around the table naturally. There was something comforting about the room being full, the voices familiar and loving. Worse things had happened to families, Abigail thought, carefully balancing the soup tureen to keep the hot liquid from sloshing over. She looked around the table. No one had died. They were all alive, and well.

"So, Josh, how's business?"

"I've got some really good records I'm working on, Dad. I have this one artist—Janna O—who is going to be the next J.Lo. Her voice is—"

"Dad, what was it like?" Shoshana interrupted. She could only take so much of her brother's infomercials. He had been on the verge of the next Madonna/Jay-Z/Beyoncé for years.

"What was it like?" Adam mused. "I don't know. Like acting in an episode of *Law & Order*. Unconvincingly dramatic. Unreal."

"They came to the office?"

Adam nodded.

"I don't understand how they can do that to someone without any kind of warning! It's like Stalinist Russia."

"What does it matter, Josh? It's in the past. My secretary, Ida, took it really hard, but she was great. She made all the calls. Your mother and my lawyer were there waiting for me at the courthouse."

"Did they put you in handcuffs, Grandpa? Take your fingerprints? Make you stand against the wall and have your picture taken?" Alex burst out.

"Shut up, brat." Ellen cuffed him.

"Ellen! Leave your brother alone! Alex, you are being rude! Apologize to Grandpa."

Adam coughed, rubbing his wrists under the table. "It's okay, Shoshana. There's nothing wrong with the child being curious." He paused, his fingers wrapping around his spoon, which he dipped into his bowl, filling it with hot, orange soup. Slowly, he brought it to his mouth, continuing to eat in silent rhythm until the bowl was empty.

No one spoke.

Finally, he put the spoon down, wiped his mouth with a napkin, and folded his hands in his lap. "It wasn't fun, Alex, but it wasn't the end of the world, either."

Under the table, Abigail reached for her husband's shaking hand, twining her fingers through his.

"Are you two still living in Century City?" Adam asked, turning his attention to Josh and Deidre.

"Yes, but we've been looking for a house," Deidre said.

"A house?"

"It's a good time to buy. Everyone says so. Before prices rise even more," Josh said enthusiastically.

"But the mortgage payments will be high, no?" Adam asked.

"Not if you can scrape together a decent down payment!" Deidre informed them excitedly, as if she'd been patiently anticipating the question and now her time had finally come. "Actually, we were hoping . . ."

"Deidre!" Josh cut her short. "Not now, for Pete's sake."

"It's all right, it's all right." Adam lifted his hand. "Don't fight."

Shoshana whistled low under her breath.

"Would anybody like dessert?" Abigail asked. "Chocolate cupcakes with candy sprinkles?"

"Me!" Alex shouted, running into the kitchen.

"I have to have some coffee," Shoshana announced to no one in particular, getting up and joining her son.

"Do you need any help?" Deidre asked, without moving.

"I'll get the water." Ellen jumped up.

"Bring some cups, will you?" Josh called after her.

"Hi, is there any food left?"

They all turned around and looked at the door.

"Kayla! Mom, it's Kayla," Josh called out, getting up and reaching out to her. "What's with the hair?"

"What's with the mustache?"

"Kayla." Abigail wiped her hands on her apron, walking behind Alex, who was carefully balancing a tray of cupcakes.

"Hi, Alex. Is that all for you, or can I have one?" Kayla asked him, her face completely serious. Before he could answer, she lifted one off the tray and took a large bite. "Hi, Mom."

"Hi." Abigail took the offered cheek and kissed it lightly. "You don't answer the phone?"

"No. I don't. I actually threw it into the Charles River after the tenth journalist called me."

"What, they are calling you? Who?" Abigail winced, astonished.

"Who not?" She shrugged.

"My poor Kayla," Adam said, reaching out and taking her hand.

She laid her head against his shoulder, letting him hug her. He stroked the shiny straightened hair so unlike the hair she was born with. She looked almost like a stranger. He lifted her chin with his fingertips, searching her face.

"Your eyes."

"I know, I know. I had no sleep last night—I have a report due. I forgot to put in drops, that's why they're so red. Hey, don't worry about me. I'm going to be fine."

"You did the right thing about the cell phone. Don't talk to them. Don't let them hound you." He looked around the room. "That goes for all of you."

"Is Seth coming?"

"Well, sister, I can't answer that, not having a cell phone and all."

"Call him now."

"Leave her alone, Shoshana!" Adam said, a little more loudly than he intended.

Alex began to cry.

"I'm so . . . sorry . . . children . . ." Adam said, leaning heavily on the table to help himself up. "I . . . I . . . don't . . . can't . . ." He shook his head, weaving unsteadily out of the room and climbing up the stairs.

"He'll be all right." Abigail nodded firmly, facing her children. "Go lie down now," she called up after him.

"Ellen, take your brother to the den! Put on a video."

"Do I *have* to, Mom?"

"Yes, Ellen. You do. Now go," Shoshana ordered her. "Mom, maybe you should check on Dad?"

"Yeah. This is so awful for him. How's he been through all this?"

"You know your father, Joshua. He never says how he feels. He's been stoic, determined."

"What happened? What's the truth, Mom?" he asked her.

"It's . . . complicated." She weaved her way unsteadily into the living room, dropping down on the sofa. Joshua followed her. Then she explained what had been explained to her, which she herself hardly understood.

"But the person who actually transferred the money to terrorists, that fund manager, has he also been arrested?"

She shook her head. "Nobody even seems to know where he is. They're looking for him. He could be anywhere—in Europe or on a yacht in the Caribbean or in Saudi Arabia. Who knows?"

"But how could it have happened? If I know Dad, he must have checked the fund out six ways from Sunday before he invested his client's money. He's very, very careful."

"He did, Kayla! He even flew to Europe and went over the books . . . He says it was all legitimate, as far as he could tell."

"All Dad did was invest the money with a reputable firm, or so he thought . . . They can't blame him if the firm transferred it illegally!"

"But they are blaming him, Shoshana! And we have to prove that he didn't know."

"Can you prove that, Mom?" Kayla said slowly. "Was there due diligence?"

"Oh, the big expert throwing around legalisms . . ." Shoshana sneered. "Why did you let Mom and Dad go to court alone? Why didn't you go with them?"

"If someone had let me know . . ." Kayla answered bitterly.

"There was no time!" Abigail shouted. "His secretary called and told me to get a lawyer and get down to federal court in Worcester. We had to make sure we made bail before the judge put him in jail . . . !"

"Why don't we all just sit down and chill?" Josh suggested.

"Why, so you and your wife can ask for more money?" Shoshana screamed at him. "Don't you get it! Dad isn't going to be able to work anymore! His clients are going to drop like flies! And by the time he finishes paying a team of lawyers four hundred dollars an hour each, he won't have a penny left to his name! What part of this don't you understand, Mr. Hip-hop?"

"Don't talk to him like that!" Deidre said.

Shoshana ignored her, turning to Kayla. "Maybe you can ask your professors to help you research Dad's legal brief. They'd know if the lawyers are taking the best approach."

"Right," Kayla said, rolling her eyes.

"Why not?"

"You don't understand anything, big sister!"

Abigail suddenly felt dizzy. "Children, children, please, don't fight!"

"Sorry, Mom."

"Yeah, sorry, Mom."

A slow burn started up beneath Abigail's left breast. "I think . . . I'll see how your father is doing. Excuse me a moment." The staircase had never seemed as steep, she thought, her heart beating rapidly as she pulled herself laboriously up each step.

"Is there some reason Matthew isn't here?" Josh demanded.

"He wanted to come but thought that the house would be under siege by journalists. He's a fund manager. He can't afford to be photographed in connection to this case."

"And I can't afford to have my professors connect me to this either," Kayla said through clenched teeth. "I am interviewing now. I will be asking for written references . . ."

Josh looked at his sisters, shaking his head. "They need you. Mom and Dad need you."

"I know that! I live here, Josh! I'm here every day practically, while you're off in California living off their handouts . . ."

"I make money too! Besides, who are you to lecture me, Kayla?"

"He's right. I don't remember you fighting tooth and nail against their paying your tuition," Shoshana pointed out.

"Like you paid your tuition for that diploma you dust off in between making dinner parties for Matthew's clients! Not to mention the bundle Dad gave you for your down payment on the Greenwich minimansion," Kayla shot back.

"Touché!" Josh laughed.

"He offered! And I, at least, have given him some joy instead of heartache," Shoshana said, looking pointedly at her brother.

Deidre put a restraining hand on Josh's arm. "I think we should go."

Shoshana blushed. "I'm sorry, Deidre. I didn't mean . . ."

"NO? Then explain it to me, Shoshana, exactly what did you mean? Because I thought I understood you perfectly," Deidre answered furiously.

"This is not about us!" Shoshana shot up, facing her brother and sister-in-law. "It's about them! About what Mom and Dad need. My God! He could go to jail." Her hands shook as she reached behind her, groping for the chair. She slid back into it.

No one spoke.

"That . . . can't . . . happen," Kayla said, shaking her head. "It just can't."

Of everyone, she alone knew how untrue that statement was. It could happen. In fact, it happened all the time to all kinds of people, for all kinds of reasons; people who were guilty, innocent, or in between. Some people were just luckier than others, or had better lawyers, or dumber judges. If there was one thing she had learned at Harvard Law, it was this: Once you entered the halls of justice, you could get anything but.

At the top of the stairs, hidden from view, Abigail leaned against the wall, listening to the rise and fall of her children's angry voices. As she listened, she looked at the family photos hanging on the landing: There they were gathered around each other at Josh's Bar Mitzvah, their faces shining, Adam's arm around Josh's shoulder, six-year-old Kayla in Shoshana's lap. Adam's parents, and her own, seated in the center, elegant and not yet frail. The big smiles, the closeness of bodies arranged for a studio portrait. A unit. Unity. She stumbled, her shoulder brushing heavily against the wall, sending the framed photo crashing.

All the king's horses, and all the king's men, she thought, bending down to pick up the pieces.

8

"You are up? Already?" Abigail asked him sleepily.

"I want to get to the synagogue on time."

She lifted herself up on her elbow, surprised. "Are you going to synagogue?"

Adam sat down on the side of the bed, reaching for her hand. "Yes, Abby, and so are you. You are going to put on your prettiest suit, and your smartest hat, and you are going to walk down the aisle and take your seat in the women's section between Helen Silverstein and Joyce Mathias, just as you've done every Saturday for the past fifteen years. You are going to sing all the songs, and answer 'amen' as loudly as everyone else, do you hear me?" His hand closed gently over hers.

"They will all stare and talk behind our backs."

He nodded. "And if we are not there, they will say worse things."

She fell back into bed, staring at the ceiling. That was sickeningly accurate. "Please!"

He touched the top of her head gently. "Abby, I need you. I need you there, beside me."

She lifted her head and threw off the covers. There was nothing else to say, was there? She stood unsteadily on the soft blue rug, her body out of proportion, the head weighing her down and pitching the rest of her forward. She opened her walk-in closet full of expensive clothes, flipping through the racks until she found a dark grey suit. Out of her hatboxes, she took a matching grey silk hat with a grey-and-white feather. It was really too elegant for mere synagogue attendance. But it certainly did send a very definite signal, a reminder that the Samuelses of Brookline, who lived in the beautiful corner house with the wide, manicured lawns, were still themselves.

He wore his best Brooks Brothers suit, a black pinstripe, with a gleaming white high-collared shirt and an apricot-silk tie. She laid her hands on his shoulders, brushing off nonexistent lint, wanting simply to feel their solid breadth.

"You ooze respectability and success," she laughed, then added, more soberly: "My handsome husband."

He kissed her hand, then cocked his head. "My lovely wife."

They walked silently, arm in arm, down the tree-lined streets, their shoes scraping softly against the pretty piles of autumn leaves. It was a walk they had made countless times, but now they felt like tourists exploring a new country.

As they neared the synagogue, they began passing people they knew. "Good Shabbes," they said, nodding. Some answered; some didn't. In either case, they smiled.

"Good luck," he whispered to her at the entrance, parting to make his way to the men's section. She squeezed his hand, then let him go.

She climbed the stairs. For the first time she could remember, she felt it necessary to reach out for the banister, gripping it firmly as she put one foot in front of the other, pulling herself forward to a place she didn't want to be.

When she opened the door to the women's balcony, she was relieved to see that she had arrived early enough to find it almost empty. Most women—herself included—usually turned up about halfway through the service, just as the morning prayers concluded and the Torah portion of the week was being read. That way, they could use the reading time to catch up on the latest gossip before they needed to fall into respectful silence for the rabbi's sermon.

Slowly, the pews around her began to fill.

The secretive, silent stares. She could feel them touch the back of her neck, then crawl down her spine with disgusting and electric swiftness, not unlike a roach scurrying down bare skin. Wherever she turned, she seemed to encounter them, like beams of high-intensity light aimed at the sky to warn away jets from skyscrapers.

Mrs. Garfinkel, who usually turned around to greet her, sat facing straight ahead. And Mrs. Finer, who sat behind her and never gave her the time of day, didn't even bother to return her nod. Or was that what she usually did? Abigail suddenly couldn't remember. Was it her imagination, she thought, or was the buzz in the women's section an octave lower than usual? She felt raw and vulnerable, like an unbandaged burn victim anticipating pain from the very air around her.

Helen came in later than usual. She reached out and hugged Abigail, kissing her on both cheeks. "Be strong!" she whispered, leaning into her. Abigail breathed in the fragrance of her good perfume and her good fortune, a life without complications, a life in which it was so easy to be strong. Not that she begrudged Helen her life. She deserved it as much as or more than anyone. She was, after all, such a good person. She baked for the poor, visited the sick, and held fundraisers for weary domestic-abuse victims.

And I, Abigail thought, no longer have that scent. I smell of scandal and failure. I've been added to the "dontinvitem" list, a person to be avoided at all costs.

Joyce came in at her usual time. She walked with the slow caution and heartrending straightness of back that is the pride and achievement of the very old, each step a defiant rejection of lurking pitfalls. She had broken her hip last year, and now used a cane. She was a great-grandmother, a small, elegant European survivor, who wore lovely gold bracelets and earrings, and always dressed like mother of the bride. She said nothing, reaching out for Abigail's hand and holding it the entire time. God bless her, Abigail thought, wanting to cry.

"It's shameful, shameful! What is the world coming to? Your wonderful husband. How can they say such things? We all know it's a lie. Really, Abigail, don't let them get to you, my dear. They are always looking to pull down the best people. Let me know, whatever you need, my dear. Anything. Anything at all," Joyce whispered during the rabbi's sermon, ignoring all shushing.

In response, Abigail reached over and kissed her cool, papery cheek.

How simple, how natural were the words. It was what one expected in such circumstances from the people who knew you, words that carved in fine relief just how badly most of the people she knew had behaved.

"How was it?" she asked Adam, as they walked home.

He looked straight ahead. "Fewer people seeking free accounting advice . . . And the rabbi wants to speak to us right after the Sabbath. Isn't that kind of him!"

"You think?" Abigail turned to him, two spots of color in her cheeks that he hadn't seen before. "Doesn't it depend on what exactly he has to say?"

"What . . . what do you mean? He's got to be supportive. He's our rabbi, for goodness' sake!"

"Right. We'll see."

"You never liked him, Abby."

"I just never saw the connection between his wisdom and his deeds, that's all." She shrugged.

"What do you mean?"

"He's very pro-Israel, right? But during the Intifada, when Israeli tourism was suffering, he canceled the synagogue's yearly trip and privately told people to keep their kids home from Israel-year programs."

"It was a difficult time, Abigail."

"The Evangelicals didn't cancel their trips. They increased them. It was a test, and he failed."

He shook his head, ready to take up the rabbi's defense once again, but stopped. There were people sitting in front of their house on their porch chairs. Strangers who jumped up when they approached, brushing wet leaves from their raincoats.

"Mr. and Mrs. Samuels? We're from WBGL Channel Four. We're wondering if we could ask you a few questions?" She was a startlingly pretty black woman holding a microphone. The man had a camera hoisted on his shoulder.

Abigail stretched out a clawlike hand, sheltering her face. "NO! Please. We have nothing to say! Now leave us alone. This is our Sabbath day . . ."

But instead of retreating, the woman moved in closer, blocking their way.

"Our viewers are interested in knowing if, as devout Jews, you have any guilt feelings about funding terror which might be used not only on American soldiers but on Jews in Israel and Jewish institutions all over the world . . . ?"

"Oh, my God, please leave us alone! We haven't done anything," Adam begged.

"Isn't it true that the money transfers were in the millions of dollars? And isn't it true that A. J. Hurling was an innocent victim of your scheme?"

"Do you know the damages they can ask for in a civil suit for invasion of privacy?" a familiar voice suddenly interrupted. "Not to mention libel. I know, because I'm a Harvard-trained lawyer."

"Seth!" Abigail cried, surprised and relieved.

The reporter and cameraman exchanged looks, hesitated, then reluctantly stepped out of their way.

"Come in, Seth!" Adam held the door open, patting him on the back.

"It's so good to see you!" Abigail hugged him. "What are you doing here?"

"I should have come over right away. I'm so sorry. It was all so confusing."

"Seth, this isn't your fault or your problem," Abigail said.

"Yes, don't worry about it, son."

"Join us for lunch?"

He hesitated, then nodded. "Thanks, Abigail. I'd like that."

"I can't tell you how sorry I am that this has touched your lives, tainted your happiness . . ." Adam said, gripping his hand.

"Don't worry about me! I'm going to be fine. But I am worried about your daughter."

"Did you quarrel?" Abigail asked, biting her lip.

Seth hesitated, then nodded. "I've never seen her like that. She was furious. I'll tell you the truth, it frightens me."

"You don't really think she'd do something reckless, hurt herself?"

Seth shrugged. "I have no idea, Adam, what she is capable of doing in her present state."

"You're exaggerating, Seth. I saw her three days ago. She was fine," Abigail protested.

"Did she say anything about me, about the engagement party?"

Abigail thought for a moment; to her surprise, she realized Kayla had not said a single word about either. Only now, thinking back, did she realize how strange that was.

"Then you don't know that she's insisting on having the engagement party on time or not having it at all? That she's insisting on publishing an engagement announcement in the papers?"

Abigail shook her head, shocked. "She didn't mention a word to us about any of this."

"I understand your mother . . . your parents . . . have a different opinion?" Adam said tactfully. "And what about you?"

He shrugged with unconvincing nonchalance. "I don't care one way or the other. I don't care about parties. All I want is for Kayla to be happy. I'll do anything you all think would be best. But I will say this: I don't understand why we have to steer directly into the iceberg."

"Have you told her this?"

"She won't listen to reason, Mrs. Samuels. She thinks postponing it will be viewed as a slap, a judgment call about your husband's innocence. She is adamant. And my parents are just as adamant. I don't know what to do . . ." His eyes glistened. "Please, I didn't mean to cause you more worries. You have enough on your plate. Can I help, by the way?"

"Thank you, Seth. But we are up to our ears in legal advice." Adam shrugged.

"I understand that Marvin Cahill is representing you?"

Adam nodded. "Our family lawyer recommended him."

"He has an excellent reputation, but I would be careful that he takes into consideration certain recent decisions about terror funding that have set some important precedents. Sometimes lawyers are lazy, even the best of them. I would also recommend going over the ruling made in the State of New York Supreme Court, Appellate Division, just this past year that had to do with money transfers . . . Has Marvin mentioned this to you? If not, I'd be happy to call him and point this out to him . . ."

"That's very kind of you, Seth, but let's get back to Kayla. Where is she now?" Abigail asked.

"Back at the dorms, I think."

"You think?"

He lapsed into an uncomfortable silence.

"Seth?"

"She isn't talking to me at all." He swallowed hard, as if he'd bitten off a large piece of food that was preventing him from speaking until he disposed of it. "Look, I said some things . . . things I didn't mean. She took it very hard."

"What," Adam said slowly, examining Seth carefully, "kind of things?"

"Okay," Seth finally blurted out, realizing all his verbal skills were inadequate to the task of finessing what had to be said next. "I told her I thought we needed to distance ourselves from your problems, or it could ruin our careers."

Adam sat down heavily.

"I'm sorry, Adam. Really. I've thought about it, and I don't care anymore. You see that I'm here. I let the reporters photograph me. I was just a little hysterical, I guess, and my parents didn't help." He stopped, gulping down a big breath. "I really love Kayla. And I do care about all of you."

Abigail put her arms around him. "Of course you do, Seth. It's all so awful. For everyone."

"I should have come here with her. I should have been there for her."

Adam nodded. "That's true," he said pointedly, less forgiving than his wife. Kayla was his princess. "But it's not too late, Seth. Remember, we're just at the beginning of all this."

"Which is why you both have to talk to her. She's got important follow-up interviews scheduled for next week with some top law firms. She shouldn't cancel. It's both our futures on the line."

"Of course she shouldn't cancel. Do you think she will?"

"I don't know, Mr. Samuels. I don't know anything. Would you call her now, speak to her?" he begged.

Adam's eyebrows rose. "You went to yeshiva. We don't use the phone on the Sabbath."

"Oh, right. Sorry. It's just that I'm not practicing anymore, even though I believe."

"Something new?" Abigail asked, surprised.

"It's the pressures of law school. But I've been thinking about it for a while."

"I once had a friend who said he was a nonpracticing vegetarian. He ate steak every night," Adam said dryly.

"Yes, well. I just wanted to see you both, to offer my help. If you need me to go over files or anything . . ."

"Thank you, Seth. Offer noted." Adam nodded gratefully.

"Come, sit down, have something to eat."

"Thanks, Mrs. Samuels. But on second thought, I've really got to get back. I've got a ton of reading to catch up on."

Abigail felt a sense of relief. She was already rethinking the hug, wondering about his behavior and what it meant for the long haul. She wanted him gone.

"Don't work too hard. Remember, the Sabbath is a day of rest," Adam said.

"Maybe after I finish law school." He smiled, backing away toward the door, then stopped. "Is there a back way out of here?"

"Go out through the garage, then hop over the neighbors' fence. They won't mind."

Seth wiped his sweating forehead with the back of his hand. "Okay. Sorry. Thanks."

They waited for him to go. "I'll get the wine," Abigail said. "And then we can eat."

"I'm not really hungry," Adam whispered.

Rabbi Moshe Prinzak was a distinguished man. Tall and slightly underweight, with the face of an ascetic made more worldly by an immaculately trimmed white beard and gold-framed glasses, he looked like central casting's idea of a spiritual leader, Abigail thought cynically. His suits were dark and impeccable, his silver hair shiny and well cut, his black leather shoes always hand polished to a mirror finish. His rabbinical degree and doctoral degree, both from distinguished institutions, hung on the wall of his synagogue study in laminated perfection among thousands of learned volumes in Hebrew, English, German, and Yiddish.

He was a man who disliked controversy, unless he could forcefully cite an opinion that most people would be eager to agree with. He was a man constantly looking over his shoulder to see if his sermons, his written halachic opinions, sown in the ground of the modern Orthodox movement, had borne any bitter fruit that would poison his reputation among his far-right-leaning brethren who had sewed up control of Israeli religious institutions. Some thought he was exactly what a rabbi should be: a peacemaker and hater of divisiveness.

While others called him a moral coward, unwilling and unable to stand up to the religious establishment. Abigail leaned toward the latter.

For example, he took a strong stance on premarital agreements for brides and grooms but refused to sanction annulments for women married to drug addicts, homosexuals, and wife beaters who couldn't get a divorce the normal way because their husbands wanted to blackmail them. And he had never expressed any opinion at all about cases of rabbinic sexual misconduct.

On the plus side, as Adam always liked to point out, he knew how to give an inspiring sermon, and he was sincerely interested in helping the ill or unfortunate members of his congregation, generously dispensing synagogue funds to those in need. Adam and Abigail had always contributed generously to those funds, as well as to other synagogue needs. Rabbi Prinzak had never been turned away from their generous home.

"Rabbi, an honor and a pleasure, please come in out of the cold." Adam smiled, taking his wet umbrella. "We are so grateful you've made the effort to come out in this weather to visit us personally. It is very kind of you."

"Oh, don't mention it. Of course, my place is here with you. We have shared so many wonderful dinners and *simchas* in your lovely home. It is only right that I come now."

"Can I take your coat?" Abigail asked politely.

"Thank you, thank you." He slid his arms out of the silk-lined sleeves and handed it to her, then rubbed his hands together. "I guess winter has arrived. It's a shame. I was hoping we'd have at least another week or two. Especially since this week started off so mildly."

"That's true. Only last Tuesday when I was doing my shopping in Coolidge Corner, I kept staring at people in shorts."

Could that be true? Was it possible that joyous, carefree walk had been less than a week ago? She looked out of the window at the falling snow now blanketing the lawn. A few days and a new universe ago, she thought, startled, turning her attention back to the rabbi.

"Can I get you something? A hot drink? Coffee, tea?"

"Straight scotch, if you've got it."

She tried not to show her surprise. "Of course. Adam, why don't you take the rabbi into the library. I'll join you both in a moment."

She poured the drink. Then she sat the glass in her palm, holding it up to the light, studying the clear amber liquid. Impulsively, she threw back her head, gulping it down. She gasped and choked, her throat burning indignantly. Then she poured two more, carrying them carefully into the library. "Here, Rabbi. And here's one for you, Adam. Rabbi's orders." She felt light-headed, almost gay. The two men laughed.

"*L'Chaim!*" they said, in unison, draining their glasses. The rabbi's face turned a pale pink. Adam coughed.

Cradling the empty glass, the rabbi began: "Needless to say, Adam, we are all deeply saddened by what has happened. We share your heartache, and hope you will feel that we are family, and will be there for you. *Kol Yisrael Arevim Zeh la Zeh.* Every Jew is responsible for every other Jew. We are still a tribe in the desert surrounded by hostile forces. We survive only because we stand together against them."

"Rabbi, I am touched. Thank you." Adam's eyes shone.

"Yes, it means a lot to us to know that you feel this way," Abigail smiled, touched.

"Such a difficult, complicated business. And the media . . . How they blow things up, twist everything around! Yes, that's the world we live in. And most people see the headlines, and become judge and jury. They blindly judge, with no facts . . ."

"Rabbi, I can't tell you how comforting it is to hear you say these things! That is the truth. Exactly that."

"I know, Adam. I know. And once they spread these terrible stories, there is no taking them back. That is why our sages were so stringent in forbidding slander and gossip. Like feathers let loose into the wind, lies and evil talk about a person can never be retrieved because we cannot know where the wind will take them. That is the society we live in. A society that relies on slander and gossip to sell newspapers and magazines. A multibillion-dollar business. Such an unjust world." He shook his head mournfully.

"Yes." Adam nodded, feeling slightly uncomfortable for a reason he couldn't quite pin down. "Well, it means a lot to us that you've come personally," Adam repeated, at a loss at what to say next.

"There was no question that I needed to come." The rabbi waved his hand dismissively, obviously in no rush to get to the point of his visit, if there was one.

"Can I get you another drink, Rabbi?" Abigail inquired.

"No. I am sure you are both very weary with all that is going on, so I don't want to keep you." He exhaled. "There is something very important I need to discuss with you both."

Adam and Abigail caught each other's eyes.

"Please, go on."

"Yes, well let me start by telling you an old Chassidic tale my *rebbe* used to tell. Once there was a king who was very wealthy and lived in a large castle at the edge of the forest. The king had everything: gold and silver, fertile fields, mines for iron and copper and rare jewels. Only one thing was lacking: He had no children. One day, an old peasant came to the king's castle. He said he was from a faraway place and begged for food. The king's servants were unkind, mocking him and turning him away. But the king was on his balcony and overheard. He came down by himself and apologized to the stranger. He ordered his servants to feed him and give him clothing and a purse of gold coins to make up for his ill treatment. He asked for the stranger's blessing. The stranger asked what kind of blessing the king wanted. 'I am childless,' the king informed him.

"'And, so, what is it you wish?' the peasant persisted. 'Isn't it obvious?' the king answered in surprise. 'A child.' 'Most noble King, I will do as you ask,' said the stranger, 'but God does everything for a reason. Are you certain you wish to ask for something He has withheld from you?' The king nodded. 'Like Abraham, I too ask for a child.'

"'So be it,' said the stranger, offering his blessing. He quickly disappeared. And the following year, to everyone's great joy, the queen had a child, a son.

"You can imagine how precious the child was to his parents and to the kingdom. He was pampered and spoiled. He learned to be cruel to the servants and mocked his parents and teachers. He was extravagant in his spending, and wasteful of the kingdom's riches. The old king was heartbroken, fearing what would happen to his prosperous and happy kingdom when the young, wastrel prince took over. But, still, his love for his only child did not alter. One day, the old king took ill. He called in his servants and told them to take the prince for a journey to a far kingdom, telling him that he was to meet his future bride there. 'But when you cross over the mountains into the far country, strip the boy of his crown and fine clothes, give him sturdy workman's garments and a bag of coins, and send him on his way. Only in this way will my kingdom be saved, and my son learn to be a man. And when I die, choose the wisest and best man in the realm to take my place.' The courtiers were amazed: 'This goes against all human feeling! How can you make such a sacrifice?' And the king answered: 'I am king. Shall I behave no better than a frog? For the frogs of Egypt were willing to jump into the Egyptians' ovens to accomplish God's will, sacrificing to help the nation of Israel be free and prosperous. I can do no less than the frogs.'"

Abigail and Adam, who had been listening with ever-growing perplexity, said nothing.

"Do you understand?"

"No, Rabbi. I'm afraid I don't," Adam said, shaking his head. "It's been a long week."

"Adam, you are a treasured member of our congregation. You and Abigail and the children are our family. But sometimes, even in families who love each other, decisions have to be made for the good of the family as a whole. Difficult decisions."

"Difficult for whom, Rabbi?" Adam said, suddenly wary.

"There is a wave of anti-Semitism sweeping over the world. I mean, right here in America, that anti-Semitic black preacher and his hate sermons were broadcast all over America."

"He was roundly denounced, Rabbi. By everyone," Abigail pointed out.

"Yes. All positive signs. And in time, we all hope, anti-Semitism will once again be ridiculed and abhorred. But right now, that is not the case. There is suspicion and bad blood. There are some who want to view your situation as one more instance of a greedy Jew destroying America. We have been getting some vicious e-mails—all the synagogues in Boston have. Horrible threats."

"I hadn't heard about it!"

"We are trying to keep it quiet, Adam."

"Rabbi, are you saying you want us to distance ourselves from the synagogue?"

He looked hurt. "Abigail, how can you even think such a thing? Of course not! All I wanted was to ask you if there is any way—of course you must consult with your lawyers—to make this go away? A plea bargain, perhaps? Sometimes, even the most innocent person has no choice in certain situations but to make compromises."

They were both speechless.

"Let me understand this, Rabbi. Are you telling me to admit I did something wrong when I didn't? To sacrifice myself for the greater good? To . . ."

"To jump into the oven with the frogs?" Abigail interrupted, furious.

He looked from him to her, hesitating. "What I'm asking of you is to be completely honest with yourself, Adam. We are all human. We all make mistakes. We can't move forward until we recognize and atone for them."

Abigail shot up. Adam reached out for her, putting a restraining hand over her arm. She shook it off. "I can't believe that I sat in your synagogue for fifteen years! I can't believe that I listened to all that stuff you said about righteousness, and faith, and courage, and helping one another. All that stuff about community, and tradition, and truth . . ."

"Believe me, I am here because I care about you and your family. Think of what this is going to do to your children, your grandchildren. They will be dragged through the mud. All of us will. Sometimes one has to forget one's personal pride and think of the wider picture."

"The moment Adam admits he is willing to negotiate with the FBI, it's as much as admitting that he deliberately transferred money to terrorists who killed American soldiers. His life will be over, and so will mine. What do you think that will do for our children?"

"You're being overemotional, Abigail. Be reasonable . . ."

Adam stood up. "Rabbi, what about integrity? What about honesty?"

"I think that's exactly what I'm asking of you, Adam. Both of those things."

Adam's jaw flinched, then tightened. "Well, in that case, I think we have nothing left to talk about, Rabbi. I think it's time for you to leave."

Rabbi Prinzak's distinguished face crumpled into the face of an ordinary middle-aged man who was five parts frightened, two parts offended, and three parts annoyed. "Adam . . ."

"No! This conversation is over. Thank you for sharing your rabbinical wisdom. But, begging humbly to differ, I don't think God—that is, the Jewish God I believe in—wants human sacrifices to appease the forces of evil, fanaticism, and prejudice. I think He'd want me to have some courage, to fight to clear my name if I am innocent, which I am. Totally. Thanks for asking. Abby, would you get our rabbi his coat and his umbrella. He's leaving."

"And Rabbi," Abigail began.

The rabbi looked at her warily.

"When you first started talking about Jews sticking together, I had this image in my head of those emperor penguins, the ones that stand together huddled for warmth, withstanding any blizzard. But I see now you weren't talking about that kind of community. You were talking about the Donner party, those pioneers in wagon trains on their way west, who got caught in the mountains during the winter; or those Argentinean soccer players whose plane crashed into the Andes, communities that survived by eating one another when the chips were down . . ."

"Never judge a man when he is suffering," the rabbi said piously, rising and hurrying to the door. Abigail handed him his things. "I hope we can talk again soon. I hope you'll reconsider. For your own sake, as well as for the community's."

"What community?" Abigail asked. "You mean all those people who are willing to feed me and eat my food Friday nights? People who collapse like a house of cards at the first puff of trouble? You don't have to throw us out of your synagogue, Rabbi. We're gone."

When the rabbi left, they called Kayla on her new unlisted number. She was cheerful, noncommittal.

"Please don't worry about me. That's the last thing you need. I'm fine. Yes, I'm in touch with Seth. And I have every intention of making those interviews. Don't worry. Everything is going to be fine."

"Seth came to see us. He said you two aren't speaking."

"He had no business doing that! Look, Mom, don't you have enough problems without adopting mine?"

It was the Kayla she knew, Abigail thought, freezing at her daughter's cold, superior tone, the tone that made her feel like she didn't know anything and had no right to an opinion.

"And Kayla, what about the engagement party?"

"I guess everyone's decided to put it off, right? I don't care anymore. Do what you want."

"Well, I am happy to make it, but you and Seth have to decide," Abigail answered, hating herself for the apologetic tone she always used when Kayla got on her high horse. I am afraid of her, she thought.

"Oh, all right. Just tell the caterer we are putting it off for the time being."

"And you're okay with that?"

"I said so, didn't I?"

Abigail forced herself not to hang up, to listen for the suffering she knew must be hiding behind this rancor. "Do you have the airline tickets to New York for your interviews?"

"It's all arranged, Mom," she answered, exasperated. "Just don't nag me about it. Okay? I'm a big girl."

She and Seth would work it out, Abigail told herself, putting down the phone. Besides, Kayla didn't seem noticeably upset, although there was something in her tone which, under other circumstances, Abigail would have wanted to explore. But now she was happy to tell herself it was her imagination, and she shouldn't go looking for trouble. She had enough of it coming to look for her.

9

Please note that Kayla and Seth's engagement party has been postponed. Please keep a lookout for updated information.

Abigail read it over a number of times on her computer, wondering if she could do better. But anything she thought of changing, i.e., "It is with great sadness that we announce . . ." or "Due to an unexpected family illness . . . ," just made things worse. She hit the SEND button, feeling as if she'd sent out a death notice.

Nobody would believe how fast a life can unravel, Abigail thought. Like a Nordic sweater of intricate and complicated design, one good tug was all you needed to turn it back into a ball of yarn.

The incessant ringing and ringing of the phone of the first few days was replaced by an eerie silence. Except for their children, reporters, lawyers, lawyers' secretaries, and people wanting bills paid, everyone seemed to have forgotten about them. She reflected bitterly on the hundreds of expensive charity events she and Adam had attended, the endless wedding and Bar Mitzvah ceremonies they had endured, the time-consuming shopping, cooking, and cleaning they'd undertaken to host guests over the years. What had come of all those social investments? The account stood empty, just when she needed to cash out. Except for a handful, like her best friend, Debra, and Joyce and Helen, and some of Adam's clients, all their friends, admirers, and acquaintances seemed to have vanished, to be glimpsed from afar across the abyss of a street, or a parking lot, pretending not to see.

She burned with anger and resentment, which was transformed into self-pity, and finally self-loathing, thinking of how Emily Kahn, her neighbor, had passed her by without saying hello. Was it deliberate? Or had she just not seen her? Of how Brenda Cohen had called her, wanting a lift to the Emanuel wedding, and how she had had to admit that they hadn't been invited. Imagine! The Emanuels, who were such old friends!

"Maybe it's going to be a small wedding. People are cutting back. You don't have to take everything so personally," Adam told her, perhaps sincerely or perhaps blindly. She couldn't decide which would be worse. He was kinder than she. He didn't see bad in anyone unless it was truly beyond a reasonable doubt. And even then . . .

How many clients has he lost? she wondered. Enough so that he would have to let his staff go, all those bright, promising young accountants he had selected and wooed with such care? Aside from the expense of the severance pay, it would break his heart. He had made them so many promises to win them over. And now, they would be unemployed, in this job market. And then there was the lease for the office space and equipment, which couldn't be broken without penalty. He never spoke about it, getting dressed and leaving for the office the way he always did.

How much money did they have in savings? She didn't know anything. Adam had always handled it all. "I just go to the cash machine, and pop, like magic, the money comes out!" she'd once told a dinner crowd of admiring friends. The women had all nodded. That was the way it was in their circles. Powerful, successful men who took care of them and their money. Why would you want to balance a checkbook, make a budget, and stick to it, if you didn't have to?

There had been moments through the years when this state of affairs had tweaked her conscience. It didn't seem adult, somehow, to be so far removed from the fiscal knowledge and responsibility on which your life rested. She had never paid bills, never balanced the budget. Not that she hadn't tried. Once, in a particularly ambitious mood early in their marriage, she had purchased a home-accounting notebook, and diligently gone through and recorded all their monthly expenses as Adam looked on, amused. "You're not buying anything we don't need" had always been his indulgent answer to her attempts at cutting back and cutting down. But not long after that, Adam had made some spectacular connections in the real-estate world, and their income had soared into the stratosphere, making her feel foolish.

The wake-up call had come with Adam's health scare. She had been terrified, realizing she didn't even know how to access their money-market funds; where the stocks or bonds were hiding; and what kind of life insurance they had. She had tried to get him to explain things to her. But he was going through radiation, and the whole subject seemed to hurt him. "So, you're that sure you'll be needing to handle all this alone soon?" he'd answered her bitterly.

And that had been the end of the subject.

Until now.

She needed to talk to Adam about money. But no matter how desperately she needed the information, she felt she couldn't ask him, that it would smack of disloyalty or—worse—distrust.

Well, at least I still have a job, she told herself. But their lifestyle could not be maintained on a teacher's salary. She lay in the dark, pondering: Were they going to have to let Esmeralda go? The gardeners? The maintenance man? And then, what would happen to their house? Even if she quit her job and worked at it full-time, she couldn't possibly keep it maintained in the condition it was in. She just wouldn't know how, especially the gardens, with all those leaves . . . ! That alone was a full-time job. It would be exhausting to even try. But then, she thought, could I be any more exhausted than I already am?

In bed, she lay awake imagining stacks of white envelopes holding bills that lay unopened on Adam's desk. She couldn't sleep. This fact dawned on her slowly.

At first she thought that she just wasn't tired. Or that she had something she really wanted to find out about on the Internet. And so at one in the morning she would browse aimlessly, going from entertainment news gossip to the latest on Fritzl and his daughter, or Madoff. Then she checked out iTunes, and Web sites about Jews and Israel and terrorism. She avoided looking at her watch. And when she finally got into bed, she could not get up the next morning. She dragged through the day, feeling like she was walking underwater, each foot-fall heavy and clumsy. It reminded her of her days as a young mother, when the clock had made no distinction between night and day, and the crying infant had disordered the universe. It was all the same, a twenty-four-hour period of wakefulness, with no time off.

She knew, vaguely, that she couldn't keep it up, that she was betraying Adam, who needed her to be strong. She wanted so much to prove to everyone that she was. She wanted so much to be one of those people about whom others say with admiration: "Through it all, she was magnificent." "She never wa-vered." "I don't know where she got her strength." It was heartbreaking to ad-mit to herself that—as much as she wanted to, as much as Adam deserved it, and as much as her children expected it—she couldn't be that person. It was a surprise, a disappointing failure for which she hadn't been prepared.

She was falling apart. If anything, it was Adam who was holding her up.

Finally, she confided in her doctor, who listened sympathetically and pre-scribed sedatives. "Now you aren't going to take these every night, are you?" He smiled, that kindly I-know-I-can-count-on-you smile, the smile that told her she was a sensible woman who could be relied upon not to take too many pills too often, because they were addictive.

Abigail, a woman who didn't like drugs, and hated to swallow pills of any kind, even vitamins, took a sedative and slept for over eight hours. It was such a deep, restorative sleep. She loved the way those little white pills made her feel—as if nothing was important. Soon, she couldn't sleep without them. But when she went back to renew her prescription, her doctor balked: "Abigail, it's not that I don't trust you. I've known you a long time. But perhaps we should be dealing with this in another way." He suggested antidepressants.

She called Debra, the only person to whom she always admitted the truth.

"I took them once, a long time ago, when Ben and I were having our prob-lems. It helped. But I didn't like the way they made me feel," Debra recalled.

"What way was that?"

"Like there was this glass window between myself and the world. I was part of everything, functioning, but I didn't feel anything. Nothing made me sad or upset. But nothing made me happy either. I couldn't stand that! I finally stopped."

"What happened?"

"I felt miserable, but so what? Isn't it better to feel miserable when you're miserable than not to feel anything at all? Yes, I was angry and upset and everything else. But at least I felt alive. You remember that movie *Tootsie*? Remember what Teri Garr says to Dustin Hoffman when he tells her the truth, that he's in love with another woman? She says: 'I'm going to feel this way until I don't feel this way anymore, and you're going to have to know that you're the one that made me feel this way, you schmuck!'"

She laughed. "But I can't sleep."

"I know. Try some Chi Qong. It's very relaxing. Or recite some psalms. You wouldn't believe how comforting they can be. Believe me, everyone who has ever lived has gone through this crap. It's part of the human condition, as our Lit professors liked to say."

She bought a book on Chi Qong. She tried standing perfectly still, her feet gripping the ground, her hands weightless at her sides, feeling her mind empty of all thoughts. She concentrated on her breathing, feeling the cool air as it entered her nostrils, making her little nose hairs quiver like sea anemones, feeling it fill her lungs and make her stomach rise and fall. She beat back her thoughts, until there was nothing left but her breath. She timed how long she could keep it up: five minutes, ten at the most, before she found herself back at square one—pain, pain, and more pain.

And then, one morning, as she was walking down the street, she crossed on a red light. Cars screeched to a halt, barely missing her. Instead of being shaken and grateful, she realized that some part of her was disappointed. How comforting it would be if it were just all over. Dying wasn't so frightening, she thought. She'd had a great life. Great kids, grandchildren. Maybe it was enough?

"I'm not coping very well," she told Adam. She was standing outside the door of his home office, watching his back hunch over the keyboard of the computer.

"Look, I'm sorry. Can we talk later?" He was brusque, abrupt.

She felt offended, brushed away. And then she felt guilty for her resentment. How could she think about burdening him even more with her own problems?

She went to the kitchen and made him some coffee as a peace offering, climbing back up the stairs with it. He was on the phone.

"This is Adam Samuels. Is George Cook there? I'll hold. . . . George, it's

Adam Samuels. Yes . . . thank you very much. I appreciate your loyalty more than I can say. But I think it would be in your best interests to find another accountant. I am innocent of these charges. I have done nothing wrong. But your company could be adversely affected by my legal battles, and it is just not in your best interests to be involved in this. . . . Thank you very much for saying that. I appreciate your honesty also, George. Yes, thank you very much. Let me know when you want to pick up the files."

She stared at him, speechless. "What are you doing?!"

"Abby, I have no choice. This is the honest thing to do. These people could find themselves investigated just for their association with me. It's my responsibility to . . ."

"What about your responsibility to yourself, to me, to this family? How can you do this? Blow off all the clients who didn't go running?"

"It's the honest thing to do," he repeated stubbornly. "I'm sorry. I have no choice."

Her hands trembled. The hot coffee sloshed over, burning her fingertips. She said, "OH!" and opened her hand, letting the cup smash on the floor.

He sat down heavily, staring at the dark brown circle widening across the blue-and-cream carpeting of his office. "I've got work to do, Abby," he said tonelessly, swiveling his chair around to face his computer.

She wanted to scream: "Explain to me why my life is falling apart! What happened? What did you do? What do they think you did?"

But she could already see in her mind exactly what would happen: He would turn around, his jaws clenched in fury. He would say: "I've already told you everything I know, Abigail."

To which she could only answer: "Tell me again!"

And he would repeat what she already knew: that he had transferred a client's money to a hedge fund in England that came highly recommended. Unbeknownst to him, this fund had a manager who had transferred that money to terrorist groups. The feds were convinced he was a venal, willing participant. "But I didn't know . . ." he would beg her, his voice growing louder and louder.

And she would have nothing left to say to him but the worst thing she could say: "Why didn't you know? Why weren't you more careful?"

So she didn't say anything, swallowing the words like a cup of arsenic.

She looked at his back, then walked out the door.

Second by second, minute by minute, her anger grew and multiplied like some splitting amoeba that infects the entire body in record time. It did not stem from any question of her husband's guilt or innocence. At most there might be a remote possibility that he had made an honest, stupid mistake, or there had been some innocent misunderstanding now misconstrued. No, it wasn't that. It was the idea that this was hanging over his head and he was doing all he could to exclude her. She felt like a child whose parents had made decisions that were only now being discovered because of the consequences which had fallen on her. She felt completely in the dark, forced to stare through keyholes and under doors, scavenging for information.

It had been like this with the cancer too, she thought, that same infuriating desire to go it alone. He'd pushed her away with both hands. What had she done to deserve this kind of dismissal? Didn't he understand? She didn't want to be separate from him. Like that old wedding vow that gentiles took: *For richer or for poorer, in sickness and in health.* She was in it with him. He was the love of her life. Her partner. How could he not understand that, not trust her enough to let her in? She thought of that old couple in the movie *Titanic* who refused to be parted even when the ship was going down, the wife refusing her place on one of the lifeboats.

It had been *their* cancer; and now it was *their* court case. They would float above it or go down together. Why couldn't he understand that? And what would happen to their marriage if she couldn't convey this to him before it was too late? Like the ball bearings in some never-quiet machine, they scraped and scraped against each other, until their nerves were raw and their wounds bloody.

Small things irritated her: a sour look on his face; the way he rose from the table after eating without lifting a finger to help clean up; the way he closed a door just a tiny bit too hard; the way he let the phone ring without answering it. And there was that look he got when the fax machine beeped—a look of anguish.

"How many eggs did you use in this omelet?"

"I don't know. Two . . . We're running low."

"Why is that?"

She could see his jaw flinch in anger.

"I . . . I didn't get to the store yesterday. I was so busy." She smiled, but he didn't respond. "I'll get to it today."

"What, are you trying to save money, is that it?"

Like being inches away from a person with pneumonia who coughs on you without covering their mouth, the germs of his anger and pain infected her.

"Why, is that such a bad thing?" she shouted back.

"Right, let's talk about it! I know you blame me for everything that's happened. We're going to be poor! Is that it?"

"I wish I could just tear these people limb from limb! That big-shot prosecutor, those FBI robots . . .'"

"Yes, that would be wonderful! Then I'd have to use whatever's left of our money to bail *you* out of jail."

"I can't help how I feel! I'm entitled to feel any way I want!"

"Really? Well, this is the way *I* feel!" He picked up his plate, flinging the eggs into the sink, then stomped out of the room.

She sat down at the beautiful marble kitchen counter, staring indifferently at the wall of crimson ceramic tiles, grateful to have been spared the humiliation of household help looking on.

Esmeralda was gone, paid off and sent packing. She'd been polite and cold when they gave her notice. The week after she left, Abigail realized her favorite gold-and-lapis earrings had gone missing. In the weeks that followed, she discovered some silver candlesticks and a small jade elephant had also disappeared.

"I'm going to report her to the police," Abigail fumed.

The idea infuriated Adam: "That's all we need now. More publicity!" When they got into bed that night, their backs were stiff and they were facing opposite walls. Some impulse made her turn around. Her fingers smoothed his brow. He reached out to her, pulling her to him, burying his face in her shoulder.

"I'm so sorry, Abby."

She caressed him silently in the dark as they clung to each other, survivors in a home torn apart by a hurricane.

In the evenings after dinner, they sat beside each other on the living room couch, drained of words. "Do you want to play some Scrabble, watch a video?"

"No, I think I'll just go out for a walk."

"Do you want me to come with you, Adam?"

He shrugged. "If you want."

She put on her down-filled parka, gloves, and a scarf. The Boston cold was already brutal as she walked beside him through dark, deserted streets, carefully picking her way through the ice. But he was walking way too fast for her to keep up, his head down as he plowed forward, oblivious. Finally, he glanced sideways. Then he turned around, staring at her, waiting for her to catch up. "Are you cold? Do you want to go home?"

"No, I'm fine," she lied, her nose blue, her fingertips numb.

"Look, why don't you just go home?"

"Why are you trying to get rid of me?"

"You don't have to do this to prove something."

"Is that what you think? That I have something to prove?"

"Well, it's true, isn't it? You need to be Mrs. Perfect. Stand by Your Man. I don't need your pity. Just go home, Abigail."

"You are such a jerk. You really are!" she said, turning swiftly on her heels, not wanting him to see the tears that flowed down her cheeks, burning like hot wax in the freezing cold as she hurried through the dark night. Turning the corner, she felt her feet suddenly disconnect with the sidewalk. With horror, she felt her body tip uncontrollably forward. She reached out one hand, but it was too late. She crashed on her knees, her breast hitting the pavement hard.

In the warm bathroom with its blue tiles, she dabbed disinfectant over her scratches. Days later, a big black-and-blue mark formed just above her nipple, together with a little lump that felt like the stuff of every woman's nightmare.

"What is that?" Adam said as they undressed for bed, alarmed.

"I fell."

"When?"

"That night, on the way home from our walk. I slipped."

"Oh. I shouldn't have let you go alone. I'm so sorry, Abby. I'm such a jerk."

"Yes, you are," she agreed.

He touched her gently. "I feel a lump. Do you feel it?"

She touched herself. "It's probably from the fall. But I'll see the doctor."

She lay in bed thinking: Maybe it's cancer. Maybe I'm going to die. She hadn't had a mammogram in years, afraid the X-rays might give her cancer, confident that she would follow in her mother's footsteps and live to a ripe, cancer-free old age.

"It's probably from the fall," her doctor agreed without examining her. He was a very religious Jew. I will have to find another doctor, she thought. But the lump disappeared after a few weeks, along with the bruise marks, healing without a trace. She had a mammogram. It came out clean, and the reprieve gave her the first joy she had felt in weeks. She knew now that she didn't want to die. She wanted to live.

And then, there was suddenly a lull. The lawyers didn't call. The fax machine didn't ring. They exhaled.

"Let's go for a picnic!" she suggested.

"In this weather?"

"Please, Adam. I'm going crazy."

He touched her face. "Okay."

She took some leftover chicken and a few slices of corned beef, a package of rolls, and cans of pickles and olives. They traveled to Concord, traipsing through Louisa May Alcott's picturesque little house, because she was Abigail's favorite writer. They parked the car overlooking frozen Walden Pond. As she unpacked the lunch and gave out paper plates and napkins, he took out a copy of *The Portable Thoreau.*

" 'Let us consider for a moment what most of the trouble and anxiety is about,' " he read aloud.

> *. . . how much it is necessary that we be troubled, or at least careful. It would be some advantage to live a primitive frontier life, though in the midst of an outward civilization, if only to learn what are the gross necessaries of life, and what methods have been taken to obtain them . . . For the improvements of ages have had but little influence on the essential laws of man's existence; as our skeletons, probably, are not to be distinguished from those of our ancestors.*

"Do you want corned beef, or chicken?"

"Chicken, my love," he said, turning the page.

> *I am a parcel of vain strivings tied*
> *By a chance bond together.*
> *Dangling this way and that, their links*
> *Were made so loose and wide,*
> *Methinks,*
> *For milder weather . . .*

She laughed. "That sounds more like me than you. I am very loosely tied together these days."

He slid over and put his arm around her. "I don't want you to worry, my love. It's going to be all right. Whatever happens."

"How can you say that, Adam?"

"Because as long as I have your love and the children and grandchildren are well, I'll be fine."

She touched his face, searching his eyes. "Really?"

"Really." He smiled.

Could it be true? she wondered. For him, for myself? "You know Thoreau was a maniac. I'm sure the mosquitoes ate him alive out here," she said gaily.

"Ah, you are such a romantic, my love!" He laughed, closing the book.

They sat quietly, watching the clouds swim by in the cold blue sky, reaching out for each other's hands. When they got home, she brought out a bottle of wine they'd purchased in the Jewish Ghetto in Venice, a kosher Italian Cabernet. She filled two of her best crystal glasses and brought it to him. In the living room, he was playing music from the Four Tops.

"Where did you find that? It's a zillion years old."

"I've had it stashed in a secret place all these years."

They had gone to a Four Tops concert the summer before they got married, driving out on country roads from jobs in Catskill hotels. Joining an overflow crowd of New York Jews sitting in the balcony of the old upstate theater, they'd sung, clapped, and roared with approval for the four suave, velvet-voiced black men.

"Remember this?" She straightened her arm, raising the palm dramatically: *"When you think that you can't go on."*

"Just reach out, reach out!" He joined her.

"Here, drink this." She handed him the goblet.

He drained it, then put it down carefully on the coffee table. He lifted her half-filled glass from her hands.

"But I'm not finished. . . ."

He put it down beside his own. Then he took her hands and pulled her up, putting his arms around her waist, entwining his fingers through hers. They took off their shoes, sliding around on the polished wood floors.

"I'LL BE THERE WITH A LOVE THAT WILL SEE YOU THRO-OOOO," they shouted, their voices rising until they were hoarse. They collapsed on the rug in laughter.

"My love."

He pushed her gently until she lay down beside him in front of the fireplace. They clung to each other, making love with a gentleness and urgency they had not felt for many weeks.

Their days took on a new rhythm. She got up early to clean the house and go to work. He got up even earlier, raking leaves and preparing breakfast before disappearing into his home office to study his case. He seldom left the house except on the days they were obliged to meet with their lawyers.

Those were the worst, looming on their calendars like black holes. She hated being there. It was like being on line for a painful procedure, worse than a root canal or a bone-marrow transplant.

Their attorney Marvin Cahill was one of the top men in his field. He was about their age, with a balding head and keen, cool blue eyes. He was not a hand-holder. The opposite. "Let me put all the cards on the table" was the way he began almost every other sentence, followed by worst-case scenarios.

"I don't know, does he really think you're innocent? Or is he just constantly covering his ass, anticipating disaster?"

"That is what a lawyer is supposed to do. He is very, very cautious. And very thorough. That's a good thing."

"But he keeps hinting that you should consider making some deal."

"That's not true!"

She said nothing, astonished. All she ever heard from Cahill and his associate, another senior partner in one of Boston's top firms, was how to avoid actually proving Adam's innocence. If he admitted to a lesser charge . . . if he could provide valuable information about Gregory Van and Christopher Dorset, who were the really big fish the feds were after . . . then it could be worked out, etc., etc.

"Let's put our cards on the table! You are facing serious jail time, and a monetary fine that will destroy your family. You should seriously consider a plea bargain."

"No, I won't. I haven't done anything wrong. I'm completely innocent. Even if it takes my last penny. Even if I wind up behind bars for life"—the words made her shudder—"I'm not going to admit to something I haven't done. As for Gregory Van and Christopher Dorset, I've told you all I know."

It took her days and many sedatives to recover from a visit to the lawyers.

"Don't come with me. I can go alone," Adam said.

The words were an echo from the all-too-recent past, from a battle just barely won against an enemy that had also ambushed them out of the blue. It had been five years, but it felt like yesterday.

Midday. Sitting at the dining-room table, reading the newspaper. The door opened, and he came in. She didn't even look up.

"So," she said, turning the page, engrossed by some stranger's tragedy, awaiting with only half an ear confirmation of that which she was already so sure she knew. "Was the biopsy okay?"

He was the kind of man who always took his time to answer a question. But there was something about the quality of the silence between them that made her finally turn her head and look up at him. She wasn't the least bit afraid, just curious, as she took in his handsome greying head, the shirt of some soft material with its open collar still showing the tan left over from Kauai, Queenstown, and Cairns.

They'd only been back two weeks. It had been the trip they'd planned for practically all their lives. Three months traveling the world, freed from years of brutal 6:00 A.M. partings and 10:00 P.M. workday endings. Making off with the loot of their stock gains, they'd shocked their doubtful children, escaping to a fabulous second honeymoon.

Awaiting his assurances she thought, as always, how very handsome he was. "No," he finally said without inflection. "It wasn't okay."

One thirty in the morning, sitting in her office scanning the e-mails from the LMS sarcoma list, a group you really don't want to belong to, typing in desperate questions. She'd spent a day at the hospital, waiting and waiting on endless lines, running down long, dreary basement passageways leading to the hallowed offices of the professors and experts who were going to save her husband with their priceless knowledge. And Adam, sitting patiently, waiting his turn, forgetting to give his file and number to the nurse who was arranging the queue. "How will they know to call you?" she asked him. He was annoyed at the question. She went in to the nurse, who was up to twenty-three, when his number was fifteen. She went back, taking the file from him and handing it to the nurse.

All their knowledge was gleaned from hurried meetings with young physicians, who, in their white coats, glanced over the files, telling them things like: "You don't have to come back to have the stitches taken out. You can do that anywhere." Or: "The margins are clean." They held ballpoint pens and added short notes onto pieces of green paper full of bad handwriting from other doctors.

In their calm routine, the doctors gave them the sense that they were not losing the world, that they were still part of ordinary life: long lines, appointments, options.

It was only at one thirty in the morning, alone in her office on the computer, that some anonymous list member, Lang09, a cancer-ridden doctor in a chat room on the other side of the world, finally explained what their doctors had not: that her husband's numbers were not good; that the margins weren't clean, they were dirty. Dirty with cancer cells. "And that is why your husband needs radiation."

And if that doesn't work, she cannot help thinking then . . . *He is going to die. My handsome love, my husband, the father of my children. He is going to die, and there is nothing I can do to stop it. The children all think I can save him. After all, didn't I find the surgeon, the best expert in the country? Didn't I?* But they don't understand that even the best, the Sarcoma King himself, is helpless.

Should I share the horror of these e-mails? But she didn't want to frighten the children. Shoshana had just had another miscarriage, after years of fertility treatments. Josh was off in Hollywood, following his dreams. Kayla was just finishing her second year in college. She had given her children too much information already.

She had no choice, then, but to go it alone. She was part of it, the strange, dark world between life and death that is called a malignant sarcoma. There were other natives here who spoke a new language which she was trying to learn: The word "stage" used in conjunction with something that has nothing to do with theater. Stage 1, 2, 3, 4, and you're out. Margins, the space you needed between the tumor they cut out and healthy skin. Do you have one centimeter or don't you? If you don't, you are in trouble.

They were in trouble.

There was a way to get out of this trouble. To zap the margins with radiation to kill the cells, to stop them reproducing. The healthy, good cells, the cancerous bad cells, zap them all. Every day, for months. Hope the technicians' fingers won't slip and get your heart, your lungs. Hope to God they know what they are doing.

The patient felt fine. The patient wasn't worried. He didn't want to talk about it.

"You are not a doctor!" he'd scream, when she suggested making copies of the X-rays, biopsies, diagnosis, and sending them to other professor genius saviors who resided in other research palaces made possible by multibillion-dollar research budgets: places where husbands lived a decade after being diagnosed with liver cancer, and brain cancer, and kidney cancer, and sarcomas and melanomas and carcinomas . . .

She'd fling her arm across her face, stretching out on the bed. "You aren't behaving responsibly. I have to take over and do what's best for you," she'd tell him, echoing the words of her shrink, lately consulted. It was not what she had wanted him to say. She had wanted her shrink to give her absolution—to say: "He's a big boy, and this is his life, his decision. You can't tell him what to do, as much as you love him."

Her chest pains (or were they stomach pains, that horrible squeezing feeling on her left shoulder that seems like a prelude to a heart attack?) began. There was the sleepless wandering around a dark house, attempts at meditation. And browsing through self-help books as the clock clicked past one, past two, and on to three. And now, after the horror had finally ended with the passage of a cancer-free five years, this new horror. This new danger. And again, there was no choice.

The day of their lawyers' appointments, they'd get up at seven.

She'd stand in front of her mirror thinking: What's the appropriate outfit for the wife of an accused felon? Nothing too revealing, but also not dowdy; you'd want them to know they had to take you seriously. It's a whole new life experience, dancing down this yellow-brick road to the wizards who hold the keys to all we want so much to keep. Like the Sarcoma Kings, the lawyers too were larger than life, legal specialists who can interpret pages of numbers, affidavits, and correspondence to distinguish between a twenty-year lockup and maximum humiliation, and absolute vindication and freedom.

The waiting room in a legal office was similar to waiting rooms to see the Sarcoma Kings. People looked each other over, trying to guess who was in trouble and who was just along for the ride. As with the cancer specialists, Abigail wanted to wear a sign on her chest: IT'S NOT ME. She didn't know why that was important, unless it was because she didn't want their interest or their pity. Not wishing attention herself, she nevertheless looked everyone else over shamelessly. In the legal offices, the eyes are troubled, or bored, or both. People seem restless, skin pinched between brows. But nearly everyone is expensively dressed, well toned, made-up. In contrast, the cancer clinic was filled with a collection of the old and overweight who made her want to comb her hair until it shone, to put some demarcation line between herself and them. She wanted to be outside this club, sympathizing and admiring its membership.

She thought of other queues: Lines in Häagen-Dazs and Ben & Jerry's. The line in the Galeries Lafayette outside the Louis Vuitton boutique. Lines in Disneyland. Now their lives consisted of waiting patiently for something they desperately didn't want to be involved in.

The lawyer has two others with him. Students? Colleagues?

He goes through the files. The initial charges confuse him. He shows it to the others. Is it money laundering? Or isn't it? Why isn't there an exact list of charges, and the names of the accusers?

Marvin Cahill gives them a litany of dangers involved in any litigation.

The doctor gave them a litany of dangers involved in radiation.

Cahill tells them what lies ahead in the best-case scenario: pretrial hearings, then the trial itself, with days for questioning witnesses.

CTs every three months. And then a colonoscopy, bone scans, etc., etc., for as far into the future as the eye can see. Endless medical tests. Endless worry awaiting the results. For the rest of our lives, this fearful thing hanging over our heads like a sword.

I can't bear it. Can't bear it.

God has thrown a brick at me to get my attention for the second time, she thinks. "What is all this supposed to teach me? What am I supposed to learn?" Abigail agonizes out loud. Adam says nothing; his faith made of a harder metal, one that apparently has no melting point because it was forged in doubt. He will never lose the faith he has because it is so tentative, so realistic. He believes in God but does not believe that God involves Himself in the tedious affairs of men. On earth, you were on your own.

They finally print out all the pictures from their around-the-world trip. They sit at night at the dining-room table dividing them into groups chronologically, then geographically, finally putting them into an album. There they are, smiling in Park Guell in Barcelona. There is the beach in the Dominican Republic. The black-and-white cactus pictures taken in Tucson. The rainbow in Waikiki Beach that fell over the whole city and into the water like a child's drawing. There she is holding a croissant at breakfast at the Four Seasons in Maui, her face tan against the white blouse, beaming at the camera. The licorice-smooth backs of whales protruding from the waters off Kauai. New Zealand bungee jumpers. Australian rain forests. The orchids in Singapore. And that picture, her favorite, of Adam in the rattan chair framed by the veranda in the Raffles Hotel in Singapore, looking like some F. Scott Fitzgerald expat. He is so young, so handsome, she thinks, in that picture. They smile, even though they know now that in every frame there had been this lump in his chest, which they kept telling each other was nothing, and anyhow, it wasn't growing. No, it was exactly the same, and, anyway, it's nothing. They were so committed to this nothing ("the doctor said it was nothing") that even when they got back home and were only given an appointment two weeks away with the surgeon, who needs to go over the results of CT scans they took before they left, they didn't think to speed it up, to call back, to insist . . .

That night, she had a dream. They are in Germany with Shoshana and Matthew. They are in a nice hotel, on vacation. Suddenly, Adam falls on his back on the floor. He can't breathe. She thinks: He is going to die, right here. She asks the waiter: "Please, get him an ambulance. Please!" But the man doesn't seem to understand her. She wants to take Adam in a taxi to the hospital, but she doesn't speak the language of this new place. She doesn't know how to help him, so she watches him gasping. And then, suddenly, he stops. He gets up. He looks fine. He says he feels fine. "But you aren't fine. We have to get you to a hospital. It could happen again. You could die!" He is upset with her. "I feel fine," he says, and they leave the hotel. It's a lovely day. And the grandchildren are with them. After all, they don't want to ruin it for them; they are on vacation. The urgency she felt a moment before leaves as her footsteps slow to match her husband's. She looks down the block at the foreign landscape, wondering which direction the hospital is in, but there is no way to know. "I'm fine," Adam repeats. There are two benches in front of the hotel, at right angles. Adam sits down on one, and she on the other. It is the kind of bench she's never seen, the kind that has to be opened up, like a convertible. When she opens it, she sees a big, sticky stain on it. I wish I could wash it, but I can't, she thinks. So she sits down next to it, trying not to let it worry her.

Later that morning, she tried to tell Adam her dream, but he didn't really want to hear it. He said: "But what does it tell you about reality? Nothing. It's just some reality in your head that has nothing to do with anything. It's all just in your head." He didn't want to interpret it, as she did, wanting to crack open its secrets like an oyster.

The other side of midnight. The barking dogs, the faint streetlight. The hope that it will be 4:00 A.M., not 2:00 A.M., so there is less time to kill until morning. Each time she touches her husband, she feels a tiny tug of desperation. Each time she looks at him, she loves him more. She can see that now. Understand it the way she never has in all the forty years they've been together. So many wretched times. So many fights. And yet, a partnership that let us run our "business" and succeed beyond our wildest dreams. The children, all grown now.

I've had that, a father for my children, a husband to help me all those years, she thinks gratefully, which is more than my poor mother ever did; more than some women ever have. A good man, who went to work willingly, and came home willingly, and cared for his children willingly, and with all his heart. An honest man. A kind man, despite his temper and unwillingness to suffer fools gladly. I wish I could sleep, and not worry, and have the courage to face God; to ask Him for things I'm afraid I don't deserve. I wish I wasn't afraid to pray, to bang down His door. I wish I had more faith that my prayers will be answered. But this terrible trouble, this is from Him, isn't it? Or are misfortunes and illnesses something we bring on ourselves by our own choices? And when, when, when will it all be over?

"There is someone at the door," Adam said.

"What?" She propped herself up on one elbow, then reached toward the radio alarm. "It's three o'clock in the morning!"

"I'll go down," Adam said, throwing off the covers and sliding his feet into slippers as he reached for his robe.

"I'm not sure you should! Be careful," she called after him anxiously, not moving, waiting to hear something. She heard the door open, and low male voices.

"Who is it? Who's down there?" she called out, jumping out of bed and pulling on her bathrobe. She ran to the landing in the stairwell, peering down. It was Seth. "What's happened?" she called out, running down the steps.

"Calm down, Abby. Seth, come in and sit down. Let me get you a drink."

"There's no time!" he said in anguish.

"No time for what? What's happened?" Abigail said, her voice at the very edge of losing control, so many horrible things flashing through her mind.

"Abby, Seth thinks that Kayla . . . that she's . . . well, we don't know where she is."

"She went to that job interview in Manhattan three days ago. And she still isn't back. And my friend Bob, who works at the firm, says she showed up at the firm but left before her interview began."

"Why would she do that? Go all the way to Manhattan and run off before the interview? It's not like her. It makes no sense." Adam shook his head.

"I agree with you, which is why I'm here. I've looked everywhere, called everyone. No one has seen or heard from her in two days. Have you?" His eyes were bloodshot and desperate.

"I feel ill," Abigail said, losing her footing. She sat down heavily on the stairs, her hand over her heart. How much more? she thought, listening to its rapid beat tattoo her palm.

"Where was she staying in New York?" Adam asked calmly.

"Well, that's just it. She wasn't staying anywhere. She was supposed to come back the same day. That was the plan."

"Have you tried her cell phone?"

"I've been dialing for two days. Nothing."

Abigail stood up. "Let's try it again."

Seth shrugged. "Why not?" He took out his phone and dialed. A look of wonderment came over his face. "Kayla?"

"Is it her? Thank God!" Adam wiped his forehead, his face collapsing from stoic calm into wretchedness with amazing speed.

"Let me talk to her!" Abigail grabbed the phone. "Kayla, darling, where are you? Are you all right? What? You're where?"

"Where is she?" Adam said.

"Kayla, when are you coming back?"

Seth and Adam watched Abigail's face as she stared into the phone, trying to read the answers in her forehead and cheeks.

"Kayla, darling, that makes no sense . . . how can you . . . when your father and I are going through so much . . . and Seth . . . he's been insane with worry . . . Kayla! Hello?"

She put down the phone. "Her battery went dead. She says she was on planes for the last two days and couldn't call."

"Planes? Where is she? Is she all right?" Seth shouted.

"She's in Israel."

"Israel?" Seth's face flushed in bewilderment and fury. "And when is she planning to come back? We are in the middle of the school year . . ." he said, barely coherent.

"That's just it. She says she's not sure she is coming back."

"Ever?" Seth whispered, his fury suddenly gone, bewilderment and hurt taking its place.

They stared at each other wordlessly.

10

How strange, Kayla Samuels mused, putting her now-dead cell phone back into her purse, that huge, life-changing decisions so often pivoted on the tiniest details. The fact that she'd taken her green and not her blue backpack to the job interview in New York. The fact that she was disorganized and lazy and the green one still contained her passport from last summer's trip to Paris. Had any of these things been different, she would probably now be back in her room in Boston arguing with Seth, studying, and dreading the next newspaper article on her father.

What luck, she thought with momentary exhilaration, envisioning the thousands of miles she had put between herself and everything and everyone familiar—all the people she knew, who knew her and her parents; all the newspaper-reading idiots of the Western world.

Or was it luck? Her mother sounded heartbroken, and her father was probably even worse off. And then there was Seth *"insane with worry."*

She couldn't let herself think about any of that, not yet! Not when she'd just tunneled out from under the avalanche of heartbreak and betrayal that had crushed and buried her over the last few months, using her own bare hands, having finally realized that the rescue dogs weren't coming; her parents and fiancé weren't coming. She was almost there, already seeing the light at the end of the tunnel. But the sides and roof, she realized, were fragile and thin. Just thinking the wrong thoughts could bring them crashing down. She just couldn't risk it.

She waited on line at passport control, filled with dread at being recognized. But when her turn came, the pretty Sabra with long dark hair just stamped her passport. "Have a good stay!" she said in heavily accented English. See, Kayla told herself, exulting. My name and face mean nothing to her!

She walked out into a wall of greeters anxious to gather some beloved wanderer into their arms, holding flowers and helium balloons in the shapes of Dora the Explorer and Dumbo. They looked her over; then they looked away. No one was waiting for her.

"Taxi, young lady?"

"No thanks."

But he wouldn't budge. "I have nice car. Big, American Buick. Where the young lady go? Haifa, Tel Aviv, Jerusalem?"

She shook her head, moving on. She had managed to avoid thinking about the answer to that question the entire eleven-hour plane ride. In any case, she couldn't afford taxis.

She'd cashed a check drawn on her college tuition account, viewing it as a personal loan she fully intended to repay. Someday. Depending on whether or not a law-school dropout could ever find employment. When that ran out, she'd be on her own.

"Jerusalem, *motek*? We have five. We need six. You come?" the driver of a shuttle service accosted her. The other passengers eyed her hungrily. They, at least, were happy to see her, she told herself climbing in. A black-clad Chassidic man began arguing with the driver about where she would sit, piously adamant that it would not be next to him. Finally, a husband and wife agreed to separate, allowing her to sit down without controversy.

"Where you are going?" the driver asked her, slamming the door shut.

He started the engine.

"Hotel," she answered, shouting over the noise. "Maybe you know someplace central, and very cheap?"

"Try the little hotel off Ben Yehuda Street," the wife offered. "My American nieces always stay there."

"Uff." The husband shook his head. "Such a hole."

"She wanted cheap." The wife shrugged.

"The place. You go?" the driver asked Kayla again, insistently.

"Okay, okay. Ben Yehuda Street." Her head swirled. Like Dorothy in *The Wizard of Oz,* a whirlwind had picked her up, hurtling her through time and space. She didn't think, as any sensible person would far from home, in a strange country where she knew no one: What am I going to do? No, she didn't think at all. Closing her eyes, she happily gave in to fatigue.

"*Geveret!* Your stop!"

Were they here already? She opened her sleepy eyes, peering out the dusty window. The white-stone walls of Jerusalem stared back at her. A shiver went up her spine. Excitement? Fear? Dread? She didn't know.

Jerusalem.

Exhausted, barely conscious of her surroundings, she found the hotel, checked in, and without even undressing fell into a deep sleep.

She awoke feeling like a desert nomad, her hunger and thirst fierce and unfamiliar, her throat a bed of gravel clogged with mud. She coughed, spitting up and half choking on phlegm. She rushed to the bathroom, washing out her mouth and bringing cupped fistfuls of water to her lips to drink. She washed her face, cleaning the pus from the corners of her eyes, drying herself. The towel had seen better days, but at least it was clean.

She pulled back the frayed drapes, opening the dusty shutters. Bright morning light streamed through. She was in the middle of a city street, with lively outdoor cafes and shoe stores and clothing shops. Even two flights up, she could smell the pizza. She was starving, she realized. And filthy.

She stood beneath the burning-hot water, imagining solar water-heating panels baking in the Middle Eastern sun. She diluted it with as much cold as possible, to no avail, finally closing the hot-water tap altogether and making do with cold. Scrubbing off the accumulated grime of the last few days, she watched with pleasure as her skin turned pink and raw. But when she was done, a heap of sweaty clothes confronted her. The idea of putting them back on was disgusting. Rummaging through her backpack, she found one clean pair of underwear, a less sweaty bra, and her dress-for-success interview suit, wrinkled beyond recognition. Even if the room had an iron, which she highly doubted, pressing it would take at least an hour, at which time she'd be dead of hunger. Taking pleasure in the underwear—an unexpected treasure—she reluctantly pulled on the dark blue skirt, slipping her arms into the white blouse, then the blue jacket. She looked at herself in the mirror, appalled. Although she knew she would suffocate, she pulled on her coat, hoping at least to keep the outfit hidden and thus salvage some self-respect, surprised she still had any left.

The hotel was far seedier than she remembered, she thought as she walked downstairs, taking in the dirty carpeting, the plastic lawn chairs stacked up on the dusty veranda, the lobby crowded with (very) used furniture, looking like a Goodwill warehouse. Even the clerk behind the front desk looked unclean, as well as sullen and a bit dangerous.

She changed some money. "What time is checkout?"

"Twelve. Something not good with room?" he accused.

"No, no. I'm . . . just . . . traveling . . . up north . . ." she improvised, realizing she now had no choice but to flee.

She followed her nose to the pizza place. Ordering four slices and two regular Cokes, she carried her tray to a sunny spot outdoors. She soon ditched the coat.

Chewing slowly, she closed her eyes, relishing the deliciousness of all that bubbling cheese and tomato sauce. The people at the next table were Russians, she saw, a pretty blond girl, a young man with close-cropped, wheat-colored hair, and a dark-haired older woman. She studied them idly, trying to unravel their relationship. Then the young man put his arm around the older woman, calling her "Mama." But that could just be a courtesy, couldn't it? If it really was his mother, why had he brought her along on a date? To the apparent delight of all, the older woman took a big bottle of something with Russian lettering out of a bag, setting it down. There was much laughter, the girl smiling at the woman and speaking in rapid Russian as they all took big slices from a large pizza and poured generous doses from the bottle.

Kayla tried to imagine herself with Seth and his mother in such a situation. There would be no easy laughter, no offering of beverages from plastic bags. It would all be terribly, terribly formal, an inspection and a judgment badly camouflaged in the thin wrappings of an outing involving people who cared about each other. With her own mother, it would have been different, but equally strained, everyone working hard to be friendly and warm.

She felt suddenly sad.

Her mother tried; she really did. She'd been a bedside storyteller, a breakfast partner. A dinner companion. A play and soccer-game audience who sat in silent approval, good performance or bad. If anything, her mother had always been *way* too interested in what she did and thought. In fact, locating dark, secret corners where her life could unfold, unthreatened by the withering, relentless sun of her mother's undivided attention, had become something of an obsession. As a child, she'd often felt like an African violet, desperately needing shade before she dared risk unfurling the delicate, velvety petals of her secret flowering self. She hated being pored over and examined, or even exclaimed over in joy. Truthfully, she hadn't feared criticism more than praise. Both were equally intrusive, a banging down of doors—an uninvited entry into the only space she could call her own.

Both her parents had worked hard at family intimacy. Her mother made those elaborate, delicious sit-down dinners. Her father paid restaurant and hotel bills, taking them all on vacation. They'd provided generous amounts for their children's educations and houses and birthdays and anniversaries. She and her siblings were grateful. They said thank you. But it was a cautious relationship—changeable, sensitive, resistant. Nothing like these Russians or those flamboyant Italian or Greek families you saw in movies.

But her mother did not expect or require her children's unconditional adoration to fill up her life. She had her own life.

Kayla both admired and resented that: Every child wants to believe she is the epicenter of a parent's existence. Yet, when she thought of her sister, who had given up everything to play perfect mom in Greenwich, Connecticut, she felt pity and contempt for such a compromised existence.

She had always envisioned a life filled with passion—for work, for love, for life. She wanted to live with intensity, to do nothing halfway, giving no quarter to life's complexities, which most people used as sad excuses for failing to live up to their own expectations.

When she was very young, she thought she wanted to be a poet. She would drift off during math classes, filling notebooks with overwrought and passionate prose: *Life stands in the distance like a great ship anchored in the harbor, calling "all aboard" for those with courage enough to face the great journey.* When she grew bored with prose, she tried her hand at poetry, often completely blocking out lessons in the Torah portion of the week as she concentrated on getting the meter and cadence of her lines right:

From golden skies I heard the cry of my enchanted rainbow friends. Their grief had seeped into my heart. I prayed and weeped, and soon fell into troubled sleep . . .

When her closest friend pointed out that "weeped" wasn't a word, and suggested "wept," Kayla had thought long and hard about the restrictions placed on art by the world, grammar, and spelling rules.

Writing made her feel special, even when her report cards came back with dismal statistics. She would hug her crammed poetry notebooks to her chest as she curled up next to her parents on the down-filled cushions of their living-room sofa, her eyes glistening with moisture as she read lines out loud:

If it darkens and bright images frequent less my widening vista
Passions will soon dry, leaving yearnings and flooding joys to but
murmur with ghostly faintness.
It is then I will sow the worldly seeds of the mundane and too soon
will a tired harvest be mine to reap.
Will I even wonder at my indifference to the crimson sunset?
Will doubts gnaw at the absence of diamonds in the snow?
God! Would that I would see the world always through the eyes
of my thirteenth year!

Her parents, of course, thought she was a genius. They tried to explain this to her teachers and were unsatisfied with their unfeeling response, but agreed to humor them by adopting their solution: a private tutor for math and science. The first two didn't last very long. But the third—a tall, blond Brandeis sophomore named Jeff—was a different story.

Jeff. She smiled to herself, remembering her girlhood passion not for the subject matter but for the man. Snobbish and sure of himself, he exuded the pheromones of worldly success. Soon, she put away her poetry notebooks, trying to learn what he was intent on teaching her, which went way beyond the subject matter.

He was very directed, regaling her with his strategy on how to get into an Ivy League law school, and how to prepare for the LSATs. He told her he already had his list. Although Yale was supposed to be the top school and the hardest to get into, he had still opted for Harvard because his uncle was an alumnus and he figured that would give him a leg up. Besides, you couldn't compare the campuses: New Haven to Cambridge. New Haven was practically a slum, he'd told her, even a bit dangerous. Because of him, she learned about the monetary value of grade-point averages and extracurricular activities. "You should really get a job," he told her. "Earning your own money is so empowering and maturing. Otherwise, you'll be a spoiled princess who is under her parents' thumbs forever."

Until then, she had never been aware of being spoiled or even of living a life of rare privilege. She took her custom-made designer bedroom for granted, thinking every Bat Mitzvah girl sat with fabric swatches and carpet samples. But then, she began to look at herself through his eyes. By the age of ten, she'd already been snorkeling at the Great Barrier Reef and Maui. By the age of twelve, she'd become so used to the wonders of transatlantic flights and eye-popping hotels, she didn't even bother asking her parents where they were taking her anymore, confident it would be one more stop in paradise.

But the summer of Jeff, she told her parents that she didn't want to drag along with them to rain forests, or the top of Machu Picchu; she wanted to earn some money. Like her friends, she found a job working as a junior counselor at a very expensive Jewish summer camp in the Catskills.

The experience was transformative.

She was assigned to a group of eight-year-olds. Two of them refused to drink anything but bottled water, which arrived by the caseload from doting parents in California. Another resolutely resisted putting on a life vest during boating exercises and swimming lessons, thereby exiling herself from water sports the entire summer. Only toward the end of the summer did the little brat finally explain why: "Orange," she said, "is so not my color."

They were self-centered, spoiled, blasé, pushy, ungrateful know-it-alls. Kayla envisioned the years stretching ahead of them—one long whine as everyone in their lives scurried around trying to squeeze a smile or a word of affection out of them. They were bored by the world, left with nothing to wish for that wouldn't be handed to them—sooner or later—tied up with a red gift bow expertly tied by a professional gift wrapper in a major department store. And in them she glimpsed—with horror—herself.

When she came home, Jeff was gone. He never made it into Harvard, her parents told her. He was in some little college in the Midwest.

She refused her parents' offer of another tutor, promising to keep up with her grades. But in a sense, every boy she'd been interested in from then on had been a Jeff.

She began to spend more time at the library, reading everything: romance novels, travel books, the poetry of Emily Dickinson. She chattered less, played less, asked for less. And her grades zoomed up. Her teachers gushed over her like doting older relatives giving Bat Mitzvah speeches. Her principal, cold, undemonstrative Mr. Arens, once even put his arm around her mother and asked: "Mrs. Samuels, what is your secret? I've never seen such a transformation in a student."

Far from being delighted, her mother had been completely unnerved. Had they solved a problem or created one? Had they come down on Kayla too hard and "broken her spirit"? Or had they assured her future?

Kayla found all the parental hand-wringing hysterically funny. "Ambition. Almost as bad as being on drugs," she'd mocked.

She looked down at her Brooks Brothers blouse where the pizza sauce had stained it an oily red. So much for ambition, so much for hard work; she sighed, trying and failing to clean it off with a thin napkin.

What had it all come to?

She got up, leaving the fourth slice of pizza untouched, and walked slowly down the street without purpose or direction. Crossing over busy Jaffa Road, she suddenly found herself in the middle of an outdoor market. The air was scented by piles of cookies fresh from the oven, newly roasted nuts, and the exotic perfume of paprika, coriander, and cumin.

Her eyes feasted on the piles of red strawberries, the passion fruit, and oranges. The exuberance of the produce was matched only by the *joie de vivre* of the vendors who sang out in praise of their wares: "Come buy strawberries, sweeter than wine, and cheaper than you deserve," warbled one. "Oranges, bright like the sun, filled with vitamins. Take some for your sons."

She had always thought of America as rich, and all other countries as poor. But as she looked at the amazingly cheap prices of fresh local produce, she realized that even the poorest Israeli could feast every day on strawberries and oranges—even in the dead of winter—something most people in Brookline could never afford.

A one-legged beggar in a wheelchair held out his cup, sobbing dramatically. She dug into her pocket, taking out a few coins. As soon as she dropped them into the can, his sobs stopped, his face wreathed in a smile of cynical self-mockery and congratulation. He had gotten his coin and kept his self-respect.

She looked at him in admiration. He couldn't care less what anybody thought of him. Her entire life, on the other hand, had been one long search for an affirmation of her worth: degrees to prove her intelligence; the trophy boyfriend to prove her beauty and desirability. So far, her life had been one big report card signed by the universe, all A's. But what kind of person are you, really? she asked herself. Do you have any quality or achievement worth admiring?

She thought of her grandmother, Esther Cantor. They had been so close, she had always told herself, remembering all those visits she had made when she was a little girl. But she wondered now if that was ever true. She would come to her, laying her accomplishments—drawings, poems, report cards, certificates of merit—on her kitchen table like offerings. And her grandmother would accept them, making her feel—as no one else ever had—that it all meant something. She told herself she was making the old woman happy. But really, she received more than she gave. She was royalty when she arrived unexpectedly, fussed over and fed and admired. But each passing year, the intervals between visits had grown, reducing their meetings to a handful or less, until the old woman had had a stroke and could no longer speak.

In the beginning, Kayla had hurried to the nursing home to hold her hand and whisper kind words. But then she'd gotten tired and bored. The week her grandmother passed away, Kayla couldn't remember the last time she'd been to see her.

And now, she had left her father, too, just when he really needed her.

Why have I come here? she asked herself. What is the real reason? Or is it just another flight from responsibility? Another ugly, unforgivable act of self-ishness?

A group of klezmer musicians began to play. A Chassidic woman pushing a crying baby in a carriage, two smaller children trailing after her, all talking at once, passed her by. From a number of different command posts, the noise of walkie-talkies from security guards blared. The rumble of traffic merged with the songs of the merchants hawking their wares.

I have to get out of here, out of the city. I need to think, to work it out. I need some peace and quiet.

Her eyes brimming, she hurried down the street back to her hotel.

And then she saw it.

She stopped, leaning against the building: a square bronze plaque dated August 9, 2001, for the victims of a Hamas homicide bomber who had blown up a Sbarro pizza parlor in the heart of Jerusalem.

She held her breath as she read the names. A sixty-year-old from Brazil. A thirty-one-year-old American tourist. Two sixteen-year-old girlfriends from Jerusalem. A Dutch mother and father in their early forties, along with their fourteen-year-old, four-year-old, and two-year-old. A young mother and her eight-year-old daughter . . .

Her heart began to beat erratically, feeling as if it might burst.

She closed her eyes, trembling, leaning against the building, imagining what it must have been like. The summer crowd filling the restaurant. The laughter. The baby carriages pushed close to the wall. The smell of melting cheese. And then the explosion. The noise and black smoke. The scattered limbs and bits of cloth. A child's screams. A baby bottle and someone's broken glasses lying in the blood. A bomb purchased by money given to terrorist organizations. A ter-rorist's family and his accomplices rewarded with thousands of dollars from terrorist organizations. They couldn't, wouldn't, do these things if they had no money. The money made it possible.

What . . . ? she thought, unbearably. What . . . if . . . ? What if her father was guilty? No, not in the sense of having deliberately transferred the money to terrorists for a profit. She would never believe that of him! Never! But some-thing else. Like running over a small child who runs right in front of your car with absolutely no warning, no chance to brake in time. You'd be blameless.

Blameless! And yet, without wanting to, without any intention, you'd killed a child.

Her father had admitted transferring the money—so much money!—and that money had gone to terrorists. Her wonderful, kind, honest father. It had gone to facilitate the worst crimes imaginable. People were dead because of that money. And, like the blameless driver who kills the toddler, her father had been part of it. And because she was his daughter, she too was now part of it.

She sat down in the triangle known as Zion Square, now the front yard of a bank high-rise. It was filled with Peruvian flute players, beggars, political activists, and homeless young people who had adopted it as their own. In the center was an ambulance from Magen David Adom, which was collecting blood donations.

She said nothing as she walked in off the street, accepting their smiles and thanks as she lay down on the table. She welcomed the pain of the needle through her skin, turning her head to watch as her blood dripped out, filling a bag.

Her stomach contracted, her throat caught, and large, silent tears streamed down her face.

"Are you feeling all right?" the nurse asked in concern.

"Yes, I'm fine, really," she insisted unconvincingly. She saw the nurse exchange glances with the orderly. She detached the tube and the bag, bandaging her arm.

"Sit up slowly. I'll bring you some juice."

She felt dizzy and strange as she sipped the sweet orange-flavored drink.

"We don't get many tourists these days. Except the German kids. The kind who had Nazis in the family. For them, coming to Israel is a kind of atonement. They also give blood," the nurse said.

She suddenly felt faint.

Like a German kid. The kind who had Nazis in the family.

She let herself be led to a chair, where she was given more juice. She sat there, dazed, until the dizziness passed, her mind clouded and blank. She took out her cell phone and dialed.

"Seth. Did I wake you?"

"Kayla? How kind of you to call, and to be worried about waking me," he said, his words clipped, his tone thick with sarcasm. "No, I wasn't sleeping. Unlike you, I have courses to study for, and a bar exam in my future."

There was a silence as loud and heavy as a bomb blast.

"Kayla, are you still there?

"Yes."

"HAVE YOU LOST YOUR MIND?!" he suddenly shouted.

"I don't know. Maybe. Seth—I'm so lost. I don't know what to do."

"That's obvious," he said coldly.

Her eyes stung with tears. "This call was a mistake. I'll let you go."

"No. You don't get to hang up on me! Do you have a clue as to what you've done? That law firm in New York you blew off is one of the top firms in the country! Do you think jobs like that grow on trees?"

"Believe me, they weren't going to hire me anyway."

"Oh, so now you're a prophet!"

"Just let me explain what happened . . ."

"Did you even care how that was going to make me look? I have friends at that firm! Do you know how many phone calls I got? You left me to clean up after you. And on top of that, you never even bothered to call me and let me know."

"So that's what you're angry about? Making you look bad in front of your legal cronies. I'm sorry, I'm sorry. What do you want me to say?"

"Oh no. You don't get to rewrite this story. You just disappeared. What was I supposed to think? I was frantic! I thought you were going to be one of those *New York Post* 'Harvard coed raped and murdered' page-one stories. You were furious at me when I suggested we distance ourselves from your father's problems, then you take off halfway around the world without a word to anyone! Where has all your much-vaunted concern for your dear old dad suddenly gone?"

"I'm sorry. I'm so sorry," she repeated helplessly. "You're right."

"We have—or should I say had?—a life planned out, a life we've both worked very hard for. I know I have. And, unlike you, *I* have student loans to pay off. You won't get a job at all if you don't come back immediately and finish the term. We always planned on two incomes. We need two incomes."

"Seth," she interrupted him, "if I don't graduate, and I don't become a lawyer, and my family is ruined, and my father is convicted, will you still love me?"

"DON'T YOU DARE CHANGE THE SUBJECT! I am not prepared to waste my time holding your hand so you can indulge your 'poor little me' fantasies."

She sobbed softly into the phone.

"Kayla? Don't . . ." His tone softened. "Please, please, just come home. We can figure this out together."

"Seth, I . . . don't know. I can't. Not yet. Try to understand."

"No. I will never understand how you could do such a thing. But I can forgive, if you just take the next plane home. Good-bye, Kayla."

She heard a dial tone. He had hung up.

What am I going to do, what am I going to do? she thought, cradling her head in her hands.

"Are you sure you're all right?" the nurse asked.

"Fine, I just have to go now." She got up. Keep focused, some still-rational part of her brain kicked in. Live one day at a time. One hour at a time. She looked at her watch. She needed to go back and check out. She needed to figure out some way to live.

She ran up the hotel steps to her room, then stuffed her dirty clothes into her backpack. The leather briefcase was lying on the floor. She opened it, riffling through her day planner, course notes, articles from *The Wall Street Journal*. And then her fingers closed over the slick pages of the magazine she had been handed by the smirking secretary while she was waiting to be interviewed, opened to the article that had sent her to the airport to catch a plane. She stuffed it into her backpack, swallowing hard, leaving the rest behind. Of one thing she was absolutely sure: That part of her life was over.

11

She needed clothes, she thought. But even that small decision seemed to demand some existential reckoning. For the first time in her life, she realized, she had no idea what she should be wearing or what she was supposed to look like. I can wear anything I want, she thought. No one knows me. I'm not trying to prove anything. But what did she *want* to wear? She could not remember the last time she had asked herself this question. A twinge of controlled panic touched her heart.

She wound up buying sweatpants and hoodies, and a few cotton tees, clothing inappropriate for all occasions except perhaps jogging, which she had no intention of doing. But they were inexpensive and practical and made her feel thrifty. It was also, she admitted, a kind of camouflage. She would look like every other foreigner backpacking her way around the world except for the expensive camel-hair coat from Nordstrom, sole remnant of her former life.

"Here," she said, slipping it off her shoulders and placing it around the back of the first beggar woman she encountered.

"God bless you," the woman called out to her, clutching it in her bony hand.

In an army-navy store, she bought an ugly green army-issue jacket called a *dubon.* She looked at herself in the mirror, satisfied. All she needed was a few more changes of underwear, and she'd be prepared for anything her new life might throw at her.

There it was, the ancient stone wall built around the Old City. Her heart beat a little faster as she saw Christian pilgrims crowding through the darkened stone archway that led inside. Is that what I am, she thought, a pilgrim? Or just another sightseer? Or maybe—she stared at the long-haired, bearded backpackers dressed in the colorful light cotton garments of India—a seeker of truth, searching for a new way to live?

She followed the crowd, a piece of cork floating on a floodtide, streaming through the dark, narrow walkways that led through the bustling Arab souk.

"Souvenirs?" Arab men in kaffiyehs fingering worry beads called out to her, holding up olivewood carvings of camels and spangled head scarves.

She shook her head, avoiding eye contact, keeping her eyes down, and flowing forward with a mindless eagerness to reach some unknown goal. She was struck with a sudden fear. How did she know she wasn't going to land in some hostile Arab neighborhood? She peered down all the forks in the winding passageways, left turns and right turns into still-narrower alleyways.

"Excuse me," she asked one of the young Israeli soldiers stationed all along the route, "which way to the Wall?" finally defining her goal.

As she followed his directions, the narrow alleyways eventually gave way to staircases and newer homes; cleaner, whiter stones. She was in Jewish territory now, she realized with relief. The Jewish Quarter. Suddenly, all at once, she was confronted by the stunning panorama of the Wall, and the golden-domed mosque above it.

It should take my breath away, she thought, wondering why it didn't. Maybe it was exhaustion. Or maybe it was confusion. But she didn't feel tired, or confused, she realized. She felt nothing, nothing at all. Could it be I have nothing left inside me, no attachments, no knowledge, no sentiments? That I've managed to put all that behind me as well? And was that a good thing, or not?

She walked slowly down the hundreds of steps that would lead her to the most sacred site in the Jewish world. Reaching the bottom, she saw everyone putting their backpacks and purses through an X-ray machine. Guarded by soldiers, they then walked through metal detectors. No one seemed to think this was strange. People just did it automatically, as if being surrounded by

Uzi-wielding guards and subjected to intrusive searches was normal. But it was, wasn't it? All over the world, millions of people now submitted to being frisked and taking off their shoes because a few madmen had destroyed human trust. It wasn't just people that terrorists killed. It was the fabric of civilized human interaction. Everyone lived in fear.

There was the women's section of the Kotel, closed off by metal barriers from the men's. "I'm not married, so I don't have to cover my hair," she remembered, preparing herself for the inspection of the pious women gatekeepers who controlled the flow to the holy site. She suddenly realized how much she wanted to be allowed inside to touch the huge, ancient stones.

She skirted her way around the blind retreat of pious women who refused out of reverence to turn their backs on the holy site. She searched for an opening in the crowded front row near the Wall. But it was packed, women of all ages swaying and weeping or silently mouthing the sacred words of Hebrew prayers read from worn, yellowing prayer books. These were the regulars, she thought, matronly women of various ages in the same uptight uniform of the fanatically brainwashed: long sleeves, dull, loose-fitting, ankle-sweeping skirts, and wigs or scarves or hats. They had staked out the choicest spots. Behind them were the bareheaded tourists like herself, with makeshift outfits to approximate modesty, keeping vigil until a spot opened up in the front row.

The young girl in front of her kissed her prayer book, then stepped backward, retreating. Kayla stepped forward hurriedly, taking her place. She reached out, touching the sacred stones, eyeing the tiny bits of crumpled paper jammed into every crevice, each one a heartfelt request.

Resting her forehead against the stones, made smooth by millennia of human caresses and heartfelt tears, she realized she didn't know what to pray for. I can't pray that Dad is innocent. That would be like a pregnant woman praying for her fetus to be a boy or a girl. It was what it was. It couldn't be undone, she told herself, clenching her fists in frustration and beating them against the hard stones in helpless fury, unable to find the words. Murmurs of shocked disapproval rose up around her. She dropped her arms, ashamed. God, show me the way; I am so lost, she finally prayed silently, her lips resting on the cold stone. She lowered her head, backing away.

"Excuse me, miss."

She was standing at the periphery where men and women mingled, readying herself for the walk back into the city and the search for a better cheap hotel. She turned around. It was a young bearded man with a large black hat and a black suit holding a large, heavy book.

"I'm sorry to interrupt your thoughts, but you seem tired and upset. I work at a women's study center not far from here. You could have a hot meal and a place to sleep. And if you'd like to attend some lectures you might find interesting tomorrow, you'd be most welcome. Of course, our hospitality is free. You are Jewish, aren't you? We are not missionaries," he added solemnly.

"Free, do you say?" Kayla answered, shaking her head. "Oh, I don't think so."

He seemed puzzled. "Like our father Abraham, our tent is open on all four sides to invite in strangers."

"To invite them in, but letting them out is another story."

"Excuse me?"

"I know all about your 'study centers.' First it's a hot meal and a bed, then some lectures. A lot of lectures. And then, eventually, you'll tell me what to eat, and how to dress, and what to think, convincing me it's all my own idea. And when I finally live up to your expectations, Yentl the matchmaker will find some ex-druggie who has seen the light to live off my earnings forever. And then there'll be the children, six of them, one after the other, with runny noses living in poverty-stricken ignorance. No thanks. I'll get a hotel room."

She heard laughter and turned around. A woman of indeterminate age, with long dark hair, wearing a skirt with pants underneath, Indian-style, was applauding.

"I'm sure that they don't hear that very often. You were a sight to behold, my dear."

When Kayla turned back, he had disappeared. She felt strangely apologetic. "I was pretty harsh. I'm sure he meant well. I guess I'm just tired."

"You look ready to drop," the woman agreed sympathetically. "Are you visiting, touring?"

"I'm not sure . . ."

"I see. I was in a similar boat when I came. I was newly divorced. I felt lost. But it all worked out so well."

Kayla looked at her. She seemed normal, intelligent, not poor, and not a religious fanatic. "What did you wind up doing?"

"I have a degree in archaeology from Oxford. Someone told me about this dig in the Judean desert. They were hiring archaeologists. The money was good, and the work fascinating. I've been there ever since."

"I don't have any skills. I'm a law school dropout. Harvard."

"We can always use some unskilled workers on the dig. They pay minimum wage, but the food is plentiful and the accommodations free."

"I don't know if I'm really qualified . . ."

She laughed. "Do you remember kindergarten? Working in a sandbox with your shovel, then sifting the dirt?"

She smiled. "I suppose so."

"That's all the qualifications you need. We have quite a few people like you there. One is an architect from Stanford. We even have a young doctor. It will be an adventure, I can promise you that."

"Do you think they'd hire me?"

"I am sure of it. A few people left just last week, and we are really short-handed. My name is Judith, by the way."

"Hi. I'm Kayla."

"Where are you staying?"

"Well, I just checked out of this fleabag on Ben Yehuda Street . . . I guess I don't really know."

"Well, I'm about to drive back to the dig. You're welcome to come with me and try it out for a few days. If nothing more, it'll be an adventure."

Kayla hesitated. Her former self would have never considered getting into a car with a stranger. But this seemed like a new universe. Looking back at the Wall, she wondered if God was already beginning to answer her prayers.

12

"You're not a smoker, are you?" Kayla asked with forced casualness, breathing in the rancid upholstery, wondering who she was sitting next to.

Judith laughed. "Goodness no! I'm one of those grow-your-own-tomatoes-in-organically-composted-pesticide-free-soil people. A tree hugger. I rescued this car from its abusive former owner. But still, the scent lingers on."

"Where, exactly, are we headed?"

"What, getting nervous? Already?" Judith gave her a sideways glance of amusement. "I promise you, it's a phone call away from numerous taxi services, who will be only too thrilled to overcharge you mercilessly and take you back into civilization. There are also public buses wandering down the road when the mood strikes them. But you won't want to leave. At least, I didn't."

"Oh, I'm not nervous at all," Kayla lied, embarrassed at being so transparent. "I just wondered about the route you were taking."

"If you reach over into that side pocket on the door, you'll find a map. Just open it to page 123. Ein Gedi."

Kayla fumbled through the pages. It was in the desert, near the Dead Sea. She glanced out the window. They were already out of traffic, going down a highway bordered on both sides by small Arab villages. As they rode, the intermittent patches of green disappeared, overwhelmed by sand dunes pockmarked by the dark growth of tiny plants.

"The hills look like they have acne," Kayla quipped.

"There is still enough water here for little bursts of vegetation. But with the way this drought is going, soon, there won't even be that."

"This is really very kind of you, Judith," Kayla said. "I mean, you are taking a chance on a stranger. You don't know anything about me."

"That's true. But I sensed we've both been on a similar journey."

"Why would you say that?"

She shrugged. "I think your defensiveness speaks for itself."

"I'm sorry. I guess I am just keyed up. Tired."

"Hopeless?"

"Is it that obvious?"

"It takes one to know one. You've got some practical clothes with you, yes?"

"Yes. I bought what they call 'trenning.' It took me a while to figure out that was an English word and it meant 'training' exercise pants and hoodies. I just didn't have time to change."

"And the jacket. It's military, no?"

"I gave the coat that went with this suit—when it's ironed, that is—to a woman who seemed to appreciate it. But I think this jacket might be way too warm for the desert."

"Ho, you have no idea! The evenings are freezing. Believe me, you'll need it." Judith glanced over, taking in Kayla's outfit. "And you're okay with it? This wardrobe transition? You don't mind?"

"I actually can't wait to change out of this," Kayla said sincerely.

"Really? I made the transition from dress-for-success to dress-for-happiness only after about six months. You did it spectacularly fast. My compliments! I guess I waited because I didn't want to burn my bridges."

"My bridges went up in spectacular flames without my even being in-volved," Kayla answered bitterly.

There was a short silence. "That's hard. Want to talk about it?"

Kayla shook her head. "But I'd love to hear your story. That is, if you don't mind."

"Not at all. Everyone I know is sick to death of hearing about this."

"Well, only if you don't feel I'd be prying . . ."

"Such an American term: 'prying.' We are all so closed, so ashamed. To make a real connection with another human being feels like a crime. We're criminals with crowbars if we're interested in what's going on inside someone else's life."

"Well, I don't know . . . I just meant . . . we don't know each other . . ."

"Some people you get to know really quickly, while others—you can even marry them and live with them for ten years and never know a single thing about them."

"Is that what happened to you?"

Judith nodded. "I was brought up in London. East Kensington. My parents own a grocery store—like Margaret Thatcher's parents! They also scrimped and saved. I was sent to public schools—for you Americans that's the equivalent of a private school. They—and I along with them—were determined that I get into Oxford or Cambridge. And I did. But then, in the middle of my freshman year, I started having these tummyaches. I thought it was just tension. I took antacids, painkillers, all this bloody over-the-counter rubbish, but the pains just got worse and worse. Finally, the NHS decided to do some CAT scans. They found a malignant tumor in my womb."

"I . . . I'm . . . so . . . sorry . . ." Kayla whispered, appalled.

There was a long silence. "Yes, well. I came to terms with it as best I could. I needed a hysterectomy. I was nineteen years old, and I would never have children."

The hot, dusty desert wind whistled through the silent car.

"I broke up with my boyfriend, whom I didn't deem sufficiently sympathetic. Or maybe I wanted to be the one to decide he'd leave, before he did. I plunged back into my studies, getting in over my head. I had enough sense to realize I needed to get away before I drowned. So I went on a dig in Turkey. The last thing I expected was to meet someone. But I did. He was an assistant professor at Santa Clara University. He had a narrow, intense face with dark hair and blue eyes that lit up when he smiled, which wasn't often. Naturally, after telling myself that it could never happen again, I fell in love . . . *we* fell in love. I told him that I could never have children. And he said: '*I don't care. I want you, just the way you are.'* Besides, he said, there are so many orphans in the world. Someone has to care for them, no?"

"He sounds wonderful."

"He *was*," she answered wistfully, without a trace of irony. "We were married on the beach at Corfu: sunset, torches, Greek dancing. The works. And for ten years, we lived and worked together. He was my best friend, my colleague, my lover. But every time I brought up adoption, he changed the subject. It was either: 'We're still so young, what's the rush?' Or there was this one really, really *important* dig he wanted to do that would put us both on the map so we could field offers from the top universities before settling down. And after that dig, there was always another, and another. Get the picture?"

"I think so."

"Finally, I said: 'You don't want to adopt, ever.' It wasn't a question, just a statement of fact. I guess I was expecting a fight, a heated denial. Instead, he looked at me, and said: 'I want my own children.'"

Kayla turned her head, looking out the window. The dunes had given way to strangely ridged sand mountains where nothing grew. Bedouin compounds dotted the surreal landscape, their tattered tents and forlorn-looking donkeys and camels a blight. And then, there was nothing, nothing at all but sand-colored mountains undulating in a vast emptiness. She turned back to Judith, feeling suddenly chilled, the goose bumps rising on her arms.

"What did you do?"

"I cried. I hated him. I wanted to kill him. And then I stopped hating him and just accepted the simple fact that he was a healthy young man, with healthy instincts, and that he had simply changed his mind."

"But there are surrogates . . ."

She shook her head with a sad smile. "He wasn't into anything that high-tech. He simply wanted to make love to the mother of his children, get her pregnant, and watch their child grow inside her. It was natural . . ."

"It was unforgivable. He had made his decision. You had let him into your life based on that decision."

"Oh right. I should've sued him. Taken him to bloody court. Have the magistrates string him up. After all, what he wanted was criminal. A wife and child."

"You depended on his word, on his love!"

"Life is a series of demolitions and rebuildings. And you can't really know anything about anyone. There is no such thing as 'ever after.'"

Kayla thought of her last phone call to Seth.

"But you should be able to figure out in advance if your partner is trustworthy and honest and steadfast, or if he will cut and run at the first sign of trouble."

"Should you? How, when he himself can't know! Okay, sometimes there are warning signs, things we deliberately ignore. In that case, you need to get out. Fast. But not always. Not in my case. Yes, my husband did cut and run. But he could just as easily have stayed or come back. There is no use in my berating myself for having chosen him, or for him to have mistakenly chosen me. People don't know themselves. They don't know what they are capable of feeling and doing. They may think they do. They may even make promises based on what they think they know about themselves. But it's building on quicksand."

"Then how can anyone ever get married? Ever decide to trust someone?"

Judith shrugged. "I had ten years with a man I loved. Wonderful years. It didn't last forever, but that doesn't mean they were a mistake. That he was a mistake."

It was so overwhelmingly simple, and yet so complex. Not to let the present color the past. To accept what is and what was without any shadows.

"If it were me, I'd be furious. I'd want revenge."

"Oh, I felt that way too. Believe me. It took me a long time to get where I am now. And I would never have gotten there at all if it hadn't been for Natan."

"Your therapist?"

She smiled. "You could say that. But more like a guru. He's the one who taught me about risking everything, about prying yourself open to let in the light, and to let out the poison. You'll meet him."

"Is he on the dig?"

"Not exactly. He's . . . well, you'll see."

"I don't believe in gurus. And I don't believe in risks."

"And yet, your bridges get burned without your even striking a match."

Kayla looked at her, startled, then looked away.

TO THE LOWEST POINT ON EARTH read a sign on the side of the road. How ironic, she thought, shaking her head. She had always thought of herself as an explorer, one with those unswerving, determined adventurers covered with frostbite, determined to reach the top of the world. But sinking down was also an adventure, she admitted to herself.

A sign pointed to Jericho on the left; then, suddenly, the landscape changed once more. Her eyes, her heart, lifted upward to the high mountain cliffs dotted with secret caves. They were so old, older than anything she had come across in her lifetime. There was something primordial about them; something overweening, dwarfing anything human. She looked at the deep canyons carved out by desert flash floods, imagining the thundering cascade of water exploding through the rocks, washing out the roads with dangerous suddenness.

Everything about this place was wild and hard and untamed, inimical to the core of the human need for nourishment and predictability. A place full of risks.

The precipitous plunge from habited to uninhabited, from human settlement to wilderness in such a short time span was awesome and terrible, especially to someone like Kayla Samuels, who had spent her entire life amid nurturing abundance. She felt small, helpless, abandoned. A stranger to herself. Perhaps, then, Judith was right. You couldn't know anyone, because you couldn't know yourself. Not completely.

"That's where the Essenes lived, the Qumran Caves, at the time of Jesus." Judith nodded in the direction Kayla had been looking. "That's where they found the Dead Sea Scrolls."

"I can't imagine anyone living here. How did they survive?"

"They didn't need much. They had desert springs for water. They had animals for milk and meat and skins. There were wild trees with dates and figs, and olives. They imported flour and wine from Jerusalem."

Kayla shook her head incredulously.

Judith shrugged. "People do strange things when they want to be left alone. Look at Venice. Those people were also running away. They built their homes in the middle of the sea! The Essenes wanted spiritual purity. They felt they were running away from the corruption of their coreligionists, and the domination of the Romans. They thought that the Messiah was on his way, and they wanted to be worthy of being chosen to survive the cataclysms of the End of Days."

People going to wild extremes, living where no one else wanted to live simply to be left in peace. Yes, Kayla thought. She could certainly understand that.

"They say the Essenes didn't write the Dead Sea Scrolls. That there were other groups, and many more scrolls still to be found. Some of them filled with prophecies . . ."

"About our future?" Kayla asked. "Or about the past, which was their future?"

Judith hesitated. "Natan once spoke about it." She didn't elaborate.

Kayla was surprised, sensing a certain discomfort. How odd, that such a theoretical question about such an obscure topic could make this very honest, open, free spirit suddenly clam up! Kayla wondered at it, her curiosity growing together with the feeling that not everything was as it seemed. There was some underlying mystery about all this, something strange, even frightening. It was more than just a desert dig.

The towering mountains dropped behind them. Looming ahead were the reddish hills of Jordan and the rising blue haze of the Dead Sea, which almost melted into the sky, making you wonder if you were dreaming of water rather than seeing it. And then the blue gave way to a shimmering silver band and the grey outline of a faraway mountain range.

"Look over there!" Judith said, pointing. "That's the mountain in Jordan where Moses stood looking toward the Promised Land that God refused to let him enter."

Kayla stared, thinking with sadness how Israel's greatest prophet had been denied his heart's desire, forbidden to complete his long journey home, condemned to die in the desert. And how she, Kayla Samuels, had made it here. It made her feel blessed somehow. How strange and inexplicably detached from our actions are our fates sometimes, she mused.

The sun-dappled waters sparkled, deceptively lovely, giving no hint of the thick concentration of minerals that stung the eyes and could even hold a person upright, making it impossible for her to drown. A group of cyclists rode past them, their taut bodies stretched out in spandex blue, their helmets low on their foreheads. Where were they cycling from? she wondered. And where was it they were they risking so much to get to?

"What if they run out of water or something? It's dangerous. Don't you feel that way? Or didn't you, when you first came here?"

"I don't know. I can't remember. It feels as if I've been here always. Besides, civilization is always just around the corner."

The car began to slow down. There was a series of low white buildings. "Come out and stretch your legs. Can I buy you a Coke?"

"Oh, thanks! Water would be great."

The pungent odor of camels permeated the air as they strode toward the roadside kiosk selling everything from cold bottled water to roasted lamb stuffed into pita bread. Underneath flapping canvas tents, an Arab squatted beside earthenware pottery, hawking his wares. Farther down the road, a Bedouin held the reins of a gaudily festooned camel, as Israeli tourists with a small child crowded around the animal, no doubt negotiating the price of a ride and a souvenir Polaroid. Kayla relaxed, a sense of familiarity flooding her with relief. There were bathrooms and phones and ice cream and cold drinks and young families. It was a tiny desert in a tiny country, not the Sahara.

"Ready?" Judith asked in her patient way. She never seemed to be in any hurry. It had such a calming effect, Kayla realized, to be around someone like that. The people she knew were the opposite—Seth, her mother, her teachers. For them, life was one marathon relay race. If you slowed down, you were letting down the team.

"Sure. Let's go. Is it far?"

She shook her head. "Less than a half hour. We should be there way before dark."

Kayla thought about being in the desert with this stranger, her sense of ease suddenly evaporating.

Was this an answer to her prayers, she wondered, or punishment for her sins?

13

It was two thirty in the morning. Portable lanterns lit their way. Long tables were set outside with drinks. Kayla counted twenty-five people waiting for the bus that would take them to the excavation site, including Judith.

"Sleep well?"

"It's a mistake to put that into past tense."

Judith grinned. "Well, your eyes are open, so good for you. It will be our secret. Come with me, and I'll introduce you."

"Uh, that's nice of you, but I'm not really up for socializing yet." She ran her hand through strands of her now-curly hair, still soaking wet from her hasty shower. She tucked a voluminous T-shirt into her sweatpants, pulling her army jacket around her. As promised, it was freezing outside. Thank God Seth couldn't see her. He'd have a heart attack. "Maybe after breakfast. There is going to be breakfast, isn't there?"

"Of course, and a really good one too. They serve it around six A.M. at the site."

"Any reason we can't get there at six A.M.?"

"It's a desert dig. By the time the sun comes up, you'll be sitting in a frying pan slowly sautéing. Professor Milstein, this is Kayla, our newest worker. Kidnapped at the Kotel. She's taking a break from Harvard Law."

He bowed with old-world courtesy, offering her his graceful old hand. He had dark eyes under great bushy brows that were halfway to grey. "Harvard Law, you say? I'm impressed. But you are missing your semester, no?"

"I'm not sure I'm going back," she murmured.

"Oh, I see. Their loss. Our gain. We'll start you out with digging, but we will find more responsible things for you to do soon enough. Can you draw?"

"Yes. I mean, basic stuff."

"Good enough. We will exploit you mercilessly, child." He kissed her hand. "You've already met Judith. And this is Carla, and Michael and Efrat, and this . . . this is Daniel."

He was a little older than the others—who looked to be in their early twenties—with a large head of unruly brown curls. His light green eyes jumped out at you, mesmerizing against the dark brown of his deeply tanned skin. His simple work clothes were stained but had the fresh smell of having been washed and hung out to dry in the desert air.

"Good to have you on board, Kayla." Carla smiled.

"Yes, we can use the help," Michael echoed, while Efrat just smiled and held out her hand. "My English. Not good. I from Haifa. Port, fishes."

Only Daniel said nothing, barely inclining his head to acknowledge her existence. Kayla nodded and smiled back at the others, but her eyes followed him, curious and a bit offended. If it had been Seth, he would have been commenting on everything from the appropriateness of her hat to the UV rating of her sunglasses, describing in detail his own very important job and how extremely vital it was to do everything just the way he did it . . .

Daniel climbed on the bus. He took a seat alone near a window, glancing out, silent and preoccupied.

Transportation was an old school bus with indiscernible suspension, every rock making its presence known as they bumped and rolled down the mountainside. She sat down next to Judith.

"Who are these people?" Kayla whispered.

"Carla is an exchange student from Bologna. She is finishing some credits at Hebrew University, and this is part of her course. Michael showed up six months ago. He's from Virginia. He has a degree in architecture from Stanford. He said he was backpacking around the Middle East, and had experience in digs. He'll be moving on when the mood strikes him, or a letter bearing more cash arrives from his parents. He's gay, by the way. Efrat is Israeli. She just started here a few months ago. And then there's Daniel."

"Are they a couple? Daniel and Efrat?" She was annoyed at how much she cared about the answer and how deeply she was prepared to feel disappointment.

"What? Because they're both Israeli? No, at least, not that we can see. He isn't involved with anyone."

Not yet, she thought, finally being honest with herself for the first time since she boarded the plane at JFK.

"The earliest remains we found were from the Chalcolithic period," the professor informed her companionably. "That's fourth millennium BCE. There was a pagan temple here that probably served as a cultic center for the tribes who roamed the region. They chose this spot because of the freshwater springs that flow down from the high cliffs. Then at some point the priests fled, leaving behind all these little idols, which are now in the Israel Museum. It's so dry, everything was preserved beautifully for thousands of years. Much later, David hid here from Saul."

"As I told you. The desert is a good hiding place," Judith whispered. "You'll find many volunteers with that idea."

"Including Daniel?" Kayla asked.

"Daniel . . . that's sort of a different story." She hesitated.

"What?"

"Not so much hiding as trying to find himself."

"The houses of the first village were crowded together on terraces," the professor continued. "They had two rooms and a courtyard. They had large clay vats for storing drinking water and beverages made from local plants. A while back we found a hoard of silver pieces!" His voice rose with excitement.

"We'll talk later . . ." Judith whispered. Kayla was disappointed, anxious for the story to continue.

"Then there were the Persian and Herodian periods. The Jewish settlement thrived. A citadel was built to protect the village and its farms from marauding nomads. All that ended with the first Jewish rebellion against the Romans in 70 CE. But during the Byzantine and Roman periods, it was once again a large, prosperous Jewish village. They credited their prosperity to the cultivation of a tropical plant from which a rare and wonderful perfume was made. They say it was Cleopatra's favorite, the source of her seductive powers. We think the plant was called balsam, but we can't be sure. Even then, it was a closely guarded secret. On the floor of the synagogue there is even a verse cursing anyone who reveals the secret formula."

"And here we are, centuries later, trying to undo all that secrecy by digging up and revealing all." Judith laughed.

Kayla shifted uncomfortably. Some things *were* best left buried, she thought, wondering if she would ever tell these people anything about herself.

The bus jolted to a halt just as the first light was breaking over the mountains.

The ground was broken into many neat craters, carefully excavated to preserve the delicate layers that separated one time period from the next.

"Here are your tools," Judith said, handing her a small shovel, a trowel, and a brush.

"These are tiny!"

"Yes, well, it's easy to replant a garden if you mess it up the first time. But if you destroy a tel, it's destroyed forever, all the layers intermingling, all the artifacts impossible to date. Not to mention that if you dig in big clumps, you run the risk of smashing a priceless fourth-century vase. So, dig carefully. Load the dirt into these buckets, then dump the bucketfuls into this wheelbarrow. When the wheelbarrow is full, you take it over to there—" She indicated, pointing. "That's where all the dirt from this particular part of the dig must go and nowhere else—otherwise, they lose track of where things were found. Then you come back and start again. Someone else has the job of sifting through this, even washing the mud through a sieve to see what remains."

"It sounds like very good exercise," Kayla groaned, eyeing the wheelbarrow with trepidation. Even empty, it looked too heavy to budge. She couldn't imagine what it would take to lift it when it was brimming with heavy earth. Judith patted her shoulder sympathetically.

"If you need help, just ask."

"What's that?" Kayla asked, pointing to a spot in the distance.

"Oh, that's the synagogue the professor was talking about. When you get a chance, go down and look inside. It has the most magnificent mosaic tile floor and an inscription naming the zodiac symbols."

"I didn't know Jews believed in astrology!"

"Actually, they believed the zodiac was simply part of nature, not the voo-doo stuff of the *National Enquirer* or psychic phone calls. It was believed that signs of the zodiac ruled the world. But they also believed that God tran-scended nature. The signs had the powers of midlevel bureaucrats, but God was the ultimate CEO. One word from Him, and everything changed."

"It's an interesting idea."

"I agree. Well, I've got to get to work. See you at break time."

"You aren't working in this section too?"

"No, I'm over there, on the north hill with your roommate Bev. But don't worry." She gave Kayla a sly sidelong glance. "You have some very interesting people assigned to your section. I think you'll be pleased. See you later!"

"Thanks for everything, Judith."

"Not a problem. Hope you survive your first day. After that, it gets easier."

Kayla watched her retreating back, then turned and looked down at the earth, the buckets, her trowel, and the wheelbarrow. She sighed, crouched, and began to dig, carefully filling bucket after bucket.

The desert air was still cold, yet she felt the sweat break out over her fore-head and under her breasts and armpits. Shedding her jacket and hoodie, she filled the buckets, dumping them carefully into the wheelbarrow, so that in the slide of earth from container to container no unforgivable damage was done to priceless objects. It was really quite a responsibility, she thought, lifting the two handles of the wheelbarrow and pushing. But nothing happened. She took a deep breath. Slowly, she once again lifted it off the ground, struggling to inch it forward across the rocky terrain. She felt every bone in her body straining and near the breaking point.

Suddenly, the load grew lighter, as strong male hands slid over her own, replacing them.

"Wow, thanks!" She looked up, startled. It was him. He didn't say any-thing, pushing the wheelbarrow swiftly down the small incline, emptying it out, and bringing it back to her.

"I . . . thanks . . . but . . . you don't . . ."

But he was already gone.

She exhaled, trying to decide if he was rude and obnoxious or modest and gentlemanly. Either description fit equally well, she noted. Each time she filled the wheelbarrow and began to push, she found him by her side, taking over. There was a kind of rhythm to it, almost like one of those elaborate court dances in Elizabethan England: a forward and backward movement, an advance and a retreat. There was something about the way his body moved in unison with her own, some indefinable way all his movements fit in with hers, solicitous, caring, self-deprecating, always sensitive to her slightest movement, discerning without being told exactly where she needed him to be, what she needed him to do. He didn't seem to want anything from her in the deepest sense; he left her free. But she felt some unseen force pulling her toward him anyway. She had never felt this way before, about anyone. Certainly not about Seth. This instantaneous burst of fire coming out of nowhere, when all around was damp and cool, was strange, magical, almost frightening. She wanted this wordless dance to go on and on.

But it wasn't right. She was still engaged. And Daniel might be married, for all she knew. In any case, he had his own work to do and because of her must be lagging behind. Besides, she hated to think of herself as weak or needy. So, the next time it happened, she was determined to have it out.

"NO. No thank you," she said, leaving her hands tightly gripped around the wheelbarrow handles, refusing to budge.

"I can't see you struggling like this. Let me help."

She was surprised at how good his English was. There wasn't even an accent.

"I'm not struggling," she lied. "I'm getting used to this."

"Well, what do you say if while you are getting used to it, you hold one handle and I the other. When we divide the work, it will be easy for both of us."

She thought about it. It sounded reasonable and left her pride intact. "Thank you, Daniel."

"You're welcome, Kayla."

"You remembered my name."

"And you remembered mine."

She blushed, rubbing her throbbing arms, examining her hands. Gone were the soft, clean palms, the expensively manicured fingernails, the glowing diamond ring. They were the hands of a stranger: reddened and dirty, the nails broken and rimmed with mud.

She took off her sunglasses to wipe off the dust. The lenses reflected back a face red with exertion, ribboned with streaks of dust and sweat. She had broken out in a million freckles.

"What I look like . . ." She shook her head.

"You look . . ." He stopped himself, as if uncertain, or unwilling, to finish the sentence. They put their hands to the handlebars, and for a moment, they touched as she chose the same side as he. He dropped his hands as if burnt.

"Sorry," he mumbled, crossing swiftly over to the other side. They walked silently beside each other until they reached the dump site.

"I'll take the wheelbarrow back for you?" he offered. It was not a command.

"Thank you, Daniel. I'd appreciate that," she said, finally dropping all pretense, accepting him.

"Dan-y-yel," he corrected her, a tiny secret smile, the first she'd seen on his serious face, playing around his lips. She could see his shoulders relax.

"Isn't that what I said?"

He shook his head. "No. You said 'Dan-yell.'"

"You know, I did go to a Hebrew Day School in Boston. I'm not completely ignorant."

"Really? So why are we talking in English?" he teased her.

"My Hebrew is not in the same league as your English. You don't even have an accent! Were your parents American?"

"No. But my father was a *shaliach*—a representative of the Jewish Agency—in San Francisco. His job was to talk people into moving to Israel. I was born there—in San Jose. I even have an American passport. I picked up the language, and it never left me. It was a great help in school. Especially medical school."

She looked him over once more, aware of having unlocked one more closed chamber, glimpsing the world within. "You're a doctor?"

"Don't look so shocked."

"You must look very different in your scrubs." The green would match your eyes, she thought. And all the while, something was humming beneath the small, silly talk between them, something deep and resonant she couldn't explain. A small butterfly threw open its wings and fluttered through her stomach. Oh no! she told herself, recognizing having crossed some tightly guarded border, knowing there was no way back.

"I haven't worn scrubs for years. And I don't think I ever will, again. Excuse me. I have to wash up for breakfast."

"Oh, sure. I guess . . . I . . . will too," she stuttered, trapped in the flow of unexpected emotion, desperate to know more.

"Hi, ready to eat?" It was Judith.

"Oh, sure."

"You look shocked. What happened?"

"Daniel . . . he's a doctor?"

"Was. A surgeon."

"What's the story?"

"Did you get a chance to talk to him?"

She nodded shyly, anxious to hide this new thing that was unfolding inside her. "But he's not very communicative."

Judith nodded. "True. But he's a special, wonderful man. It's just so tragic."

"You said before he was looking for himself. What did you mean?"

"I guess what I meant to say was that he was looking for a way to heal himself."

"Is he . . . was he . . . ill?"

"Not physically."

"Details?"

"All I can tell you is what I've heard here and there. He was married. He had a child—a daughter. Both his wife and child were killed by a suicide bomber."

Kayla held her breath, feeling as if she had started to slip down a long flight of steps, not yet seeing the bottom. "Really?"

She nodded. "After that, he just up and left everything behind in Tel Aviv and came here. That was three years ago."

Picnic tables were laid out with enormous bowls filled with salads, piles of warm pita bread, cheeses, yogurts, and urns filled with piping coffee. Large jugs of cold orange juice and icy lemonade with fresh mint were passed around, as were hot croissants and little Danish pastries.

Although she had been starving a moment before, Kayla somehow found she couldn't eat a thing.

Hours later, when the midday sun was at its hottest and most relentless, the bus came back, mercifully rescuing them. Back on top of the mountain, a hearty lunch was served in the cafeteria. She joined the others, but was almost too tired to chew. She limped back to her caravan, took an icy shower, then crawled into her hard bed. It was heavenly. She slept soundly until four in the afternoon, woken only by her British roommate Bev singing, "*When I see you cry it makes me smi-i-ile.*" She sat up, suddenly discovering every bone in her body, because all of them were shouting out complaints. She could hardly move.

Bev looked at her with glee. "You'll get used to it. You'll get stronger."

"Or not."

"That's a negative attitude. Have you ever read Norman Vincent Peale's *The Power of Positive Thinking*?"

"No. Have you ever read *The Horrible Experience of Painful Blinking*?"

Bev was silent. "Oh. That's a joke, right? I mean like a pun or rhyme or something?"

There is a special place in hell for humorless people who dissect and kill jokes, Kayla thought, particularly the ones who say . . .

"Very funny," Bev said.

No court would convict me . . . "Now what?"

"Some days we have off, and some days we go back and mark all the pottery sherds . . ."

"What does that mean?"

"Every piece of broken clay has to have a code number which says where, exactly, it was found. Then we can date them, and even have a chance of pasting them back together."

"It sounds very exciting."

"It's not worse than dumping dirt in a wheelbarrow. You might even enjoy it. And afterward, in the evening, if you want, you can join them."

"Them?"

"The religious hippies."

"What?"

"You mean Judith hasn't tried to convert you yet?"

"I have no idea what you are talking about."

"They call themselves 'The Talmidim.' They dress like flower children in a time warp. And they have this guru, except he's a rabbi, who gives them lectures. They live in this commune up on the mountain, about a five-minute walk from us up the hill. A lot of the workers come from the commune. And a lot of the people from the dig wind up there. You mean to say she hasn't dragged you to one of Rav Natan's lectures yet?"

Kayla shrugged. The too-rapid ingestion of all this information gave her the mental equivalent of heartburn. She had actually been looking forward to meeting the mysterious, all-wise Natan, before she found out he was a *rebbe* . . . But remembering Judith's reaction to her telling off the religious recruiter at the Kotel, she felt she must be missing something. " 'Commune'? Is that another word for cult?"

Bev paused, considering the idea. She shook her head. "They don't have enough discipline to be a cult. And there is no money changing hands that I can see. And people come and go all the time, so if it *is* a cult, it's not very well run. They need some lessons from Sun Myung Moon."

"I gather you, yourself, haven't checked it out? Is it cynicism?"

" 'Realism' would be a more accurate word. Oh, I went to a few lectures. Honestly, they were fascinating. But I'm very shallow. I learned everything I need to know about self-improvement from Norman Vincent. Give me a good *Hello!* magazine with pictures of Prince William to read on my time off, I say. Or a story in *The Sun* about poor Jade Goody with pictures of her going bald from chemo, then marrying her bloke, and saying good-bye to her kids."

Kayla winced. "When does he give these lectures? Can anyone just go?"

Bev shrugged. "Go if you want. He gives a talk almost every morning and every afternoon. You see that path over there?" She pointed to a white-gravel road nearby. "Just follow it up the hill. You'll probably see a queue going into this big, round tent. He's very popular. No accounting for tastes."

Every afternoon she considered going. If Bev didn't like him, Rav Natan couldn't be all bad! But something held her back, something she couldn't put her finger on. Perhaps she was afraid of any kind of introspection, ashamed to look.

The days took on a surprising rhythm. She got used to going to sleep early, waking in the dark to cool showers, and friendly banter under inky skies. After that first day, she noticed that Daniel had begun working on the other side of the tel. At meals, he sat at the other side of the table.

It was almost as if he knew about her, she thought, knew that she was the enemy. She was hurt. Insulted. Yet in some ways also relieved. What would he do, if he knew? It was better this way. Better for them to be apart. Yet, she could not keep her eyes away from him, or her thoughts. At night, she dreamed of his tragic green eyes looking out at her from his dark face; his lean body standing at a distance, aloof and still. She didn't understand it herself, this strange obsession. It was chemistry, she thought. That outer ring of electrons always seeking to be completed, to have the perfect eight; looking for the exact match that could supply what they lacked. Like oxygen and hydrogen.

Or perhaps the attraction lay simply in the mystery he posed. All things are imaginable under the cover of darkness, she told herself, allowing one's mind to furnish all the right details to make a stranger irresistibly attractive. Reality, she scolded herself, which supplies its own details in the cold light of day, is not always so accommodating to our fantasies.

What did she know about him, really? That he had experienced a tragedy not of his making? That he had been on the road to a good life when evil forces beyond his control had made him swerve disastrously, destroying it all? That he had abandoned years of study, a profession, running away, because he felt unable to face the life he had worked so hard to achieve?

It suddenly dawned on her who else that could describe.

14

Then one afternoon, when she was off, she walked the white-gravel road up the hill, aware that all around her people she had never seen before were converging on the same path. They wore long skirts and turbans, bell-bottoms and cotton shirts with cowboy boots. Some of the men wore bright knitted skullcaps that covered almost their entire head, while others wore white crocheted caps. The long fringes of the men's *tzitzis,* four-cornered garments worn under shirts, dangled down their sides. Everyone greeted everyone else with a smile.

"Hello, Sister!" "Hello, Brother!" they called out in Hebrew as they passed by. "*Shalom Achi. Shalom Achoti.*"

To her surprise, the tent was almost full when she got there. She sank down in lotus position on one of the many colorful pillows, looking around for familiar faces. There was Judith in the back, quietly conversing with a grey-haired woman in a magnificent cotton turban of peacock blue and green. They were laughing. And there, in the far corner, his face suffused in the light of one of the many candles that lined the floor, was Daniel.

He looked beautiful and tragic, she thought, studying the strong lines of his weathered face in the candlelight, which imparted a gentleness and vulnerability to him she had sensed but not yet seen. His eyes were intelligent and searching. He wore the same dusty clothes he had on the dig. She wondered if he owned another outfit.

A low murmur began as a tall man entered and walked swiftly to the podium.

Suddenly everyone stood. "Blessings, Rav Natan!" someone called out.

He was much younger than she'd imagined, like one of those Israeli paratroopers who take off to India the moment they get out of uniform, returning with a beard and a mission.

"Please. Everyone sit," he said in Hebrew, waving his hand with a self-deprecating smile. "Especially the people who dig all day. Sit before you collapse."

Easy laughter washed over the crowd, as people made themselves comfortable.

"How do we know what our Creator wants of us?" he began with no introduction. "If God had told us directly, it would have taken away our choice, and choice is the most precious thing a man has. Yes, we must take ideas and directions from our wise men, but we must add of ourselves. We cannot copy.

"Each man must sing his own song. As long as you live, that song is being written. Your life is your song. No matter how low you have fallen, even if your life is full of misery, find in it one good thing, and that tiny spot of goodness will grow and widen. In an instant, you can reach the truth, see the good inside you. And the moment you find that, you will find God."

He bent his head. Lifting his legs into a lotus position, he balanced on the chair, his hands extended forward, cupped open.

Kayla looked around her, surprised. The entire roomful of people had taken the same position.

"Close your eyes. Let your worries go. Imagine tiny paper boats holding little candles sent off on a dark river, each boat carrying another worry. Watch them float away into the distance. You know they are there as they sail past you, but you are no longer connected to them. You are cleansed, empty of cares. They are distant. Listen to your inner voice without worry or sadness. Stifle for a moment your own human noise. Listen to the Divine conversation."

The room went absolutely silent, the only sound the intake and exhalation of human breath.

Kayla imagined Bev's cynical face. Defiantly, she closed her eyes. What will become of me? she thought. I've ruined everything! I've left school. She put that thought into a paper boat and watched it flow down the river, distancing itself from her. I've abandoned my parents in their time of need! How will they win their court case! My father could go to jail! We will be all over the newspapers. Our family will be ruined! This thought too she lifted and placed in a tiny boat and sent off. Seth! She saw his furious face, his pain, his humiliation. She lifted the worry from her mind, placing it gently in a paper boat of its own, giving it a gentle push to cast it off far from her.

And as each unsolvable problem rose to her mind, she gently lifted it and sent it off, until all that remained was an empty space, a dark river full of tiny points of light like distant stars, detached and irrelevant.

She sat there quietly, at peace, filled with a strange sensation that her hands were no longer empty. Like a lost child whose parent has come to claim him, she felt them tingle with the warmth of connection.

Everything was in ruins. But her soul was still intact. God was with her, on this hill, in this room, commingling with the souls of these strangers.

Oh God, don't let anything bad happen to my family, to everyone I love, Kayla sang in the silence of her ravaged heart, tears streaming down her cheeks, the prayer so long dammed inside her suddenly breaking free. Let them forgive me, and let me forgive them.

"Now, very gently, open your eyes. Connect to the world again," Rav Natan said.

She opened her eyes. Across the room, she saw Daniel. He too was weeping, as a lost child weeps.

She walked down the starlit path back to her room filled with a sense of having returned from a long, transforming journey. She was elated, and weary, her heart wrung with grief and hope. Footsteps came up behind her. She turned: It was Daniel. She waited for him to catch up, wanting to reach out to him, to know him. But he passed her without looking up, his eyes fixed on the ground, his back bent, his footsteps weary and slow, as if each movement forward was filled with uncertainty and pain.

"Daniel," she called out after him.

He turned around slowly, taking her in, his eyes searching hers. She took two hesitant steps toward him, but he shook his head. "I can't, Kayla. I just can't," he whispered, turning around and walking away.

Weeks went by, the days running one into the other. Mornings and evenings splendid with mountain sunrises and sunsets which blazed across the skies, extinguishing themselves in the sparkling blue sea. Day after day she found herself walking to the white tent, listening as she had never listened before. This was not a classroom, nor was this the kind of knowledge you wrote down in words on lined paper. It was something that melted into you, the way water melts into sand, she thought, invisible yet changing the texture of your being forever.

Wherever she was, she searched for Daniel, homing in on him with some strange instinct, longing to know every moment where he was in relation to herself. This morning was no different. He lifted his head, his eyes acknowledging her wordlessly. As usual, he sat in the back of the bus alone.

Impulsively, she followed him. "Do you mind?" she said boldly, amazed at herself.

He looked up, startled, his body stiff. Slowly he shifted over, making room for her. She sat down next to him. The flaps of their open jackets touched. He seemed uncomfortable, shifting over farther. She felt suddenly furious.

"Look, have I done something to offend you, Daniel?"

"Why would you think that?"

"Well, since that first day when you helped me with the wheelbarrow, you've done everything you can to avoid saying a word to me. You pass me by as if I were air."

He was silent, shocked, she imagined, beginning to feel like one of those pushy, obnoxious American tourists who insist on getting their due from the natives.

He shook his head. "I'm sorry you feel hurt. I know by American standards, I have no manners. We Israelis are not big on 'have a nice day,' 'please,' and 'thank you.' We behave honestly."

"Even if it's offensive?"

"Have I offended you?"

"You've ignored me. I'd say that's offensive, yes."

"No. I've been aware of you every single day. Painfully aware."

She inhaled. "What, exactly, is that supposed to mean? That my existence here pains you?"

"Yes. It does."

She was mortified.

"But it's not personal, not you. It's . . . Americans."

What a jerk! "What do you have against Americans?"

"Wide green lawns, July Fourth parades, Memorial Day sales, and national mourning over the rising price of gasoline."

"Real tragedies happen even to people with wide lawns, parades, and sales," she said softly, rising and moving deliberately away. She sat down near Judith.

His eyes followed her, then looked out the window.

"I can't believe I just did that!" she told Judith, humiliated.

"Leave it alone, Kayla. There are so many things you don't, can't, understand."

"Maybe." She nodded, not up to a battle with Judith, but disagreeing completely: What was there not to understand? Rejection was rejection. It was a universal language.

The morning's dig went forward with excruciating slowness. Her whole body felt weary, her mind shutting down, doing the tasks by mindless rote. She was bored with digging, weary of the heat and dirt. And lonely. So very lonely. When break time came, she moved away from the others, impulsively walking down the hill to the ancient synagogue Judith had mentioned. She would be late getting back to work, but so what? What could they do, fire her? Not exactly the worst thing that could happen, she thought bitterly. Perhaps that was what she really wanted.

The area was deserted, being too hot in the day for most tour buses. She stepped inside the flapping plastic covering stretched over the roofless structure. The mosaic floor was magnificent. Dating back to the fourth century, it had a leaf pattern surrounding four birds with long, graceful necks. She wandered around, looking at the sea framed by every window. And then she came upon an inscription. The ancestors of humanity were listed—there was Seth's name, right after Adam's! She would have to tell him this, if he ever spoke to her again. And there was the list of the zodiac signs, but not the symbols, which were considered idolatrous, she read in the brochure from the Antiquities Authority that lay scattered around in piles. Next to that were the names of Daniel's three companions, the men who by legend upheld the world. Adam, Seth, Daniel, she thought in wonder at the strange coincidence. She read the rest of the inscription:

> *Warning to those who commit sins causing dissension in the community, passing malicious information to the gentiles, or revealing the secrets of the town. The One whose eyes roam over the entire earth and sees what is concealed will uproot this person and his seed from under the sun and all people will say Amen.*

"This person and his seed," her mind repeated, shocked. Children punished for the sins of the father.

She went outside, looking up at the path that led back to the dig. She turned in the opposite direction, toward the date palm orchard. Their swaying plumes were regal, their shade tempting and mysterious. They beckoned like a mirage amid the shimmering heat.

She climbed easily over the low fence, ignoring the KEEP OUT—DANGER sign, assuming it was meant to scare off potential date thieves. For what could possibly be dangerous about a date orchard? Falling dates? She smiled to herself as she wandered through the magical forest with its cool green shadows. She stopped now and again, looking up at the large orange-hued bunches at the very top of each tree, wondering how people could get up there to pick them once they ripened.

She walked forward, pondering this, and almost without noticing it, her foot hit a tiny hole in the road, a small inconsistency in the texture of the ground. Her toes dug in idly as she looked down. There was a small scraping noise and then, without warning, the astonishing plunge downward as her body was swallowed by the collapsing earth. In shock, she groped the dark earth that rose up all around her, her stunned mind unable to grasp what had happened. One second she had been on top, and the next she was on the bottom, the lower half of her body covered with debris.

It was so dark, with only a tiny pinpoint of light, like a forgotten star, above her. How far down had she fallen? Had she struck bottom, or would any sudden movement, any attempt to free herself, simply plunge her deeper into the abyss?

She thought about that. What a fitting metaphor for her life!

And then a sudden idea came to her: This is what it must have been like for them, those people in the pizza store in the center of Jerusalem: the solid familiar ground giving way with shocking suddenness, plunging them into darkness, pain, horror, and uncertainty.

She tried to dig out her legs, but a terrible stabbing pain in her wrist made her cry out in agony. Her head throbbed. She lay back, afraid to move, looking upward.

Am I going to die? she wondered, at first with clinical detachment and a touch of defiance, and then with horror and panic. She was buried alive in a place as silent and cold and dark as a grave.

Please, God, I don't want to die. I don't deserve to die!

She looked inside herself. Why do you want to live? Because I'm not finished. I'm not finished writing my song. I haven't even started.

She closed her eyes, her life, all her struggles, suddenly too heavy for her to carry any further. She released them, falling to the bottom of her existence, as low as it was possible for a human being to fall. She felt something had ended. Whatever was going to happen was going to happen. I am not in control of anything. She felt a sense of strange acceptance, of reconciliation. Without willing it, she slept.

When she awoke, she felt hungry and slightly wet. How much time had passed? Minutes, hours, days? Then suddenly, there was a faint noise. Human, animal, imagined?

"Kayla!"

A voice. A real voice, not a hallucination!

"I'm down here!" she screamed, looking upward. She saw the pinpoint of light suddenly widen.

"We're throwing down a rope. Grab on to it, and we'll pull you out!"

It was Michael and Judith!

She saw the rope dangling in front of her, but the pain in her wrist was too great for her to hold on. "I think my wrist is broken!" she shouted. Could they hear her?

And then suddenly the rope rose, disappearing.

She closed her eyes, afraid. What would happen now? She heard shouting, then the scrape of legs forging down the abyss toward her.

"Kayla."

"Daniel!"

"Can you move your legs?" he asked.

She shifted her body and found to her astonishment and relief that the earth covering her gave way easily. She pushed her legs free of the debris, wiggling her toes and flexing her ankles and calves. She tried to stand.

"Don't!" he shouted. "The earth might give way even more! Just gently, move closer to me."

She inched her way toward him in the darkness. Suddenly, his strong arms were around her, pulling her up to him.

"Up!" he shouted, tugging on the rope.

They hung in space, his body encircling hers as if they were no longer two people, but only one, dangling in thin air, suspended and lost. She leaned against him, breathing in the sun-dried odor of his soft old T-shirt, feeling the strong, comforting bones of his shoulders and chest.

He said nothing, but she could hear the quickening intake of his breath as his unshaved cheek pressed into hers. She rested against him, exhausted, allowing herself to be rescued.

"Thank you!" she whispered.

His arms pulled her closer, his heart beating fast against hers.

Then it was bright day again as they suddenly reached the top. Many hands reached for them both, pulling them apart and into safety. Despite the sunlight, her body suddenly felt cold.

"Oh my God! Are you all right, Kayla?" Judith called.

"She's all right," Daniel answered, exhaling, his hands touching Kayla's body professionally as he gently probed her wounds. "Her wrist isn't broken, just sprained. But she needs to be examined and bandaged, and just to be sure, a head X-ray. Hey"—he smiled down at her—"you're going to be fine, Miss America." Gently, he brushed her hair out of her eyes.

She looked up into his face, so strange and so distant, yet so familiar. "Daniel, thank you . . ."

"You thanked me already on the way up, remember? You're welcome. You see, I do have manners after all." He grinned. "But don't make a habit of falling into sinkholes, okay?" He brushed himself off and walked away.

On the way back from the hospital, where they confirmed Daniel's diagnosis and bandaged her wrist, she finally got an explanation of what had happened.

"The drought has shrunk the Dead Sea. The retreating waters have left behind a high level of salt. When freshwater comes along and dissolves the salt, these underground cavities are formed, called sinkholes. They are all over the place. Didn't you see the sign?" Judith told her.

"It said danger, but nothing about sinkholes," she protested, feeling like an idiot. "I'm sorry for causing such trouble."

"I should have warned you . . ." Judith bit her lip. "If anything had happened to you . . ." She shook her head, horrified.

"It didn't. You heard the doctors."

"But it could have. Thank God for Daniel."

"He didn't seem to think it was such a big deal."

Judith looked at her, astonished. "Kayla, he risked his life for you! All we had was a simple rope. None of us really knew how much weight it could hold. At any moment, it might have given way, dropping you both. And then who knows how far down the two of you would have plunged!"

"Then why didn't you just wait until you had better equipment?" Kayla complained, feeling enraged that he had put himself in such danger.

"Daniel wouldn't let us. He said that every moment you were down there, your life was at risk."

"He's hardly said ten words to me! He thinks I'm some spoiled American princess. Why would he do that for me, risk his life?"

Judith shook her head patiently, patting Kayla's hand with an innocent smile. "Such a mystery!"

15

She spent the next few days in bed, feeling both embarrassed and grateful. Everyone came to visit her, except Daniel. Even Rav Natan stopped by to bring her some fresh fruits.

She felt embarrassed, overwhelmed by the Rav's presence. But when she looked at him, she realized he was just a young man, not a prophet. And his eyes were kind.

"How are you?" he asked.

"I feel sore, but most of all, stupid. I don't even know what I was doing there." She took a deep breath. "In fact, I don't even know what I'm doing here at all, Rav. I'm so confused. I want so much to change, to be a better person."

"Our lives are sometimes hard, difficult to change. So change the easy things first. Fix one little thing you don't like about your life."

"I don't know where to start!"

"The starting point doesn't matter! Find a teeny-tiny spot you'd like to change for the better. Maybe it's the way you answer the phone, or how you greet people on the street. Be consistent. Follow that one little spot, until you've transformed your whole life. Because you can't change just one thing without it changing everything." He got up to go. "Well, I have a tentful of people waiting for me! May God bless you and heal you."

"Thank you so much," she murmured, sitting up, feeling as if she had swallowed some medicine that was already giving her new energy.

She got dressed and went outside. The air had turned bitterly cold. Her breath made white smoke as she breathed, reminding her of Boston. A feeling of homesickness swept through her. She walked down a dimly lit path, her mind meditative, still full of the Rav's stirring words.

"Kayla."

She turned. It was Daniel. Her heart thumped, her palms suddenly warm and moist.

"Are you in a hurry?"

She hesitated.

"Another time then? I don't want to bother you." He turned around abruptly, walking quickly away.

She caught up with him, taking his hand. "Don't."

They walked side by side through the starlight, breathing in the sharp scent of the cold desert air mingled with the intoxicating perfume of honeysuckle and jasmine. She felt light-headed.

"Look how tall the trees and bushes are, how lush! No one would believe that we are in the middle of the desert!"

"The wind carries the rich nutrients from the Dead Sea and deposits them on the soil. All it took was for someone to realize that and to plant something and add a little water."

"It's like magic," she murmured, looking at him, wondering at the hidden richness in the most unprepossessing of places and human beings.

"This is where I live, Kayla." He gestured toward rough-hewn wooden chairs on a little porch in front of a tiny white house. "Will you come in and sit for a moment?"

He sat on the bare floor, his back to the wall, his sandals and the hems of his dark trousers covered in dust. His hair too was dusty, she thought, sitting on his one chair, unable to stop herself from wondering how it would feel to run her fingers through the wild dark curls. But something about the cautious way he held his body—in stiff, almost brutal, control—made her put her hand in her pocket.

"How are you?" he asked her.

"Fine. Thanks to you. But tell me, Daniel, are you just one of those hero types, the kind that jumps into swollen raging rivers to rescue cats and little old ladies, or are you simply suicidal?"

He grinned. "Both." His face became serious. "I couldn't let anything happen to you. You must know that, Kayla. You are the first person . . . the first woman . . . I have allowed myself to feel anything for since . . . I couldn't lose you, too."

She was absolutely stunned. "What? But all those things you said . . . I thought you had only contempt for me, for Americans."

"You misunderstood me completely! When I first saw you with your clean, fine, healthy body, that curly hair and pretty, freckled face, I thought of all those American college students so carefree and sheltered in their peaceful, ivy-covered dorms. Beer parties and spring breaks to Mexico . . ."

"Oh, please!" She shook her head wearily.

"No, no. You don't get it! It isn't contempt. It's envy, Kayla. Don't you see? How could I taint your easy, innocent world with my mourning and pain and tragedy? I wanted you to stay just the way you were, to protect you. But it wasn't easy. I was telling you the truth when I said your presence here was painful. It's torture."

"So your goal was to protect my innocent freckled happiness from the sordidness of life, the scourge of terrorism?" She shook her head slowly. "You have no idea how funny that is."

"Funny?" he asked, stunned and confused by her reaction.

"Tell me this: Is it *my* presence that's painful, or any woman you'd be attracted to?"

"There hasn't been any other woman in my life . . . until you."

"Am I in your life?" she asked, bewildered.

"More than you can ever know."

"Then why push me away like that?"

"Because it can never, ever be allowed to happen again! If it hadn't been for that sinkhole, I would never have allowed myself to touch you. Don't you see, I simply can't risk it."

"Risk what?"

"Loving someone again that much."

Her heart somersaulted. They sat together in silence, the sound of the fierce, wild desert wind rattling the flimsy windows, demanding to be let in.

"Tell me about her."

He stared at the floor. "Don't ask me to talk about that."

"I have to! I want to understand you. And she is part of you. Even if the past is just this fading watercolor portrait, I need to see the shape, the outline of the two of you together. I need to know how it was."

"Oh . . ." he said in anguish, holding his head in his hands.

She felt a stab of guilt. "I'm sorry . . . I have no right."

He looked up at her, shaking his head.

"Is it so hard to let yourself remember?"

"It's not that. I think about it all the time. And it gives me pleasure to remember. It's just that . . . I don't know if I can explain it to anyone else. It was . . . just so . . . ordinary." He took a deep breath. "I was standing on a bus stop on Strauss Street, just outside Bikur Cholim Hospital in the center of downtown Jerusalem. There was a patient I went to see. All of a sudden, it started raining. It was late September, when it hardly ever rains. No one, except one very old lady, had come prepared with an umbrella, so everyone was crowded inside the bus shelter. There was not an inch of room left. Esther"—he swallowed hard—"was standing out there in the middle of the rain. Her dark hair was heavy with water. Her lashes looked like she'd been crying."

He stopped, his chest rising and falling with deep breaths. She wanted to reach out, to hold him, but stopped herself.

"I asked her if she was all right, offering her my spot in the bus shelter. She looked up at me, her face shining and warm and soaking wet. She laughed. She said: 'From the end of April until the end of October, there are only blue skies. Every single day. Even the wind hardly blows, except if it's a *hamsin* . . . To tourists, Americans, that sounds wonderful. But the thing is,' she said, 'it isn't. It's relentless, that blue sky and that hot, beating sun and the summer wind. Like a movie you are forced to watch again and again until you know every line by heart. And something inside you longs for rain—for grey clouds and thunder and flashes of lightning. It's thrilling—those first few drops of rain. And when you watch it, you just want to laugh and dance and hug somebody you love, and crawl under warm covers because you are just so happy the movie is over and the reruns are gone. It's new, amazing, full of possibilities—even bad possibilities. Still, it promises a new year, all the old hurts washed away . . .' Then she laughed and looked up, opening her mouth and drinking it in. I've never seen anything so . . . so beautiful."

He let out a sharp, quick sob.

She moved off the chair, slipping in beside him on the floor.

"It was Passover. We went to the hotel where my grandparents always stayed for the holiday. That way we could join them for the Seder. My whole family was there, sitting around the table upstairs, laughing, waiting for the Seder to start. And then my daughter said she had to go to the bathroom. We were in the middle of toilet training, and we had this thing about encouraging her. I offered to take her, but she only wanted her mother. A few minutes after they climbed down the stairs, I heard the explosion. It blew out all the windows, like in some kind of cartoon: The slivers just flew inward toward us. But not a single person at our table was hurt. No one even had a scratch. I ran down the steps. It was black with smoke. I couldn't see anything. There was blood everywhere, and dripping water, and hanging disconnected electrical wires, and dead bodies. I finally found them. They each had a slight pulse. I had to decide who to work on first. I chose my wife. But I couldn't save her. And when I turned to my daughter, it was too late.

"I loved them so much. So much. And yet, I couldn't save either one. My baby. She was only three. Nothing. Their hearts were not beating. I tried and tried and tried, but I couldn't get their hearts to beat . . ." He shook his head. "It's too fragile."

"Too fragile? What?"

"That thin, flickering flame inside us. One gust, and poof! It's out. And no skill in the world, no mountain of books, no years of study, can teach you how to rekindle it."

Wordlessly, she placed her hand over his strong, beating heart. Then she took his hand and placed it over her own. "We're alive," she said.

He held her close, stroking her hair, breathing her in. "Kayla, Kayla. Who are you?"

She moved away. "I am nothing. A failure in every way. I've abandoned my fiancé, turned my back on my parents when they needed me most. I've been looking and looking inside myself for one tiny spot of goodness, like Rav Natan said, but I can't find it."

"You are full of good!"

"You don't know anything about me."

"Well, then I guess it's your turn now to talk about all those things you came here to hide."

She thought about it. He might despise her. And he'd probably be right. She shrugged. It had to be done. "Come with me."

They walked together back to her caravan. He sat down on her bed.

"Here, read this," she said, handing him *Newsweek*. "Page thirty-five. That man in the handcuffs? Samuels? That's my father. And that girl on the left in the family photo? That's me. You see how ironic it is, your worrying about tainting my peaceful, happy world?"

He sat, gripping the magazine in both hands, his eyes straining in the dim light to make out the words. He looked up, his face horrified, his hands shaking. "Has he done these things? The things he is accused of?" he asked her searchingly.

"He is the most honest person I know, Daniel." Her voice caught. "He would NEVER have transferred money knowingly to terrorists. NEVER. But that doesn't mean his innocent mistake hasn't helped kill people."

"And I drove my family to that hotel. And if I had been faster, more decisive, or more skillful, perhaps I could have saved my wife or my baby. So if it's only consequences that matter, not intentions, then I guess you could say I'm also guilty of actions that got people killed."

"No! A terrorist killed your family!"

"And terrorists are responsible for taking the money your father transferred and using it to kill. That's the way they work. They take innocent people and destroy them to get what they want. So why have sympathy for me, but not your father, or yourself?"

"Because what happened to you is so clear. But my father can't explain what happened to him. He doesn't know. And if we can't find out and prove his innocence, he's going to wind up in jail for the rest of his life."

He was strangely silent. "Can I hold on to this magazine, Kayla? I have an idea."

"About what?"

"There is a familiar ring to your father's story. I can't really say more. I need to check it out with the people who would know for sure. But you must promise me you will never reveal to anyone the source of the information I give you."

"I understand. I'll give it to my father without any explanations . . ."

He hesitated. "Kayla . . . I . . . that is . . . it shouldn't come from you at all."

"Why not?"

"Think about it. This information can only help your father if he takes it seriously, if he passes it on to his lawyers."

"And if it comes from his silly, capricious daughter who has gone off the deep end and is in some desert hippie fairyland, he won't."

"Exactly."

She thought for a moment. "It's all right. I know exactly the right person."

16

Shoshana's baby was born in December, a beautiful little girl they named Annie. Adam and Abigail drove down to Greenwich in the snow to see her.
Shoshana seemed exhausted. Matthew was correct and cool. Abigail and Adam
held the baby, left their presents, and drove home, their hearts heavy as much
as they tried to pretend otherwise.

The federal grand jury indictment came in January, just as one of the worst
snowstorms hit the East Coast. There was a phone call from Marvin, then the
dreaded ring of the fax machine that Abigail had come to view like the tolling
of doomsday bells in some Victorian tragedy. Out spewed pages and pages of
closely typed text in the shocking language of the law.

She did not read them. Could not. But sometimes, as the wind howled,
driving huge icy sheets against the windows which piled up on the front lawn,
barricading them against the world, she'd peek inside Adam's office, studying
his wrinkled forehead and intense gaze as *he* pored over them, hoping to absorb
some of their meaning secondhand by watching him. He gave almost nothing
away.

And when, finally, she asked, he answered curtly: "The lawyers say this is
standard. Nothing to worry about."

She knew she shouldn't believe him, but it was easier to pretend to herself she did. "So, what's next?"

"I have to go to court for the arraignment and to enter my plea."

The day of the court appearance, Abigail woke up weary after only a few hours of exhausted sleep, and even that made possible only by overgenerous doses of tranquilizers. They were due in court at ten.

All these weeks, the vision of Adam in handcuffs, that angry red welt on his damaged wrist, had stayed in her mind. She remembered their first court visit, that feeling of defeat they got by merely walking into those paneled rooms under the wary gaze of unfriendly guards; the very walls seemed to impose their authority over the fragile human beings they enclosed.

A chill crept up her back in her well-heated bedroom as she stood at the window in her nightgown looking out. The sky was silver, the branches of her majestic oak iced with a white-crystal glaze like some bakery confection. It was freezing, a Boston winter day. Here inside we are still safe and warm, she thought. But the moment we walk out the front door, all that will change. Nothing will shelter us but the hired guns of our uberexpensive legal team. She hugged herself against the goose bumps that sprouted on her arms. Were their lawyers up to the task? Would they stand firm, holding the line, keeping the vicious tidal waves from sweeping her and Adam out to sea? Or like the dikes of New Orleans, would they give way to the ferocity of the storm?

The feds had so many lawyers. As for the judge, some "helpful" acquaintances had explained that federal judges back up federal investigators and federal prosecutors. "That's their job." More probably, federal prosecutors had no reason to lie, while well-paid defense attorneys certainly did. Who would anyone find more trustworthy?

Being targeted by the legal profession was like being hunted by a redneck wearing an expensive suit and carrying a machine gun, she thought. She would have loved the prosecutor to look like a bulldog: short and stocky, with heavy-lidded, wide-set eyes, a bulbous nose, and a large, mean mouth. Instead, he looked like Thomas Jefferson, an elegant lanky WASP, a Supreme Court Justice to-be.

He was just doing his job, she tried to tell herself. But she couldn't help hating him when she remembered his cool, convincing arguments before the judge, which twisted some facts, made up others, and wove the whole into a garment that looked seamless. Would the judge—a beleaguered éminence grise, who seemed amused and entranced by the prosecutor's performance— examine the underside of the prosecution's case, discovering all the ugly stitching that held it together?

She didn't know. And so she clung to the last and only hope they had: that there really existed such a thing as *justice.*

She rolled the term around in her mouth like a tiny expensive button fallen off a beautiful blouse, a button you do not want to lose. It seemed such a fragile, abstract term when pitted against the concrete reality of iron bars, steel handcuffs, armed guards, and the powerful juggernaut that was the American government's legal team, paid for by billions of tax dollars.

Years ago, in the fifties and even the sixties, she had believed in America, believed in its systems, in living in a just and free land among an educated, free, and decent people.

Did that country even exist anymore?

It was as if she'd woken up one morning and the world she had grown up in had disappeared as completely as any medieval village sacked by invading barbarians. But it was not just America. It was everywhere.

She had long ago ceased to feel at home in the world, which was unrecognizable compared to the place she'd grown up in. Her own country had become a brutal, foreign place. Her own culture had become alien to her, all the touchstones of her childhood turned upside down.

Take movies. In her childhood, plotlines had had a hero and a villain. The hero was usually kind to women and children and animals. He was honest and helped other people. Now, the opposite was true. The heroes were drug lords, murderers, and con men. Instead of villains, they battled the worst thing you could be in the modern world: a chump, a loser, a patsy. In fact, Hollywood— and the rest of the world—seemed to be saying that any good deed you did was a mistake that would cost you dearly. Those who triumphed over these clueless do-gooders were to be cheered.

The message of all these things—which ran through the culture like a spine holding up the entire body—was that all things were relative. There was no good, no evil. There were such things as honest thieves and praiseworthy, deeply religious mass murderers.

If you wanted to watch and enjoy movies or read the news, you had to learn to push down your disgust, to argue away your queasiness, to reeducate your tastes, making allowances for how things were now.

No one was interested in hearing this. She didn't like to talk about it openly because people treated you like an old fogy. "The good old days," her kids would groan. When racism, sexism, and tobacco smoke filled everyone's lives and living rooms!

That was also true, she had to admit. But the fact was, it had gone too far now. It wasn't a question of censorship, or turning back the clock. These twisted values had become part of Western culture, deforming it until people had no idea what was right and what was wrong, no matter how clearly they saw both happening in front of them. They had no memories of another time, of other values, another way of life. The outrage against those endangering human life had died out.

Instead, people were outraged about climate change. They were outraged against oil prices. They were outraged against land ownership claimed by native peoples. You had to be on the right side of any conflict for your life to be worth anything. You had to be on the trendy side.

The lords of the media, whoever they were, helped to nudge people in a certain direction. They taught people when to close their eyes, to close their hearts. She, too, could no longer hear that voice inside of her, that keening over the world's misery. It had been silenced; a heavy blanket of cold had settled over her feelings. If you wanted to survive in this world, you had to filter out the daily atrocity count. You had to grow numb.

Some people made themselves feel better by joining a group or a political party that would tell them what to care about and what to ignore, helping them to relinquish their individual responsibility in making those decisions. You could believe what you were told rather than what your eyes saw and ears heard. You could trust others to be the guardians of morality, the moral repository of the human race. They would decide, then you could write your checks, join the demonstrations when you had time, or compose the occasional letter to the editor when you had an idea. You could sweep your desk clean, order your mind, and sew a nice blanket for your heart, tucking it into a warm bed at night, allowing yourself to cry over what *The New York Times* deemed worthy of your tears.

And now this world, this new world, which she had helped create through laziness, indifference, and moral fog, was about to judge her and Adam.

The idea terrified her.

"You look nice," she told him.

He took her hands, kissing them. "Shoshana called, and so did Josh."

"What did they say?"

"They were sweet. Concerned."

"But not enough to actually pick themselves up and come . . ."

"Shoshana suggested it, but I absolutely forbid her to consider it. Do you want your daughter taking her new baby out on these icy roads? And Josh doesn't have the money for the fare. You know that."

No one brought up Kayla.

Except for a few one-line postcards from Israel over the last two months that imparted such information as "Not much rain. Working hard," they knew nothing. It was a sore point, too painful to touch.

"It'll be all right, my love. Get dressed. Have something to eat. This is just the beginning. Be brave." He hugged her.

He is comforting *me,* she thought, feeling guilty and useless.

She poked through her closet. "Clothes to be judged by," she whispered to herself. She looked for a dark, respectable suit. Black was too funereal. Why should she project mourning? She and her husband were guiltless, she reminded herself, like a child who assures himself there are no monsters.

There was a dark pink suit. Ashes of roses the color was called in a novel she'd read years ago. She held it up against her chest. It was very plain except for a brooch, but still, it looked expensive—no doubt because it was. Would the judge look at her and think: rich bitch, clothed in ill-gotten gains? She put it aside. Finally, she came across an old brown skirt with a matching blouse and vest, the kind of thing she wore to teach on cold winter days. She held it against her. Was it too obvious an attempt to dress down? Would it look like a pretense? Most of all, would it wound her husband, signaling her belief that she found it necessary to hide the truth of who they were, as if that in itself was incriminating?

She went back to the pink suit, slipping it off its hanger. She stepped into the skirt, then added a simple white shell with short sleeves. She put her arms through the jacket, then buttoned it as she carefully scrutinized herself in the mirror. The brooch—a glittering crystal eye-catcher worn above her heart—would definitely have to go, she thought, unpinning it and placing it on her night table. The jacket still looked expensive. I can always slip it off in court, she told herself, giving up.

In the kitchen, Adam was sitting at the counter drinking his coffee. This amazed her. How could anyone own a stomach that allowed one all that caffeine in such distressing circumstances? She made herself a cup of pale yellow chamomile tea and chewed halfheartedly on a dry whole-wheat biscuit. Even so, she hoped she wouldn't have to ask the taxi driver to pull over to a gas station restroom on their way to court.

She envied people with iron digestive systems. People who needed prunes. Ever since she had been a child, she never knew when her bowels would turn to water. Everything affected them. A test at school, a new spice, getting up early and having to leave the house and be on the road. Soon, she was afraid to go anywhere unless she knew exactly where a bathroom would be. Long car rides through unfamiliar places were torture. A doctor once diagnosed her with IBS, or irritable bowel syndrome. She got little yellow pills, and they actually did seem to work.

But more than once she had recognized in her fears a wider significance: She was afraid of being humiliated publicly. Soiling oneself was simply the most obvious manifestation of that. Why she cared so much what others would think of her, she could not immediately diagnose. But she had some ideas. It had something to do with her parents, that horrible mess her mother called housekeeping. The chronic sense of shame at things over which she had no control or responsibility.

Her mother, Esther, had been born in 1933 in Jerusalem, the child of young parents who wound up there after fleeing German anti-Semitism when that was still possible. But the raw new country had not suited the sophisticated

Europeans, and as soon as they got the coveted entry permits, they had journeyed to the U.S., leaving the struggling Jewish Promised Land behind.

Thirteen-year-old Esther had never actually learned to be comfortable with the English language—her third language after German and Hebrew. And having spent her formative years among simple, hardscrabble pioneers, she was equally unhappy with what she always considered American snobbery and materialism.

She didn't know what to do with material things. She was an unorganized woman who never liked taking care of a home. A hoarder, she would keep things well past their prime, stocking new clothes, furniture, and knickknacks beside the old until the closets were overflowing, the bedrooms like a warehouse. Abigail was embarrassed to bring friends home. It was the beginning of a lifelong sense of inferiority. And a chronic case of IBS.

Her father, Joseph, was born in 1922 in Chicago. A printer with no ambition, he seemed fascinated by his opinionated foreign wife, and only too happy to indulge her. Often, he cleaned up after her, creating some order out of the chaos. But her father had died young, and her mother had mourned him until her dying day, forty years later. After his death, things in the house had gone from bad to worse, until finally they put Esther into a nursing home and locked up the house. The first and only time the house was clean was when Abigail had gone there after the funeral, bringing mops, brushes, and detergent, and many, many garbage bags.

She looked around at her own clean, orderly home. I've made my own life, she thought proudly. Still, the terror of disclosure hung over her head. It probably always would no matter how much she invested in her home, or how beautiful it was. She would always feel that *ping* of alarm when company came over, afraid things were not good enough. She shook her head, musing at the insanity of human beings. No judge looking at their expensive lifestyle from the outside would ever be able to grasp that.

"I'll make us some sandwiches," she told him, taking off her jacket and putting on an apron. "Goodness knows how long we will be there."

He said nothing, reading the paper, bringing the cup methodically to his lips. Only the sound of the clattering saucer made her look up, realizing that he had placed the cup in the wrong spot, almost sending it flying. His hand shook.

She put down her knife and walked toward him, wiping her hands on her apron. She slipped her arms around his neck. They stood there, unmoving, until the doorbell rang. It was their car service, waiting to drive them to court.

They arrived before their lawyers.

"For the money we are paying them, they should be sitting here waiting for us," she fumed.

"Shush. They are good people. They are doing the best job possible. Be grateful, can't you?"

"We'll soon see about that," she hissed. "If they had done the best job possible, why would we be in court at all?"

"If you are going to be unreasonable and childish, maybe you should go home," Adam said through gritted teeth.

She felt wounded and chastised. She had wanted it to be them against the world, but that was not what he wanted. He had invited the lawyers—who were bleeding them dry—into their inner circle, preferring them to her. Of course, he was right. For what had she to offer in his defense but her childish love and useless faith, both worthless in the eyes of the law?

They waited outside the huge doors of the courtroom, realizing that inside another trial was still in progress. When someone left, she peeked inside. She saw lawyers standing at attention, interrupting each other, and a judge angrily banging his gavel. Her heart sank: He will already be in a bad mood, annoyed by the previous case, when it is our turn. Bad luck! But maybe he wasn't the same judge at all, not *their* judge? She tried hard to conjure up his face from the first time in court, but could recall nothing more than a halo of salt-and-pepper hair hovering above black robes.

The prosecuting attorney arrived together with four assistants and cartloads of papers. Marvin came in, with two assistants, also carrying a cartload of documents. The doors opened wide, and they went inside.

It was part theater, part waiting room for open-heart surgery, she thought, her heart beating erratically as she found her seat. She looked over at the other side. There was a hush in the courtroom as the doors opened and A. J. Hurling strode in. He was impressive, with a face both large and majestic, a model for something to be carved into a mountainside. His body too was on a grand scale at well over three hundred pounds. But with the advantage of his height and expensively made custom suits, he exuded more Henry VIII than obese trailer trash on line at the all-you-can-eat buffet.

Adam tensed physically, his eyes lowering in shame. Without meaning to, had he brought this honorable man into contact with something ugly, something shameful? Hurling did not look in his direction, inclining his head toward the man next to him.

"Who is Hurling talking to?" Abigail whispered.

"It's James Williams Jr."

"The attorney that represented O.J.?"

He nodded.

The attorney was a legend. And he was here to protect his client's rights even though it wasn't A. J. Hurling who was on trial.

"Hurling has no reason to blame you for anything. You didn't know! It wasn't your fault!"

"Abby, be reasonable." He cradled his face in his hands.

Abigail stared at Hurling, trying to catch his attention. She didn't understand why she needed to make eye contact with this man. Maybe just to see what was going on inside him; to understand just how much of an enemy he was going to be. Or perhaps simply to nod in shamed acknowledgment of their shared connection to this ordeal. But he continued to stare straight ahead. She had almost given up when suddenly, without warning, he turned his head in their direction, looking at Adam. She had been prepared for almost anything: anger, vengefulness, betrayal . . . anything but what she'd glimpsed: indifference.

She found that shocking on many levels. First, it made no sense, except if there was a piece missing, something they didn't understand, hadn't thought of. And second, it was contrary to human nature. If he thought for a moment Adam was guilty, Hurling should have been furious.

"All rise!" the bailiff demanded as the judge entered, a faceless man in black robes who held their lives in his white hands.

A wave of sound washed through the silent room as people jumped to their feet.

"Docket 5890-89. The United States versus Adam Samuels."

The words cut through her like an ax. The United States! The country they and their forebears had looked at as the fulfilled promise of all their dreams! Now, they were pitted against each other, enemies. She could see Adam's eyes well with tears. Now it begins, Abigail thought, the longest, most treacherous ordeal of their lives, putting at stake all they owned, or could ever own, all they were or could be.

There was some procedural bickering between the lawyers and the judge that she didn't understand; then the prosecutor said he wanted to read the indictment out loud before the judge took Adam's plea.

Their lawyer, Marvin, jumped to his feet. "Your Honor, this is most unusual. We have all read the indictment carefully; there is no reason to waste the court's time . . ."

But the prosecutor didn't budge. "It is our belief that the public should be reminded at every opportunity of the seriousness of activities such as those Mr. Samuels stands accused of. With the court's indulgence, we would like to use this courtroom as a public forum to emphasize the despicable nature of this particular crime."

The judge waved a dismissive hand. "Just make it quick. Sit down," he told Marvin. "I've made my decision."

" 'That Adam Samuels did knowingly, intentionally, and willfully conspire and agree to commit offenses against the United States.' "

She saw her husband tremble.

" 'That he knowingly and willfully violated and evaded and attempted to violate and evade regulations issued under executive orders of the International Emergency Economic Powers Act, Title 50, and U.S. Code 1701 an offense under Title 18 U.S. Code Section 1956 a 2 A. And that said offenses included Boston, Massachusetts, and Amman, Jordan, and Iraq. That his intent was to promote the carrying out of specified and unlawful activity to organize, equip, and promote groups designated as terrorists and enemy aliens of the United States of America, including Hamas, Hezbollah, and Al-Qaeda, in excess of $150 million.' "

There was a collective intake of breath, or perhaps it was simply her own lungs she heard urgently gasping for air. She saw her husband slump, as if, balloonlike, he had been physically pierced by the enormity and hurtfulness of the charges brought against him. Unthinkable, unthinkable, that Adam should "knowingly and willingly" have done any of these things.

What followed she barely heard. Dates and amounts of monetary transfers to Gregory Van's Organza Group, Ltd., in London. Dates and transfers of money from the Organza Group to the Jordan Islamic Bank, payable to Zimbal Trading Corporation. Transfers and canceled checks from Zimbal to Aba Musa Rantisi, Mohammed El Bargouti, and Halib baba Faheed, high-ranking members of outlawed terror organizations, including Hamas, Al-Qaeda, and the Islamic Martyrs Brigade.

But it was only toward the end, when they read out what they wanted if Adam was convicted, that she was made to finally grasp the enormity of what they were up against, and what they stood to lose.

"'Present Forfeiture. If the defendant is convicted he shall forfeit to the U.S. the following property: all right, title, and interest in any and all property involved in each of the offenses. Any and all property traceable to such property of a sum not less than $150 million representing the total amount of funds involved. All funds on deposit with Organza and the Jordan Islamic Bank. The defendant shall substitute property up to the value of the amount described if any portion of the amount cannot be located upon exercise of due diligence, or has been transferred, sold, or deposited with a third party, or placed beyond the jurisdiction of the court or has been substantially diminished in value or has been commingled with other property that cannot be divided without difficulty . . .'"

She heard nothing more. One hundred and fifty million dollars! And they wanted Adam to repay it! Every penny. They would lose everything. Not only their own home, but Shoshana and Matthew's, because Adam had given them money for their down payment. Not only their own savings accounts, but those set aside for the children and grandchildren. The more she thought about it, the more her horror grew. From a life of luxury to a life of bankruptcy and penniless want.

"In addition, each count carries a penalty of not less than ten years in federal penitentiary."

Each count, that is, each monetary transfer. And there had been dozens.

She began to understand now about the lawyers. Only they stood between her and Adam and the braying vicious pack waiting to be let loose to tear them to pieces. *Everything* was at stake.

Finally, the judge turned to Adam for the first time. "Are you ready to enter a plea?"

"Yes, Your Honor. I am not guilty."

"Duly noted."

The prosecutor stood up. "Your Honor, the State requests that Mr. Samuels be taken into immediate custody until the end of the proceedings against him."

"Your Honor!" Marvin jumped up, earning Abigail's unending gratitude. "My client has been out on bail for over four months and has done nothing in violation. We ask that this arrangement be continued."

The prosecutor rose to his feet. "Your Honor, the situation has changed. The defendant's daughter has already fled the country."

"Your Honor! Kayla Samuels is not accused of anything! She is perfectly free to travel. She is taking a trip abroad. A child on vacation cannot be accused of having 'fled the country.' Besides, Mr. Samuels has a wife, two other children, and grandchildren, all of whom presently reside in the United States. He has close ties to the community. He has no priors. He has surrendered his passport."

The prosecutor was furious. "Your Honor, this is no vacation. Kayla Samuels left with no warning in the middle of a semester in her final year at Harvard Law School! Furthermore, in the days of computers, the State believes Mr. Samuels needs to be under constant supervision to see that he does not continue his illegal money-transferring activities."

"Leaving Harvard Law in the middle of the semester is not a crime, except if you are the one paying the tuition," the judge said with deadpan humor. "Can you present any evidence of illegal activity conducted by Mr. Samuels over the past four months?" he asked the prosecutor.

"No, Your Honor, but . . ."

"Well then . . ." He waved his arm dismissively. "If the situation changes, I will consider changing my ruling. But until then, bail will continue."

Adam took her hand as they walked out of the courtroom. The flashing lights of television cameras and photographers blinded them. She did not bother to cover her face, walking stoically forward. She had forgotten, she realized, to take off her jacket. But what did it matter? The reporters, once their most formidable enemies, seemed like mosquitoes to her now. For what could they actually do? Put you in jail? Steal your home? Your life's savings? No, only the court could do that. The U.S. government, her own government, her own justice system.

Marvin motioned silently for them to follow him. They walked down the corridor into a private office. "Close the door behind you," he told Adam. "They have to prove 'knowingly, intentionally, and willfully.'"

She winced. "Can they?"

"Look, the feds would not have put themselves on the line like this if they didn't think they could prove it. A prosecutor generally does not want to arrest somebody that he can't establish is guilty beyond a reasonable doubt. Arresting someone starts the 'speedy trial clock' which means that if you arrest a defendant, you have to be prepared to take him to trial soon. I don't know any prosecutors who authorize arrests on white-collar-type cases in the hopes that evidence will materialize to enable them to prove their case. They believe they have a case against you, Adam, and a good one."

Their hearts sank. "How can they prove something that isn't true! What if that prosecutor is just trying to make a name for himself?" Abigail demanded.

"Look, there is always theoretically the possibility of a 'rogue' prosecutor, who wants an indictment or an arrest to make himself look good. But in my experience, that possibility could not arise in a situation such as this. Sensitive cases like these have oversight from a variety of different stakeholders, including FBI headquarters overseeing the local FBI field office, and Department of Justice headquarters overseeing the local U.S. Attorney's Office. This is all in addition to the oversight performed by the management chain in the local U.S. Attorney's Office . . . No U.S. Attorney wants his Assistant to bring a case that will blow up in their faces, causing them embarrassment and humiliation if the government loses . . ."

"What you are saying? That they have proof? A witness? Do you have any idea who they are going to bring?" Adam asked.

"So far, I know about one. Christopher Dorset, the person Adam says introduced him to Van. Attorney Dorset is claiming the opposite. They have an affidavit from him that says Adam not only introduced *him* to Van, but also asked *him* if he wanted to help bring in additional investors. He claims Adam explained the whole operation to him, how the transfers were made and to whom. He says Adam offered him huge fees to bring in other clients."

"He's lying!" Adam shouted.

"That's what we have to prove, Adam. I won't sugarcoat it. It won't be easy. Dorset, Hurling. They are all very high-profile."

"And I'm just a stupid, gullible little accountant from Boston. But what about Gregory Van, the fund operator who made the actual money transfers? Surely, if anyone knows the truth, it's him!"

"Interpol is still looking for him, but it's by no means certain he'll ever be found. He could be holed up indefinitely in Saudi Arabia or Syria or Iran. And another thing—this case has become a political football. The State Department is anxious to show the British government that British help in Afghanistan and Iraq is appreciated. In turn, we have to cooperate fully in prosecuting any terror funders from our side."

Adam's face went white. "What is it you're trying to tell me, Marvin?"

"Look, I know you both don't want to hear this again, but as your lawyer, it's my duty to tell you that it would be in your best interest to plea-bargain. They have a strong case. A trial is much too risky for you. As I keep telling you, it's not really Adam they want. They have bigger fish to fry. They'll be lenient."

Abigail saw the blood rush to Adam's face. "Let me get this straight, Marvin. You want me to admit I knowingly transferred a client's money to fund terrorism? Admit that I introduced Gregory Van to Christopher Dorset, when the opposite is true? Admit that all the horrible lies they have been spreading all over the world about me have some kernel of truth in them?!"

"I understand how you feel, but we can't afford to be emotional about this, Adam. Look at what you're facing if you lose! You'll be behind bars for life! And financially, your family will be wiped out forever. If we plea-bargain, maybe we could get them to satisfy themselves with a few years in jail or even to waive any prison time at all—although I'll be honest, that doesn't look likely. And financially, perhaps we could get them to agree to limit fines to just the amount you got in fees for doing these transactions, not the principal."

"*We* can't afford to be emotional, Marvin? There is no *we* here. Just *me*. And if I plead guilty, *my* family, *my* life, will be destroyed, not yours."

"Yes, of course." Marvin looked uncomfortable. "Certainly, it's up to you. But if you lose, the penalties will be staggering."

Adam grasped his lawyer's shoulder. "Which is why, Marvin, we have to win. I don't care what it costs. I'm innocent, Marvin, I swear to you. Please believe me."

"I do, Adam. Of course I do. But as your lawyer, it's my ethical responsibility to explain to you—to both of you—what you are up against. Do you understand?"

"Yes. We understand. Thank you," Adam said.

Abigail didn't contradict him, but her mind was in turmoil. Adam was innocent. She believed that with all her heart. But it was equally true that his decisions and actions, however innocent the intention, had gotten them entangled in this horrible nightmare. His endless ambition, she thought bitterly.

She tried to bury that knowledge. She had to support him, to take care of him, to protect him. She slipped her hand through his, squeezing it hard. This was her role in life. What other choice did she have?

17

On the ride home, they held hands in the back of the taxi, engulfed by a thick, exhausted silence. It was like coming back from a funeral, Abigail thought, except that there would be no friends and family bringing plates of food with sympathetic smiles, no condolence calls as they sat in stupefied grief, overwhelmed by loss. There would be only their beautiful silent house to welcome them in its comforting arms.

No one had shoveled the walk, she realized in shock, remembering that all these things were now their responsibility since their housekeeper and gardeners had been let go.

"Hold on to me," Adam said. They clutched each other, slipping and sliding over the treacherously icy stone walkway. Broken branches littered the fallen snow, and the paint on the banister was peeling.

They tried not to see.

Adam reached up to the mailbox. Bills, catalogues, more bills, then something else.

"It's a letter. From Israel."

It had been three weeks since they'd heard anything.

They didn't bother taking off their coats, hurrying into the living room, tearing open the envelope. Adam carefully unfolded the sheets of yellow, lined paper.

The edges were roughly torn, as if hurriedly snatched from a notebook. The words too seemed hasty, scrawled and crowded together as if it had all spilled out in a rush. Nothing about it reminded him of their meticulous daughter.

Dear Mom and Dad,

I am sitting here writing by the light of a single candle so as not to waken my room (tent?)mates. Believe it or not, outside, the desert air is fragrant with the scent of flowers. This place is a little miracle, full of fertility and growth where you'd least expect it.

We haven't found anything of importance to the world yet. But everything we find is precious to us: vegetable and fruit pits and bits of metals. They are the clues left behind by the ancient people of Israel who built this place, revealing what they ate, and how they lived.

I have to say, I am not crazy about archaeology. It tells you too much about houses, tools, food, plants, and climate, and too little about who people were, what they thought or believed. It is just a job I'm doing really, unskilled labor I undertook for a roof over my head and all the chicken cutlets and tiny cut-up tomatoes and cucumbers I can eat. Truthfully, I would have left here long ago if not for Rav Natan . . .

"Rav?" Abigail repeated softly with horror, already imagining her daughter forced into uncontrolled childbearing to a black-coated-Talmud-scholar wannabe, living on handouts in poverty-stricken superstitious ignorance . . .

"Don't jump to conclusions, Abigail. This is Kayla, our Kayla, we are talking about." Adam raised his voice, as if to shout down his own fears.

Rav Natan, and of course, Daniel. But before I go into any details, I want to apologize to you both. I realize now just how much I've hurt you by abandoning you in your hour of need. It was a great avera . . .

"*Daniel? Avera?*" Abigail grabbed the letter shaking her head. "My God!"

"Let me just finish this, will you?" Adam said through clenched teeth.

He was pretty much at his limit, she saw, frightened.

"I'm sorry. Go on."

A great sin. The beginning of all spiritual growth starts with grati-
tude toward those who gave you life. First God, then your parents.
But please try to understand that I did these things not out of, God
forbid, disrespect, but simply to save myself. I felt as if I were drown-
ing and had no choice but to swim to shore. The way I chose to do this
was, I admit, reckless and inconsiderate and no doubt caused you
much pain. I'm sorry for that, truly. But I hope you will be happy for
me when I tell you that I have found a safe shore, a solid piece of
earth. Sometimes, it even feels as if it's for the first time, as if all my
life I have been floating in some amniotic sac, waiting to emerge into
responsibility and clarity. What a foolish, selfish, indulgent life I've
lived until now! If not for everything that has happened, I would
have probably stayed that way, never having a shot at a real life.

I am newly born, really.

Adam put down the letter and wiped his forehead. Abigail helped him slide his arms out of his coat, then took off her own, folding them beside her on the couch.

The people around me are going through the same metamorphosis.
They are all special people from such different backgrounds. I know—
Mom and Dad—you'd like them. Together, we are learning so much
about life and God and the universe, and where we all fit in, our role
in the world as human beings. We're a colony of caterpillars turning
into butterflies!

Abigail shook her head slowly from side to side. A sudden sharp pain cut through her elbow, radiating up her arm. She massaged it secretly, not wanting Adam to notice.

I'm so sorry that you and Dad are suffering, but for myself, I am
grateful for this intervention by the universe. Yes, it was devastating

and embarrassing—all the newspaper stories, the way people looked at me in the offices where I was supposed to interview for the high-paying jobs that were my due. I remember learning that everything that happens to us is somehow for the best, but until now I found that hard to believe. Now I know this is really true. I see the fog I have lived in all my life lifting, the way it lifts over the mountaintops just as the sun breaks through.

Rav Natan teaches that all our lives are a song we sing to God. No matter how low we fall, that song goes on simply because we are alive. Life itself is the song. And no man's song is like another's.

Anyhow, I just wanted you to know that I am alive and singing.

And now the hard part, the part you are probably guessing and dreading, although you shouldn't be. You should be happy for me, your daughter, who has finally found joy in her life.

Well, there is no easy way to tell this, so I'll just blurt it out:

I am not coming back. My song is here. There was no song in my old life, only silence, because I was living someone else's life. I could never get her tune right, her lyrics were never natural in my mouth. For so long, I thought misery was just inevitable, part of the road to eventual happiness and success. Now I understand that I was on a bad road. And as the Ladino proverb says: "A bad road cannot lead to a good place."

Thank God, that is over.

I'm sorry about the tuition fees for Harvard. I hope you can get them to refund at least part of it. And I'm sorry I took part of the money in my tuition account for my trip and expenses. I know you will be needing it. I want you to know I consider it a loan, and I fully intend to pay it back.

As for Seth, we have been in touch a number of times. But I'll be honest with you: The fact is, I've met someone else, someone like me, bitten by tragedy, emerging from his own fog. I will deal with Seth in my own way, so please don't get involved.

I don't want you to think that you and the ordeal you are both going through haven't been constantly on my mind. Dad, I know you

are innocent of what you're accused of, that there is an explanation
for everything that happened. I just hope we can find it in time. But
whatever happens, you will never lose my love and respect or that of
the people who really know you. And I know that is what you care
about most.

All my love,
Kayla

P.S. Cell-phone reception here is erratic. So write to me at this
address:
Kayla Samuels
Metzuke Madragot
Dead Sea, Israel

Adam sat without moving, the letter crumpling in his hand. Then he reached for the phone.

"She said she doesn't have reception . . ."

"I'm not calling her. I'm calling our travel agent."

"What? You can't go anywhere!"

"No, but *you* can. And must. Abby, go and bring her back. Bring my daughter back to me. It's my fault this happened to her. Please, if you love me . . ."

"No, NO, NO! How can I leave you alone when you are fighting for your life? It's too much; too much, I'm telling you! You heard what the prosecutor said: 'Fled the country'! If I go running after her, too, then that awful man will have further proof of his theory! It could get you thrown into jail, convicted!" She shook her head adamantly. "I'm not budging."

His shoulders shook with shocking violence as he rocked back and forth. Like an infant whose sobs are too deep to voice, it took a moment for his strangled cries to emerge. Shockingly, he got down on his knees, taking her hands and kissing them. "Kayla. Our baby. Our beautiful little girl . . . Our Kayla. She has always given us such *nachas*. She would have been so happy. Gotten her degree. Gotten married to Seth. I've ruined everything for her. EVERYTHING! And she doesn't say a word of blame or reproach. She should be shouting at me! She should hate me! Instead, she's begun to hate herself, to abandon everything she's worked so hard for. We can't let this happen. Please, my love. Please."

She shook her head, her heart stiff, unforgiving.

It was bad enough that Kayla had abandoned them in their darkest hour. Bad enough that she'd stolen their money when they were hemorrhaging money and squandered it on running away. But on top of that, to write such a letter . . . *There was no song in my old life, only silence.* After all they'd done for her! It was like a knife in Abigail's heart. But even that was not the worst.

She looked at her husband. What all the public humiliations, all the accusations, the snub of friends, the draining of their resources, the ruination of his life's work, had failed to do their own daughter had accomplished, finally bringing him to his knees, his heart cracked wide open.

"Don't," Abigail soothed, stroking his greying head. "Don't, my love. My love."

"Please, Abigail. Please. For me. Please."

18

She caught the 7:50 P.M. JetBlue flight from Logan to JFK, and from there ran to catch the connecting El Al flight to Ben Gurion Airport. By the time she boarded the flight to Israel, she had ridden the roller coaster through fear, anger, exasperation, and impatience—and was simply numb. Or so she told herself until she realized, to her horror, that she'd been assigned a window seat and that she'd have to climb over two big men spilling over the center and aisle seats to get there. Getting to the bathroom was going to be impossible. She felt a panic attack coming on as she tried and failed to reconcile herself to the world's worst eleven and a half hours in the air. Then, suddenly, the linebacker cramped in the middle seat called over a stewardess.

"Is the plane full?"

She shook her blond curls and smiled at the big handsome lug. "No, it isn't."

He smiled back flirtatiously. "So, is it okay if I change seats?"

She smiled again and nodded. To Abigail's amazement, he picked himself up and disappeared into the back of the aircraft, never to return. The other man soon followed suit.

Three seats to myself! she exulted in disbelief. That meant she could stretch out and lie down, even sleep. It meant no swollen ankles, no distended bladder.

She hoped it was a portent of things to come, that even the worst scenarios could be turned around in the blink of an eye.

She strapped herself in, anticipating takeoff and the steep climb upward that would eventually result in the freedom to pull back the armrests and stretch out full length. In the meantime, desperate for sleep, she closed her eyes and tried to relax. The outraged shrieks of a distraught infant made that impossible. She opened her eyes, annoyed. The baby was only two rows ahead, flailing to get out of its mother's arms. What bad luck! But it was such a young infant, she saw with sudden pity. As tired as she was, her grandmotherly heart went out to it and its tired and frantic young mother.

She remembered those days. Exhausting, she thought, closing her eyes again. And here I am, once again pushing myself to the limit to help one of my kids. When did it end, motherhood? When could you retire?

If it just wasn't such a waste of time! What good would she be once she got to Kayla? When had her darling, spoiled daughter ever listened to her advice about anything?

She tried hard to place her free-floating resentment in specific settings that would justify it. Kayla kicking a plastic lawn chair and actually breaking it, in a fit of temper because Abigail had complained that she'd used up all Abigail's shampoo. Kayla picking out several pairs of expensive colored contact lenses and having the optometrist send them the bill. But the more Abigail tried to nurse her anger, the more her mind was crowded with opposing images: Kayla announcing her engagement to Seth. Kayla in black robes, valedictorian of her high-school graduation. Kayla breaking the news that she'd been chosen as youth ambassador and would be touring the Netherlands. And further back: Kayla, at two or three, watching a woman in the park nursing her baby.

"What is she doing?" Kayla had asked.

"She's nursing. Giving her baby milk."

"I also want milk," Kayla had demanded.

And Abigail had explained patiently: "When you were little, like the baby, I had milk for you. But now that you are all grown up, Mommy doesn't have any more milk."

Kayla had looked up at her with those beautiful big eyes: "Do you have apple juice?"

Abigail chuckled to herself. And then there was the time Kayla had flung herself on the floor weeping: "My Barbie has nothing to wear!" Or the time she'd given a very detailed explanation for how they made Coca-Cola: "You take a black cat . . ."

She watched the unhappy baby cuddling in her mother's arms, almost feeling the warmth of the soft cheek against her own, the fluid movements of the soft limbs.

The seat-belt sign went off. She tore the blanket out of its plastic wrapper, plumped up all three pillows, and stretched out. Despite the engine noise, the screaming baby, she slept.

When she opened her eyes, she saw that the stewardess had left some food on one of the little fold-down tables. Acquiring a rum-spiked Coke, she tore open the little tinfoil packages of beef and pasta, dipped a warm roll into the sauce, and sipped her drink, totally content. She opened the video screen. They were somewhere over the Atlantic Ocean, near Europe. She felt a calm come over her. All her problems had been left far behind her, and Kayla was still so far ahead. Right now, she had nothing to do but watch all the movies, eat the delicious, cholesterol-filled brownie iced with fudge frosting, and ask for more alcoholic beverages. It would take hours and hours for the plane to land, she thought contentedly, perfectly happy to float between earth and sky, where nothing could touch her.

The plane was sailing smoothly through the sky and even the baby was finally sleeping. It was a girl, and she looked like an angel.

19

It was 6:00 P.M. local time and already pitch-dark when Abigail emerged from the terminal in Tel Aviv.

"I need to go to the Judean desert, near Ein Gedi."

The taxi drivers shook their heads. "Maybe someone else." They melted away, searching for an easier fare. She finally waited on line at the official taxi stand, where by law they were obligated to take you anywhere you wanted to go.

"I need to go to Metuzke Madragot near the Dead Sea."

The driver looked her over. "Two hundred dollars. No meter. Okay?"

"Do you know how to get there?"

"I know what I know. I'll get you there."

She was not about to bargain.

They rode for an hour before she saw any signs of the desert. Then, suddenly, dark monoliths rose on her right, towering with menace. At every turn, something in her resonated with danger and a strange thrill. But each time she felt the word "STOP!" rise in her throat, she forced herself to swallow hard. There was no turning back.

Then the swift flow of the road beneath them slowed as they turned off the highway and headed up a narrow mountain pass. She strained with the car as it inched its way upward. Terrifying visions of Grace Kelly and her daughter plunging off a mountain road in Monaco alternated with panic-filled memories of a wild ride up the Rock of Gibraltar with Adam. Against her sounder instincts, she turned around, looking out the back window. It was all black, except for a reflection of light, elongated and shimmering, which sank into what could only be a black expanse of water.

She rolled down the window, trying to get her bearings. The air had a faint chemical smell and something gritty and abrasive.

"What is that odor?" she asked the driver.

"The Dead Sea. Good for you. "

She doubted that.

The turns were hairpin. She gripped the upholstery and tightened her seat belt. They seemed almost vertical at times, submerged in black ether. Then, finally, she saw some lights in the distance. But as they drew closer, she was disappointed to find it was not a sign of life but simply a towering metal structure, some kind of hardware in the middle of nowhere to facilitate transmissions to faraway places where people actually lived. Its red bulbs glittered festively, like sequins, against the blue-velvet sky.

They continued climbing until the road disappeared, and there was only the crunch of gravel beneath the tires.

"It will ruin car," the driver grumbled. "Where is place? You have address? Why no address . . ." he went on, growing angrier and angrier. Finally, the taxi's headlights picked out a huge gate of thick yellow metal that blocked their advance. There didn't seem to be a soul around to open it. A hand-lettered sign in Hebrew gave them a number to call.

He took out his cell phone, but there was no reception. He shrugged, snapping the phone shut with disgust. "You get out here, walk around gate."

"Here?" She looked around desperately. She was in the middle of the wilderness as far as she could see. "Absolutely not! You can forget about it! You are not leaving me here. Wait. I see an intercom."

She got out of the car and pressed the button. "Hello?"

"Yes?" A voice answered her in English.

A wave of relief washed through her. "I'm Mrs. Samuels. Kayla's mother."

As if by magic, the metal gate began to slide open.

The taxi rode on in silence except for the sound of popping gravel as it pressed the rough stones beneath its wheels. This went on for at least ten minutes, then abruptly stopped.

"*Higanu* . . . Uhm, we here," the driver said.

She rolled down the window. "You've got to be kidding!"

A makeshift group of caravans and shacks with corrugated tin roofs huddled together as if for warmth from the desert night. They were deplorably ugly, she thought, her heart sinking, feeling a strange sense of betrayal. Not a single human being was in evidence.

The driver turned around, a big grin on his face. "I drive you to five-star Dead Sea hotel? Only sixty more American dollars! Only best . . ."

For a fraction of a moment, she was tempted.

"No, of course not!"

He shrugged, resentful of being robbed of his extra sixty dollars. He got out and opened up the trunk, tossing her heavy suitcases on the gravel with a thud that echoed though the windswept hills.

"Careful!" she said helplessly, getting out of the car. She shuddered from the icy desert blast, hugging her coat around her. "I thought it was hot in the desert!"

"Not at night, lady." He laughed. "You pay me now."

"Hold on a minute. Can you just wait here until I find someone?"

Before he could answer, she turned and walked quickly toward the only lit window she saw. It was in a low building made of concrete blocks painted Popsicle orange. Crossing a makeshift veranda crowded with potted plants and orange hammocks hung from the branches of a giant tree, she knocked urgently on the pale blue door. Behind her, she could still make out the driver's grumbled complaints.

A shaft of light cut through the darkness as the door opened. Standing on the threshold was a tall, slim young man wearing a colorful knitted helmet from which unruly dark curls cascaded down to a small dark beard. He wore a fringed white-linen tunic over his shirt and white-linen pants.

"*Baruch HaBah!*" he said with a shy smile.

Abigail stared. Faded scars covered his forehead and chin. He went silent, staring back in confusion, his blue eyes as calm and lovely as a summer lake.

"Who is it?" a voice behind him said. A woman suddenly appeared by his side. She was slim and youthful, wearing a long Indian skirt and a turquoise head scarf. Her blue eyes were beautiful and familiar, Abigail thought, her eyes shifting between the woman and the young man.

"I'm sorry to bother you. I'm Mrs. Samuels. I'm here to see Kayla."

"Kayla's mother! *Baruch Hashem!* Come in. Can I get you something to eat, or drink? You've had a long journey. God bless your safe arrival." She spoke in English with a French-Canadian lilt.

"The taxi is waiting . . . If I could just . . . where is . . . my daughter . . . ?"

"Ah, the taxi! Your suitcases! Let us help you. Kayla is on a desert trek with Natan. She'll be back in the morning . . . She mentioned you might come."

Abigail gave a confused half smile. "She did?"

She nodded. "But I don't think even she imagined . . . that it would be this soon . . ." The woman grinned. "I'm Ariella, by the way. Let me see . . . Here's the key to caravan eight. It's the best one we've got at the moment. Would you like to have a meal with us?" She spread out a welcoming arm. "Or if you're tired, I can make a plate for you, and you can take it back to your cabin . . ."

Abigail didn't hear anything, busy with the slow percolation into her brain of the information she had just been given. Finally, it sank in. Her daughter—and everyone else here apparently—had been sitting back waiting for her to show up. As if there had been no other choice she could have made!

Was Kayla's letter, then, just a cynical exercise in manipulation? And were these people expecting her because that was what all the parents of potential or actual cult inductees did? Was it simply experience that informed their expectations? Or had Kayla regaled them with intimate tales concerning her family life (no doubt at Abigail's expense) that had led them to this conclusion? She found both possibilities equally infuriating. Like one of Pavlov's dogs, or that mouse in the maze that keeps going for the cheese, did Kayla really think her parents were that pathetically predictable?

Then another idea took over, shoving out all the rest: Here I am in the desert on some godforsaken mountaintop with a bunch of refugees from Woodstock. And Kayla is nowhere to be found.

The taxi honked viciously.

She saw the woman and the young man glance at each other in sad understanding. "Ben Tzion, be a *tzadik* and get Mrs. Samuels' suitcases from the car?

She is probably very tired. In the meantime, I'll prepare something for the driver."

"It's all right. I'll take care of him . . ."

"I'm sure you will . . ." The woman smiled. "Still, he needs something more. Something to sweeten his soul."

Abigail paid the driver, who continued to mutter beneath his breath. Behind her, she heard the quick footsteps of the woman. Ariella put her arm around Abigail's waist and leaned into the driver's window, handing him a handmade ceramic box covered with amulets. "Fresh zaatar, from our gardens. Put this on your salad, your hummus . . ." She smiled.

The driver opened the container and sniffed. His hard eyes softened.

"From your own gardens? You can grow something in this hole?" He smiled.

"*Baruch Hashem.*" She smiled back.

"*Todah, geveret.*" He nodded.

"*Bevakasha, adon.*"

He reached into his pocket, then handed Abigail a card. "Lady, this is good place. But anyway. Here is name, number. Anytime, I get you out of here."

Abigail pocketed it, forgetting all about the driver's bad behavior, thinking only what a relief it was to be a phone call away from rescue, even if Prince Charming on the white horse was a cabbie with thinning hair and a bad temper who didn't speak English.

The revving of the engine pierced the quiet. The rough sound of rubber flattening gravel grew fainter, until swallowed by the night. She felt a quiet desolation settle over her. She was really and truly stuck now. "Well, I am tired. I think . . . I'll just . . . go now. Thank you." She put out her hand to Ariella, who ignored it, giving her a hug, which Abigail found intrusive and inappropriate.

"Ben Tzion will see you safely there. It's just a short walk."

Abigail followed the young man and her suitcases up a poorly paved and meagerly lit path to what looked like the prefab concrete boxes you see on building sites. White paint peeled off the badly fitted wooden door.

The young man said nothing, lugging her suitcases without complaint, standing patiently outside her door until she finally realized it was she who had the key. She fumbled through her purse in the dark, finding it, certain it would jam. To her surprise, it turned smoothly in the lock. Blindly fingering the walls, she found the light switch. A bare bulb illuminated the distempered walls. With a touch of fear, she peeked into the bathroom.

"You have one of the few houses with its own bathroom," he told her cheerfully. "Just . . . don't drink the water from the faucet . . . It's not drinking water."

She thought of the scene in *Sex and the City* when the girls are in Mexico and Charlotte mistakenly opens her mouth in the shower . . .

He carefully brought in her suitcases, which took up half the room. "My mother will bring you some bottled water and some food." He was silent for a moment, at a loss. "Everything will look better in the morning," he promised kindly.

"Oh, yes. Thank you." She opened her purse to tip him, but he was already gone.

The floor of the shower stall had peeling whitewash, revealing the cracked tiles beneath. There was also a claw-footed bathtub that had seen better days; a sink with a faucet that reached out almost beyond the basin; and an old toilet with a plastic seat that seemed straight out of black-and-white prison movies. Two beds hugged opposite walls—slabs of hard foam rubber on simple wooden pallets that raised them barely above the floor. Two small, chipped Formica night tables filled the gap in between, and a rattan bookcase on a third wall held rough white towels and brown blankets. The only other piece of what could loosely be called furnishings was yet another foam mattress wrapped in a colorful fabric with several beaded pillows placed against a wall like a sofa. Old curtains covered the single window, which looked out at the concrete block behind it. There was also an old air conditioner, and a wall-mounted spiral heater. She pulled the dangling cord and took some comfort as she watched it turn fiery red. The room was freezing. A smell of bromide drifted in from the bathroom.

She sat down on the cold bed, shivering, hungry, heartbroken. There was nothing she wanted, she thought, nothing that would make her feel better. She thought of all the things she had done for Kayla over the years. And this was what Kayla had done for her! But even in her anger and despair, she knew it wasn't only Kayla. She had come to the end of some strange, twisting road, ending up in this dump, surrounded by darkness and strangers, far away from everyone she loved. Without even willing it, she began to sob, her whole body aching with longing to be home.

But where was that, she wondered? In the neighborhood of people who had shown her no compassion in her time of need? In that huge, expensive, barely inhabited pile of bricks, filled with things slowly falling into decay? Or at the side of her silent, broken husband who shuffled around like an old man and went to bed at nine, if he went to bed at all? If home was to be defined as a place of comfort and sheltering warmth, compassion, and well-being, then she was, for all intents and purposes, homeless.

She heard a gentle tap at the door. It was Ariella. She held a covered tray and a large wicker basket. The scent of warm bread and meat and potatoes wafted into the room. Abigail opened the door wider, letting her in.

"It's still warm," the woman said as she placed a large white plate covered with a napkin on the night table. "And here is mineral water, wine, and juice. We'll move a refrigerator in here in the morning. And maybe a chair and table." She looked around, her eyes alert. She picked up the basket and began to unload its contents onto the bed. "Some soaps and body lotion. They're full of Dead Sea minerals. Wonderfully healing. And some scented candles you can light to relax when you take your bath." The woman looked at Abigail, her beautiful eyes filled with compassion. "Kayla is a lovely girl. I'm so happy you've come. You must have missed her very much."

Abigail nodded cautiously, watching the woman's bustling hospitality with suspicion. She'd heard about these kinds of cults, where they first drew you in, disarmed you with kindness, then wound up robbing you of your children and every last cent. She pressed her lips together.

Ariella reacted, becoming still. "I'm sorry we can't offer you a more luxurious room. You know, most of us sleep in tents."

"Kayla too?" She was shocked.

"Kayla was actually assigned a room. But she said she liked the tent better."

Abigail stared at her, speechless.

Ariella grinned: "You look amazed! Your daughter is not a spoiled American. She's wonderful. She's one of us."

"And when did you say she'd be coming back?"

"Tomorrow morning, or maybe afternoon. You never know."

Abigail's heart sank. "Why is that?"

"Well, these treks are so organic. They start out as one thing, then things happen you don't expect, and so they grow into something else entirely." She shrugged.

What did that shrug mean? Abigail wondered. Did it mean, "Oh those crazy kids, you can never tell what they'll do next"? Or was it sad, resigned, even a little frightened?

"It's not dangerous, is it?"

Ariella smiled. "Well, that would depend on what you consider danger and how safe you think our lives usually are."

Abigail's head began to swim.

The woman cocked her head and said nothing for a few moments. "Don't let the food get cold. You're tired. Everything will look different in the morning."

That was the second time she'd heard that phrase tonight, Abigail thought. At least the Moonies had gotten their story straight. Then she remembered: The young man had said his *mother* would be bringing some food. The two were mother and son. The woman looked too young.

"I'm sorry. I am tired. Very tired. Good night." Abigail opened the door and waited, a rude gesture that fit her mood. The woman smiled and kissed her on both cheeks, then walked out into the night. Abigail swung the door shut, almost slamming it, turning the key twice in the lock.

"I should throw your tray out the window," she said in fury. She sat down on the bed and looked at it, breathing in the delicious aromas. She lifted the napkin off the plate.

There was warm pita bread with zaatar; a mound of minutely chopped fresh tomatoes and cucumbers, grilled chicken, and rice with lentils. There was a small ceramic bowl with hummus and warm chickpeas, and another with a few pieces of Arab pastry dipped in honey and filled with pistachio nuts. She opened the thermos. It was filled with fragrant green tea.

She washed her hands in the bathroom, then dipped the pita into the hummus. Her stomach growled with joy. Before she knew it, she had finished off the entire contents of the tray, leaving behind empty plasticware. She licked the honey off her fingers.

A bath did sound good, she thought. The tub was chipped but clean, she saw, wondering if there would actually be enough hot water. She turned on the taps. The hot water came in immediately, so hot she pulled her hand away. She lit some candles and shut off the lights, pouring in some bath salts and some perfumed oil. Shedding her sweaty airplane clothes and underwear, she slid softly beneath the bubbles.

It is so quiet here, she thought, closing her eyes. There was only the sound of the wind through the mountains and the call of some evening birds. The water was so soft, like cream, smoothing her dry, aging skin.

She found her mind wandering in darkness until it finally stopped, settling down in a quiet spot of indifference.

The towels were scratchy and thin, but clean and dry. Her skin felt like silk as she slipped on her pajamas and crawled beneath the clean sheets. She felt she shouldn't fall asleep too easily: that it would betray her anger and frustration. But as soon as her eyes closed, she drifted off.

20

The noise that woke her was a bird's deep-throated call.

Light was streaming through the old curtains, turning them to bronze. She put on her slippers and bathrobe and wandered toward the front door, opening it. She gasped.

There was the sea surrounded by red mountains beneath a red-gold and lavender sky. She stumbled along the gravel path to where a cliff edge gave one an unobstructed view of the entire area. Blackbirds unfurled their long, graceful wings, floating effortlessly in flocks from cliff to cliff. A family of gazelles grazed, the females nursing their babies, the males polishing their antlers as they nibbled on vegetation. The faint strains of Zen music drifted down to her. She walked up, curious to see where it could be coming from. Just above, on a small plateau that jutted out from the mountainside facing the sea, there was a large circular tent. People must be inside, she thought, doing yoga, or practicing Chi Qong as they took deep breaths and feasted on the view. It must be lovely, she thought, cleansing your mind and heart each morning, then filling it with such a view!

Voices drifted down to her. Praying? Chanting?

She pulled her bathrobe around her more tightly, suddenly self-conscious, making her way back to her caravan. In the morning light, it looked, if possible, even worse. But for some reason, that no longer bothered her.

She unpacked her clothes, wondering what would be appropriate. Even though it was the height of winter, here it seemed like spring. The full sun in a blue sky—something she wouldn't see in Boston again for at least another few months—had warmed the cold night air. For some reason, she found herself amused by that, the idea that all the people she knew were freezing, and she was warm.

She took out her jeans, then hesitated. What kind of community was this? Were they like the ultra-Orthodox who obsessed over how pants outlined a woman's crotch and behind (they did the same to men, but no one seemed to mind about that), outlawing them for women, calling them "men's clothing" and an "abomination"? A place which had multivolume rule books on everything from the proper length of a woman's sleeves to the colors she could wear? And if so, should she care?

She sat down on the bed, the jeans in her lap.

She wasn't here to be polite—or to be recruited. She was here to rescue her misguided daughter and show her the way home. While she was doing it, why should she care if these obviously manipulative strangers on a hilltop in the middle of the desert approved or disapproved of what she was wearing or anything else about her?

She pulled on the jeans, topping them with a sweatshirt that read: THANK GOD FOR NOT MAKING ME A MAN. If they are religious fanatics, that should certainly press their buttons, she thought with cheerful maliciousness, girding herself to do battle.

She walked down the path defiantly, but people simply looked at her and smiled, calling out: *"Boker tov"* or *"Shalom."* The men and women both wore sandals, long tunics over pants, and hair coverings: the men, bright knitted helmets that she realized must be stand-ins for the little crocheted skullcaps worn by most modern Orthodox men; the women, turbans or scarves.

Not a single person wore black.

For Abigail, that was both a relief from her worst fears as well as an unsettling fact that demanded more investigation she would have happily forgone. Black would have made everything so simple and clear-cut, relieving her of any responsibility to be fair and open-minded.

The community was small, she realized, the concrete-block houses and tents few and far between, spread over the mountaintop. Just beyond the last group of houses, one could already see the encroaching desert that lay like a vast backyard, inscrutable and overwhelming in its wildness.

Her stomach began to grumble demandingly, insisting on food. The easiest thing, of course, would have been simply to knock on Ariella's door. But since Abigail had practically chased the woman away and slammed the door in her face without even bothering to say thank you for the wonderful dinner, she felt awkward about asking for more favors.

She saw a young man getting into a pickup truck. "Excuse me," she said, wracking her brain for the Hebrew words . . . "*Selicha* . . . ?"

He looked up at her, taking his hands off the steering wheel.

"Are you one of . . ." she began, then thought better of it. "I mean . . . do you . . . live here?"

He nodded, unsmiling.

"I am a mother, the mother . . . of . . . Kayla Samuels is my daughter."

A slow smile spread over his face. "*Shalom.* We like Kayla very much."

"So do I," she wanted to shout, "and you can't have her!" Instead, she controlled herself. "Can you tell me where I can buy some food? I mean, where do you all eat?"

He pointed back in the direction from which she had come.

"There is a kitchen and a dining room. After prayers, there is breakfast," he said in the swift Hebrew of the native. She was surprised she could understand almost everything.

"Prayers? *Tefillot?*"

"Yes, we pray together in the mornings, afternoons, and evenings."

A chill went up her spine.

"Do they make you pray before they feed you?" she asked him in English.

He examined her, his eyes wide. "Make us?" he repeated in English. "*Mah zot omeret?*"

She blushed. It was the Hebrew equivalent of "What the hell are you babbling about?"

"I just wanted to know if I'll also have to pray before I can get some food."

He shrugged, amused, shaking his head, then started the engine, pulling out and starting down the road.

Well, he wasn't very nice, she thought, oddly relieved. Maybe he hadn't read the cult handbook on how to treat visiting parents. She wandered back. It couldn't hurt to check out the food. After all, they couldn't *force* her to do anything she didn't want to. Besides, they all seemed to really like Kayla. It would make sense for them to treat her mother well in the hope that she'd go away, leaving her daughter and lots of American dollars behind.

"Mom!"

She turned around. A young woman was running up the path. She had a head of wild red-gold curls tied back with a green bandana and wore a turquoise blue Bedouin galabia, embroidered with tiny red sequins. When she walked, there was a lightness to her steps that made it seem as if she were dancing to some unheard music. Her face was tanned dark gold, but even so, you could still make out a hundred freckles. Except for that, she looked like a goddess in some Italian Renaissance painting.

"MOM!" Kayla reached out, taking her mother's hands in hers and squeezing.

"Kayla!"

Abigail longed to reach out and enfold her taut young body, banishing the distance between them, but Kayla made no move to come closer.

They stood there, studying each other silently.

"You look so different," Abigail finally said, smoothing down Kayla's hair.

"Is that a bad thing?" Kayla smiled.

"No. You look like you did in high school, like your natural self. I always thought that was more beautiful than the beauty-parlor hair," she said, surprised to be voicing something she had always kept to herself.

Kayla looked surprised.

"Oh, so you two have found each other?"

It was Ariella. This time she was wearing a bright orange shirt and a long, purple skirt. On her head was a long, elaborately tied purple-and-orange head scarf. Her smile was bright. "Good morning! What a great shirt!" She pointed at Abigail. "I'd love to get one! Are you feeling better now?"

The woman's getup was ridiculous, Abigail thought, but somehow, it suited her. She looked exotic and ageless.

Ariella turned her attention to Kayla. "So, are you shocked?"

"No." Kayla shrugged, grinning. "I knew she'd come."

Abigail fumed. Did she think this was a big joke? Or was she once again, and as usual, thinking only of herself, expecting the entire universe—or at least her hapless parents—to magically adjust reality into a more congenial and accommodating place for her capricious and changing needs?

"We really need to talk, Kayla. Alone," she said pointedly.

"Ariella, I'm sorry . . ." Kayla apologized.

"Of course, no problem!" Ariella nodded. "You two spend all the time you need together. Kayla, I'll have someone cover your chores. You need to be with your mom."

Abigail watched as Kayla reached out and hugged Ariella with all the warmth that had been missing from their own greeting.

"Come," said Kayla, leading the way.

21

"Where were you? When did you get back? Did you really expect me?" Abigail said breathlessly, trying to keep up with her daughter's hurried pace. "And where are we going now?"

"I don't want you to miss Rav Natan. He usually speaks at nine thirty. I'm still at the dig at that time, so this is a real treat for me."

Abigail stood still. "The only person who I am interested in listening to is you, Kayla! You have a lot of explaining to do!"

"I know. But you'll understand more of what I tell you if you sit through just one class. I promise you."

Abigail shook her head firmly. "I'm not going anywhere. That's final." She saw her daughter's face fall, the light go out. "Look, honey, I'm exhausted. I haven't even had breakfast yet . . ."

"Of course. I'm so sorry, Mom. I've forgotten what that long flight is like. And that jet lag! Forgive me? Come, let's sit in the dining room, and I'll get you breakfast. We can talk then. Anyhow, Rav Natan gives another class in the late afternoon—the one I usually go to."

They walked slowly side by side, Kayla allowing Abigail to create the pace. "It's down there, the house with the blue flags."

It was on the side of the mountain that overlooked the most magnificent view, so that the house itself, its concrete slabs and ugly metal shutters, seemed to disappear from the picture. Inside, it was surprisingly homey, with hand-painted wooden paneling and large, framed oil paintings of scenes from the Bible done in the manner of Chagall. An Arab chef with a black-and-white kaffiyeh around his neck was arranging a small buffet table, laying out salads, cheeses, yogurts, and warm, crusty breads.

"Where do I pay?" Abigail said, filling her tray.

"It's not a hotel, Mom! It's a home. You're my guest. Our guest."

"So, how does this work? It's like a kibbutz?"

"Well, maybe, a little. But more like—"

"And the way people dress. That Ariella and her son Ben Tzion. What's their story anyway?"

"Ariella is one of the most wonderful people in the world, Mom . . ."

"I wasn't being derogatory. It's just . . . those turbans! Those colors!"

"She's a convert. Just a small-town girl from Montreal who went to visit a friend in Alaska one summer, as a lark. She had a summer romance, and wound up marrying a local boy from Anchorage who turned out to be an abusive drunk. She divorced him, and they had joint custody, until one day he took Ben Tzion out for a drive and smashed up the car. Ben Tzion was only three. He nearly died—you can still see the scars! That's when she decided to take her son and flee, going underground. One of the families that sheltered her was a rabbi and his wife, who talked to her about the Holy Land. She got on a plane and came, fell in love with the country and with Judaism. She and her son converted. She's been here for five years."

"And the ex?"

"Finally got the car crash he was looking for. He took his second wife and baby with him."

Abigail shuddered. "Horrible."

"I'm sorry. I shouldn't have told you. Here, have something to eat."

They sat quietly, eating, drinking coffee and tea made with garden herbs. Abigail felt herself grow warm and drowsy and satisfied.

"That soft white cheese was excellent," Abigail said, yawning. Even though she was no longer hungry, she spooned a little more on her pita. "What kind is it?"

"Lebanah. It's low-fat, and made from goat's milk. We make it right here in our dairy."

"You raise goats here? You have a dairy?"

"This is a fertile, self-sustaining little world, tucked away inside this awesome desolation."

The penny dropped. "It's a commune, right? These people are hippies. And this *rebbe* . . ."

"Rav . . ." Kayla corrected her, rolling her eyes.

"This *Rav* Natan . . . he's your guru?"

"Mom! These sixties concepts! Really. I feel like I'm on a rerun of *Happy Days*." She fidgeted with her paper napkin, tearing it into tiny pieces, which she then rolled into bunches that turned into flower petals. "Origami."

"Very pretty. Do they have belly-dancing classes here too?"

"MOM!"

Abigail smiled, and suddenly Kayla broke out into peals of laughter.

"I guess it does sound pretty crazy. Pretty sixties-flower-child. I never thought about that before, how you with your cultural biases would view it. I should have realized."

"Don't be so dismissive."

"I'm sorry, Mom, it's just . . . I was born two decades after the sixties. I can't relate to any of that. All I know is what I've experienced here."

"And what is that, Kayla? What have you experienced here?" Her tone rose, her face growing hard and tense. What did her privileged daughter who had been given everything have in common with these unfortunates?

Kayla looked around at the startled faces turned in their direction. "Mom, if you're finished eating, maybe we could take a walk and find a more private venue?"

Abigail put an irresistibly beautiful apple into her pocket and got up. "Let's go."

They walked silently toward a deserted spot behind a group of tall trees.

"Look how angry you are, Mom! Already! We haven't even been together twenty minutes! Why did you come at all if all you are going to do is criticize? You could have done that in an angry letter. All it would have cost you was a stamp."

A furious, bitter retort rose to Abigail's lips, full of condemnations and accusations and expressions of deep disappointment. Not useful, she told herself, feeling Adam's steady hand grip her shoulder. She took a deep calming breath, then swallowed hard. "You're right. Please forgive me. It's just that . . . with all that's going on in our lives right now . . . it wasn't easy leaving your father. I feel guilty and upset even being here."

"How is Dad?" Kayla asked, suddenly less sure of herself.

"Devastated. He is under charges that could put him in jail for life, and could cost him—us—everything we own. Shoshana could lose her home . . ."

"What?"

Abigail nodded. Let her get this through her head, she told herself, mitigating her own misgivings about destroying Kayla's newfound peace and happiness. It couldn't be helped. She was part of this, part of this family. "Anything purchased with money from the proceeds of these money transfers is liable. Your father gave your sister and her husband a considerable amount for their down payment. Your college tuition also. It would all have to be repaid to the government."

Kayla slumped, her back rounding. "I had no idea."

"No? What did you think?"

"I thought . . . I just . . ." She took a deep breath. "Look, the truth is I don't think I ever let myself think about how much was at stake, or what was hanging over your heads. I guess I was hoping that they would have so little evidence the whole thing would just collapse, like a house of cards."

"That was what we were hoping for too, of course. But in the meantime, they now have a witness."

Her heart sank. "Who?"

"That lawyer, Christopher Dorset."

Kayla was silent, gnawing her lip. "What possible reason could someone like that have to lie?"

"What? So you think he's telling the truth? You don't doubt your father, do you?" Abigail asked sharply. "Is that what's really going on, Kayla? Is that why you ran away?"

"I'd rather jump off this cliff than find out Dad's guilty, Mom. But be real! The circumstantial evidence is overwhelming! Dad admits he transferred millions, got millions in fees, met with the hedge-fund operator, in both Boston and Europe. And the hedge fund was unquestionably a cover for terrorist operations; the British have already closed it down. There's no question they made direct transfers to vicious organizations that are responsible for horrible crimes, for the deaths of hundreds—Israelis, American soldiers . . ." Her voice shook. "Gregory Van has disappeared. Apparently, Van and his fund were under British Intelligence surveillance for months when Dad stepped into the picture."

Abigail paled. "How do you know all this? It hasn't been publicized. Did Dad tell you?"

She looked at her mother, confused. "You told me, didn't you?"

"Not that I remember."

"Well, then, maybe it was Dad," she hedged. "But I didn't know about Dorset's testimony. That must be new."

"It just happened yesterday"—Abigail nodded—"though I still can't believe that anyone will take that Vegas-partying bimbo chaser seriously."

"Don't kid yourself, Mom. He's a tax attorney who knows a lot of people in high places. He knows all the ins and outs of the court system. In the hands of someone like Dorset, the law is a lethal weapon. There is no one more dangerous than a crooked lawyer." She shook her head, then suddenly looked up. "Didn't you tell me a while back that this whole thing started at the mixer for Harvard Law parents? Gregory Van doesn't have a child in Harvard Law, and as far as I know, Christopher Dorset doesn't have any children. So what were they both doing there? And—"

"Look, Kayla," Abigail cut her off wearily. "I'm glad to hear that you haven't forgotten your father and are analyzing his case. But this is not what I flew halfway around the world to discuss with you. Kayla, your father sent me here because he feels your being here is a tragedy and that it's his fault. He feels he's destroyed you."

"WHAT? That's so not true!"

"And I can tell you, of all the things he's suffered, your leaving hurt him the most."

Kayla's eyes stung. "Really? But why?"

"Come on, be honest! You know that without this court case, you'd be at Harvard right now, studying hard, planning your wedding to Seth, with a job offer waiting for you at graduation."

"Yes, exactly. So you can tell Dad this court case, this wrench in the works, was the best thing that could have ever happened to me!"

"You can't mean that!" Abigail countered, flabbergasted.

"Rav Natan says that one of the reasons God gives us troubles is to soften our hearts and make us open up to the truths we have been shutting out."

"What truths have you been shutting out, Kayla?" Abigail demanded.

"In the past, so many of the choices I've made were based on wanting people to think I was doing really well. I'd gotten into the habit of listening for unspoken messages from everyone about what I should do—from you and Dad, teachers, guys, whomever. I always felt as if everyone was giving me assignments I needed to complete with honor to earn their respect and love. And so, whether or not it mattered to me, I tried really hard so that everyone would say to themselves: 'Look at that Kayla Samuels! How well she's doing!' I never realized how hollow that was. How meaningless. For a long time, I just felt empty. I mean, I knew I was doing all the things everyone else thought was great, but in the end, it was just so stripped of any joy or meaning for me."

"I never knew . . ."

"No, how could you? I didn't know myself. Until recently."

"And now, you are sure that this"—she waved her arms in a sweeping circle—"is what you want to do?"

"I'm not sure what 'this' is or what 'to do' means. I'm not up to that yet. All I know is that I have been searching and I've found a few answers. I can't imagine leaving here before I find the rest."

"How long is that going to take?"

Kayla tensed, looking over her mother's shoulder at the desert landscape, so stark and unforgiving, altered only by eons of wind and water pressure. Some things could never be changed in your lifetime. But you had to try.

"Mom, can't you just try, for a minute, to understand what happened to me?"

"I'm listening."

Kayla sighed. "One minute, you are on top of the world, and the next your name and face are all over the place as the child of a national traitor. Millions of people you don't know hate you and your family. Your phone doesn't stop ringing. Your professors give you strange looks . . . You go for job interviews and . . . I don't want to talk about it! Look, I just needed to get away, at least until the media frenzy died down. I admit it was impulsive, and my plan was vague, even to me. But I think deep down all I wanted was to give myself a little time to pull myself together before coming back. But then something happened . . . something I didn't expect . . ."

"What? What happened to you, Kayla?"

"I started to figure out a little bit about who I am and what I don't want to be. I came here to hide. But I stayed because it's a better place, and because I'm a better person when I'm here. That's what happened."

"What possible future can this life hold for you, my darling? Whatever its charms—and I admit the view is magnificent and the people I've met so far incredibly kind—what kind of life do you envision here that will fulfill you in the long run? It's not a few weeks we are talking about. It's not summer camp. Life is a long, hard, drawn-out business, Kayla! What can a place like this possibly offer your ambition, your intelligence, your deepest needs?"

"I don't know. I just know that I'm not distraught anymore. I feel whole, and calm, and full of energy and creativity."

"Look, Kayla. You went through hell. We all did. I'm happy you've gotten back some strength and clarity. Why not use those things now to regain all you've worked so hard for, all the things you've always wanted, instead of giving up?"

"Aren't you listening to me, Mom? I don't know if I want them anymore . . . if I ever wanted them."

Abigail leaned forward, stunned. "How can you say that? You always chose your own paths, made your own decisions."

Kayla looked at her sideways. "Is that right? Is that what you remember?"

Abigail stared at her, confused. "Yes. That's what I remember."

"Well, I remember writing poetry, and how next thing I knew, I was being dragged off to math tutors, who convinced me poetry was a waste of time . . ."

"Your math grades were pulling down your entire average! We didn't care if you studied English, or writing. We just wanted you to have the opportunity to choose the best college . . ."

"Yes. You were only thinking of me . . ." Kayla snorted, humming the tune from *Man of La Mancha*: *. . . Whatever I may do or say, I'm only thinking of you. In my body it's well-known, there is not one selfish bone . . .*

It was disgustingly unfair, Abigail thought. "We encouraged your writing!"

"But as a hobby, right?"

Abigail hesitated. "You were the one who stopped writing! You were the one who decided to study law!"

"Because there was no money in poetry! Look at how you treat Joshua. Like a loser, no matter how he struggles."

Abigail wiped beads of sweat from her forehead. "We've supported your brother. But there are limits. An adult has to take responsibility for himself at a certain point."

"Mom, it has always been about money. That house we lived in, all that money we spent fixing it up to impress the neighbors. What was that supposed to teach me? And so, big surprise, I did everything I could to prepare myself for a life of moneymaking and money-spending, and rich-husband-attracting . . . And that was the real message you and Dad were so good at, with all those big Sabbath dinners with so many people Dad hoped to impress and butter up and reel in as clients. The Sabbath wasn't a day of rest at all, just business as usual, no?"

Abigail felt breathless, so hurt she could not speak.

"How can you paint this ugly picture of us?"

"I'm not painting anything, Mom. It's a photograph. I'm sorry the lighting isn't better, and you find it unflattering."

Abigail felt her stomach ache. She was suddenly weary. God, she realized, might be compassionate and forgiving, but children were not. Their delicate antennae picked up every lapse, every hypocrisy, every gap between what one preached and what one practiced.

Was that really all it amounted to? All those years of trying, sincerely, so hard to bring up a family that honored tradition and were upstanding members of the community? Were all the things she and Adam thought they were doing really just a façade? And now, because of some unexpected outside force, had the camouflage been ripped away? Was the portrait her daughter had sketched the truth, or an ugly distortion? Worse, was it the picture of Dorian Gray?

"If that is how you really feel, that your father and I are moneygrubbing hypocrites, then there is nothing left for me to say. I wish you well, Kayla. You were my youngest child, my little heart. I spoiled you. Made excuses for you. You were always such an extremist. The year you decided to be a poet, you woke up in the morning and wrote poetry. You wrote poetry during algebra and refused to participate in gym. You barely passed math and science, and they were even talking about having you repeat the year. Did we complain? No. We sat on the sofa and listened to you read. We went to school and battled your 'insensitive' teachers. We accepted everything you thought; everything you said about yourself. You were so convincing all the time. And every few months you were convincing about the exact opposite. And we let you get away with it. We paid for tutors. Paid for classes. Begged published authors to read your incoherent, childish scribblings as if you were the next Carl Sandburg. We were in awe of you. And, I'll admit, a bit terrified also. You always knew better. And now you also know better. Well, let me tell you something . . ."

But she couldn't say another word, feeling a sudden, almost frightening loss of control, her stomach throbbing as she gave in to unwanted, uncontrollable paroxysms of grief-filled tears.

"Mom . . ." Kayla reached out, touching her shoulder.

Abigail shook her off. "All my life, I believed in God. I tried to be hospitable and kind. Yes, I invited your father's business contacts, because that's what your father wanted. Yes, maybe I did get too caught up in redoing our home, making beautiful rooms for you and Josh and Shoshana because that's what I thought my children wanted! That's not a mortal crime! All I ever thought I was doing was making everybody happy! It was NEVER what I wanted. Never!" She choked, blinded.

"Mom, I'm so sorry . . . I didn't mean . . . I just felt . . . It was that woman in the lawyer's office, that day I went to New York. She was staring at me. And then I saw her call another one of the secretaries over, and they sort of put their heads together and looked in my direction. I finally got up and went over to them. 'Is there something wrong?' I asked.

"They pushed a copy of *Newsweek* at me. 'We were just wondering if you were that Samuels.' It was a picture of Dad in handcuffs being led from his office."

"Oh, Kayla!"

"I didn't know what to do. But it finally dawned on me that I WAS that Samuels. And that my life, as I knew it, whatever happened, was over, everything I worked so hard for, everything that I'd invested in. And it wasn't because of something I'd done, or hadn't done. There were simply forces out there beyond my control. And so, I decided, given that that was the way the world really worked, as opposed to the way it was supposed to work . . . the way you'd brought me up to think it worked . . ."

"The world has changed. That's not my fault or your father's . . ."

"Exactly! Which is why I decided right then and there to finally take some control, to do something that made sense to *me*. I saw all those dead fish washing up on the shore and knew I had to get as far away as possible from the tsunami coming my way . . ."

"Abandon us? Abandon your father?"

"I wasn't thinking about you," she admitted. It sounded shameless in her ears. Shameless and honest. If she'd learned nothing else, it was that the two often went together, and it was just as well to be truthful about it and stop kidding herself that she was a nice person. She wasn't. Nothing in her spoiled upbringing had punished selfishness and lack of consideration. And even though she liked to tell herself that she was a better person than she could have turned into—which, all things considered, was probably true—at the present moment, she didn't feel particularly proud of that.

"So you've changed your mind. Again. And we are to blame. Is that it? So, tell me, Kayla, what is it now? What do you want, or think you want, now?"

Kayla stiffened, bracing herself as if against a strong wind. The negating maternal power turned in her direction with full force would take all her strength to withstand, she thought a bit desperately. But to let her mother win was to lose her life. It was all or nothing. "I know why you're here. But it won't work. I'm not coming back to your and Daddy's idea of the perfect life. Mom, look at your own life. Where has all this dogma, following all these rules, gotten you?"

It was as if her daughter had deliberately taken aim and jabbed viciously at a broken arm or leg swathed in bandages.

Where was she, indeed?

She tried to think of a response that would be so devastatingly brutal to her daughter's ego it would end the conversation then and there. But it would have taken an energy and sense of righteousness she no longer possessed. Instead, she took the apple out of her pocket and bit into it. It was deliciously sweet and a bit tart, with that perfect crackle and spurt of juice. "Do they grow these here as well?"

Kayla nodded, relieved. "Yes. Apples in the desert. We're like the people who lived here thousands of years ago. They also fled society. They lived simple lives, provided for their own needs, and left behind scrolls that still have the world in awe."

"And that's what you want to be? An Essene? Living in the desert, writing prophetic scrolls for the next century?"

She smiled, shaking her head. "I don't know what I want to be. That is the greatest gift of all. Uncertainty. Time to choose, without pressure. Time to commune with my own soul. And whatever path I choose, I understand now, as I never have before, that the path itself has to be its own reward, no matter where it leads. Because you and Dad are living proof that anything can happen along the way. You can sacrifice, and sludge through and suffer, and spend most of your life doing things you hate, to reach some elusive pot of gold. Yet no matter how much you follow the straight and narrow, you might never get there. The journey itself is your life, and that has to be good, whatever the eventual goal that may or may not be reached. It doesn't matter if you succeed or you fail, because the journey is everything, and they can never take that away from you."

Abigail listened to her daughter. Unwillingly, she felt something suddenly resonate in her soul, something unexpected. "I would like to join you in those classes, Kayla."

22

The tent, large and bright, seemed like something that should contain three rings and a clown, Abigail thought as she made her way toward it. It was late afternoon. She had managed to fall back asleep after breakfast and to awake just in time for a late lunch. She looked around for Kayla, but she was nowhere to be seen.

The sun was going down over the mountains.

She took out her cell phone. Kayla had suggested that she try to catch the phone signal, as the tent was the only place on the mountain where it was sometimes strong enough to use. There was a dial tone.

"Hello?"

"Abigail?"

Adam's voice, coming to her on this hilltop in the desert, was a shock.

"Yes." She gripped the phone, the distance between them suddenly unbearable.

"How are you?"

"I'm here, in the desert. I'm with Kayla. She's fine, Adam, really. You wouldn't believe it. She looks tan and peaceful and happy. It's not what you think . . ."

He exhaled. "Are you telling me the truth?"

"Yes. I'm not sure what this place is, but it's not a simple thing like a cult. At least, I don't think so. I'll know more after I meet the Rav who leads the group. Tell me about yourself."

There was silence.

"Adam?" Her brows contracted as she stared into the darkness of the little plastic receiver.

"Abby, someone has firebombed the synagogue."

The sky suddenly seemed to darken. "Oh God, no!"

"No one was hurt. But they burnt down the study hall. The books, hundreds of them, have been destroyed."

Her stomach ached. "Do they know who did it? Or why?"

"No . . . but . . ." He stopped.

"Adam . . . please!"

"There was graffiti."

She didn't say anything, hardly daring to breathe. "Tell me!"

"It said: 'Jews are the real terrorists. Hang Samuels . . .'"

"Adam . . ."

"This is exactly what the rabbi was afraid of."

"If it wasn't about you, it would have been about something else. Every time Israel defends itself, the nutcases scribble their filth all over the world. It happens."

"Yes. Just not in Boston. Not on Beacon Street." The words were strangled.

"Did the rabbi call you?"

"No. I called him."

"What did you say?"

"What *could* I say? That I'm sorry. So very, very sorry."

"And what did he say?"

"He told me he was very busy and couldn't talk. Then he hung up."

"Adam . . . I should be with you."

"Abby, you are exactly where you need to be—with our daughter. Have you met the *someone* yet?"

"Who?"

"The someone of 'I've met someone.'"

Honestly, she hadn't given it a single thought. "No, no, not yet. But I can't believe it's serious. Kayla is so confused."

"I've spoken to Seth. But I didn't tell him everything. I was hoping you could convince her to come to her senses before he realizes what's going on . . . He has been just wonderful to me, Abby. He has been doing the most amazing research. You wouldn't believe the information he's come up with! Even my lawyers are shocked. I can't tell you . . . Abby? What do you think?"

She wasn't thinking anything. She stood before the sun sinking down into the mountains. Every moment, it presented a different face, a new creation, its colors merging, deepening, then fading; shapes coming into focus, then transforming, melting, fading into the background. To miss such a sunset was to miss a hundred masterpieces that would be lost forever, she thought, breathless, drinking it in moment by moment, letting it fill her with quiet joy. She felt mesmerized, almost hypnotized.

"Abigail?"

"I'm sorry. I was just . . . the sunset . . . I'm on a mountaintop facing the sea. Adam, if you could be here with me . . ."

"I didn't realize you had time for sightseeing." His voice was cold and strained.

She crossed her arms over her chest, hugging herself, chilled. "Adam. I'm still alive. I'm not going to apologize for that. I'll do what you want me to do, but don't take that away from me."

"I'm sorry," he said, and she thought his voice sounded suddenly husky. "I'm just . . . it's so hard. I miss you."

"Adam . . . I love you. I'll hurry. Take care of yourself. Don't forget to take your pills. What are you eating . . . ?"

But before he could answer, the phone connection suddenly went dead. She tried to redial, but it was too late. The signal had disappeared.

"We're about to start," someone whispered in her ear.

She looked up. It was an older woman with the lean body of a teenager wearing all blue with a red-cotton scarf and long, dangling earrings. She smiled, beckoning. "Come."

Oil lamps and candles lit the interior, which was filled with pillows and a few scattered plastic chairs. Floor space, she saw, was already filling up.

"Would you like a chair?" the woman asked. Abigail nodded gratefully. She sat down, waiting.

Suddenly she saw everyone jump up. She automatically joined them, unsure what had happened. Then she saw him.

He looked like a kid, she thought, his body strong and beautifully proportioned, like a trekker's. The long sidecurls spilling down to his shoulders from beneath a white knitted skullcap reminded her of an Old World Chassid's, except for their silky blondness. His eyes, wide set, were of indeterminate color in the dim light, but she imagined they must be blue. A honey-colored beard outlined his slender face and high cheekbones, surprisingly delicate for such a large man. His wide forehead glistened with light and also (she admitted to herself almost reluctantly) with intelligence and youthfulness. He wore a plain white button-down shirt whose long sleeves were neatly folded just below his elbows, and simple dark pants. He wore no black hat—that easily noted symbol of religious affiliation with the ultra-Orthodox. And yet, she noted that the fringes of his *tzitzis* hung out over the waistband of his pants, clearly marking him as one who was not modern Orthodox either. The skullcap was the white cap of the Breslavers, those lovers of Jewish mysticism and song, followers of the dead *rebbe* buried in Ukraine who had left behind only his cryptic books, but no Chassidic dynasty.

Where, exactly, this person fit into the gradations of religious observance she could not decide. In fact, he reminded her of guitarists sitting on the pavement in Haight-Ashbury in the sixties although that was years before he was born.

She leaned over to the woman in blue. "Who is that?"

"Our teacher. Rav Natan." Her face shone.

Abigail shifted uncomfortably. She'd expected someone older, greyer, fatter, swathed in the usual black uniform. Looking around the room, she realized nothing was as she'd imagined. In front of her, a woman in harem pants and a Himalayan Arveda Yoga sweatshirt sat next to a black woman in a red turban. An Asian girl in boots and a red beret and pink tights, her legs stretched out before her, gently massaged the forehead of a young blond girl whose head rested on her knees. A man with a grey beard, wearing a huge purple-and-orange skullcap, sat in a lotus position. Next to him sat a grandmother in green-and-black pajama pants topped by a black-flowered skirt and a purple blouse. Silver chains dangled around her neck. A heavy woman in boots and a jeans skirt was leaning against her, hugging her. And in the back, among the men, Abigail was amazed to see the Arab chef, his kaffiyeh wrapped around his neck, standing and waiting for the lecture to begin.

"No matter how dark our lives may be," Rav Natan began, "one need never despair. Real despair comes from feeling abandoned. The source of all sadness is in this loneliness. You feel there is no God, and this belief is the source of anger, depression, destructiveness. But in that fog, in the lowest depths, that is where He is, waiting for you. And what your heart desires most is to find Him, as a baby seeks its mother, a child its father."

Abigail listened, watching as he drew his long fingers gently, contemplatively through his beard. His smile was lopsided and charming.

She looked around her at the rapt faces. They were all in love with him; that was plain. Their eyes were dark and wide; they rested their cheeks on folded fingers, like young women in Monet paintings. They looked at him as she had recently gazed at the sunset.

"But in order to connect with God, you first have to find yourself. Self-discovery is the purpose of creation, and ordeals are the way God stretches us, showing us, who we really are."

Abigail suddenly sat up.

"The Hebrew word for ordeal, *nesayon,* contains the word for miracle, *nes.* A person looks at a wall and says: 'I could never climb over it.' But if that wall imprisoned you in a concentration camp, and you were being chased by Nazis and their guard dogs, you would scramble up that wall and jump to the other side. You would find that you did have it in you all along. You just didn't know it. But as wonderful as that would be, it wouldn't be miraculous.

"Where, then, is the miracle in our ordeals? It is when God asks you to do the impossible."

Abigail felt her heart beat faster, the sweat break out on her forehead.

He suddenly stopped, looking up and into the faces of everyone in the room.

"If God told you to jump off a cliff and promised to catch you, would you jump?"

There was an exchange of anxious, amused glances, as people tried to decide the right answer, the answer he wanted.

"If you knew, absolutely, that it was God talking to you, and you weren't hallucinating, of course you would! God can ask you to do the impossible, because it is impossible for *you,* not for *Him.* When we are faced with such an ordeal, we should not ask if it's *possible* for us to overcome it; we must ask if it's *necessary.* If the answer is yes, and you are willing to make that leap, then He will catch you. But you have to make the first move. You have to lift up your feet. You cannot see who you are meant to become from where you are standing now. You can only see it once you arrive, when you allow God to stretch you beyond your real limitations."

Abigail felt light-headed, as if she'd been given a great revelation.

"*Lech-Lecha.* Leave who you are now and go to who you were meant to be."

She felt the tears suddenly, unexpectedly flow down her cheeks. Like the Mona Lisa who gave all onlookers the sensation that she was staring directly at them, and only them, Rav Natan looked to Abigail as if he was talking to her, saying those words only to her. She searched vainly in her purse for a tissue.

"Here." Someone handed one to her.

"Thank you." She blew her nose, and wiped her eyes.

"Do you need another?"

She looked up. It was a young man with tangled dark curls, tragic green eyes, and a three-day stubble.

"I'm Kayla's mother," she whispered with some strange instinct that he already knew.

She got up, wanting desperately to go somewhere private. Her feet wobbled as if they'd been frostbitten. Her back ached. Her heart felt as if it had grown in her chest. She placed her hand over it, counting the beats.

"Are you all right?"

It was him again.

"I don't know," she answered. He took her arm and led her outside. He brought a chair out for her, and she sat down.

"I'm Daniel," he said. "Your daughter's friend."

"Yes," she murmured. "I thought so."

"Really?"

He spoke in English, which surprised her. He looked so Israeli. "Is Kayla here?"

"Yes. She's inside. You were measuring your heartbeats. Do you have heart problems?"

"No . . . that is . . . I have a mitral valve prolapse. But so do millions of others. It's not dangerous."

"Maybe you should lie down. Is your heart racing? Do you take beta blockers? I'm a doctor," he said simply. "Let me help you. Was there something in the lecture that upset you?"

"I don't know." She shook her head. "It's just that . . . I'm too old to jump, too old to grow. The trials God has given me are really too hard for me. Impossible." She felt the tears welling over. "I'm not a bad person. And God is about to strip me of everything I have, including my self-respect, and my good name."

"Rav Natan once taught us that when God removes our familiar boundaries, when He changes the landscape of our lives, it's the scariest thing in the world." He nodded. "But also the most blessed. A second chance to be born—not like a baby, but with all our knowledge. A chance to start over."

"I was happy with who I was!" But even as the words left her lips, she felt the sting of regret, wanting to take them back. That isn't true, she admitted to herself.

"You will be happy again."

"How do you know?"

"You are already in the air. You've already leapt."

She stared at him, and past him at the little holes poked in the sky letting in the abundance of celestial light that had traveled from billions of light-years away. She felt a strange sensation as this light poured through her, entering through a tiny crack in her desperation that she hadn't known existed. It would not stop. Undeserved, unearned, it refused to listen to reason, gathering strength, flooding all her senses with unearned hope.

23

"Mom?"

The sound of Kayla's voice brought her back to earth.

"Kayla. I'm here."

She saw her daughter exchange intimate glances with the young man, the unspoken expression of married people and lovers. Her heart sank. He was glue. Superglue. And she had been assigned to pry her daughter loose.

"So you've met my friend Daniel."

"Yes. He's been very kind, but I really think I need to lie down. Will you come with me?"

"Of course." Kayla reached down and took her arm, helping her up.

"Here, let me . . ." Daniel offered.

"NO! I mean, thank you, it won't be necessary. I think I need a little alone time with my daughter, if that's all right. I don't mean to be rude."

She saw the two of them signal to each other with their hands and eyebrows. She imagined it must be code for "meet you later, honey, when the old lady is disposed of." She felt like the meddling busybody in some Noel Coward comedy, trying to thwart the obvious. She would no doubt achieve the same farcical results. Besides, she had her own problem, she realized. A gigantic one. She actually found Daniel more congenial than Seth, who had always intimidated her a bit. Also more attractive. He seemed more rugged, more manly. Seth had always secretly reminded her of those male dolls manufactured to serve as Barbie's boyfriend. She secretly blamed him for Kayla's leaving. If he had been more of a man, if he had supported her . . .

"I'll see you later." Daniel nodded to them both, turning back into the lit tent. She watched Kayla's eyes follow him greedily until he disappeared.

"So, how did you like the lecture?"

Abigail was silent for a moment. "Tell me, Kayla, you didn't say anything to him . . . your Rav Natan . . . about . . . our situation, did you?"

"What do you mean?"

"Ah, I was just wondering if that speech was custom-designed for me . . ."

Kayla shrugged. "As I've already told you, Mom, lots of people here have had ordeals. It's that kind of place."

"So I gather. A place to run away to. What is your friend Daniel running from?"

She met her mother's eyes. "Sorrow."

"Yes. He has sad eyes."

Kayla nodded, some of the brightness fading from her own.

"He says he's a doctor. A medical doctor?"

She nodded. "But he doesn't practice. Not anymore."

"He seems a bit young to have retired."

"It's a long story."

"And what's the story with the black woman and the Asian girl? And that Arab chef with the kaffiyeh who comes to lectures? They aren't even Jewish."

"They aren't. There are people here from all over the world."

"Really? How did they even find out about this place?"

"Through the Internet. Rav Natan's lectures are online, translated into several languages. Anyone can read them, or hear them."

"Why would a Muslim or Christian or Buddhist be so fascinated by what a rabbi has to say? And why, in Heaven's name, would they travel all the way here just to be near him?"

"Why did Madonna start learning Kabala?" Kayla shrugged. "People all over the world are overwhelmed. Things are happening too fast. Awful things. All the red lines have been crossed. There isn't a single person alive who isn't terrified about the future. No place seems safe anymore. People are searching for a way back, a way out. The old religions seem so helpless."

"So, you're founding a new religion here?"

She grinned. "Nothing so exciting, Mom. We are just listening to some of the old wisdom that has been forgotten. Trying to figure out a better way."

That actually makes sense, Abigail thought. "But what's with the clothes?"

Kayla laughed. "I also thought it was weird at first. I think people here just shed whatever they'd brought with them because the climate here is so different. And then, a certain style just evolved: comfortable, modest, sun-friendly . . ."

"But why the turbans? And those colors?"

"A few of the married women decided to follow Orthodox Jewish tradition and cover their hair. But they made the custom their own, doing it with elaborate headdresses and bright colors. My own theory is that it's sort of a protest against the idea that women should cover themselves up in order to become invisible."

"They do look pretty!"

Kayla nodded, pleased.

"But why Israel? Why the desert?"

"Some people say that just like some places have an abundance of sunshine or rain, Israel has an abundance of God."

Could this be true? Abigail thought, strangely elated and even a bit frightened by such a concept.

"And the desert has always been God's crucible, hasn't it? It's got no distractions. It's easier to find God here. Easier to find yourself. That makes sense, doesn't it, Mom? And if you're honest with yourself, you'll admit that you're in the same boat. We all are."

Abigail was silent.

"So, what did you think of the lecture?"

"He's a very stirring speaker. But maybe that's because I am so vulnerable right now."

"Did you do the meditation? That would have clarified things for you."

"What meditation?"

"He always ends each session with a guided meditation."

"No, I left before that. It's . . . I'm . . . too . . ."

"What? Too skeptical?"

"Let's just say I don't know if I could force this stiff body into a lotus position."

"Mom, I know you're afraid. But that's normal. It's terrifying to open yourself up like that. I was so frightened the first time. Being alone with your thoughts is the scariest thing in the world."

Abigail stiffened. "I'm not afraid."

Kayla looked at her mother with compassion: "You've never had a real communication with God, have you?"

Abigail felt her insides contract. The words scrambled hotly to her lips: "Don't *presume* to tell me what kind of relationship I've had with God! Do you really think you are the first person to discover 'the meaning of life'? I've been around a little longer than you! Everything you think you've just discovered is old news."

"I can see I've hurt you."

Of course, that was true.

"Promise me you'll try to meditate. Just for ten minutes. It isn't hard. Just cleanse your mind of everything."

"I've had enough . . ." Abigail said firmly, rushing down the path back to her room, her heart beating wildly. She slammed the door, then leaned back against it, feeling dizzy with anger, and sorrow. Could Kayla be right? Was she terrified of facing a God she didn't really know, had never encountered despite a lifetime of faithful ritual observance? Or was it herself she was afraid to meet? Had it all been a waste, then? Years invested in faith with nothing to show, and one minute alone with herself and God too much to bear?

She walked out of the room into the night. There were so many, many stars! A kaleidoscope of diamonds that had been hovering over her for a lifetime unseen, hidden by city lights. An amazed shudder went through her.

She closed her eyes, sinking down to the ground, her back resting against a tree. Her mind went suddenly blank—a white screen with no subtitles, a white nothingness, an emptiness. This is stupid, she thought, jumping up and opening her eyes. But some mysterious force pulled her down again. She closed her eyes once more, leaning back. She sat awkwardly at first, sensitive to the slightest discomfort, shifting to make her legs more comfortable, taking her elbows off her knees. Gradually, she found a place for all her limbs, which seemed to melt away, moving out of her consciousness. She was no longer a body, she realized, just a yearning soul crying out in the wilderness in its terrifyingly separateness. She took deep breaths, trying to keep herself from panicking.

Then came the images. She glimpsed a sea turtle gliding along the ocean floor in the Great Barrier Reef. Giant sea lions basking in the sun on a riverbank in Alaska. The sunset over the ocean in Kauai.

Maybe this is what it's like to die—she suddenly thought. Your consciousness lives on with all its experiences and memories, detached from anything physical. You have no arms with which to embrace, or build, or fight. No legs to carry you from place to place. No eyes to see outward, only inward toward memories. No taste, but the memory of taste.

The living were blessed with powers to create. When these powers were gone, they never returned, she understood for the first time, startled at how simple a thing that was, how simple and true. She felt like mourning everything she had not yet done, filled with a new ambition to use her lips to pray while she still could; her tongue to taste delicious fruits while she still could; to dance, to kiss, to speak, to sing a beautiful new song. So many things that only the living can do for such a short time.

"Dear God, help my family. Help me to find You again."

For the first time in a very long time, she could hear God listening. She understood how distant they had become, and how lonely she had been for Him. And how lonely He had been for her.

"Mom, there you are! I was so worried . . ."

Abigail got up and held out her arms, enfolding her daughter's young body, all the years stored up ahead of her to feel and experience, all the years to create those things she would take with her into eternity. Who was she, or Adam, or anyone, to take those choices from her, the essence of being alive, the freedom to choose?

"I'm so sorry, Mom! I never wanted to hurt you or Dad! I've been incredibly selfish. Dad needs me. And . . . Seth. I've treated him really badly. Maybe you are right. Maybe I should go home."

"NO! NO!" Abigail wanted to shout: "Don't do it! Don't weaken! Don't listen to me! Or your father. We don't know anything!" Instead, she found herself thinking of Adam, alone in the house thousands of miles away. She was here to plead his case, to wrench her daughter back to familiar ground, to the only life they had both ever known.

"That would make your father and Seth very happy, Kayla," she said, betraying them both.

24

When Kayla rose for work early the next morning, her body felt heavy and her mind dizzy with uncertainty. For weeks, she had been jumping out of bed joyfully, eager for the day to come. She had come to love the tingling cold as she walked to and from the showers to her tent, the hot cup of coffee, the easy conversation with Daniel and the others as they bumped down the road to the tel. Recently, the dig had begun to yield some fascinating artifacts—coins, utensils, even a gold ring. There was a growing excitement in the act of plunging her shovel into the ancient earth, as if it were a treasure hunt, or a story whose exciting plot unfolded day by day.

But now she was torn. Was it merely obligation and guilt? Or were her parents right? If she went back now, she could talk to her professors, even patch things up with Seth. She might even be able to redeem herself with her father although she was undoubtedly more useful to him exactly where she was. But he didn't know that. By moving back into the house, she could give both her parents true moral support. In no time at all, she could get her old life back. The question was: Did she want it back? Were those words she had spoken to her mother true, or a cover? Was she tossing away her future on a childish whim, an act which could never be undone? Or was staying the most adult decision she had ever made?

She looked up at the great mountain towering over her, and it seemed to look back, as if it were trying to tell her something. But what? It wasn't like looking into a mirror, she thought, which reflects back what you want to see, the sum of all your artifices. The opposite. It somehow forced you to look inside at all the things you wished to hide, even from yourself. Was it not enormous hubris, she asked herself, to even try to live in such a place? It was so harsh and pitiless, forcing human beings to draw a line in the sand between life and nothingness. Only so far, we say to the desert. Here, at this line, life begins and flourishes. We can do this, make this bloom, because we are human. We can keep back the tide of encroaching death. We are stronger than the silence. We can fill the air with sound.

Equally hard to believe was that a settlement filled with people who had had the same religion, rituals, and God as her own family had lived and flourished here two thousand years before. They had come here looking for purity, brotherhood, and peace. They believed it was possible, if not for themselves, then for future generations, prophesying in their scrolls about the coming of a different age, a holy age when mankind would once again find its way, undoing all the human harm that had been wreaked on Eden.

She thought about The Talmidim, this strange community in the middle of nowhere, led by its strange preacher, a man who had roamed the ashrams of India and the mountains of the Himalayas, only to find that all he learned pointed him back to his own roots and the land of his birth. Like those before him, he had come with some followers to this place, trying like them to plant the seed of a new kind of human community, based on old rules that had simply been forgotten. And others, hearing about it, had followed, many of them drifters, most of them wounded, in one way or another, by human selfishness or violence, people who had tried and failed to find a home elsewhere in more hospitable surroundings. In this unforgiving, almost inhuman environment, they had finally found community, and friendship, and hope. As they huddled together on this small mountaintop, they nourished these things, the way a man lost in a snowstorm fiercely nurtures and protects a small flame he has managed to ignite.

It was impractical, silly really. How would they ever support themselves?

From goat's milk? From tourists? From selling tapes of Rav Natan's lectures on busy intersections to indifferent drivers? From their savings? And when the savings ran out, then what?

She looked around at what they had planted: the baobab tree, brought as a seed from Africa; the ficus and the fast-growing cotton silk; the myrrh and frankincense bushes; and the Sodom apple trees, which let loose thousands of pieces of fluff, each holding a seed in its center that the wind carried for miles. She looked up at the top of the mountain, where the fig trees flourished. Fed by an artesian well that had taken a hundred years to travel through the mountains from Jerusalem, the water had finally reached this spot to nourish their roots. It was unimaginable.

Looking at all this flourishing growth made you think God had changed His mind and decided to bless this place after all, plucking it out of desolation. It made you believe in miracles, in taking leaps of faith.

She loved it.

But what of tomorrow? she thought. What would it be like here in the summer, if it was so hot in the middle of the winter? The heat would be unbearable, although there were those who had borne it. And what of next year, and the year after?

Once again, she felt that tightness in her chest she thought she had left behind her forever, along with her textbooks and day planner. It made her want to cry. She didn't know what to do. Her gut was telling her one thing, her mind another.

"Kayla, the bus is here," Judith said, touching her shoulder lightly, peering into her face, concerned. "Are you all right?"

"I don't know. I didn't really sleep much last night."

"Sometimes that happens to me too after Rav Natan's lectures. My mind just keeps running in circles, trying to absorb everything."

"It's that too, but . . . My mother is here."

"Yes. I heard."

"She wants me to leave."

Judith pouted, making a funny "sorry" face. "And what do you want to do?"

"I don't know." Kayla shook her head. "I'm beginning to wonder if I haven't made a terrible mistake."

Judith seemed disappointed. "Kayla, it's not a question of a mistake. Nothing is lost. You can leave anytime. I told you that. As long as you think the time is right for you, that you've taken all you can, all you need. As long as you don't go back to the old life."

"If I leave here, I don't know what other life I *can* go back to, Judith. It's the only one I've ever known. I have no idea what another life would even look like."

"It would look like this." She spread out her arms.

"Not in Brookline . . . Not in America."

"You can make changes. You can make it look any way you want. It's up to you. But if you are still unsure, then you shouldn't go. At least not yet."

"But my parents need me. I'm abandoning them."

"Is that what your mother said?"

"Yes, more or less."

"Or is that just what you heard? Do they want you to go back to help *them*? Or do they want you to go back because they think *they* are helping *you*? It's not the same thing, you know."

Kayla thought about it, winding her way thoughtfully toward the bus.

Daniel was waiting for her.

"How did it go? How is your mother feeling?"

"She wants me to go back with her."

His face fell.

They sat down side by side on the rickety seats.

"Daniel, I don't know what to do," she whispered, leaning against him. The strong young bones of his shoulder held her up.

He leaned his head toward her, kissing her forehead. "I know," he whispered back.

Abigail felt the sun warming her eyelids. She sat up, a smile on her face as she looked around her at the small, dismal room. Who would have ever thought she could be happy in such surroundings? My real wants are so small, so basic, she realized suddenly. A roof over my head. A bed. A bathroom. Clean clothes. Simple food prepared simply. She washed her face and brushed her teeth, then opened the door. The glorious view of the mountains and the sea filled all her senses.

She would call Adam. She would explain this to him. She would explain that their daughter Kayla had found something precious and real and that she should be left alone to reap all the joys of her discovery. She would tell him that he mustn't pressure Kayla to come back. That it would be a selfish thing, not a kindness, not to her benefit. They mustn't push her back into the old life. It wasn't going to make her happy.

It hadn't made them happy.

He wouldn't like it, she considered. He might even be a bit sad at first, at the thought of his daughter having chosen so different a path from their own, from what they'd envisioned for her. But he would get over it. After all, he really did love Kayla, and all he had ever wanted for her was a good life. Talking her into coming back now would only fulfill a selfish need for companionship, someone with whom they could share their misery. Why would he want that? After all, he had sent her, Abigail, away, willing to live in that house all by himself, for Kayla's sake. He had prevented Shoshana from coming to visit for her own good. Why would he insist on having Kayla there if it wasn't in her best interests? That wasn't like Adam.

She would straighten this out with him today, then she would talk to Kayla. She would tell her how she really felt, that she mustn't go anywhere. That she must explore the things she had discovered and her relationship with this Daniel. Just the fact that she had formed another romantic relationship so quickly meant that her feelings toward Seth did not have the depth and passion needed for a long, happy marriage. It was a blessing Kayla had realized it now rather than after ten years of miserable married life filled with innocent children who would have been damaged beyond repair by their parents' incompatibilities, no?

She smiled at the mountains, the green treetops, the sparkling sea. "*Boker tov*, Brothers and Sisters!" she called out to passing strangers in sandals and long skirts and knitted skullcaps, who waved and smiled back.

She didn't know anyone here, and no one knew her. There was nothing to be ashamed of, nothing to explain or justify. She put one foot behind the other, improvising a little dance, twirling in the cool mountain air. Maybe it was all that bromide that was acting like tranquilizers, but she suddenly felt fantastic.

25

Adam opened the door to his study. Thick, open folders covered his once-pristine work space, and boxes of legal documents were piled high on the floor. Just the sight of it made his heart sink with misery. And yet, what choice did he have?

He had been targeted by forces he had not known existed in the world, forces that wanted to destroy him, everyone he loved, and all he had worked to achieve over a lifetime of honest toil. For what purpose or possible benefit, he could not imagine.

But then, he had never been a man with a prolific imagination, preferring nonfiction to fiction, history and biography to novels. He was a man who, until recently, slept well at night, untroubled by visions of mysterious disasters lurking in the shadows that kept more sensitive souls awake. He had actually always been rather proud of that. Now he thought that perhaps such a life and such a temperament had not prepared him for the world he lived in, a world in which the suddenness of change had replaced the slow, incremental buildup of transitions made naturally from one state to the next, a life where rewards and punishments flowed inevitably from one's own choices and actions.

Now the world seemed hopelessly muddled, good and evil mixing together like paint, producing hues of neither color. Accusations and innuendos ruled the airwaves, and the people most talked about were those least admired. No one cared about guilt or innocence anymore, just consequences. Would the murderer sit in jail, or be playing golf when his lawyers got him off? Would the famous, useless party girl arrested for DUI face lockup, or community service? Would the rock star arrested for assault, pedophilia, or indecent acts sell more or fewer records?

He could not accept that. Whatever the consequences, what was most important to him was his good name. He was willing to sacrifice almost anything to protect that. Reluctantly, he pulled back his chair, confronting the documents as one would face off with an enemy with whom one was in mortal combat.

He had gone over them again and again, reading the carefully constructed lies meant to convince the world of his culpability in the worst crimes imaginable to a man of his character and position in life.

It had been so hard.

His lawyers had ascertained that everything Dorset had told Adam was untrue: He and Van weren't old college buddies, nor did either of them have children in Harvard Law. So what *had* they both been doing there?

The answers had been brewing inside him, rising up slowly from deep within his consciousness. And then, one morning, he had opened his eyes and found the solution staring him in the face: It had not been a chance meeting at all. Both Van and Dorset had been there simply because they knew *he* was going to be there. The whole thing had been a careful, lethal, setup. He was simply the "mark"—as he knew con men like to call their victims.

This idea, so long resisted, overwhelmed him with fury and fear.

Why? he asked himself a million times. What had he ever done that Christopher Dorset, with whom he had had only brief, cordial relations, and Gregory Van, who was a complete stranger, would want to ruin his life? What possible good had come to Dorset from A. J. Hurling's money being transferred to Van? There was proof that Dorset had known Hurling, even worked for him. Why would he want to hurt Hurling? Dorset's bank accounts had been examined. He had not received anything from Van. What malice, then, what benefit or self-interest could such a plan serve? Adam couldn't imagine it. And neither, so far, could his lawyers.

In fact, they weren't even searching for the answer. All they wanted, they told him, was to prove that Dorset and Van knew each other before Adam's involvement. Such evidence would destroy the prosecution's most damning witness, and more or less decide the case. Adam had wracked his brain to no avail. As far as he could see, the only one who could possibly answer that question was Gregory Van himself, and he—despite the considerable efforts of British law-enforcement agencies to lay their hands on him—was still missing.

The only person who had really been any help in all of this was, surprisingly, Seth. He had brought up an intriguing topic no one else had yet touched upon.

"Listen, Adam. Who's the one person in all of this that is deeply involved that no one has investigated, or even accused?"

Adam shrugged. "Who?"

"A. J. Hurling."

"Please. He's the victim. I feel badly enough already."

"Hold on a minute! Don't you think it's a bit convenient that he contacted you out of nowhere, then soon after—out of nowhere—Dorset introduced you to Van? I'll tell you something else. I have information about Mr. Hurling that is not widely known. Did you know that he was arrested for drug possession? He did time."

"Everybody knows that. It's part of the A. J. Hurling legend: Convict becomes community leader, millionaire software technology genius, businessman, and philanthropist."

"Did you ever look into how, exactly, he did it?"

"His company, Survivor Systems Technology, is privately owned. There is not much out there."

"There are a number of people on the board with Islamic names."

Adam caught his breath, leaning back in his chair. "Are you serious?"

Seth nodded. "Right after 9/11, their V.P. of sales went to the FBI in Boston and said he thought there might be a connection. Their software is installed in everything. It lets you forage for information, and it lets you change codes . . ."

"Who gave them security clearance?"

"That's a question, isn't it?"

"What else?"

"Their main stockholder is Muhammad Al Mafouz, who is the director of the Saudi Cooperative Relief Organization, which gave Survivor Systems Technology over $50 million in loans, and another $50 million in investments."

Adam's face paled. "Where did you find this out?"

"That's not important. The point: It's true. The FBI raided Survivor Systems a few years ago based on the information. But they didn't make any arrests. And there's something else. About the same time he founded Survivor Systems Technology, Hurling converted to Islam."

Adam leaned back, drained. "Really?"

"He doesn't advertise, but it's a fact."

This information intrigued Adam's lawyers, who said they would check it out with the feds. Miraculously, it had all turned out to be true. His lawyers were in the process of working out a much more effective defense strategy. But in any case, Marvin ordered him to come up with character witnesses, people willing to testify to his blameless life and activities.

He had imagined that that would be easy. After all, how many people had reached out to him over the years for help, free financial advice, loans, charity, letters of reference, referrals? How many people had been guests in his home and his family celebrations?

He went down the list of the many who had been eager to take his hand when he was on top of the world. Very soon he found himself reduced to humiliation and self-abasement as he begged those same people to reach down and help pull him up now that he—through no fault of his own—was down at the bottom of a pit.

"May we never need the help of our fellowman" went the prayer. Only now did he understand its full meaning. The cautious to outright-cowardly responses of people he knew and had considered friends, people he had not only helped but sincerely admired, had been downright shocking, ripping the mask off the world he thought he knew. And no matter how many times it happened to him, the terrible necessity of having to beg and abase himself, the shock and disappointment of being refused, seared his soul, making him realize that the world as he thought he knew it had never been real.

Eventually, he had become more forgiving. No matter how good you have been, he discovered, however righteously you have lived your life, however generously, no one wanted to get involved with a court case. No one wanted to be called to the witness stand to be badgered by an accusing lawyer.

There had been some exceptions, people who had said, without hesitation and most willingly: "Of course. How can I help you?"

Their simple decency, more so for having been so rare, had brought him to tears. It was what he himself would have done, he knew. But at this point, it felt like a miracle. It was something he would never forget, or cease feeling grateful for.

The only bright spot in all this darkness was the thought that soon Abigail would be bringing Kayla home. A shiver of loneliness passed through him. Abby. He missed her scent on the pillow next to him when he woke in the morning and went to sleep at night. He missed slipping his hand around the small of her back as they sat next to each other sipping their morning coffee. He missed looking into her eyes when he spoke to her. He missed her small, ladylike hands, with their familiar engagement and wedding rings, curling around a book as she leaned back on the sofa in the lamplight in the evenings.

They had been married close to forty years. And yet, his feelings for her were still the same as they'd been when as a young college student he had crossed a crowded room to make a beeline to her.

Sending her off had been a considerable sacrifice. But more than a husband, he was a father. Whatever the personal cost, whatever happened to him in the end, at least his daughter would be all right, her life back on track. You can deal with much suffering as long as your children aren't harmed, he thought. If all this had irreparably destroyed her life . . . He slumped down in his chair, his bones liquid. He could not bear to even imagine it.

He looked at his watch. It was even possible they'd boarded the plane already, which meant they'd be home for the weekend! He'd have to order more food, he thought, reaching for a pad to jot down a shopping list: drinks, paper napkins, roast chickens . . .

Then he let the pen slip, laying it down in front of him. He got up restlessly, stretching his arms above his head, leaning down to touch his toes. He was completely out of shape, having canceled his gym and country-club memberships.

Exercise and networking and friendship had all been interwoven; to lose one was to lose them all.

He walked through the empty hallways, peeking into the rooms with their stale, neatly made-up beds where once his children and guests had slept. No one had used them for months. He climbed down the regal, winding staircase, studying the now-dusty photographs of a lifetime of joyous family occasions, everyone dressed up and smiling, and young. So young.

The house was silent, except for his footsteps and the occasional creak of a floorboard beneath the plush carpeting. A house was an enclosure, he realized. Nothing more. You infused life into it. And that life made it worthwhile. Otherwise, it was an empty shell, no matter how beautiful. You couldn't buy a home. You could only buy a house. Both had been taken from him, he thought, suddenly filled with rage.

He had always been a religious man. He prayed, if a bit hurriedly, three times a day. He belonged to a synagogue. He was charitable. He was honest. He loved God. He loved other people. And yet, all this had happened to him. Where, then, was God? Was it true, as some said, that He was like a watchmaker who had set the world in motion, then gone off? Or a distant observer, who did not involve Himself in the tiny details of each man's existence, allowing nature to take its course? He didn't want to believe that. But the truth was, he didn't know.

He could no longer hear God's voice. And thus, perhaps, God had stopped hearing his, his prayers falling like rain into the sea.

Be patient, he told himself. Isn't that what you would tell your children if they came to you wanting instant results? *The wheels of justice grind slow, but they grind exceedingly fine.* He felt his fingers tingle from the terrible tension of forced inaction. Terrible to be targeted by evil men, a fly caught in their web, struggling to break free. Terrible to be at the mercy of a system that was blind and often cruel. Terrible to be dependent on the goodwill of others. And most terrible of all was to face all these things alone.

It was 5:00 P.M. when the phone rang.

"Abby, is that you?" He gripped the phone gratefully, almost feeling her beside him. "I was just making up a shopping list in case you and Kayla are going to be here by the weekend . . . What? What did you just say?"

It was her beloved voice, yet so far away, he thought. So distant. It was hard to hear. Or perhaps his ears could just not absorb what she was saying.

"Abigail, I'm trying to understand. What do you mean we should leave her alone, that she's happy? Have you lost your mind? You are on a hilltop in the middle of nowhere. Your daughter has a brilliant legal career, a successful and loving fiancé, waiting for her. Why would you encourage her to give all that up? Why would you betray me like this, just now?"

He listened intently, shaking his head. It was all new-age spiritual mumbo jumbo. She sounded like some groupie. His sensible wife! His beloved help-mate! What had they done to her? Was she on drugs? he wondered. Or had the cult gotten to her, too?

"Listen to me carefully. I don't know what you are smoking, or what detergent they have used on your frontal lobes. You are killing me. I want you to take Kayla and get on the next plane out of there. We can talk about all of this at home. Don't say that! You can't mean it! ABIGAIL, IF YOU DO THIS, I WILL NEVER, EVER FORGIVE YOU FOR AS LONG AS I LIVE. Abigail?" He shook the phone, but it had simply gone dead.

He sat still for a moment, considering his options. Hesitantly, he reached for the phone, then hung up. He sat back, thinking. Then he leaned forward, reluctantly picking it up again. "Seth, this is Adam. Can you come over right away? It's an emergency."

26

On Friday night, Abigail joined The Talmidim in the dining hall. She lit Sabbath candles and heard the blessing over wine. She sat down at a long table next to Kayla and Daniel. Platters of steaming meat, chicken, and vegetables were brought. There was a burst of Sabbath songs, and conversation, and suddenly Rav Natan stood up, and everyone settled down to listen:

"Reb Chaim Vitale says: Every blade of grass has its own song. Every rock, every tree. The prophets sang their message. Rabbi Carlebach says: We have the words of their songs, but we've lost the melody. The Talmud says mankind has ten songs to sing, and we have already sung nine. There is not much time left. We must find it again before it is too late. Together, mankind must sing their tenth and final song."

Someone began to sing:

Da diddy da da
Da diddy da da
DA DA DA
Ashira l'Hashem b'chayai
Azamra l'Elokai b'yodi

Ye'erav alav sichi
Anochi esmach b'Hashem

The voices grew louder, the rhythm tapped out on tabletops, with clapping hands and stamping feet jumping up and down on the floor. Again and again, the words were repeated, until they became almost hypnotic. People closed their eyes, swaying ecstatically.

Some of the men began to put their arms over the shoulders of other men, and then some of the women did the same with other women so that the entire room was now connected physically. And when the room seemed ready to burst with the intensity of communal joy, someone left the swaying row and began to dance. Immediately, circles were formed, men on one side, women on the other. The song turned into a swirling dance of dizzying speed. In the background, the Arab chef danced too, clapping his hands with the others.

Then all of a sudden, someone said: "Shush!"

There was complete silence. No one moved.

The silence and stillness were startling after so much sound and movement. And then this same person began the song again, starting with a whisper, barely audible. The rhythm was firm, deliberate, each word following the other slowly, as if it was only one note, and there was no song at all, just one emphatic statement following another.

Da

Diddy

Da

Da

Eyes were clenched shut, hands became fists, as people sucked into themselves, their concentration frightening in its intensity. Some continued to hum the notes, while others sang the words, and the two combined in a rousing harmonic chorus of amazing strength.

Abigail found her mouth forming the words. Her eyes too had clenched shut. She was no longer an observer she realized, completely caught up.

Ashira (I will sing) *l'Hashem* (to God) *b'chayai* (with all my life)

Azamra l'Elokai b'yodi (I will praise Him as long as I have being)

Ye'erav alav sichi (Sweet will be my words)

Anochi esmach b'Hashem (And I will rejoice in God)

A woman in a swirling purple skirt, her hair covered in a blue head scarf, reached out a hand to bring Abigail into the circle. She grasped it, like a climber about to fall through a crevice, pulling herself up.

She had nothing holding her up, she realized. She was a dust mote, floating in the air. Everything solid had disappeared beneath her feet. Her place in the world had been snatched by robbers in the night, her niche wiped out, her feet with no resting place.

Suddenly, the steps of the hora from her days in Zionist youth groups came back to her. Her feet were not the feet of the grandmother, but the girl, she thought. They did not need to rest, but to go forward. She closed her eyes, and mouthed the words:

I will sing to God with all my life

She felt her heart shed its heavy burdens, like a young sheep shorn of its winter growth. She felt lighter.

I will praise Him as long as I have being

She held on tightly to the hands reaching out to her. They knew nothing about each other except that they were human and alive, filled with human hopes and passions and heartaches. They had drawn her into their circle because at this moment in time, she was alive, and so were they. That was a miracle in itself. Of all the generations that preceded her, and all that would follow her, she was part of this one.

That was the connection every human being had with every other human being: being alive at the same moment in time. And whether it was a tsunami come up from the splitting mountains on the ocean's floor to drown and destroy or an evil army of barbarians raping and pillaging small villages in remote African regions, every single person alive was affected by it. It tore holes in the fabric of human existence, and all who were alive were part of it and—if they were truly human—suffered.

But the most difficult connection of all was to the person next door, or next to you on the bus, or at your own dinner table. The closer someone was, the harder it was to reach out to them, because one's own flesh was vulnerable, one's own soul fragile.

The fear of "getting involved," of catching disease, or worry, or misery from someone else, of draining the resources and energy needed for one's own problems, was the fear of her generation. Only when that wall of fear could be pulled down and the ocean of compassion allowed to flood through, encompassing all human beings, could anyone alive in any generation feel safe to live until he died.

The medicine to any disease, the poultice to any wound, the magic elixir to any heartache was in those waters. But like the waters in biblical wells, they were covered with a stone too large for only one person to lift. It needed collective effort. It needed mankind moving together, shoulder to shoulder, with combined strength, to take away the barriers to the endless supply of cure and comfort available. It needed resolute resistance against evil, brutality, savagery, and lies. It needed courage.

She walked to her daughter, putting her arms around her.

"Don't go back to the old life, Kayla! There is nothing there for you, for anyone. It is a dead place, full of dead ideas, filled with misguided ambition and unreal dreams. Don't waste your life chasing them, as I did. Don't marry Seth out of obligation or because he's a 'catch' if you don't love him! Don't be a lawyer if you want to be a poet!"

Kayla held her breath, listening to this outpouring. "Mom?"

Abigail said nothing, pulling her daughter into the circle. They danced, singing the same words, each time with a greater intensity.

27

"Of course, Adam. I appreciate your calling me. I don't know what to say. I'll think about it and let you know. Good-bye." Seth hung up the phone. He turned off his computer, slammed his textbook shut, then put on his coat.

"In this blizzard?" Medgar asked, concerned. The drifts were already a foot deep, and the sky had turned the color of dirty water.

"Yeah, well," Seth answered distractedly, pulling on a scarf and gloves, and closing the door behind him.

His nose hairs hung like icicles and the frigid air filled his lungs. He walked quickly, oblivious to his surroundings, the fury burning inside him like a furnace, keeping him warm.

How had it come to this? Who was responsible? His perfect life, slipping through his fingers. She wasn't coming back. She might even, her father had hinted, be involved with someone else.

He smashed his fist into his palm. He'd kept telling himself all she needed was a little distance from the stressful situation for a little while; that it was temporary. It had never occurred to him that she might also, at the same time, be distancing herself from him. And most of all, it had never crossed his mind that this might be permanent.

He had never imagined that he might lose her forever.

Up until the very moment of that desperate phone call from her father, he had sincerely believed he knew Kayla Samuels as well as he knew himself and that they wanted the same things out of life. After his initial outburst of fury—a tactic which had not proven very useful in achieving his goals—he had regrouped, deciding on a different tactic. He had taken her late-night phone calls and done her bidding, spending time with her father and passing on the information she gave him in his own name. It had cost him some precious time, true, but little else to indulge her cloak-and-dagger fantasies of saving her father from thousands of miles away. Besides, if the information turned out to be false, it wouldn't be his problem. And if it was true, he'd get all the credit. At the very least, he thought it would regain him her forgiveness and her love.

How could he have misjudged the situation, misjudged *her,* so completely? On some level, she'd been his mirror. But perhaps he had not been honest with himself. Perhaps he had seen what most people see in a mirror: what they are looking for, ignoring all the rest. Had he edited out all those things about her he hadn't liked or understood or agreed with?

He suddenly had an image of her, sitting in a movie theater watching something that stirred her emotions—the soft rise and fall of her breasts, the way she sucked in her breath and her lovely lips trembled at something actors in a pretend story were faking for their paychecks. He had never understood that part of her, her vulnerability, her willingness to suspend her intelligence and have her emotions manipulated. He had leaned over, and whispered: "Don't cry, honey. After this scene, he goes back to his mistress and his cocaine stash in Hollywood, and his dead girlfriend will be getting breast implants." She had responded to his teasing with fury, calling him a coldhearted bastard. "You are perfect lawyer material," she had hissed contemptuously, as if that were an insult. He'd been shocked, but had soon laughed it off as inconsequential.

She had been his trophy woman—beautiful, bright, rich, argumentative, and fun; a little confused perhaps, but wasn't everyone? Still, he'd always found her malleable. But then, was he in love with a real person or a fantasy of his own creation? Certainly, the Kayla Samuels of his fantasy would not have dropped out of Harvard Law in favor of a desert commune.

Adam's phone call had been a wake-up call: "Seth, if you love her, don't wait! You need to fly to Israel now and bring her back home! If you hesitate, put it off for even a few days, it may be too late."

"But I thought her mother was going to do that, bring her back! What happened, Adam?"

There was silence. "I don't know. But Mrs. Samuels is apparently going through some kind of breakdown of her own. Or perhaps they are all smoking something up there in the desert . . ."

"Adam, you can't mean . . . !" He was shocked.

"No, no, I don't mean it. I'm being facetious. At least that is what I'm telling myself. But I have never felt anything more strongly in my life. It's now or never, Seth. It's all up to you. Go. Bring my daughter back."

"But why? What's happening?"

"There is someone up there—one of those charismatic types—irresistible apparently, even to my levelheaded wife. And Kayla has always been impulsive, easy to manipulate, you know that. She is so vulnerable right now. Just the kind of person who gets preyed on by charming opportunists in such situations. In this condition, she could ruin her life in a minute. Please, Seth, if you love her . . . she needs you now more than she has ever needed anyone. She needs to be reminded of all she has to lose."

He had papers coming up. He had work to do. He was at the end of a long, hard slog upward. And now, he was being asked to risk losing it all for emotional reasons. He was being asked to be impractical and selfless.

It went against every bone in his body.

But even after how she had treated him, he knew he still wanted her, very much. And he wasn't used to losing the things he wanted. He was angry with himself. He had been given a choice, and he had, for a split second, made the wrong one. He had wavered. And she had seen that. He didn't know if that split second could ever be undone.

When he reached the corner, the snow began to blow in earnest, frosting his eyelashes, blinding him. It seemed as if the universe had chosen him as its foe, throwing all it had against him. He turned around, feeling defeated, retracing his steps toward his comfortable room and the warm lamplight shining on his notebooks and study sheets. Then, in a moment of decisive contempt for his own weakness, he swiveled, marching forward across the street and entering the offices of the campus travel agent.

He woke up in Tel Aviv just as the plane began its short descent, having taken pills his research had found to be the answer to jet lag. The cloudless skies and blue sea filled his heart with irrational spring-break joy. Coldly, he reminded himself that he was not by any means on a legitimate leave from his studies. He had not even had time to notify his professors, something he planned to rectify by e-mail just as soon as he landed and could connect to the Internet. He hoped they would have a touch of romance in their souls. Besides, the third year wasn't like the first or second year in law school. There was a certain amount of flexibility. At least, this is what he told himself.

But none of that was important. He now applied the secret formula which had garnered success for him ever since he could remember: He resolutely set his goal. He always took on only one goal at a time. Once he pinpointed what it was he wanted to achieve, he was absolutely focused and relentless. His goal now was to bring his fiancée back home, convincing her to pick up their lives where they had left off. Nothing else mattered.

"Do you speak English?" he asked as cab drivers accosted him left and right at the exit gate. "Listen, I need to get to this address—" He held out the piece of paper.

"Two hundred dollars," one answered in perfect English.

"What? Forget it." The others shrugged when they heard this, walking away toward more amenable customers.

He walked along, collaring a few more drivers, until he realized that all they heard was his American accent and all they saw was his cashmere sweater and North Face jacket. It was way too warm for this climate anyhow, he thought, taking it off and stuffing it into his backpack. Finally, a woman who had overheard stopped him. "Why don't you just take a bus to the central bus station in Jerusalem, then grab another bus to the Dead Sea? It will cost you a fraction and won't take much longer," she said kindly.

"Thanks very much!" It sounded like a plan.

He changed some cash at a money changer's and got directions to the buses. It didn't take long for the bus to Jerusalem to pull up. He was a little hesitant about leaving his suitcase and backpack in the luggage hold at the side of the bus while he boarded, but overcame it. If it got stolen, it got stolen. He touched his inside pocket, feeling the reassuring bulge of his credit cards and passport.

He had never been to Israel. Not once. Not that he hadn't wanted to go, but there never seemed to be the right time. When all his friends were doing their year after high school, he was in summer school getting advanced placement in calculus and working as a lifeguard at a local pool to save for tuition.

He looked out of the bus window. The landscape seemed almost countrified, with farms and open fields all along the route to Jerusalem. This surprised him. He had imagined a bigger place, taller buildings. After all, Israel had the reputation of being a whiz in high-tech and biotech companies. A world leader even. As a Jew, he had always been secretly proprietary about that, as if somehow he too deserved credit simply for being of the same race.

Jerusalem piqued his curiosity. So much fuss. So many battles. So many people wanting a piece of her. The ambition of the world in laying claim to her made him wonder what great natural resource she held that would stir such deep and unrelenting drives across the planet and history. That wasn't immediately apparent when the bus pulled into Jerusalem's central bus station. The much-touted, worldwide source of coveted real estate looked awfully ordinary: a bus terminal inside a shopping mall, with a food court, bakeries, a record shop, clothing stores. He sat down and ordered a pizza, washing it down with a Coke. The crust was a bit soggy, and the cheese some cheap substitute for mozzarella. Still, he was hungry enough to find it satisfying if not delicious.

He wandered around, asking directions, until he found his way to the information booth. He pushed the paper with the address inside the glass barrier, but the girl shook her head. "Wait; I check." She leaned over and spoke to the other person manning the booth, who stared at the address and shrugged. She picked up the phone and had an animated conversation with someone— perhaps her supervisor. "Okay, okay, okay," she finally said, hanging up. "Look, mister. You take bus to Ein Gedi, or to Dead Sea. That is as close as you go tonight. Tomorrow, you take bus from there to Metzuke Madragot, at six A.M. Only come once a day."

"Once a day?" He thought about this. "Okay, what bus will leave me off near a hotel down there?"

"The bus to Dead Sea. Near all hotels. You stay night?"

That just might wind up happening, he thought. Hotels were going to be damn expensive. Maybe I should rent a car. It couldn't be more expensive than a hotel room, he thought. That way, I could also drive us all back to the airport as soon as possible.

More and more, the idea began to appeal to him. He knew his credit-card company had some kind of deal with Hertz and Avis. He managed to find a phone book near public phones but couldn't get them to work. He took out his cell phone and managed to negotiate a good deal on a week's rental. He made his way down to the rental offices by cab.

It was a Subaru, but a nice color, and fairly new, with adequate trunk space if Kayla and her mother didn't have too much luggage. They gave him a map, marking off directions carefully in red.

"But I think you shouldn't go at night . . ." The girl smiled, shaking her head, looking over the handsome young American in his beautiful preppy clothes, thinking: Brad Pitt. "It's the desert. Wait until morning. It will be easier."

"Thanks for the unsolicited advice," he said irritably, taking the keys. "Now which way do I turn when I get out of this parking lot? Right or left?"

"Right," she answered, insulted.

"Thanks." He walked out the door, not looking back.

"You tried," her supervisor comforted her.

"*Amerikanim.*" She sighed, switching to her native Hebrew. "Imagine, going to that *chur* in the middle of the night! Anything could happen."

"*Chalas,*" he answered, the Arab equivalent of "forget about it." "Did you see how he was dressed? He will find it all right. Nothing ever happens to people like that."

"How can you say that?"

"Success. It clings to them, like deodorant. They can't shake it even if they want to."

"That makes no sense," she replied, mystified.

"It's the Yankee-Doodle dandy in them. The 'can do' in them. They always figure things out, whether they are on top of a mountain or diving in dangerous waters. They are always the ones who come back with the fabulous stories about near disasters, their pants still pressed, their fingernails still clean."

"You are just jealous," she snorted.

"And you are in love." He touched her forehead with his forefinger.

She blushed, looking through the frosted glass as Seth started the car and pulled into traffic. "Good luck, Brad," she whispered, shaking her head.

28

Kayla awoke earlier than usual, stirred into consciousness by the sound of muffled voices that seemed to come from everywhere. "What?" she said aloud, but the tent was empty, the two other women who had been sharing it with her gone.

She pulled a rough blanket around her shoulders and stepped out into the soft moonlit night. Shocked, she saw a crowd had gathered. In its center was Rav Natan. She moved closer, jostling for a position that would allow her to hear what was being said. She looked around, realizing it was not only The Talmidim that were there, but also the people from the dig: Judith, Michael, and Efrat. She looked around for Daniel, but couldn't place him in the crowd. Her mother too was nowhere to be found.

"What's going on?" she asked Judith.

"Haven't you heard? There's been a find! Something amazing."

"Really? What?"

"A cave. We need to get there before it's closed off by the Antiquities Authority, or vandalized."

"There are writings, they say. Ancient prophecies," Michael joined in, his voice shaking with excitement. "We'll be the first in history to read them!"

"That's fantastic! Who found it?" Kayla responded, tingling with a strange excitement mixed with doubt. Could any of this be true?

"A young Bedouin looking for a goat!"

"Can you imagine?" Judith laughed. "The same exact story as the discovery of the Dead Sea Scrolls! Some Bedouin kid in Qumran threw stones into caves trying to chase out his lost goat, then heard a crash and went in to investigate! He found a jar full of ancient scrolls, which he sold to antiquities dealers. Luckily, this time our Bedouin has a father who once worked here, helping in the dairy. He brought the boy and his findings to Rav Natan. The Rav got Professor Milstein involved. The professor has examined some findings. I heard he was stunned."

"I heard he'd called it 'the greatest find of the generation,'" Michael interjected, excited.

"Rav Natan is going now. He's bringing his whole family. He has invited all of us to join him. They've sent camels and donkeys ahead carrying enough food and water for everyone. Even a few tents for shade. But we should all bring our own sleeping bags and extra water. You never know." Judith was ecstatic. "They are saying it might even be the End of Days manuscript."

"What's that?" Kayla asked, intrigued.

"The scrolls that are supposed to prophesy how and when the world will end, and what will come after. The writings were hinted at in the Dead Sea Scrolls but have never been found! So far, that is." The tension among the listeners became almost palpable.

Could any of this be true? Kayla wondered, her analytical lawyer's mind clashing with her ever-hopeful, believing heart.

"It wouldn't be just a coincidence if the End of Days scrolls turned up now!" a woman's voice exclaimed just behind her. Kayla turned around. It was Ariella. "It's God's will, because the earth and mankind are so fragile and vulnerable. There's so little time left. There is so much corruption, such injustice, so many lies and wanton murders, the whole earth sunk in immorality, overtaken by new barbarians with no one to stand up to them."

Kayla heard the rambling speech, feeling a shiver crawl down her back. She had found Ariella a kind and intelligent woman for the most part; but this kind of talk made her cringe. She couldn't help wondering, though, if there might just be some kernel of truth in it.

"You are coming, Kayla, aren't you?" Judith asked.

"Yes, you must!" Ariella exclaimed. "You can't miss this!"

"I don't know," she murmured, looking around for her mother.

"Your mother is coming. So is Daniel." It was Ariella's son, Ben Tzion. He wore a full backpack with huge bottles of water. In the dim light his facial scars seemed to fade.

"How do you know?" Kayla asked him. "Have you seen my mom?"

"She and Daniel were both just behind me when I was coming up the path. They're on their way here."

"How far away is the cave?" Kayla asked.

"About a day and a half journey by foot," Ben Tzion informed her.

"By foot? You mean we are all walking through the desert, now, in the middle of the night, and all day tomorrow? That's a hike for paratroopers, not for families with kids and older people. It's crazy!"

"There's no choice," Ariella explained. "It's through the mountains. There's no road. No vehicle could make it."

"You don't have to go. Nobody has to go," Efrat reminded them.

"Of course I'm going to go!" Kayla exclaimed. "But I first need to find Daniel and my mother."

"Isn't that them over there?" Michael pointed toward the road up from the caravans.

It was. Daniel was holding her mother's arm. She looked pale in the moonlight. Kayla ran down to meet them. "Have you heard the news, Mom?"

"Yes. Some miraculous prophecy risen up out of the desert earth . . ." She smiled.

"That's what they say." Kayla nodded, smiling back. "Rav Natan is going with his family. Daniel, are you coming?"

"Of course," he said, nodding. "But I think your mother should stay here and rest."

"I'm fine." Abigail shrugged. "Just a little indigestion. I wouldn't miss this for the world."

"Are you sure?" Kayla asked, concerned, feeling a sudden new softness for her mother, feeling for the first time in her life that they were equals, on a journey together through a wilderness of wild possibilities. She respected her mother's journey, and felt validated in her own, touched by her mother's sudden revelation during the dance circle. For the first time, she had suddenly glimpsed her mother as a fragile, aging human being, not some invincible, all-knowing pillar of authority cast in immutable stone. In her hug, she had felt unconditional love, the kind she had despaired of ever receiving. It was also, simultaneously, an acknowledgment that her mother considered her own perfect life a failure.

This confluence of ideas had both shocked and thrilled the daughter. For Kayla, who had been throwing herself against the unyielding wall of her parents' perfection and expectations her entire life, that wall had suddenly collapsed, opening up vistas of freedom that she had never dared glimpse in the past. She was grateful that her mother had allowed her this vision, feeling the stirrings of something new in her heart toward her that was selfless and true. A real connection.

"Well, we need to get ready then," Daniel urged. "Take as much water as you can. Some food, head coverings, sleeping bags. It could take a day or two."

"Two? As much as that?" Kayla asked, worried.

"Well, it depends on how fast we walk, Kayla." He smiled.

"Mom, do you really feel up to this?"

"I'll walk at my own pace. I'm not so over-the-hill that I can't get over the hills, my dear. Don't worry so much!" Abigail laughed.

Daniel took Kayla's hand and pulled her aside. "It's not a good idea," he whispered.

"Why not? Is she ill?"

"Well, she isn't used to the desert heat. I don't know if she's been drinking enough."

"I'll make sure she drinks, Daniel. I know her. If we insist she stay behind, she'll take it personally. And I think she'd go anyway. She seems to need to do this."

He took her hand, nodding in understanding. "Then we'll both watch over her."

She reached up and kissed him. "Thanks. Let me get dressed and packed then."

She hurried to her tent, packing what she needed, and taking spares for her mother. She layered her clothes, starting out with the lightest layer and covering it with her baggy, faded sweats that she could shed as the sun rose. She filled empty bottles with water, packed some crackers and cans of hummus, then went outside to join the others.

There in the pale moonlight, looking as dapper as if he'd just stepped out of Harvard's Old Austin Hall, was Seth.

At first, she thought it was a mirage.

"Kayla?" Seth said.

Mirages didn't speak. "Seth! What are you doing here?"

As he moved closer, she saw he was red-eyed, shivering in the freezing desert air. His face was streaked with sweaty grime, his pristine striped Brooks Brothers shirt collar stained by drying perspiration.

He stared at her, rummaging furiously through the image of the woman before him for something that connected her with the lovely, cool, sophisticated girl he was engaged to marry. "Your hair!" he said, reaching out to finger a few strands of the curly, undisciplined tangle. Was it the lack of light, or was she really almost unrecognizable?

She stepped back, tossing her head defiantly. "When did you fly in?"

"About five hours ago."

His teeth were chattering from the cold, she saw with sudden sympathy. "Let me get you a blanket. You're freezing. Come in; sit down!"

"Come in? You mean, this is where you live, in a tent?"

"You're tired. Here, take something to drink?" She gave him an unopened bottle of mineral water. He uncapped it, gulping greedily.

"I drove for hours. Got lost at least six times . . ."

"You drove yourself here? That's crazy!"

"I didn't want to waste a second. I had to see you . . ."

"And you found the place, in the dark." She shook her head in wonder.

"You know I'm good with directions. At least, I thought I was. The ride was terrifying."

"You shouldn't have driven straight after the flight! Especially here! You could have fallen asleep at the wheel; something could have happened to you, God forbid!" She felt a horrifying surge of guilt and terror as various tragic scenarios flashed with lightning speed through her mind.

He put down the bottle and took her in his arms. "Would you have cared?" he whispered.

"Seth . . ." She lowered her eyes, wondering how she really felt, which was by no means simple or clear but a muddled combination of feelings. She could make out surprise most of all, and a streak of trouble and complication, and yes, a bright yellow tinge of happiness. In the middle of the desert, in the middle of the night, at the beginning of an odd and perhaps painful quest to discover the world might just be about to end, here was a familiar face from home representing sanity, and ease, and practicality. A fallback position.

She leaned forward, hugging him. "It's good to see you, Seth."

He hugged her back, then separated, his lips seeking affirmation and familiarity in hers, but she pulled back. "Please . . ."

"Yes, all right. I respect that you're confused. But I'm not . . ." Then he drew upon the words he had practiced all through the flight as he imagined this moment, saying them by rote: "I love you. I want you back. That's why I'm here."

"After everything I've done? The way I've treated you?"

He didn't respond from the gut. The important thing now, he told himself, was not to hash out the truth. That would come later. What was important now was to accomplish the task he had set for himself any way he could. He swallowed hard. "I'm not exactly putting up my candidacy for sainthood either. I also did horrible things. I abandoned you when you needed me most. I put other considerations in front of our love for each other. I'd do anything if I could turn back time, Kayla. It's not too late. Is it?"

She had never seen him so vulnerable and uncertain. It was unnerving. "Why didn't tell me you were coming?"

He shrugged. "Why didn't you call me before you left?"

She fidgeted with the straps of her backpack. She hated to have to answer such a valid question. "I could say because I was angry and confused. And that wouldn't be a lie. But it wouldn't be the whole truth either. The truth is, I didn't call because I believed you were part of a world I didn't want to be part of anymore."

He was stunned. That, of all things, had never occurred to him. "And what do you think now?"

"I think that I'm exactly where I should be for now. I think that you shouldn't have come."

He felt as if she'd reached out and slapped him.

"Well, I don't happen to agree with you. And neither does your father. This is just killing him, by the way, in case you need a reminder."

Her lips tightened. "NO, no. You don't get to use the guilt card on behalf of my parents! Not you who told me that I—we—had to 'distance ourselves.' Remember that?" She felt some of the goodwill he'd earned with his bloodshot eyes and perspiration stains dissipate.

"Listen, it was your father who called me, begging me to come and rescue you!"

"My dad told you to come?"

He nodded. "I've grown really close to your father over the past few weeks. I care about him. And I care about you. That's why I'm here. Not to pass judgment."

She softened. "How is my dad?"

"He's been through hell. And he is all alone. I tried. I've been over there often, telling him the things you wanted me to tell him. But he needs you and your mother."

"Seth, I don't know how to thank you! It . . . was so good of you to get involved. I'm so grateful . . ."

He took her in his arms impulsively. "Come home, Kayla," he said simply. "All of this will soon be over. Your father will be exonerated. I'm sure of it. I've rented a car. A Subaru with plenty of trunk space. There's enough room for you and your mother. We'll drive to the airport in the morning and get the next plane out of here. You can be with your father for Friday night dinner. We can have the engagement party in two weeks, with an announcement in the paper—and my parents can just go to hell if they don't like it . . . As for school, you can start again next year. So it will take you a little longer to earn your degree. There will still be plenty of firms still hiring."

Voices grew closer.

"Kayla, we are just about to . . . Oh." Daniel stood still, his eyes flicking in confusion from Kayla to Seth.

"Daniel, this is Seth; Seth, Daniel," she said breathlessly.

The two men nodded at each other, staring like boxers waiting for the starting bell. Daniel took in the tall young man's clothing, the good cut of his hair. He had the clean-shaven look of the prosperous, judgmental Americans who travel the world simply to reassure themselves they couldn't live anywhere else, Daniel thought, particularly places where natives don't speak English and have less-than-pristine bathrooms. Was this the man Kayla loved? Still loved? And what did that say about her? And where did that leave him?

Seth stared back. Here he was, the "someone" Kayla's father mentioned. He put out his hand. "*Shalom*, Daniel. *Ma nishmah?*" he said forcefully, his hand-shake firm and committed.

"I speak perfectly good English," Daniel replied, smiling. He would have liked Seth more if he hadn't smiled so brightly, hadn't offered his hand. He would have respected a fist flying, an angry shout, something primal and real. All this phony gentlemanly civility was a bit nauseating to him. "So, you've come to take your fiancée back home?" Daniel said, looking questioningly at Kayla, who looked away, mortified.

"That's the general idea." Seth nodded cheerfully.

"And your fiancée, she is ready to go home?" The question was directed at Kayla, who said nothing. "By the way, Kayla, your mother is looking for you."

"Could you ask her to come in here please, Daniel?"

He nodded, turning around to leave, when Abigail burst in.

"Oh, there you are. Are you ready? Because people are beginning to move out . . ."

"Mom, look who's here."

Abigail turned, squinting in the dim light. She stood stock-still, doing a double take, something elaborate and theatrical like an actor in a situation comedy. "It's not my imagination, is it?" she asked Kayla, who shook her head. "Seth, is that really you?"

"Yes, Mrs. Samuels, it's me. Regards from your husband."

"OH!" Abigail sat down on Kayla's mattress, hugging herself. She looked up: "What are you doing here?"

"He's come to take us to the airport, Mom. He's rented a car. A Subaru. With plenty of trunk space. Dad sent him."

Abigail looked up. "But we can't go. Not now. Everyone is leaving with Rav Natan. You are still coming, aren't you, Kayla?"

Kayla didn't move.

"Well, I'm going. I wouldn't miss this for the world." Abigail reached out to Daniel. "Here, give me a hand."

Daniel pulled her up gently.

"Good-bye, Seth." Her voice was curt and cold. Adam had sent him, to force her into doing his bidding, she thought resentfully. As if she were a child. All she had told him had meant nothing.

"Mrs. Samuels, Abigail . . ." Seth called after her, but she was too fast for him, disappearing into the night.

Kayla adjusted the straps of her backpack. "I'm going, too."

"Now, in the middle of the night? To where?" Seth protested.

"There's been this incredible archaeological find. Some say a book of prophecy. I can't explain it to you, Seth. You'll just sneer. But I have to go. I'm sorry."

"When will you be back?"

"I don't know. A few days."

He got up. "I'm coming with you."

"Don't be ridiculous. You're exhausted."

"I'll be fine."

"You're not dressed for the desert."

"I'm not letting you out of my sight. Not after I've found you."

"I wasn't lost," she said softly. She filled up two more bottles with water. "Here. Take these. Do you have a backpack, a hat, some warmer clothes, a sleeping bag? Some shorts?"

"I've got some stuff in the car. I'll go get it and meet you back here."

Kayla nodded, about to tell him to hurry, but thought better of it. He'd come so far, all for her. The least she could do was wait patiently for him for a few more minutes.

She walked outside and looked at the gathering crowds: women in long, flowing skirts and head scarves, or shorts and jeans; men in knitted white skullcaps or baseball caps. They were an odd bunch of pilgrims, not at all as she envisioned the Israelites embarking on their epochal journey from one existence to another. Yet, like that ancient desert tribe, the desert would also be the medium that washed them clean of their old lives, preparing them to absorb the demands of the new era ahead of them.

She crossed her arms over her chest. Would Seth's presence allow her to be part of the group, or force her to look at them through his outsider's vision? Would the force of habit, the long-established patterns of her old self, reassert themselves to reclaim her, demolishing her fragile new knowledge of the world and her place in it? And what of Daniel? Was their connection as tenuous as it was new? Would it, too, be unable to withstand the threat of serious inquiry into what was real and what was transitory?

She stepped out onto the long, moonlit path that led to the edge of the inhabited space she had come to know and be part of. Someone was already opening the locks on the iron gate that separated them from the wilderness. People began flowing through it, down to the path that led through the unexplored mountains and valleys.

"Ready?" It was Seth. He wore jeans now, and a warm jacket, a backpack thrown over his shoulder.

Slowly, they joined the human stream, floating out into the unknown.

29

They walked slowly at first, like water slowly spreading out on the ground from an overturned bucket. There didn't seem to be any urgency, and were an observer to have come upon them unawares, he would have judged them a group of strangers who had paid an indifferent guide from the Society for the Protection of Nature for a night excursion to explore exotic desert flora and fauna. The moonlight cut a swathe like a magical yellow-brick road through the dark shadows of high mountains, the water-cut wadis, the flinty ground. They wandered through a dreamy moonscape punctuated by dark tufts of flora, and even, surprisingly, an occasional tree. The hard, jutting rocks hurt their soles, tripping them up, and small, painful gravel wedged inside the sandals of those who had been foolish enough to wear them. But the cool night air smelled like it had been washed clean with ice water, scented by night-flowering plants. Tiny creatures scuttled frantically across their paths, burrowing into the earth. A mountain goat stood still, waiting.

"I somehow thought the desert would be sandy, like the beach," Seth said.

"The little rainfall we do get here goes a long way," Daniel replied.

"You are . . . an archaeologist?" Seth turned, studying him.

"No . . . that's just a job . . ."

"Did you go to college?"

Daniel nodded, offering nothing more.

"What did you study?"

"Many things, some more useful than others."

"I see." Seth shrugged, too weary to pull the information out of him with any more polite questions. "So you're an unskilled laborer?"

Daniel smiled. "I'd agree with that. 'Unskilled.' A good word."

"Well, in America, we don't think much of that word or the people it describes. Mostly high-school dropouts, illegal immigrants. Americans are very big on education, professions. You know that Kayla has almost finished her law degree at Harvard?"

"She told me all about it. All about you, too."

Seth stiffened. "Is that so? And what did she say?"

"Oh, I think you'd better ask her that yourself. It was a private conversation. I don't think she'd appreciate my gossiping like an old lady. I'm not big on gossip."

"Well, I'm very big on gossip. You learn the most interesting and useful things from the casual way people shoot their mouths off. But I suppose you're right. It is between me and *my fiancée*."

"So, you still want to marry her, even though she is doing unskilled labor?" Daniel smiled.

Seth straightened. "She's a bit confused right now, but she has a brilliant future ahead of her as soon as I can extract her from all of *this*." He waved his arms, his voice heavy with disgust.

"And what if you were to find out that she isn't confused, Seth? That she knows exactly what it is she wants? What if you were to find out that you are the one who is confused?" He spoke softly, with no anger, in a tone that was respectful and mildly amused.

It was that tone, more than the words, that infuriated Seth. "Now you listen to me, Mr. Mud-Digger. I have known Kayla Samuels for a long time. She is still wearing my engagement ring. I don't know what kind of brainwashing has gone on here for the past few months, but make no mistake, I'm a man who gets what he wants, and I'm not leaving here without her."

"I'm so glad life has smiled on you that way, Seth. Not many of us get what we want most of the time. But—and I mean no disrespect—I don't think that decision is up to you, Seth. I think that decision is up to Kayla. And, by the way, the last time I looked, she wasn't wearing any rings at all."

Seth's face turned red, matching his bloodshot eyes. He looked around for Kayla. She was walking ahead of him, talking softly to a woman in a bright orange dress.

He grabbed her elbow. "Kayla, can I just talk to you for a moment?" He steered her to a private spot behind a rock. Then he reached out and took both her hands, staring at them in the moonlight. The nails were chipped and the skin coarse and tanned. She wore no rings.

"Kayla, your ring!"

"Don't worry, Seth. I didn't lose it, and it wasn't stolen."

"That's not what I'm worried about! Why have you taken it off?"

"It wouldn't have been too smart to keep it on during all this digging," she tried, smiling. "It's in a safe place. Don't worry."

He held her hands, caressing them. "Was there any other reason, Kayla?"

She didn't want to lie. She didn't want to tell the truth. She wanted to walk toward the unknown in this strange place with peace of mind, readying herself for the future, however difficult or shocking it might be. She wanted to gather her resources, not dissipate them by fighting random battles on all fronts. She had decisions to make, and did not want to be forced into them before she was ready.

"Seth, I'm not ready to talk about this now. You are also exhausted. Let's talk after we've both had a few hours' sleep."

"I think the answer shouldn't require that much thinking," Seth pressed, realizing it was unwise yet unable to stop himself.

"Well, if you must know right this minute, I took it off because I'd decided to send it back to you," Kayla blurted out. "That's the truth. I wanted some time to reconsider before I told you now, but since you insist on knowing, there it is!" She was upset with him, and with herself, her feelings raw.

He had had no experience with this kind of rejection. All his life he had been a winner, used to people choosing him. He felt demeaned, insulted, humbled. But was it his heart that was hurt, he asked himself, or his vanity?

"Is it because of him, that Daniel? That unskilled laborer?" he spit out, furious.

"Daniel, unskilled?" she repeated, confused.

"Yes, your Israeli mud-digger . . . !"

"Who told you this about him?"

"He did, himself!"

Her response was the very last thing he expected: She laughed.

"Yes, I suppose it is pretty ludicrous: a Harvard Law School student and an unskilled Israeli workman. But if you are planning to throw your life away on him, I don't see the humor in it."

"Not that it matters Seth, but he's a doctor. A surgeon."

"But, he said . . ."

"He's got a strange sense of humor, and no ego."

"I suggest you check out his diplomas first and not accept everything he tells you blindly since he seems to change his story depending on his audience. Besides, if it's true, then what is he doing out here with a shovel?"

"It's a long story."

"Right. I bet," he sneered. Why would someone hide his accomplishments? Especially in a debate with a rival? It was incomprehensible to Seth.

"Is there a problem?" It was Daniel. He put his arm around Kayla.

"Yes, she wants to see your medical diplomas!" Seth seethed. "And take your hands off her!" He lifted Daniel's arm roughly off Kayla's shoulder, flinging it backward.

"Seth, stop! What's the matter with you? Daniel, it's not true! I don't care. It doesn't matter to me!" But even as she said it, she wondered what the truth really was. Would it matter to her if she discovered Daniel really was just an unskilled laborer? Yes, because it would mean that he'd lied to her. But what if he had never told her about his medical degrees? Would she still feel the same way about him? Or was she still stuck in the status consciousness of her upbringing? Was she still the same old Kayla, simply trading in a lawyer for a doctor?

Slowly, deliberately, Daniel once again put his arm around Kayla. "Are you all right?"

She nodded, patting his hand and lifting it gently off her shoulder. "I just don't want any trouble. I just want to get through this, Daniel."

He nodded, putting his hands into his pockets and strolling away. He began to whistle slowly under his breath. The people in front of him heard it, and they too began to whistle. Suddenly someone broke out in song:

Ashira l'Hashem b'chayai
Azamra l'Elokai b'yodi
Ye'erav alav sichi
Anochi esmach b'Hashem

Through the vast silence of the dark wilderness the sound began to roll, the way rare rainfall thunders and rolls through parched desert wadis, gathering strength as it storms through the arid stretches of uninhabited wilderness where moisture is a rare blessing. Their voices, too, blessed this place, rising with joy, invigorating their tired footsteps along the rocky pathways as they walked toward the unknown, following their leader, and each other. Their song voiced their connectedness to each other, to the world, and to their place in it at this moment in time, the sound echoing at the bottom of the deep canyons, bouncing back from the mountaintops, until they felt as if they were walking through it, suspended in it, wafting upward with the notes. Above them, a billion stars blinked, staring, as if the curious eyes of the entire universe had decided to focus on this one strange and wonderful scrap of human activity.

Seth trailed behind silently, moved and yet stubbornly resisting the temptation to feel the astonishment that was welling up inside him. He fought it with every rational tool he had. "I'm just tired, and this is just weird," he told himself. "A bunch of crazy old hippies marching through this godforsaken pile of dirt in the middle of nowhere, toward another pile of dirt in the middle of nowhere." His heart was bitter with resistance toward this thing he could not explain, which had no rational explanation, which could not be explored or measured by any of the criteria he was used to.

Abigail felt herself float through the sound. Bathed in moonlight, the ground beneath her seemed to soften and flatten, rising up to meet her. This was a shared journey, she realized. But it was also a solitary road. Whatever they were experiencing together, each of them was going through a separate path. She and Kayla were each on her own journey, disconnected from anyone else's. Each step Kayla took led her forward on her own chosen path. No one could stop her, Abigail realized, no longer afraid for her.

The road began to narrow, rising upward, until it turned into a footpath where people had to walk single file, clinging to the side of the mountain, because the other side was a sheer drop down into a wadi, hundreds of feet below. Abigail felt suddenly paralyzed with fear. What if I slip? she thought, looking down, horrified. Ariella reached for her. "Take my hand, and don't look down. Look at me."

She hesitated. Could she do that? Sometimes, you simply had to admit that you weren't in charge of the universe. True, she risked falling. But if she hung back, sitting on a rock, who was to say she wouldn't meet a yellow scorpion?

What you did or didn't do, each thing had its own path, its own rewards, its own risks. The only way to absolutely avoid dying was to die. If you lived, you were vulnerable. Whatever happened, good or bad, it was there to teach you something. If you were so afraid of death, of pain, that it paralyzed you, then you might as well already be dead. Because nothing was more terrible than stagnation.

The time had come for her to lift up her feet and trust God to catch her.

She reached out, grasping Ariella's strong, womanly arm. They smiled into each other's eyes and began to inch their way along the path that led upward.

"Mom!"

"Are you coming, Kayla?" Abigail called back, reaching out for her.

"Kayla, don't! This is crazy!" Seth, an experienced climber, shouted out. "It's too dark to see anything, the drop is treacherous. This is insane." He took her arm, holding her back.

"Don't be afraid to move forward, Kayla. I won't let anything happen to you," Daniel said suddenly. He was in front of her, holding out his hand.

Impulsively, she reached forward, grasping it.

"I trust you, Daniel. I'm ready to move forward. But are you?"

Even before he answered, she felt his reply in the way his hand tightened around hers.

"I'm ready, Kayla."

Kayla looked at him. "What about Seth?"

Daniel looked back. "Are you coming, Seth?" He moved to Kayla's left, reaching out his hand generously toward his rival, as if it were the most natural thing in the world. "Kayla, take your mother's hand. She's just ahead."

Seth turned away, looking behind him. What was more dangerous? He calculated. Trying to find his way back to the caravans, thus risking getting lost in the desert? Or taking his rival's hand to navigate a dark, treacherous mountain pass? Cursing softly under his breath, he took the offered hand, terrified and humiliated. Who, he thought, would get the brownie points for this effort? Would Kayla view him as brave and self-sacrificing, or as the recipient of his rival's generous good nature? Was he making himself, or his rival, look good?

He tried not to look down, expecting any moment to hear screams and the thud of falling bodies. But the only thing that met his ears was the gentle scrape of careful footfalls. Daniel held on to him firmly, supporting him at every step, whispering encouragement. This surprised him. After all, Daniel's behavior was just between the two of them, hidden from disclosure. Kayla would never know what passed between them. Daniel could just as well have jerked him around, or ignored him. It was hard for Seth to fathom the other man's behavior. Were the situation to be reversed, he couldn't imagine being as generous.

Finally, they reached the summit. The road suddenly widened, spreading out in the moonlight like the sea.

Kayla and Abigail hugged each other, then reached out to Ariella and Daniel.

Seth dropped to his knees, his whole body shaking.

He felt Daniel's hand on his shoulder. "Are you all right, Seth?"

"Yes, thank you," he said stiffly, jumping up and brushing Daniel aside.

"Really, Seth?" Kayla asked him, the back of her hand brushing his cheek.

"I did it for you, Kayla. All of it. I hope you know that. I want to see what it is you see."

"Yes." She nodded, wondering if he was telling the truth yet stricken with guilt anyway for all she had put him through. She had at one time thought she loved this man; that she wanted to spend the rest of her life with him. What was it she had seen in him? she asked herself, searching to find it again.

The first light of the breaking dawn began to spread through the darkness.

The horizon was black, then deep violet, crimson, and finally gold. They bathed in the light, like people diving into water after a drought. They held their palms upward, closing their eyes and turning their faces toward the rising sun. What had been frightening, even life-threatening, just moments before became benign, then joyful.

It was still cool, and the breaking day illuminated the still, magical vistas of ancient mountaintops, the green-black outcroppings of tenacious desert flora. In the distance, they could see the faint outline of caves embedded in the mountainsides like pencil drawings.

They picked up the pace, singing intermittently, but gradually they were overcome by weariness, dragging themselves forward. The sun rose quickly, the heat supercharged and unbearable as it beat down on their heads. It was like some gigantic hair dryer set at the maximum temperature blowing against them, Abigail thought, feeling her knees buckling.

"Mom, are you all right?" Kayla grabbed her.

Daniel quickly took her other arm. "Come, sit down here in the shade. Have some water."

"Rav Natan says we are only a few hours away. He says we will rest now," Ben Tzion told them. "We will reach the cave before nightfall."

"Imagine. We are only hours away!" Ariella rejoiced. "Ben Tzion! Let's make some coffee!"

He reached into his bag and brought out a little portable gas burner and a small pot. Soon they were resting beneath the shade of the tents, drinking the thick, sweet brew, chewing on granola cookies, pita-bread sandwiches, and apples that volunteers brought back from the supplies sent ahead.

Abigail leaned back against a large rock, exhausted, her body aching everywhere. Adam's silent disapproval, his sense of betrayal, had pulled at her, weighing her down, she realized, making every step forward a statement of rebellion, and thus an ordeal. Still, she had no regrets. This journey had been her choice. She was anxious for it to continue, excited by her place in it and filled with curiosity and hope about what she would find at its end. But she had to admit: It had taken a toll on her.

Why did it have to be this way? She argued with Adam silently, filled with anger and a touch of bitterness. Why did she need to stop growing to feel loved? To remain his obedient good child? Was she still that same young girl who had tossed her food money into a young man's hands to win his approval and forestall his contempt? When was it going to end, this feeling of having to prove herself again and again to earn her husband's love?

And it didn't just end with Adam, she realized, startled. Every move she had ever made was calculated to win someone's approval: her friends' and neighbors', her children's, the rabbi's, her parents'. God's. When was it going to end? When would she be able to see herself as a finished product, something whole and beautiful, fashioned in her own image, not someone else's?

She looked at her daughter, a flood of sudden understanding filling her heart, like the light now filled this wild uninhabited place. They had forced Kayla into the only life they'd ever known, the same life they had been forced into by their own parents. Buying that plane ticket out of it was the first real act Kayla had chosen freely to please herself. It was a real sign of growth. Why couldn't Adam understand that?

She saw Seth curled up in the shade of one of the tents, his hand flung over his eyes, fast asleep. Nearby, Kayla sat talking intimately to Daniel, looking tired, but exhilarated.

How would I feel if they got married, settling down in this wild, unpredictable little homeland in the Middle East, so far from home? Abigail wondered, swallowing hard, close to tears. Her little girl. But it wasn't about herself, or Adam. She loved Kayla enough to hope she would find her place, and not reach sixty before realizing how much of her precious time on earth had been frittered away chasing phantoms: other people's dreams for her, other people's ideals of safety and prosperity and happiness. She closed her eyes, weary with trying to figure everything out.

"Did you mean it?" Kayla asked Daniel.

"Mean what?"

"What you said back there when you took my hand. That you were ready to move forward."

"You understood me perfectly, Kayla." He took her hand in his, kissing it. "I will always love my first wife and my baby. They will always be a part of me, of my life."

"Yes." She nodded, her eyes soft with compassion.

"But something has opened up inside me. I've made the climb at the edge of the cliff. The road has widened. I can go forward. I must go forward."

"What does that mean?"

"It means I love you," he whispered, winding one of her curls tenderly around his finger.

"How will we live? Will you go back to practicing medicine?"

"Will you finish your law degree?"

They looked at each other, startled into laughter.

"We have to do something in the world, no? Why not something we do well?"

"Everything you do, you do well, Kayla. Did you love the law? Was it what you wanted, expected?"

She hesitated. "At first, it was all about the terror of flunking out, the competitiveness of outranking others . . . But then, I began to see some things. I've been thinking about all my father's been through. When you are targeted by evil, sometimes only the law can protect you from being eaten alive. Whatever else it may be about, fundamentally the law is about pursuing justice, as it says in the Bible. Of course, some people become lawyers to protect the wealthy, and to become wealthy themselves. But that is a choice. It doesn't have to be that way. I was free to choose what kind of law I wanted to practice, what courses to take. I think I didn't make the right choices for myself. That is also why I ran away. But it's not too late for me to go back and correct that. What about you?"

"Medicine is not like law. There are no stays of execution. When you make a mistake, people die."

"But how many more would die if there were no doctors? And is it always about saving lives? What about comforting the sick, and giving them hope, whatever the final outcome? What about applying skills and trying?"

He took both her shoulders in his hands and held them, looking deeply into her eyes. "I just don't think I can do it anymore, Kayla. I don't think I have the courage or the arrogance to play God."

"So, what's next then?"

He shrugged, releasing her. "Live. As best I can. Doing whatever I can. My needs are simple and few. I can retrain. You know, being a surgeon isn't all that different from being a plumber. The pipes get clogged, you unclog them."

He smiled.

She didn't.

Would it be possible? Kayla Samuels, married to a plumber, living in a little rented walk-up in unfashionable Brighton or a run-down two-bedroom in a working-class suburb of Jerusalem? She would run free legal-aid clinics, and he would fix drains. She would buy cotton dresses from discount stores, and they would go to free concerts in the park, or take long walks? She tried to look at the idea dispassionately but found she couldn't. The old Kayla was sitting on her shoulders, horrified.

Seth opened his eyes slowly, taking a moment to focus. Where am I? he thought, his head aching almost as much as his feet. His throat was parched. From the corner of his eye, he saw Kayla. She was sitting next to Daniel. They were talking quietly and, it seemed to him, passionately. A sudden flash of hatred coursed through him for them both. The more he tried to fathom the connection between this unwashed failure and his lovely fiancée, the more unfathomable it became, and the greater his feeling of betrayal.

Had Daniel been extremely handsome or successful, he would have felt less betrayed and humiliated. But to be thrown aside for this scruffy loser with a hard-luck story? It made no sense. It was a random kick in the behind, an "anyone but you" choice. He found that unforgivable.

And then there was Mrs. Samuels! He sat up, searching for her among the resting hikers. She was supposed to be his ally! Yet she had incomprehensibly changed camps with no warning. He would never forgive her for that.

And, last but not least, what of Kayla? Did he really want her back? He was too confused to know at that moment what he would do given the opportunity, but that didn't mean he couldn't pursue his real goal: More than he wanted her to choose him, he realized, what he really wanted was the *status quo ante.* He wanted to be in a position to accept or reject. He wanted power and control over his fate.

He sat up, splashing water on his hands and face. He found his comb and ran it through his dusty hair. He saw Kayla raise her head, looking away from Daniel in his direction, alert to his every movement. He smiled to her, waving.

30

They gathered their things together, helping each other up, as the message went through the camp that it was time to continue. They moved slowly out of the shade, as one dips a toe into water to test its temperature. The sun had released its fierce, destructive power, leaving behind only a hint in the form of a brilliant white light that soon darkened.

The rapid transformation was mystical—even a bit frightening—to one unaccustomed to such intensity, Abigail thought. There was something strange and primordial about this place, its scents, its sound, like entering through a magic portal to a lost kingdom. Even time was altered, moving more slowly, the days and nights stretching on endlessly. She felt a shiver go up her spine. How would it have been to have died without ever having experienced this? To have lacked so much without even having realized it? If you didn't know what you were missing, did that mean it didn't matter? Or was it a tragedy?

The trek had taken its toll, she thought; the pains in her stomach were getting worse. All this tension, all the unaccustomed food, she thought, vowing to eat very little and to drink some of Ariella's chamomile tea. Along with fears of her irritable bowel attacks, she had always been terrified of getting sick on a trip, far from medical care.

"I refuse to be afraid anymore," she told herself. "It's enough! Fifty years of being afraid. And where has it gotten me? Did I save myself from humiliation? I was the pillar of the community until all this happened to me, something I had nothing to do with and couldn't have prevented. So who cares if I make in my pants now?"

She smiled to herself.

"Mom, are you sure you're all right? You don't have to do this, you know. I'll take you back to the camp. You can see a doctor. Don't feel you need to prove anything."

"Kayla, I'm fine. I'm wonderful," she told her daughter, making herself believe it. "I feel like I could walk a million miles if I had to. Don't let me hold you back."

"The cave is only minutes away, just over the hill. But Rav Natan says we're to stop and sleep until daybreak, because it's too dark to enter at night and the artifacts are too fragile and precious to be surrounded by torches. Besides, I wanted a chance to talk to you."

Abigail looked at her, surprised. "Sure. About what?"

"Mom, what's gotten into you?"

"What do you mean?"

"Why aren't you trying to talk me into going back with Seth? I mean, that's the reason you came here, isn't it?"

Abigail said nothing.

"Mom?"

"Don't put me on the spot, Kayla! Honestly, I don't know what to say. I came here because your father sent me. Begged me. Put me on a plane. I did it for him, not for you."

"So, you thought I was doing the right thing all along?"

"No. The truth is, I just didn't care."

Kayla inhaled, shocked. "What is that supposed to mean?"

"My darling, what it means is that I was finished mothering you, Kayla. There is just so much you can take from a child. You know we—your father and I—called you Her Majesty between ourselves."

"I didn't know that." She found, surprisingly, that this hurt her deeply. "So, you didn't care if I was throwing away my expensive education, my perfect Jewish, Harvard-educated fiancé?"

"No, I didn't care." She shrugged. "Maybe this will surprise you a little, darling, but I've been through something myself these last few months, Kayla dear. And before that, with your father's cancer. I've learned about loss, and about limits. I always did what I thought was best for you. But I was ready to let go, to let you make the worst mistake of your life, if that's what it turned out to be. I wasn't coming out here to rescue you."

"So, all those things you told me when you first came . . ."

"That's what your father wanted me to say to you. That was my job. To get you to come back."

"Then I'm confused. You did a very bad job!"

"I had pity on you. And your father will never forgive me for it. I betrayed him."

"What do you mean?"

"He expected me to get you and myself on the next plane back. I told him it wasn't going to happen. I guess that's why he sent Seth. I guess he thought Seth would have more of an incentive. Does he?"

"What's that supposed to mean?"

"Does he really want you back? And do you want him back? Is it love? Or is it just pride, power, jealousy, fear of poverty?"

"He says he wants me back."

"Do you believe him?"

"Why shouldn't I?"

"I don't know. It's like those photos of smiling people. If you cover their mouths, can you see the smile in their eyes? How deep does it all go?"

"I have no idea what you're talking about," she said petulantly.

"Oh, your pride is hurt at the very thought that your fiancé might be faking it."

"I can't believe this! You were the one who was skywriting about this engagement! He was your dream son-in-law! The CEO of your *nachas* factory."

"Maybe I've gotten over waving my achievements like a flag to win the approval of a bunch of hypocrites who proved they could turn against me on a dime," she said bitterly. "Look, don't get me wrong. I am extremely grateful to Seth for how he's helped your father with this case. I understand he's done some incredible research that might just turn the whole thing around. It was amazingly generous to invest his precious time like that . . ."

"Oh, whoa, wait a minute. Who told you that?"

"Your father. The lawyers say the information Seth came up with is all true and could make a world of difference."

"Really . . . ?" Her heart leapt.

"Kayla, my dear, your life is your own. But if you are interested in my opinion, I'd be happy to share it with you."

Kayla thought about it. This was just the thing that she had only recently convinced herself she didn't want to know at all costs: her mother's smothering opinions. But ever since the dance circle, this person seemed different from the mother she knew, a person whose opinion would be based on real things, not superficial ones, whose opinion would be worth hearing and considering.

"Tell me."

"With Seth, you will never be hungry. You will always live in a beautiful home. But you will never make a single decision that is not colored by what he wants. You will live in his shadow. Some women like that. Freedom terrifies them. They crave a life like a fifties sitcom: *Husband Knows Best.*"

"Seth can be pushy. But I can hold my own. And what do you think of Daniel?"

"I think he has tragic eyes, and I think it will take him a long time to heal, if ever. But you tell me, Kayla, since you are the one working in archaeology, don't you sometimes find when you put together the pieces of a shattered pot that it is more beautiful than the new whole ones you can buy for a few shekels all along the Dead Sea road? That it was worth the effort?"

Kayla stared at her mother. Slowly, she moved closer, putting her arms around her and resting her head on her shoulder.

"Come, child; lie down next to me and look at the stars."

They lay next to each other, their arms entwined, sharing the wonder.

The light broke softly. It was as if the world lay under the rays of a gentler, kinder orb—less fierce than the sun, less cold than the moon—whose rays painted the sky with a thousand colors. Opening her eyes, renewed, gave Kayla the feeling that the world did not yet exist, but was in the midst of being created, and she had a front-row seat. She hugged her knees against the cold.

Looking up the hill, she watched as Daniel put on his skullcap and rolled up his sleeve, winding the strange leather straps of his *teffilin* around his arm. He turned his face to the east, toward Jerusalem. As he prayed, his look was somber, then yearning, then finally at peace. She waited for him to finish, then walked to him.

"Daniel," she said, putting her arms around him. "How can I ever thank you?"

"For what?"

"All the information you gave me about my father. How did you . . . where did you . . . ?"

"I told you, Kayla. I can't say. But my contact told me that Israeli Intelligence has been following Hurling and his connections for a long time. I believe your father was set up. They chose him deliberately. He had no way of knowing."

"My mother says my father's lawyers are astonished. It might make all the difference."

"I'm so glad, Kayla."

"How can I ever thank you?"

"If a blameless man is freed, that will be my reward."

She laid her hand over his heart. "Daniel, can you free another blameless man?"

He covered her hand with his own.

"So it was you all along?" Abigail interrupted, astonished.

"Mom? Where did you come from?"

"I was just bringing you two some breakfast . . ." She held up a thermos and some cookies. "Kayla, why didn't you say anything? You just let me go on and on about Seth . . ."

"Someone once said that you can achieve almost anything if you don't care who gets the credit," Daniel interrupted her. "What does it matter? Isn't the important thing that we are helping to bring justice to an innocent man?"

"It matters to me. How can I ever thank you?"

"There is no need."

"Well, I have a need." Abigail leaned over to kiss him. "And another favor; if you're finished, can I borrow your prayer book?" Abigail asked.

He kissed it reverently, handing it to her. "How are you feeling, Abigail?" he asked.

"Never, never better," she lied, willing it to be true, going off to be alone. She closed her eyes, feeling the healing warm rays turn the darkness behind her lids to gold. Her breathing slowed as the clean desert air filled her lungs with peace.

I am happy, she thought. It was startling. Nothing was different, after all. Adam was, no doubt, still furious. Financial and social ruin still loomed. Nothing had changed, and yet everything had.

Because I have changed, she thought, filled with hope.

The time had come to speak to Seth, Kayla thought. Although the information he had relayed to her father was not his own, still, he could just have easily refused. If her mother was right, he had made this breakthrough possible.

He was sitting by the edge of the mountain, seemingly engrossed by the view. "Amazing, isn't it?" Kayla said softly, putting her hand lightly on his shoulder. He flinched.

She took it back, startled. "What's wrong?"

"Oh, why should anything be wrong?" he said, his voice heavy with sarcasm.

"Right. Dumb question."

He reached up and took her hand, putting it back on his shoulder. "You know there isn't much time left, Kayla. We are on this make-believe quest for some imaginary revelation, then the sun will set and come up again after your *Rav* tells you how the world is coming to an end. And you'll be hungry and dusty and tired. And your new boyfriend will go back to digging in the mud, and you'll lie down in your tent, brushing away the flies. But I won't be here to rescue you. No one will. Even if your mother is in the middle of her own postmenopausal breakdown, your daddy—who is the only sane one left in your family apparently—will be fed up with you, at long last. Even he won't be able to buy you out of this one."

She felt pierced and bruised, the angry hurtful words slashing at her like weapons. But he could not destroy her, she realized, startled. He doesn't have that power. Not anymore. No one does. She turned, walking away. She felt her shoulders gripped firmly. Seth turned her around. "Kayla, I'm trying to help you! I've come all the way out here, jeopardizing everything I've been working for all these years, to help you through this! Don't brush me off. Listen to me!" He shook her urgently.

She looked deeply into his eyes but could read nothing. They were the same blank, cool blue they had always been. It was like trying to read meaning into a poster of the Caribbean. "Please, Seth," she said so softly that he had to lean his cheek in closer, almost touching hers. "Get your hands off me."

"I'd expected at least some gratitude," he said stiffly.

"I am grateful. Extremely grateful."

"Then show me!"

She went limp. "Knowing you, Seth, I guess I should have expected this. After all, only fools work pro bono, right?"

He dropped his hands abruptly, turned around, and walked off.

She found Daniel getting ready to go. Next to Seth, he looked like a wild man, she thought, the uncombed curls, the thick stubble, the frayed T-shirt and jeans, the worn sandals. She looked into his brown eyes. They were full of concern.

"Everything okay?"

"No." She shook her head.

He put his arm around her. It felt like an answer.

31

They spent a fitful night, unable to sleep from the excitement of what lay ahead. And when the first light broke, they packed up their things and began to walk slowly upward along an unmarked path. Unlike the beginning of their journey, it no longer felt like being part of a tourist group. It felt like being part of a tribe, Abigail thought, as she walked along trying to keep up.

She had to admit to herself she felt weary, and older than she'd felt when leaving Boston. Pitching yourself against others gave you a certain energy, all the fight-or-flight endorphins kicking in. But battling yourself left you drained.

Suddenly, Ben Tzion called out: "We are here!"

The words echoed through the desert down the long line of people scrambling up the hillside.

"I don't see anything," Seth grumbled, looking around. "But, hey, thank God it's over."

"It's just up ahead," Ben Tzion told him. "The cave entrance."

Kayla held her mother's arm in hers, helping her along the rocky path.

"You're trembling, Mom!"

"I'm . . . I don't know. Excited, I guess. Worried. It's so unlike anything I've ever been involved in. Such a strange place, such a different kind of people. Such a different concept of success and failure."

She squeezed her mother's arm.

"It must be how the Israelites felt in the desert the day before God gave them the Torah," Ariella said breathlessly.

"As I recall, they were terrified," Seth murmured.

"No, that was the next day when the mountain thundered and flamed, and the voice of God came blasting down," Ariella corrected him. "That's when they started backing away and telling Moses to go up by himself."

"And when Moses didn't come back, they found a substitute, a golden calf, to mediate between themselves and the irascible mountain," Seth observed, laughing.

"Not the mountain. Between themselves and God," Ariella said seriously. "That's what idolatry is, when you need some intermediary between yourself and God."

"Like gurus and *rebbes*?" Seth asked innocently.

"Needing an intermediary comes from fear and lack of faith, neither of which we suffer from, thanks to our *teacher*," Ariella chided him.

"What do you all expect is going to happen exactly?"

"Nothing you could sum up in a sentence, Seth," Daniel replied softly.

"If you can't sum something up in a sentence, that's a sure sign it makes no sense."

"Not everything makes sense, Seth," Kayla challenged him. "Not everything fits into a day planner and a study outline. The universe is not such a neat, predictable grid. When you come right down to it, what do human beings understand about anything? Can you understand what it means that you didn't exist, then you were born? Where do we all come from? And what does death mean? What happens to that part of us that is 'us'—our ideas, our feelings, our memories?"

"Wheeet," Seth mocked, passing his hand in the air over his head. "You got me there. Way over my head!"

"Don't mind him," Kayla said, turning to the others. "He thinks he's a wit, but he's only half right."

"Now, now, Kayla dear. Sarcasm may be the lowest form of wit, but it's the highest form of intelligence," Seth countered.

"That's Oscar Wilde, isn't it?" Daniel smiled.

"Why, Daniel, I had no idea you were so well-read!" Seth said with mock amazement, shaking his head.

"Oh, I read a great deal. Didn't Wilde also say: 'I'm so clever that I sometimes don't understand a single word of what I'm saying'?"

Everyone laughed but Seth.

"Well, this has been most enlightening," Seth finally said. "And I'd really like all these fun and games to continue until the great revelation, which I am somehow guessing will be no laughing matter at all: all fire and brimstone and Kool-Aid. So I guess I'll take the coward's way out and just go to sleep for a few hours or whatever, until we are summoned. Bye all." He turned his back and walked off.

"I'm sorry, Seth, it was just a joke," Daniel called after him apologetically.

"Whatever," Seth called back over his shoulder, disgusted at his rival's uncanny ability to earn points at every turn. He felt his stomach churn. He had underestimated Daniel, he realized. He was not just some country bumpkin. He was a challenge, and a formidable one. Seth just hoped that this revelation had not come too late.

"I didn't think he was so sensitive," Daniel said, worried. "I didn't mean to hurt his feelings."

Kayla shook her head. "For Seth, conversation is a blood sport. Don't worry about it."

"Well, I guess he's right, though. We should all try to get a little rest," Ariella said.

"Yes, I think I will too." Abigail nodded. She was drained.

"Mom, are you okay?" Kayla asked searchingly, taking in her pallor, the strange knot between her brows. She exchanged worried glances with Daniel.

"Now don't you two worry about the old lady." Abigail smiled, reaching out for her daughter, holding her close and kissing her. "I'm fine. Thank you for your concern. I'm sure I'll feel better after a rest."

"You're probably right," Daniel agreed cautiously. "But I'd be happy to check your pulse . . ."

"Let me help you get settled," Kayla offered.

Abigail waved them both off. "Thanks, but there's nothing either of you can do to help me." She pointed to a shady spot nearby. "I'm just going to set myself down there and cool off," she murmured, walking off.

Kayla started after. "Remember to drink, Mom!" She handed her a cool thermos of water.

"Thanks, Kayla, but I've got plenty of water in my own canteen."

"Let her go, Kayla," Daniel said quietly, putting a restraining hand on her arm. "She needs rest. And so do you."

"I *am* exhausted from all the anticipation," Kayla admitted. "We all are."

Daniel folded his fingers through hers, leading her to higher ground near a large, flat rock. "We can see your mother clearly from here." He spread their sleeping bags on the ground under the shade of the mountain. Kayla sat down, studying her mother, who lay motionless, one hand flung over her eyes, the other cradling her stomach on the right side.

"Go to sleep."

"Well." She yawned, stretching out gratefully, her head resting on her lumpy backpack.

Daniel took his jacket out of his backpack, folding it and placing it gently under her head.

"Daniel!"

"Hmm?"

"Daniel," she repeated softly, her eyes closing.

He stayed up, watching Abigail uneasily.

"Rav Natan says it's time," Ben Tzion announced.

Kayla felt an electric thrill course through her body. She squeezed Daniel's hand as he helped her up.

He looked worried.

"I don't like the way your mother's holding her stomach."

Kayla took another look. "I hadn't noticed. What do you think is wrong?"

"I don't know for sure. Even if it's only a precaution, she needs a real medical workup. Soon."

Kayla nodded. "I'll make sure of it."

They began the slow upward climb of the last leg of their journey. It was their steepest climb yet. Someone had hung ropes for rappelling. They held on tightly, their hands blistered as they pulled themselves up, their knees scraping against the jutting granite and sandstone. Progress was slow and painful as they navigated the tiny stones and big rocks that blocked their path, holding on to the thorny charmless shrubs clinging tenaciously to life through the crevices. Daniel and Kayla helped pull Abigail up, each grabbing one of her hands.

Seth, an experienced climber, was up there waiting for them.

"Well, there it is." Seth gestured toward the opening in the side of the mountain.

The cave entrance was several meters tall and round, as if the mountain had opened its mouth in an expression of wonder. Rav Natan and Professor Milstein stood next to the entrance.

"Talmidim, friends, please come up and come inside. There is room for all of you," Rav Natan said. A young boy with platinum blond hair was clinging to his leg. The Rav laughed, reaching down to lift his small son up in his arms. The child wrapped his hands around his father's neck.

Abraham and Isaac, Abigail thought, looking at the two of them. Somehow, it made the whole scene less intense. Natan was just a man, after all—not a prophet; a young man with a small child in his life, and a wife too, no doubt, one of those slim, tall women swathed in a colorful Indian skirt and cotton turban. Whatever would happen would be part of the real world of children and families, despite the exotic locale.

Kayla climbed the last few steps toward the cave entrance, then hesitated, shuddering. It was so dark inside in contrast to the brightness of the day. She crossed the threshold hesitantly. It was huge, she realized, startled. Outside, there had been no hint. However many people entered, they were immediately swallowed up. The air was cool and dry, a bit rancid with dust.

"Find a place to sit!" Rav Natan called out.

Kayla was shocked. The emotional pitch of his voice was startling and unfamiliar. She had never heard her teacher sound like that. His voice seemed to bounce off the walls, the echo intensifying and doubling their impact. She walked farther into the cave. People were pointing and gasping. There, on the back wall, were four stone monoliths engraved with Hebrew lettering.

They crowded around the tablets, fingering the indentations, all speaking at once in amazement. The cave began to fill with an intensity of sound that Abigail found frightening, the noise discordant and unrecognizable as human language, all the words nullified as they overrode each other.

She held her ears, feeling her body begin to sweat. She had to get out of here, she thought, feeling faint.

"Please, silence," Rav Natan ordered. And as quickly as the noise had started, it suddenly stopped. The silence, too, was intense.

"Everyone, sit down. The professor is an expert on the Dead Sea Scrolls. He is going to read these words to you, translating them into modern Hebrew. Afterward, we will discuss their meaning. But we need silence; otherwise, the echo will destroy whatever we say."

There was a scraping of feet as people found places on the floor. A child cried. Rav Natan's small son pulled insistently on his leg and was again lifted into his arms.

"A time is coming . . ." the professor began, tracing the letters with his finger,

> *when children of light will have lost their way.*
> *Man, woman, and child will honor the dishonorable*
> *Laud and seek the indecent*
> *Praise corruption.*
> *Hands will be raised in solidarity with purest evil.*
> *The day is coming when God will look at His world and ask:*
> *What have you done?*
> *Then will come the time of reckoning:*
> *The sky will darken, and the sun will be hidden as the earth turns*
> *cold. A cataclysm will strike the North and South beyond human imag-*
> *inings. East and West will be devastated. The earth will disintegrate like*
> *a caterpillar, all its vanities, ugliness, beauty, truth, lies destroyed. It*
> *will lie dormant until the movement of rebirth begins. And then, as the*
> *earth reaches its purification, the time of resurrection will start.*
> *The graves will open, the blameless dead will rise, all their wounds*
> *healed.*

Time itself will be reborn: Every moment that did not show God's glory will be resurrected to live again. All moments of cruelty or ugliness or injustice will be reborn and relived in kindness, beauty, and justice.

Every unworthy conversation, every unworthy deed, every unworthy gesture or thought will be reborn again in worthiness.

Then the earth will sing, as it fills with the knowledge of God, leaving no room for doubt, for wrong or evil choices.

And then no man or woman will wish their will to be separate from God's will.

And death and evil will be banished forever, and tears shall be wiped from all faces.

The words, repeated and intensified by the echo, were like thunder, making their bodies shake. Like a powerful drug, the ideas coursed through their minds, a river that had broken its banks and refused to stay in its bed, gathering everything before it in a wild rush.

Seth got up abruptly, feeling his way through the crowd, his hands clutching the walls to steady himself.

He sat outside in the light, his heart pounding, his mouth dry. He felt almost as if he'd been hypnotized. He took deep breaths, trying to clear his mind.

He felt frightened. Words written thousands of years ago by ignorant people, who thought the world was flat . . .

Yet . . .

Maybe I am just tired, he told himself again. The long flight, the harrowing car ride, the shock of seeing Kayla with another man. And then this long desert trek. The heat! He was not himself, his mind repeated calmingly. In a few days, in his dorm, he would tell his roommate all about this. They would laugh.

But he couldn't budge his fear. He thought of what Kayla had said to him earlier: *What do human beings understand about anything? Can you understand what it means that you didn't exist, then you were born? Where do we all come from? And what does death mean?*

There were things he had not thought about for years. Even as a child, looking at the stars, when he had tried to imagine God, infinity—the larger it grew in his mind, the more frightened he'd become. How can a person imagine something endless, or something that always existed? It was impossible. He had never allowed himself to think about it again.

But that didn't mean it didn't exist or it wasn't the truth.

I am a coward, he realized. Afraid to face the big questions, the true meaning of my own existence, and thus the meaning of my life and all my actions.

He didn't want to be here, didn't want to be forced into it. He looked around him desperately for some way to escape. But all he could see in every direction was desolation and death. Only here, inside this cave, on this mountaintop, was life immediately possible. There was no place to run to. No place, he finally admitted to himself, he wanted to run to.

Slowly, he turned around and walked back into the cave.

Rav Natan had taken the professor's place. He was speaking.

"The people who wrote this prophecy lived two thousand years ago. And yet, their vision of the world is not very different from our own. Everywhere they looked, they saw evil. And what was their solution? They left their communities, cut their ties to their families, and went to live in the desert, hoping that while others succumbed and were destroyed by evil, they would survive. They did not succeed. History tells us that it was these desert communes whom the apocalypse found first, whether in the form of Roman soldiers or an earthquake. They died out; nothing is left but their scrolls and stone tablets, their olive and date pits.

"It is we, the descendants of those who stayed behind to struggle with the world as part of it, who have survived to read their words. Our community in the desert is not a final destination. It is a place to become the best you can be, so you can return and transform your little corner of the world for the good, to make the world a better place one good deed at a time.

"Men despair at how little they can do. *Do that little thing, the tiny thing you know you can do!* Each of us has a true and authentic song as old as the earth, but when it rises from our souls and is lent our voice, it becomes new again, and is renewed as we grow spiritually from day to day. When all seems lost, sing that song, the Tenth Song, to save yourself and the world."

Kayla reached up, touching Daniel's cheek. It was wet with tears. She wiped them away with her thumb. He kissed her fingers.

They staggered from the cave, exhausted, yet feeling that a nugget of gold had been thrown into their laps, a private treasure to be cherished that would enrich them forever.

"What now?" Seth asked without his usual arrogance. He too looked pale, subdued.

Abigail took two steps toward them when the pains in her stomach suddenly turned lethal. She doubled up, clutching her body.

"Oh God!" she moaned.

"Mom?"

"Lay her down here," Daniel demanded. He felt her head. She was burning up. "Abigail, Abigail, where does it hurt you exactly?"

She moaned. "I can't stand the pain."

He gently probed her abdomen. "Does it hurt here?"

"Oh God," she screamed.

"I think it's her appendix." He took out a strange-looking phone from his bag. "It's a satellite phone, for places that have no cell-phone reception."

"Who are you calling?" Seth demanded.

"I'm calling the army base nearby. They'll need to send a helicopter immediately to evacuate her."

"Is that really necessary? Maybe she's just dehydrated?"

"Seth, shut up!" Kayla shouted at him. "Mom, Mom!"

Abigail heard her daughter's voice as if it were coming faintly through a bad long-distance phone connection. "I'm dying," she whispered.

"What? What did you say?" Kayla repeated, filled with a sudden panic.

It couldn't end now! Just as they were on the same path to discovery. It was too soon, they were both too young! I will never get to know you, Kayla thought, horrified.

They waited twenty minutes. It felt like two days. Finally, they heard the sound of helicopter blades whipping against the wind, creating a sudden sandstorm as it hovered, then landed.

Abigail cried out in pain as they lifted her body onto a stretcher, every jostle and footstep agony.

"There is only room enough for two of you besides the patient in the helicopter. Who's coming?" an army medic shouted.

"I'm her daughter!" Kayla shouted back above the din, jumping into the helicopter. She looked at Seth and Daniel, reaching out impulsively. "Daniel, get in!"

"No, Kayla." Daniel shook his head. "You and Seth have unfinished business."

She looked at him, stunned.

Seth took two steps toward the helicopter. Then he put his hands behind Daniel's shoulders, pushing him forward. "She needs *you*. Not me," Seth said. "And I think whatever business we once had together is over. Right, Kayla?"

"Thank you, Seth. Thank you so much! For everything. Forgive me." She reached out to him, and he moved toward her, letting himself be hugged and hugging her back. Then he caught Daniel's arm, helping him into the helicopter. "Take good care of her," he said hoarsely.

The doors slid shut, and the helicopter lifted.

Kayla looked out of the window. She saw Seth move away, covering his eyes from the swirling sand and dust that darkened his bright gold hair. Then she saw him look up, lifting his hand in a final farewell. She raised her hand and waved back, watching his figure shrink and fade into the distance as they flew over the mountains, her eyes blurring with tears.

She felt Daniel's arms around her.

"Is my mom going to be all right?"

"We'll be in the hospital in minutes," he assured her, not answering her question.

"Daniel . . ."

"Yes?"

"I think I've found that one good thing inside me I've been looking for."

"What is it, my love?"

"It's how I feel about you." She put her arms around him and wept.

Ten minutes later, they landed.

Am I going to die? Abigail wondered calmly as she was wheeled down the hospital corridors. Somehow, it was not the awful thought she had always imagined it would be. She felt at peace as the pains lessened with the drip from the intravenous tubes. Perhaps they had put in some kind of painkiller. Or perhaps you didn't feel pain when you were about to die.

She was given a CT scan, confirming Daniel's diagnosis.

"It's her appendix. But there are all kinds of hazy lines around it. It may have burst, or be infected. In any case, it has to come out immediately."

"Mom, they are going to operate. It's your appendix. You are going to be all right, Mom!"

It all seemed so far away, Abigail thought, the voices, the visions of people scurrying to and fro. She didn't feel part of it anymore. She felt detached, as if she were in an audience watching this on some giant screen.

She looked up at her daughter's young, beautiful face, so drawn and pale, reaching up to caress her freckled cheeks. She beckoned her to come closer. "You were always my pride and joy, my precious, spoiled little Kayla," she whispered into her ear. "I never worried about you. You were so smart, so successful. I just assumed you were all right. I should have taken more care to see that you were happy."

"Mom, no one can make another person happy. You are a great mother. You did your best for me, for all of us. Please, don't . . . !"

"I'm not going to die, God willing. I still have my Tenth Song left. I haven't yet sung my Tenth Song," she murmured, the preoperative sedatives beginning to make her words blur one into the other.

She felt them wheel her urgently down the corridor, Kayla on one side, Daniel on the other.

The massive operating-room lights hovered above her like UFOs. She closed her eyes. She felt frightened, murmuring a desperate prayer to God, asking Him to hold her hand. They put a mask over her face. "Breathe in and count to four," she heard a voice say, "and that will be the last thing you feel until you wake up."

She had a moment of deep understanding that surpassed anything she had ever experienced before. Whatever this "thing" was she had been involved in, this consciousness, these waking moments—sight, smell, thought, understanding, love, activity, desire, pain—the light that came at intervals, replaced by darkness and the overweening sense of space, objects—sky, moon, mountains, sea, earth—whatever this was they called living, it was finite. It would come to an end. And all she had experienced and known would leave her. This certainty came to her as a dream, a nightmare, and a deep sense of peace. She was reconciled to it, to leaving all she had known behind. She felt quiet inside, ready, giving up her possession of body and mind, ready to forfeit it all if that was ordained, laying it at the feet of her faith. What would be would be. She could not fight it. She was small, finite. And her fate too was finite.

She did as she was told, breathing deeply, wondering if this was the last thing she would ever do on this earth; wondering if all this time she had been singing her Tenth Song.

32

Adam squirmed in the leather conference chair in his lawyer's fancy conference room, his hands gripping the wooden armrests. He was in the place he least wanted to be in the world, except the courtroom. The whole legal team seemed to be there. For some reason, he thought of the words "gang rape." Except that unlike most victims, he'd be paying each one of them four hundred dollars an hour for this experience.

"Adam, you are due back in court tomorrow. We, your legal team, really want to impress upon you the risks you are taking. Are you sure you wouldn't rather reconsider now, and let us talk to the federal prosecutors and work out an advantageous deal for you? When we get to court, it will be too late."

They sounded like an old record, Adam thought, furious, considering all the money he had spent on this case so far, nearly bankrupting him. He thought about all the horrible headlines and how unimaginably quickly a single article in the newspaper or on the Internet had turned longtime friends and clients into distant accusers. He had steeled himself to go through the horrors of the court trial by dreaming of the day when the newspapers would declare his innocence, bringing shame and chagrin to all those who had thought the worst of him. To do what they were now suggesting would mean the end of that dream forever; it would mean new headlines, ones which read BOSTON AC-

COUNTANT PLEA-BARGAINS ON TERRORIST FUNDING CHARGE. It would be the same as being convicted.

He looked across the room at the expectant faces of the men he had hired to protect him. He saw pity and compassion in their eyes, along with doubt. Even they, he realized in despair, didn't believe he was innocent. Not completely.

"Do you remember John Proctor, that character accused of witchcraft from *The Crucible*?" he said, and they looked at him, puzzled. "All John needed to do in order to go home to his wife and children was to confess to something he didn't do. Imagining the terrible death awaiting him, his separation forever from all those he loved, he broke down at a certain point, ready to lie. But then they asked him to sign his name to his confession. And that he could not do. *'Because it is my name! Because I cannot have another in my life! Because I lie and sign myself to lies! . . . How may I live without my name? I have given you my soul; leave me my name!'"*

They sighed, leaning back in their chairs.

"We understand," Marvin said. He, among them all, seemed to look at him with a newfound respect. "But it is my duty as your lawyer to tell you that there is a more than even chance that you will lose."

"But what about all the new information you've found? About Hurling's terrorist connections? About Dorset's gambling debts in Vegas that were suddenly paid off anonymously?"

"It is all conjecture, not facts. We don't have any witness who proves that Hurling knew Gregory Van. And without that, we have no credible defense."

Adam slumped, all his resolve rushing out of him like stale air from a punctured balloon, leaving him crumpled and weak.

"There are no leads at all on Van?"

Marvin shook his head. "He is obviously connected to terrorist regimes. He could be anywhere by now, in places that no one will be able to look.

"Adam, this is, of course, your choice. But I beg you to reconsider," Marvin implored, while the others nodded in agreement.

Wasn't that always the story? Adam thought. The criminals are always the ones who are smart enough to elude the law. Only innocent people are stupid enough and honorable enough to get caught and put through the legal wringer. "I will need to discuss this with my wife. She's abroad right now."

The lawyers shifted uncomfortably.

"That's another thing, Adam. Your wife and daughter have both left the country. You remember what happened last time in court? I'm afraid this time the judge will be less charitable and easier for the prosecution to convince. You could be taken into custody immediately. Isn't there some way you can get her and your daughter to return in the next few days?"

His lips twisted into a bitter smile. He shrugged.

"Well, please try!"

He nodded. "Can I go now?"

Marvin looked at the others inquiringly, but their faces were blank. "Yes, I guess so. But if you do reconsider about the plea bargain, I'll need your answer before we go to court tomorrow."

Adam stood up, offering his hand to his lawyer and to the others, who shook it solemnly, like people saying good-bye to someone about to begin a life-threatening journey.

At home, he sat down in the silent dark kitchen drinking a straight scotch, his throat already burning with vague regret as it poured into his stomach. He was steeling himself for the desperate conversation with his wife and daughter when suddenly the phone rang.

"Dad?"

"Kayla?" How strange that was, as if she had read his thoughts. "I was just about to call you. I wish I didn't have to tell you this . . ."

"DAD!" she interrupted him fiercely. "Mom is in the hospital. It's an emergency. Her appendix has burst . . . We were in the middle of the desert . . . Daniel called an army helicopter . . . She just went into surgery . . . Dad. I'm scared!" She sobbed.

He slid to the floor, the phone in his hand. This was the last straw.

"Dad, are you still there?"

"Yes. I'm here."

"I will call you when she comes out of surgery. Dad? DAD!"

He cleared his throat. "Is she getting the best care? Kayla, make sure . . ." he said hoarsely, barely able to speak.

"Dad, it's an emergency, so we can't exactly shop around. But we're in an excellent, modern hospital. Daniel says he's heard of the surgeon, and he's very good. He just happened to be on duty."

"Don't leave her alone for a moment. I don't want her to be alone."

"I won't, Dad. Daniel and I are both here. We aren't going anywhere."

"Tell her . . ." His throat knotted. "Tell her I love her," he said, barely above a whisper.

"Dad? This connection is terrible. I can hardly hear you . . . What's happening with you? With the case?"

"Tell your mother not to worry. It's going to be fine. Fine. You'll tell her that, won't you? Don't worry about me. This is nothing . . . It doesn't matter."

"Dad, my battery is about to die, tell me what's going on!"

"We need to find Van. Nothing else will save me. But this is not your problem. Call me as soon as she's out of surgery?"

"All right, Dad. Good-bye." She hung up the phone, turning to Daniel. "It's my dad. He says we have to find Van. Now."

He had never expected a wonderful life. No one had a life with only good things. But to go from such a good life to one that stripped him of everything felt like a Divine blow. It couldn't be a coincidence, all these things happening at the same time. He was being punished, he thought. But for what? For always wanting more? Was that a crime? For working hard and being clever and successful? Was that suddenly evil? He pounded the wall with his fist, then leaned his forehead against it, wracked by sobs. No. It was for sending her away. For making her do what I asked her to do. For not keeping her safe.

He walked through the silent house, taking inventory of his life. The lovely armoire, now full of dust. The beautiful dining-room chandelier that had not been lit for months. The silver-framed photos on the grand piano, outlining a life rich in family, friends, and good times all over the world. And now, as he was nearing the last stretch of his lifetime journey, when all his good deeds, all his blessings should have been there to cushion him against the ravages and losses of old age, there was nothing left but bare, cold planks.

He remembered something Abigail once told him years ago. Sometimes, she said, you go to great trouble preparing a meal you are not destined to eat. She was referring to an actual dinner party she had planned her first year in college to celebrate the end of midterm exams. She'd detailed the way she'd carefully washed the mushrooms and sliced them; the way she'd sautéed the onions and garlic and tomatoes to a thick, delicious paste; and how, in the middle, she'd reached into the fridge to steal one of the éclairs she'd purchased from a famous New York bakery for dessert. One hour later, she'd moved permanently into the bathroom, vile odiferous fluids pouring out of all ends, experiencing the kind of stomach pains you'd expect during labor. An emergency room doctor diagnosed her with gastroenteritis. When she recovered, she found herself in the kitchen disposing of the lavish, never-consumed feast.

Sometimes, one was never destined to reap the rewards of one's efforts. If you did, you should consider it a blessing, not a natural outcome, he realized.

The word "*be'shert*" went through his head, a word religious Jews turn to for comfort when faced with accepting such dismal outcomes. It was no one's fault. It wasn't a punishment. It just *wasn't meant to be* in the vast, celestial plan, and thus must be accepted without undue rancor or hair-tearing disappointment. It was a word equally, if not more so, weighted to explain the happy chance accidents that befall us all, leading to wondrous matches with excellent life partners, lucrative business deals, and happy encounters with long-lost relatives, friends, and coworkers. Things we don't deserve.

He sank into his down sofa, its marshmallow softness mocking the unforgiving, hard reality of his almost destroyed life. He was, he realized, helpless. Like the winds and tides that swirl and beat against each other, creating storms, typhoons, and hurricanes, a man's fate was outside his hands. There was just so much you could do, and the rest was up to what some called fate, and others, more courageously, were willing to call God.

Why was it so hard for human beings to pray? Because no human being wishes to admit helplessness, he thought. Perhaps because to be human is so terrifyingly fragile to begin with, he thought, so we surround ourselves with illusions of power: money, friends, and shrewd knowledge about how the world works. And clothed in this brittle armor we march out into the world daring to face its uncertainties. It was only when the perfect storm enveloped you, threatening all you had, that you were reduced to shedding all hubris and facing the true nature of being human.

Pressed down into the depths of despair, he felt himself drawn to the old remedy that had been the elixir of so many facing destruction, whether through inimical human opponents, or faceless acts of nature, conditions of want, or disease. When all human efforts had been expended—all expertise, all plans, all bribes—and only one thing was left.

He walked to his bookcase and took out a book of Psalms.

> *He will deliver you from the snare that is laid, from the deadly pestilence.*
>
> *He will cover you with His pinions, and you will take refuge beneath His wings*
>
> *. . . For He will instruct His angels on your behalf, to keep you in all your ways.*
>
> *They will carry you upon their hands, lest you hurt your foot upon a stone . . .*

He read and read, his soul raw with unhealed wounds, weak with helplessness.

The words poured into him like a salve. Alone, but not alone, he thought, wanting so much to believe in his faith, wanting to feel worthy of being listened to. He did not want God to be that far-off clockmaker who did not interfere with human beings, leaving them to their fate. He needed God to be near him, with him, controlling the universe.

Oh, God, oh God. Take everything I have if I deserve it; just don't take her from me. Please, God, please.

He needed miracles. He prayed for miracles.

Exhausted, he slept.

The ringing phone woke him.

"Dad?"

He held his breath. "Tell me, Kayla."

"She's out of surgery. They say she had a very close call. But they think she is going to be fine."

He put the book of Psalms to his lips, kissing it. *Thank you, God,* he mouthed silently. *Thank you.*

He had gotten one miracle. He could not depend on another.

He sat down at his computer and composed an e-mail to Marvin.

Marvin. I am ready to settle. Just make sure my family will be taken care of.

Best,

Adam

33

"Mom?"

The voice came from a distance.

Fear clutched Abigail's heart. Am I still alive? she wondered. She did not want to die. She did not want peace, she admitted to herself. She wanted the uncertainty and pain of living. She wanted to live until her throat was dry with singing and she could not utter a single new note.

"Mom, are you all right?"

Kayla stood beside her bed, holding her hand. Her eyes were bright with tears. "What happened to me?"

"You were very, very lucky."

Luck, she thought, had nothing to do with it. "Thank you, God." She closed her eyes and slept.

The room was dark when she awoke again. Kayla was sitting at her bedside along with Daniel. "Water," she said weakly.

"Here."

She felt her head lifted gently by a strong male hand. Her eyes focused.

"Adam?"

"How are you, my love?"

Was she dreaming? She pushed herself frantically off the pillows. "You can't be here! They'll arrest you . . ."

He pushed her shoulders back gently.

"Abby, it's over."

"What?"

"They've dropped the charges. The CIA picked up Van in an airport in Nairobi on his way to Libya. I guess life in Saudi Arabia didn't appeal to him." He chuckled. "He was carrying a bunch of documents that prove I was set up. Hurling and Van were longtime accomplices, longtime Hamas and Al-Qaeda supporters. They wanted a Jewish accountant to do their dirty work. Dorset was blackmailed into helping them: Hurling's friends paid his Vegas gambling debts. It was Dorset who suggested they pick me. The feds have asked me to testify against them!"

"Thank God! I can't believe it. That is so wonderful! But how did it happen?"

"The feds told my lawyer off the record that the CIA got a tip from a foreign intelligence agency. Isn't that wonderful? He couldn't tell me anything more. If Van had made it to Libya, that would have been the end of me. Is Seth around? I'd like to tell him."

Kayla took her father's hand. "He's on his way back to Harvard, Dad."

"So then, is it over between the two of you?" Adam winced.

Kayla nodded. "It's over."

Abigail examined her feelings. She tried to remember her sense of joy as she walked down the street planning her daughter's engagement party to the perfect son-in-law. But it was so distant a memory, something that had happened to someone else, someone she had known long ago.

"And where is Daniel?" Abigail asked.

"He just went out for a minute to talk to the doctors."

"I want to thank him for saving my life. But most of all, I want to thank him for saving my husband and our family."

Adam stared at her.

"For saving me?"

"It wasn't Seth, Dad, who found out about Hurling. It was Daniel. But he made me promise I wouldn't tell anyone. And it's probably Daniel who is responsible for the CIA being tipped off just now as well . . ."

"You're joking!"

"No. I'm serious. He's never said exactly how he got the information, just that he was in a special unit in the army and that he has what he calls 'contacts.' I asked Seth to pass the information on to you because I knew you wouldn't take anything coming from me seriously."

Daniel walked in.

"Dad, this is Daniel."

Adam looked in confusion at the wild-haired young man.

Daniel looked from one to the other, equally confused.

Adam walked over to him, hugging him wordlessly. "Thank you!" he said, his voice husky and full of emotion. "Thank you, thank you, thank you."

She saw the tears well up in Daniel's eyes. She squeezed his hand: "Just say '*bevakasha.*'"

He took Adam's hand in his: "*Bevakasha.* You are most welcome!"

"And what now, Adam?" Abigail asked.

"I've bought plane tickets that are good for the next two weeks. Whenever you are feeling up to traveling."

Abigail nodded, feeling her eyes closing. She would talk to him soon, explain things when she had the strength, explain that like those animals that shed their skins, she had shed hers. The old life was over, an empty shell that she couldn't, wouldn't, crawl back into.

What would happen to her? she wondered. What would her Tenth Song sound like? Rav Natan was right. She couldn't imagine it. She would only know that answer once she was in the middle of singing. All she knew was that it would be the best song she had ever sung.

She closed her eyes, giving in to sleep.

Epilogue

When she was released from the hospital, Abigail and Adam took a hotel room in the center of Jerusalem, in an unimposing but friendly little place. It had a small balcony that overlooked a street full of waiters scurrying to serve leisurely tourists and laid-back natives sitting in open-air cafes. Religious women in hats wheeling baby carriages, soldiers, Abyssinian priests in long, dark robes filled the avenues. She watched, fascinated by the variety, the energy. It reminded her in a strange way of her birthplace, New York City. Tiny as it was, Jerusalem was still a bundle of energy, optimism, and diversity.

In the afternoons, she and Adam would take long, slow walks that brought them to stone archways and rows of very old stone dwellings, which looked both mysterious and strangely familiar. She couldn't explain that: the familiarity; the sense that she had always been destined to live in this place, of all the places on earth; the feeling of comfort and relief at having been lost and now having been found, or rather, finding herself. A feeling she had never once experienced in her own birthplace.

These low stone houses, built at the turn of the century by wealthy, kindhearted Jews for their poor immigrant brethren, somehow whispered her name, inviting her to partake of whatever magic they held in the matrix of history, community, and tradition. In the dark shadows of a bare streetlamp, she touched the stones, and they touched her.

When it finally came, the inevitable conversation with Adam had been harder than she'd imagined. He was not a man who lost his temper or cried easily. And yet, there had been shouting and tears. Later, in the many conversations that followed, he seemed to have spent his anger and his grief, and was simply bewildered.

"We have lost a great deal of money, it's true," he told her. "But we have some left. Especially if we sell the house. It's too big for us now anyway," he said. "And I know now you never really liked it; I forced it on you."

She didn't protest.

"I called home last night to get my phone messages. The rabbi called. Apparently he's read the newspaper stories exonerating me. He even apologized."

"You aren't going back to that synagogue, are you?" she asked, appalled at the thought.

"Why not? So many of our friends left messages congratulating me. My clients called, wanting me back."

"Of course they did," she murmured. "But how can you just forget what you've seen, Adam, the faces without the masks?"

"I don't know. If the situation were reversed, I don't know if I'd have acted any differently."

That was so Adam. She had no doubt he would have acted completely differently. He would never have betrayed anyone the way he himself had been betrayed. As for herself, what did it matter how she would have behaved in a theoretical situation that had never occurred? What did it matter if she would have been no better? The facts remained the facts. Even if she could find it in her heart to forgive the people who had behaved so unfeelingly, still, she didn't want them in her life anymore, just as they had not wanted her in theirs when the situation was reversed, and she'd needed them the most.

"I want to put it all behind me, Abigail. I want my life back, exactly as it was."

"Adam, that's the difference between us. I want nothing back. I only want to go forward."

"Abby, be reasonable! At least come back for a little while. Help me to sell the house. Come with me to visit our children and grandchildren . . ."

It sounded perfectly reasonable. But the thing was, she just couldn't. She didn't even know why. It was like something written in stone that had been chiseled and completed, impossible to change. "I'm sorry, Adam. I can't."

"Ever?" he asked her, flabbergasted.

"Ever," she answered honestly. "I want you to come here. I want the children and grandchildren to come here, at least for a visit."

"Maybe, in a few years . . ."

"Now."

There was nothing left to say. At the end of the two weeks, when she was feeling better, he took a plane back to Boston.

"Will you take care of yourself, Abby?"

"I will. I'm happy, Adam. I will wait here for you. For as long as it takes."

They held each other close; then he was gone.

A week later, she found an apartment. It was tiny, especially by American standards. A small kitchen with ancient appliances and wooden windows that barely closed. A claw-footed tub, and a handheld shower wand the Israelis called a "*tush*." That always made her giggle. It came furnished with a beat-up table and some unmatched chairs. To complete the décor, she bought a used convertible couch she found for sale on a local English-language Web site, and a new, comfortable bed she found in a mattress store in Talpiot.

Her life took on a kind of rhythm. In the mornings, she would cross the street to the Machane Yehuda shuk, where she bought pita bread with zaatar still warm from the oven, fresh figs, and Israeli goat cheeses. For lunch, she would do the same, except buying fresh Nile perch, or St. Peter's fish, ripe tomatoes, and strawberries.

She read a great deal, books she found in one of the many English-language used-book stores that dotted the city. She was always surprised at what people brought in: almost new hardcover novels, signed first editions, paperbacks so yellow with age that the pages crumpled even as you turned them. A few times a week she taught English to adults. The money was enough for most of her expenses. Not that she was worried about money. She had transferred enough to her Israeli account to last a long time, money she had earned as a teacher all those years, which Adam had insisted go into a separate account in her name. On Sunday afternoons she took art lessons with a young woman, a recent Bezalel art-school graduate. And on Tuesdays, she took music lessons, learning how to play the clarinet. She had no television. Instead, in the evenings, she went to local concerts and lectures and art galleries, or simply visited with newly made friends. Ariella sometimes called with news about Metzuke Madragot, and sometimes she traveled into Jerusalem to visit. They would sit over coffee and delicious cakes in Beit Ticho, talking about the strange turns that lives take.

She never ceased to marvel at how easy it was to make friends even if you couldn't invite them over for ten-course gourmet meals in a palatial dining room. Abigail knew her living conditions were temporary and that eventually she would buy something larger and more modern. And yet she felt no rush to change anything. She was strangely, perfectly, content.

She and Adam spoke almost every day. In the beginning, they'd ended every conversation the same way: "When are you coming home?" he'd ask plaintively. And she would answer gently: "I *am* home, and I have no intention of leaving." But finally, he'd stopped asking. Now, mostly they discussed Kayla and Daniel.

The day after Adam left for the States Kayla had broken the news that she and Daniel had also decided to go back to America. It had come completely out of left field. In Abigail's mind, there had only been two choices: Seth and America and law school, or Daniel and Israel and no law school. Kayla and Daniel had chosen door number three. It had been hard for her to accept at first.

"But why, Kayla? Aren't you happy here?"

"Happiness is a by-product of doing the right thing. Moving on with your life. I've looked into my life, and I know what I need to do now. I'm a mediocre poet and a worse archaeologist. But I was a very, very good law student. I realize it was never practicing law I rejected. I just didn't want to practice Seth's kind of law. It took me a while to understand that. So I'm going back to finish my degree with the same intent that I started it: to change the world, and make it more just, one lawsuit at a time. This is what I know how to do. I just have to learn how to do it better, as Rav Natan said."

"And Daniel?"

"He's coming with me."

"Really?" She was stunned. "And what is he going to do in Boston?"

"Daniel has also come to realize that he loves medicine, because even if you can't save someone, you can give them comfort and help to make whatever time they have left a blessing. And that is an awesome skill. He's going to retrain in geriatrics, to specialize in hospices so he can help people sing their Tenth Song. In the meantime, he's planning to get a job in a nursing home. We'll live the student life for a while, and then who knows? It doesn't matter."

"You aren't going back because of your father, are you?"

She hesitated. "I admit, partly. I owe him. But no, the decision was mine and Daniel's, and it was made for many reasons, ninety-nine percent of them selfish."

It was painful to know she was leaving, just as they'd become friends. But Abigail felt, instinctively, it was the right decision.

"Will you ever come back here?"

Kayla's face lit up. "Always."

They'd been back in the States now for two months.

"Kayla got a job working at the Family Advocacy Center. She loves the work and is putting aside money to refill the hole in her tuition account," Adam informed her. "She's looking forward to starting law school again in the fall."

"Did she mention what courses she has in mind?"

"She says she's looking at Introduction to Advocacy; Child Exploitation, Pornography, and the Internet; and Law and Social Change . . ."

"Wonderful! I spoke to Daniel also. How does he seem to you?"

"He likes his job at Beth Israel Seniors Home, even if he is only an orderly. Geriatrics seems to be the right place for him. In the meantime, he's started studying to pass his American Medical Boards so he can go back to practicing medicine."

"I'm so proud of him. He's come such a long way."

She heard him exhale.

"They are talking about a wedding."

"Kayla told me. I understand they want to get married at the end of this coming June in Israel at that ancient synagogue near their dig. They want Rav Natan to marry them."

"That's only two months away!" There was a pause. "You were right about Kayla, Abby. I don't know what happened to her in the desert, but she is a better person. And I really like Daniel."

She was glad for him. "Are you in touch with Seth at all?"

"Not really. But I heard through the grapevine that he is seeing someone new."

"A law student?"

"No. I think she's a Ph.D. candidate at Boston University studying gender equality. She's Israeli. A friend of Daniel's sister. Kayla set them up."

"Really?" She smiled to herself.

"Seth's parents are having a hard time with it. They've called me a number of times, pushing for Seth and Kayla to get back together. And each time they call, they casually ask me for free investment advice. Apparently, there has been a drastic downturn in their income from some really bad investments . . ."

"Madoff?" she asked hopefully, relishing the idea.

"They're not saying. But their house is in preforeclosure. Apparently it was mortgaged to the max, and their loan is now underwater. The banks are pressuring them."

Well, well, she thought, smiling and shaking her head. "Will you be coming to see me before the wedding?"

"I . . . still have to testify, you know. So I can't come right away. And then there are all my clients coming back, so I'm drowning in work. I'm actually thinking about hiring someone as an associate. Or even getting a partner."

"I hate being without you. Give the house to an agent and sell it," she told him. "Retire. Come live here, in Jerusalem, with me."

"But . . . what about the children . . . the grandchildren?"

"How often do you actually see them now? They'll see you just as often if you live in Jerusalem."

"But to leave America . . . my work. Don't you miss it?"

"Yes," she said honestly. "Sometimes terribly. When I think about the children, my grandchildren, my students. Or when I want a library or a good steak, or a visit to Filene's Basement . . ." She laughed. "But if I went back, I would miss my life here more."

"Are you still in touch with that rabbi . . . ?" Adam always pretended to forget his name, holding him responsible for the upheavals in his family.

"Natan. Every once in a while, when he comes to Jerusalem to give a lecture at a little place in the center of town. We sit on the floor with big pillows, and my back aches, but my heart soars. Come, Adam," she pleaded with him. "It's time to let go of the past."

He wasn't ready. Not yet, she thought sadly, missing him. But her days of following him around, of letting him decide her life for her, were over.

She walked down the street already planning the wedding, thinking about flowers, and food, and the dress she would wear. Thinking about Adam sharing her apartment, walking to the shuk with him hand in hand early in the morning. She would teach him everything that she had learned. She would open her life and her heart to him, welcoming him in and hoping he wouldn't want to leave.

June was not so far off.

1. *The Tenth Song* takes place in both America and Israel. In your opinion, why did the author choose to tell the story this way? Had the characters remained in America, would it have been a different story? In what way?

2. Describe Abigail and Adam's relationship. What are its strong points? Flaws? How does their ordeal affect that relationship?

3. Who was your favorite character? Your least favorite? Why?

4. The characters in *The Tenth Song* all go through difficult, life-changing trials. In the end, was their suffering constructive or destructive to them? Why?

5. Describe the relationship between Kayla and her mother, Abigail, before and after their sojourn in the desert.

6. Describe your own worst trial and how it affected you. What do you think the author is saying about surviving ordeals?

7. Kayla has to choose between two men. Do you think she makes the right choice? Why or why not?

8. What is the meaning of the title *The Tenth Song?* Describe your own Tenth Song.

For more reading group suggestions, visit
www.readinggroupgold.com.

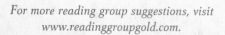

A
Reading
Group
Guide

St. Martin's
Griffin

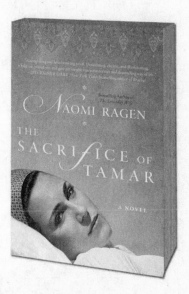
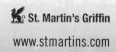